A SURFEIT OF GRIEF

A SURFEIT OF GRIEF

THOMAS BERRINGTON TUDOR MYSTERY
BOOK 5

DAVID PENNY

RIVERTREE PRINT

2025.12.02 11:08

SEVILLA, SPAIN: DECEMBER 1502

ONE

When Thomas Berrington caught Queen Isabel of Castile's gaze on him, she turned away to speak with the handsome man beside her.

"She cannot approach you, not here," said Jorge Olmos, who had reluctantly accompanied Thomas across France and Spain to Sevilla. "The right time will come, trust me."

"Can you read my mind?" Thomas asked.

Jorge smiled. "You, my friend, are an open book."

"Except you cannot read books."

"Ah, but I read people." Jorge turned away and moved through the crowd. A smile here, a touch there, spreading pleasure without effort and making everyone like him. Thomas knew he would need Jorge at some time for just this ability. As tall as Thomas, but far more handsome, Jorge might charm the dead to rise.

The gathering of over a hundred people, some exalted and others who wished to be, was taking place in the Real Alcazar palace. It amused Thomas how the tables were arranged to enhance the position of Queen Isabel and King Fernando. Most of the party were assigned places in the Ambassadors' Hall, while royalty currently stood beyond the marble pillars in the corridor that led to their private quarters. Long curtains threaded with gold prevented entry from the corridor. It was a less than subtle stating of their power. It also provided a measure of protection. Thomas suspected it was a result of the attempt on King Fernando's life in Barcelona two months before. It had come to nothing, but measures had been taken to protect both him and his wife. Ten years had passed since the defeat of Moorish Spain, and the glitter that once surrounded *los reyes católicos* had worn thin. Plots came thick and fast from surrounding countries, particularly Portugal, which skirmished with Spain over control of lands across the great ocean.

A corpulent, finely dressed man approached Thomas.

"You are Berrington, yes?" His voice was slurred and full of entitlement. Thomas saw a man half a foot shorter than himself, and three times wider. A half-empty, ornate silver goblet was clutched in his fist, and the floridity of his face hinted it had been drained more than once.

"I apologise," Thomas said. "I have been absent from Spain for several years. You are?"

"Dominguez," the man said. "Don Alejandro Dominguez. Advisor to King Fernando. Do you not recall me?"

"I am sorry, sir. I do not."

The man scowled. "I recognised you in an instant. No matter, you have no power in Spain anymore. I was surprised to find you here in such exalted company." He half turned away, pointing with the hand that held his wine, spilling some in the process. "I assume you do not know my deputy, Don Rodrigo Vargas, either. Or the guest of honour tonight, the Infante Duarte de Beja."

Thomas looked in the direction indicated but it took him a moment to work out who Don Alejandro meant. The room had grown increasingly crowded. Servants wound their way through with plates of food and drink. Thomas had also seen natives of the new world among them but was unable to work out if they were also servants or something else. Their shortness and unusual dress set them apart.

And then he saw the Infante. A boy of medium height, a little plump and with average looks, though the expression of entitlement on his face told Thomas all he needed to know. He was talking with a well-dressed, dark-haired man Jorge would no doubt approve of.

"The infant?" Thomas asked.

"Infante," said the man. "It is his title and indicates he is close to the Portuguese crown. The boy has eighteen years. He arrived in Sevilla a month ago and has been kicking his heels since. I was asked to obtain an invitation for him so he could press his case."

"His case?"

Don Alejandro shook his head at Thomas's obstinacy, perhaps regretting starting the conversation. He drained his goblet and held it out without looking. It was filled by a rough-looking cupman who appeared to be almost as drunk as his master. The man's clothing was ill-fitting and seemed to have been cut to fit someone taller.

"Portugal proposes a marriage between the Infante and Princess Catherine." Don Alejandro waved the man away. "It will bind our countries closer together and, between us, we can lay claim to the entirety of the new worlds across the sea." Don Alejandro leaned close. "You have heard of those, I assume?"

"I stood on the dock to watch over Columb when he sailed on his initial voyage," Thomas said. "And welcomed him on his return. Are the servers some of the natives he brought back with him?"

"Those?" Disdain filled Don Alejandro's voice. "They are nothing. An amusement the King enjoys bringing out to attend us. It demonstrates the power of Spain that we can bring them across the great ocean. Why are you here, Don Thomas?"

Thomas smiled. "To plead the same as this Infante, but in my case for Prince Henry of England. A far more suitable husband for Catherine."

"England is nothing. Spain and Portugal are where the power now lies, and where it will grow even stronger in the years to come. England is a backwater whose small power will wither to nothing." Don Alejandro turned away. Clearly, he had had enough of the tall Englishman and wanted to find someone of more influence.

Thomas remained where he was, watching the Infante Duarte. His companion had moved away, and now he looked lost. People stood close to him, but he spoke with none. After a moment, Thomas made his way across and stood before the lad.

"I hear you wish to press for the hand of Princess

Catherine. I assume you have arrived with ambassadors and gifts?"

The boy looked Thomas up and down, and Thomas knew he would not impress. Despite having purchased the best clothes, he always looked too uncomfortable in them to impress.

"Who are you?" The lad spoke passable Spanish, which would go in his favour.

"Thomas Berrington, Duke of Granada." Thomas used his formal title, unsure whether he was still allowed to, but no one had yet told him otherwise.

"Well met, sir." The lad offered his hand, which Thomas took. "I am the Infante Duarte de Beja, nephew to King Manuel of Portugal. And no, I have no ambassadors, only a request to make. And I know of you. I lived for a time in Granada after the defeat of the Moors, and your name was well spoken of there. Perhaps you might introduce me to King Fernando."

"Or the Queen?" Thomas said.

"If needs be, but the King would be better. And your Prince Henry of England is little more than a child, and an unsuitable match." The Infante's gaze was drawn aside, and Thomas turned to find Jorge approaching, as always the centre of attention.

"Have you seduced everyone already?" Thomas asked. "This is the Infante Duarte de Beja. He is here to plead his case for the hand of Catherine."

"I take it you have told him you are here to do the same?"

"He seemed unconcerned. That is correct, is it not?"

"Portugal and Spain have far closer ties than Spain and England."

"Except Catherine remains in England," Thomas said. "And she sees young Henry several times a month." It was not quite the truth, but Thomas was sure this lad would not know that.

"I hear he is a crook-back," said the Infante.

"Then you hear wrong," said Jorge. "He is most handsome, and strong for a lad of eleven years."

"As you are most handsome, sir," said the Infante to Jorge. "I hear Spain in your voice. Will you not come to my aid?"

"I will not cross Thomas," said Jorge, putting an arm over his shoulder. "He is my closest friend in the entire world."

"Ah, I see. That is a shame. The ladies of the court will be most disappointed." The Infante turned away.

When he had gone far enough Thomas broke into laughter. "He thinks us lovers," he said.

"Of course," said Jorge. "I trust he does not spread rumours, or it will indeed ruin my reputation as a ladies' man. The boy was, of course, interested in me, as he believes now you are."

Thomas considered the information, not doubting it because Jorge was never wrong in such matters. He stored it away in his mind for future use if needed. Should such knowledge get out, it would spoil any chance the lad had of winning Catherine's hand.

"You have worked the room?" Thomas asked, shucking Jorge's arm from his shoulder and tugging at his velvet jacket, trying to pull out the creases he seemed to have made in it.

"I met someone who asked about you," said Jorge.

"Only one?"

"You forget you are growing old, Thomas. She wanted to know who you were. I would say she showed some interest in you despite your age and lack of grace."

"I make up for it in knowledge and the ability to fight," Thomas said.

"Then perhaps she seeks a man to protect her."

"In that case you should offer yourself."

Jorge laughed. "She showed no interest in me, which I admit came as a surprise."

"You cannot make all women love you."

"I have no need to. The only woman I love already loves me. She may even be with child by now, thanks to you."

Thomas had no intention of asking where this woman, unusual enough to ask after him, was but Jorge insisted on pointing her out. She stood talking to a small group of men, who gave the appearance of being interested in her words. As Thomas studied her, she looked his way and held his gaze for longer than a casual glance might allow. Her face showed no expression as her eyes remained on him. She was not beautiful, but he found her most attractive. Not that he was looking for a relationship, or even friendship. He had one task to complete, and one only. Ensure the marriage of Catherine of Aragon and Prince Henry would take place. And that the balance of her dowry, still due, was paid. King Henry had told Thomas he did not expect another payment for his second son, which was wise considering Spain would refuse, despite its new wealth.

"Who is she?" he asked.

"You will admire her, Thomas," said Jorge, "for she is a woman in a man's world. Her name is Luisa Mercado, and she controls the *Casa de Contratación* in Sevilla."

"Which is what?"

Jorge shook his head. "For a clever man, sometimes you cannot see what lies in front of you. We have been to the docks several times. There is a building under construction there which is where all imports and exports to the city are managed from. That is the House of Trade, and Luisa Mercado its head. A woman. I thought you would approve."

"How do you know all this about her?"

"Our paths crossed earlier, and she made sure to approach me." Jorge smiled. "You know it is not unusual for a woman to do so, but in this instance, it was not me she was interested in but you. We talked. She revealed more to me than perhaps she meant to, but that is what happens, is it not?"

"It is. Why is she interested in me?"

"Perhaps she has heard of your reputation."

Thomas laughed. "In that case I would expect her to run in the other direction as fast as her feet can carry her."

"She struck me as a strong woman. To be in her position, she must be. And there are times, only a few, I admit, when you can be almost human." Jorge shook his head at the wonder of such a thing, but before he could say anything else Luisa Mercado turned away and servants began to usher people to their tables as the cathedral bell tolled noon. Thomas found himself seated close to the marble pillars, beyond which Isabel and Fernando were taking their own seats. The corpulent man who had spoken with Thomas was doing the same beside the Queen. As he sat, he slapped at his neck as if bitten by an insect, which would be no surprise. The late afternoon was warm, and even this late in the year mosquitoes swarmed above the gardens. Smoking pots scattered through the rooms should have kept them away, but some always managed to get inside despite the thick drapes. It seemed Don Alejandro's goblet was once again empty. The cupman serving the top table leaned in with a fresh bottle of wine and brimmed the goblet. Don Alejandro drained a good half of it as the cupman glanced around, then backed away to disappear behind the drapes. Perhaps to fetch more wine because he had served only Don Alejandro, completely ignoring the rest of the royal table.

Thomas looked around for Jorge but instead found Luisa Mercado's eyes on him once more. He deliberately looked away, and as he did so Don Alejandro rose to his feet. Thomas hoped he was not about to make a long speech of welcome for the English ambassadors. The man drained his wine glass, swayed a little, then before he could speak fell backwards. His body hit the stone floor with a loud thump.

Someone screamed.

Thomas pushed his way through the crowd. A guard tried to block him, but Queen Isabel said, "Let Thomas through. He is a physician."

By the time he reached Don Alejandro the man was gasping for breath and clutching at his throat. Believing he might be choking, Thomas rolled him onto his side and struck him between his shoulder blades, to no effect. Don Alejandro's breath shortened and he convulsed.

Thomas checked his pulse. It was rapid, erratic. And then ... nothing.

Don Alejandro's body went still, his eyes open but vacant. Thomas dragged him beyond the drapes to the terrace bordering the gardens, where he would be out of sight. When he turned, Queen Isabel had followed, and her sharp gaze met his. She had seen everything. Behind her, King Fernando stood, a scowl darkening his face.

TWO

"No one is to drink the wine," Thomas said to Isabel.

"We all drank the same toast," said the Queen. "Tell me, how sick is he?"

"As sick as a man can get, Your Grace. Don Alejandro is dead."

Isabel raised a hand to her face. "How?"

"I suspect he was poisoned. I say again, people should not drink any of the wine until I can determine the cause of his death."

"This is no simple banquet," said Fernando. "It has a purpose we cannot abandon before it even starts." Fernando turned to take in the room. "Don Rodrigo!" He motioned to the man Thomas had seen earlier in conversation with the Infante Duarte. "Take command of the situation. Don Alejandro's duties are yours until a decision can be made on his replacement."

"It is not my place, Your Grace," said Don Rodrigo. "There are others here more suited."

Fernando scowled. "You are Don Alejandro's deputy. Who better to take command."

"I am not liked, Your Grace, you must know this. There are more senior men in this room who expect to assume the position."

Still scowling, Fernando surveyed the room. "Yes, there are, but they all want it too much. You do not, which is why I ask you to obey me."

For a moment Thomas was sure the argument might continue, but Don Rodrigo took a deep breath and finally nodded.

"There is a perfectly serviceable room nearby we can move the body to, then the banquet may continue, Your Grace." He spoke as if he knew the layout of the palace better than Fernando. "You and the Queen must return there."

"I agree," Thomas said, feeling able to speak now. "I cannot examine Don Alejandro here where people may see us. I suggest you replace the wine on your table. No one has eaten anything yet, so the food should be safe."

Don Rodrigo looked him up and down, a frown forming between his dark brows. "Who are you to give orders here?"

"This is Thomas Berrington, Duque of Granada," said Queen Isabel. "He is also a skilled physician. You must introduce yourselves to each other. I am sure there is much you might both learn." She glanced at her husband. "We should do as both Don Rodrigo and Thomas suggest, my dear. I am sure more wine can be found." She looked at Thomas. "Are you sure the food is safe?"

"I believe so."

"Have the natives taste some," said Fernando.

Don Rodrigo turned away and began to issue orders. Thomas watched as people mumbled, complained, milled about and generally got in each other's way. Don Rodrigo went into the crowd and returned with one of the barely clad native women.

"This one speaks passable Spanish," he said. "Yariel, show this man where Don Alejandro's body can be taken. Stay with him to ensure nothing untoward happens."

The woman glanced down at Don Alejandro's body, then at Thomas and said, "Come with me." She turned away and Thomas had to walk fast to follow.

"Is this room far?" he asked as he caught her up.

"Not far." She did not look at him but was as good as her word. She stopped and opened a door to reveal a finely laid-out room. "Will this do?"

Thomas looked around. "Yes, it will do. I need to fetch Don Alejandro's body but might need help if it is to be done without drawing attention."

"I will find someone." Yariel left the door open as they started back.

People were once more taking their seats and conversation had started up as though nothing of import had taken place. Yariel went to speak with others like herself and brought two men back.

"This is Jayuya and Iacaco. They are strong and will help. I will return to the room and wait for you there."

The two men stared at Thomas, one with a sour expression, the other with patience. Both were dressed alike, their burnished skin smooth, with only a narrow wrap to cover their manhood. The women were the same but had a second wrap to conceal their breasts. Within the palace it was cool, and Thomas wondered if they felt the cold or not. He suspected they had been told to dress this way to enhance their strangeness.

"Do either of you speak Spanish?" he asked.

"A little," said Iacaco. Jayuya only stared.

"We need to carry this man's body to a nearby room. You will help?"

Iacaco nodded. Jayuya continued to stare, this time at Don Alejandro.

Between them they managed to lift the body. In the room, Thomas told the men to lay Don Alejandro on the floor and told them they could leave.

"He is dead?" asked Jayuya, remaining after Iacaco had gone.

"Yes, he is dead," Thomas said. "Do you have any idea who might have wanted to kill him?"

Jayuya smiled, but there was nothing of humour in it. "He was an important man, so would have a thousand enemies." He glanced down, knelt and brushed a hand across Don Alejandro's throat.

"What are you doing?" Thomas asked.

"Releasing his soul," said Jayuya. He rose and left the room.

"Take no notice of him," said Yariel. "Jayuya was born with a great strangeness inside him. He remains in the palace only because of the man who now lies before us."

"They were friends?"

Yariel laughed. "How could they be? He..." she nodded at the body, "...was second only to the King. Jayuya is one of us – torn from our homeland. It was Don Alejandro's idea to bring us into the palace. For the amusement of those who live here. Jayuya could not control his anger and went too far more than once. He was going to be expelled, but Don Alejandro convinced others he should stay."

Thomas studied her face for any sign of hostility at her position but detected none. Jorge might have seen something, but he did not. Her features were pleasant, her face unlined, making it impossible to guess her age. A grown woman, but that was all he could tell.

"Have you been here long?" he asked, knowing it was a bland question, ashamed of himself. The woman disturbed him in ways he did not understand. Perhaps her otherness, her near nakedness, or her acceptance of her fate.

"Many years," she said.

"Would you return home if you could?"

She offered a small shake of her head. "It is half a world away, and who would carry us there?"

Thomas knew he had work to do, but he was also prey to curiosity. He tried to set it aside.

"I need to check the wine Don Alejandro drank. Do you think you could bring me some? If the remnant of the bottle or his glass remain that would be best."

"I was told to stay with you," said Yariel.

"What am I going to do, kill him again? I will start to examine Don Alejandro, but I need to know how he died."

Yariel looked down at the body. "It is clear how he died. He is old and fat. He was also a pig with too many hands. I am pleased he is dead. I will do as you ask." She started to turn away, then stopped. "What is your name?"

"Thomas."

She nodded and left the room.

Thomas knelt and loosened Don Alejandro's clothing but left his hose in place to protect what little modesty remained to him. Naked above them it was clear the man could well have died from his age and poor condition. His skin was waxy, mottled in places. When Thomas opened the man's mouth and sniffed, he recoiled from the stench of rotten teeth. He ran his fingers along the neck and found a small mark on one side which must have been the insect bite he had slapped at.

Yariel returned with a wine glass still holding a remnant of liquid. "I could not find the bottle," she said.

"The cupman took it," Thomas said. "I will need to find him later."

"He brought a cart into the small courtyard at the back of the palace," said Yariel. "No doubt you can find him there when you are finished here. And the Queen told me she wants to speak with you later."

"When?"

"It is not my place to question her." She held the wine glass out to him.

Thomas sniffed, swirled the small amount of liquid around, then sniffed again. He dipped a fingertip into it and tasted. He learned nothing. It was wine. If it was poisoned it had not affected him, but he was reluctant to try more.

He glanced at Don Alejandro, raised the glass, then lowered it again. No. The risk was too great. Thomas needed to know more.

"Do you know who provided the wine?" he asked Yariel.

She shook her head, not bothering to waste words.

Thomas returned and knelt beside the body. This time

his examination took longer, and he stripped Don Alejandro completely. When he glanced at Yariel, she had taken a seat and watched without expression as Thomas worked. Don Alejandro had a nasty case of the pox and little regard for hygiene.

"Do you know if he was married?" he asked.

"He was. His wife is most beautiful."

"I hope he did not lie with her, then."

"I would not know that."

No, Thomas thought, *I expect you would not.*

Still he did not know what had killed the man. Possibly his heart, for it would be under great strain. A bleed to the brain. Something sick inside him? Thomas knew if he cut into the body, he might discover the truth but was unwilling to do so. Instead, he rose to his feet and brushed himself down before pulling a drape from the window and covering Don Alejandro.

"I want the body left as it is until I return. Do you also need to accompany me if I leave?"

"I was told to watch you in this room, Thomas, so no. May I go?"

"You may."

Alone, Thomas hesitated, unsure what to do next. A glance at Don Alejandro's covered body told him there was little he could do here. He was sure the death was murder and not due to sickness, even if Thomas judged the man would not have lived much longer. He needed to question people. To find out who might have wanted him dead, and, perhaps more importantly, why.

THREE

When Thomas returned to the banquet he stood out of sight and surveyed the rooms. He saw Jorge talking with two women, one either side of him. No doubt they were married, but from their expressions willing to put such minor facts aside for the night.

Isabel and Fernando sat at the top table. Don Rodrigo Vargas was on his feet beside them, delivering his version of the speech Don Alejandro was meant to give. Whether it was the same, better, or worse, Thomas could not tell, only that the man spoke well, with a strong, clear voice. He looked to be in his thirties, handsome, with dark hair and a small beard neatly trimmed. His body was slim, and Thomas suspected he would be an object of attention for many of the women in the room. Even more so now he had inherited an important position. He knew he would have to question the man, because such a promotion might be motive enough for murder. He had known men killed for far less. Sometimes it took nothing more than the wrong kind of look or a misheard word.

Don Rodrigo mentioned the English ambassadors, in particular Richard Foxe and Thomas Savage, and thanked them for risking the wild seas between their country and Spain.

Thomas was surprised when he added, "And we must, of course, welcome the return of Don Thomas Berrington, Duque of Granada. Don Thomas accompanied Princess Catherine as her protector when she left Spain for England. He has now returned to report on her experience in that cold and distant land." With that Don Rodrigo took his seat and the banquet continued.

Thomas could not decide between returning to his seat, which remained empty, or starting his investigation. It was the latter he felt obliged to do but knew people he needed to speak with were in these chambers, so he tried to walk as casually as he could to his seat. It was almost an hour before the first courses of the banquet ended. People rose from their seats and gathered in small groups, some discussing what might be brought as a second course, and what would come later. A few left without making farewells. Thomas walked to Jorge, who had managed to extricate himself from the attentions of several women.

"Have you taken care of the dead man?" asked Jorge.

"Do you think it as easy as that? I moved him to where he will not be stumbled on, but now the hard work begins. Finding out what killed him and who is behind it."

Jorge offered a heartfelt sigh. "Again, Thomas?"

"Yes, again."

"Then I will do what I can to help, provided I do not need to look at any more dead people."

Thomas smiled. "I will try to spare you that." He

looked around, aware of important people discussing important matters. None were as important as murder.

"I need to speak with that man over there," he said.

"Don Rodrigo? I was surprised he mentioned you in his speech. Do you think Don Alejandro would have done the same?"

Thomas made no reply. He turned aside and weaved his way to where Don Rodrigo was speaking with the King. He was aware of Jorge following him, which was good. He would be able to note any falsehoods spoken.

Queen Isabel stood at a small distance from her husband. When she saw Thomas approach, she came to intercept him.

"Have you dealt with Don Alejandro, Thomas?"

"I have, Your Grace, but would speak with Don Rodrigo when he is free."

Isabel smiled. "They are talking of a forthcoming hunt. Fernando is unsure whether to invite the English ambassadors or not."

Thomas returned the smile. "Not, Your Grace. Both are men of God, and I doubt either have ever hunted."

"Perhaps he should invite you, then." She waved a small hand. "It is of no matter. Do you believe Don Alejandro was poisoned? It is one reason I forbid mushrooms to be served at my table."

Thomas frowned, having to work through what she had said before understanding. He knew mushrooms well, both the benign and dangerous kind. He was also aware of how some people lacked the knowledge to choose which were safe to eat.

"I believe poisoned wine killed him, which is why I

want to speak with the cupman who served it. I have not seen him since he charged Don Alejandro's glass. He took the remains of the bottle with him. I tasted a little of that left in Don Alejandro's glass but dared not try too much. Which is why I need to know the cupman's involvement. Something could have been slipped into the glass at the last moment. I assume Don Alejandro was close to both you and the King. A trusted advisor. Can you think of any reason someone might want him dead?"

"Don Alejandro is..." Isabel broke off, "...was a valued member of our court. As such it is possible he made enemies. It is difficult to reach such a position without doing so. As you should know."

Thomas was not sure he did. The attainment of power was never anything he sought but seemed rather to search him out.

"Who would know if he had any enemies, and who they might be?" he asked.

Thomas watched the clearing of plates of food, glasses, empty bottles of wine.

A door banged open and a short, sturdy man dressed in a leather jerkin strode into the room.

"Here is someone who can answer your questions, Thomas. Do you know Diego Serrano?"

"I have heard the name, but we have not met, Your Grace."

"Of course, it is some time since you left Granada. Diego is captain of my guards. He knows everyone, and most of their secrets. I must join my husband, so will leave you in his capable hands. I will tell Don Rodrigo you wish to speak with him once he is free."

Diego Serrano offered his hand to Thomas, who shook it.

"You are Thomas Berrington, yes? It is said you are close to the Queen, but that King Fernando dislikes you."

Thomas smiled. "You are well informed, sir."

"I need to see Don Alejandro's body for myself," said Diego, his voice firm, used to issuing commands.

"Then follow me. Jorge, you had best come with us."

In the side-room, Diego glanced at the body when Thomas revealed it. "I take it Don Alejandro is dead, otherwise I would not have been sent for." He leaned a little closer before glancing at Thomas.

"He is about as dead as a man can get. I believe he was poisoned."

"He is enormously fat and very old," said Diego. "Are you sure it was poison and not simply age or infirmity? Many have been expecting him to die for some time."

"How many might want him dead?"

Thomas's question brought Diego upright to face him. "Don Alejandro's position was exalted, so of course he made enemies, but none I know of who would stoop to murder. I expect he did indeed die of natural causes. This is work for an undertaker, not me or my men."

"But you will make enquiries?" Thomas asked. "I saw a cupman fill Don Alejandro's goblet with wine offered to no one else. That man should be questioned."

"I expect it will prove a simple enough matter," said Diego. "I will set someone to the task. No doubt when he is spoken to, it will become clear this is not murder."

"It will take but a moment to confirm it," Thomas said. "I tasted a tiny amount of the wine. It was sour, but whether that was due to poison or bad wine I could not tell. Only the cupman will be able to tell us if it was. I have been told his cart sits in the rear courtyard. Find the man and I suspect you will find Don Alejandro's killer."

"I have men to do such things. What you choose to do in your own time is not my business, so long as you do not interfere with my enquiries."

"In that case, I would suggest you send these men of yours to the kitchens to ask about the wine, and also the food. Find the cupman before he flees, though it may already be too late. The man took the bottle with him, which I thought odd at the time. I suspect Don Alejandro was deliberately targeted. His position makes it unlikely this was an accident."

Diego Serrano said nothing, and Thomas knew that whatever little patience the man had shown so far had been exhausted.

"I will not keep you from your work, sir," Thomas said. "But Queen Isabel has asked that I be kept informed." It was a small victory of sorts, letting the man know Thomas was close to the seat of power. Whether it would do any good or not was another matter.

FOUR

Thomas lacked confidence that Diego Serrano would conduct any manner of rigorous investigation, so determined to do so himself. He knew it was a trait that had brought him trouble in the past, but he could not turn away. He was about to leave when the far door opened again, and Don Rodrigo Vargas strode into the room. Thomas noticed a brief scowl pass across Diego Serrano's face. He concealed it, turned and walked away, offering a brief nod as he passed Don Rodrigo, who approached Thomas and Jorge.

"I assume Diego is going to instruct his men," said Don Rodrigo.

"Possibly," Thomas said.

"Queen Isabel told me you would still be here. I am curious what interest this death is to the Duque of Granada."

"Queen Isabel may also have informed you I have been of assistance to her in the past in matters relating to suspicious deaths."

"This is murder, then? Don Alejandro was a slave to his weaknesses. Women. Food. Wine and spirits. Not to mention other vices that I have heard only rumours of. I am surprised he has lived as long as he has. Can you be sure this is murder and not a case of overindulgence?"

Thomas wondered if the entire palace would rather pretend Don Alejandro's death was the fault of the man himself.

"I would prefer to make my own decision on that."

Don Rodrigo shook his head. "Do what you will, then. I am going to be too busy to even think about it. Don Alejandro's passing has left a chasm in the hierarchy of the court that, if I am being honest, has been there for some time. King Fernando has asked me to manage his affairs during this difficult time." Don Rodrigo glanced back to where he had come from. "It seems Diego has not taken to you, Don Thomas."

"It is a state of affairs I am well used to, sir."

"You are right in what you said. Queen Isabel informed me you have served her well in the past in regard to matters such as this. That you have knowledge few others possess, which makes you a man to be admired."

"I think the Queen claims too much of me. I have some small talent, that is all."

"And your companion?" Don Rodrigo turned his attention to Jorge. "He is exceedingly handsome."

It was a strange comment, but Thomas was aware that Don Rodrigo was also handsome, and clearly wealthy judging by the quality of his clothes.

"Jorge Olmos is my closest friend in this world, sir. He

is a eunuch from the harem of the Alhambra Palace, when it once housed such a thing."

Don Rodrigo tilted his head, his sharp eyes making a fresh study of Jorge.

"I would not recognise him as such had you not informed me." He addressed Jorge. "Do you not mind Don Thomas referring to you in such a way? Is it not demeaning?"

"Demeaning?" said Jorge. "A eunuch is what I am. I cannot, and would not, make a pretence to be something I am not. Thomas made me a eunuch in order to save my life when I had little more than twelve years."

"Did he by damn? Well, well." Don Rodrigo shook his head, then dismissed the subject from his mind. "Do you have any initial thoughts regarding Don Alejandro's death, Don Thomas?"

"A few, and Thomas will suffice."

"Yet you are Duque of Granada. But so be it, Thomas. And in that case, you should call me Rodrigo when it is between ourselves. How did he die?"

"Poison, I believe, but need to confirm it. I had intended to visit the kitchens to speak with those who prepared the meal and supplied the wine but have been told it is none of my business."

"I expect my new position means I can override any order given by Diego," said Don Rodrigo. "Speak with whoever you need to."

It surprised Thomas the man was so open in his comments. His experience in the past had been that those in positions of power – and the higher the position, the more so – chose their words carefully, and their friends even more so. Perhaps it was nothing more than Don Rodrigo's sudden, unexpected promotion that made him speak so openly. On short acquaintance, Thomas found the man likeable and, more importantly, clever.

"Was Don Alejandro skilled in his post?" Thomas asked. It was an impertinent question, and he chose it deliberately to see what the reaction might be.

"Do you expect me to answer that?"

"Of course not, but I believe you already have."

Don Rodrigo smiled. "You were testing me, yes?"

Thomas offered no reply.

"Thomas likes to judge the mettle of a man," said Jorge. "It is why he keeps me close, for I am a good reader of character."

"What do you read in me then, eunuch?" Don Rodrigo held up a hand. "No, do not answer. If you are truly what you claim I am not sure I want to hear your response. Apart from which, an important man lies dead not three score paces from us. I will have Diego send someone to take the body away and have it prepared for burial."

"Did you know Don Alejandro well?" Thomas asked.

"We worked together these last two years, since I was appointed a member of court, so well enough. Do you have questions?"

"Too many."

"Then perhaps I am not the right man to answer them. I have duties I must attend to in my new position. I want to help but cannot now. I will have someone come to tell you when I have the time. Are you staying in the palace?"

"We are not so elevated and have taken a small house in San Vincente," Thomas said.

Don Rodrigo pulled a face. "Why there? I am sure rooms could be found for you in the palace, or if not here then somewhere more ... civilised."

"We prefer less fuss to be made," Thomas said. "The house suits our purpose."

"Thomas prefers less fuss," said Jorge. "I do as I am told."

Don Rodrigo laughed. "I like you, Jorge. You are my kind of man."

"Oh, I doubt that," said Jorge, which only made Don Rodrigo laugh the more.

"Come, I will take you to the kitchens where you can ask your questions, but then I must leave. They will be busy down there. Much preparation and cooking remain to be done tonight. Do you want me to speak to Diego and ask him to keep you informed of his investigations?"

"Let me see what tonight and tomorrow bring."

Rodrigo nodded. "Then let me take you to the kitchens and introduce you."

FIVE

Don Rodrigo led Thomas and Jorge to a large space at the end of a long underground chamber, filled with chaos and heat. Women shouted and called out as they pushed past each other. Chaos it might seem, but Thomas recognised the deep organisation of it. Nothing was spilled or wasted. Nothing knocked over.

Don Rodrigo approached an older woman giving orders to a small group of three. He waited until she had finished.

"Thomas, let me introduce you to Rosita Perez, head cook of the palace. Rosita, this is Don Thomas Berrington, and you are to answer any questions he has." Don Rodrigo glanced at Thomas. "If you learn anything, come and find me or send a message."

When Don Rodrigo had gone, Thomas turned to Jorge. "Speak with the others. Find out what you can. I need to know who the cupman was."

Thomas knew Jorge would charm the women and girls, capable of teasing secrets and information from them few others could. He watched him cross the room, weaving between those who worked to prepare food, then turned back to the head cook. She was glaring at him.

"Whoever you are, and whatever Don Rodrigo says, I am too busy to talk now." She shook her head. "Do you know someone came here and accused us of poisoning Don Alejandro? I tell you, there will be a reckoning come morning, if not before."

"This will not take long."

"It will take no time at all." She turned her back on him and strode away, issuing instructions as she went.

Thomas considered trying again, but suspected she would respond the same way, and he would have made an enemy of her. He needed answers to questions, but that would have to wait until whatever they were working on was done. However, he watched Jorge move slowly and elegantly among the mostly young women. He leaned close, bringing a flush to most faces, speaking without disturbing their work. The head cook approached Jorge, most likely to tell him not to disturb her staff. Thomas was amused at how she, too, was quickly won over. Of course she was. Even so, he would have to wait, so went out into the gloomy corridor and found a place to lean against the wall.

Jorge emerged a quarter-hour later, a sweet pastry in one hand which he popped whole into his mouth, an expression of bliss on his face.

"What did you find out?" Thomas asked curtly as he pushed away from the wall.

"I will tell you when you are more amenable. A thanks would be appreciated."

"You know I value your skills," Thomas said. "And yes, my thanks. Now will you tell me?"

"You will be able to speak with Rosita as soon as the last plates are sent out, which will be some time yet, but no more than an hour."

"Rosita, is it?" Thomas smiled. "It has not taken you long to be on first name terms."

Jorge scowled. "She controls that kitchen like a general controls an army, but one of the girls told me once the first rush is over Rosita will be more approachable."

"By you or me?"

"She will respond better to me than you, of course, but it is you who knows what to ask. I will stay back so as not to distract her. In the meantime, I have other information you may want to hear. The kitchen has nothing to do with the wine. There is a cellar where the vintner controls which bottles are sent to which tables." Jorge smiled. "It seems the likes of you and me get the vinegar, while the table of the King and Queen is sent the good stuff. It should make it easier to identify the man who poured wine for Don Alejandro."

"It did not seem to me the wine served to Don Alejandro was the good stuff," Thomas said. "Do you know where these cellars are?"

"Of course. We have enough time to go there before returning to the kitchen. I suspect the longer we are away the easier it will be to talk with Rosita."

Jorge led the way, which took them outside through the side of the palace facing away from the gardens. It gave on to a narrow space hemmed in by a stone wall. A few paces presented them with a door, which in turn led down steps to an extensive cellar. A man of indeterminate age looked up as they entered.

"Do they want yet more wine? How drunk are they?"

"You are the vintner?" Thomas asked. "And no, no more wine is needed."

"Good, for I will need to have more stock brought in. Yes, I am vintner César Romero, and you have the advantage of me, sirs."

"I am Thomas Berrington. My companion is Jorge Olmos."

"An Englishman and a Spaniard. Working in the palace brings many wonders, even down here. What can I do for you? If it is wine you wish to purchase, none is for sale. This cellar is kept for the court."

"You provided the wine for tonight's banquet?"

A nod. "Was there something wrong with it?"

"A man died." Thomas watched the man's reaction, seeing only a moment's shock. He assumed Jorge was looking for the same things.

"It would not be my wine that killed him." Romero's voice carried obstinacy, and Thomas knew he would feel accused of poor management, which was not his intent. However, he needed answers, so chose to ignore the man's pride.

"That is what I am here to determine. Did you provide all the wine for the banquet?"

"Almost all, yes. These cellars contain wines of the most exquisite quality. Wine of Spain, Portugal and France, as well as more distant lands. But tonight, a request was made to bring six bottles in from outside, especially for the royal table."

"I was at the banquet and there were no more than a dozen people on that table, and I know at least four of them do not partake of wine."

"Six bottles is what was brought here. It is not my place to question a direct order."

"From whom?"

"Don Alejandro Dominguez. If you want to know the reason why then you must ask him, not me."

"I cannot ask Don Alejandro," Thomas said. "He is dead. Poisoned, I suspect, by the wine he drank before making a toast."

César Romero took a step backwards. "You did not say it was Don Alejandro who died. Are you sure it was the wine?"

"Was this special wine served by the same people who worked the other tables?"

The man shook his head, a sour expression on his face. "It should have been, but Don Alejandro insisted on bringing his own cupman to attend to the Royal table."

"It displeased you?"

"Of course it did. I have worked in the palace twenty years, and such a thing has never happened before."

"I take it you saw this cupman?" Thomas asked.

César gave another shake of his head. "I did not. The bottles were brought in from somewhere else. They sat outside on the back of a cart. I hope it is all shaken up and sour by now. At least it was not my wine that poisoned him." Romero's gaze tracked Thomas before shifting to Jorge then back. "Your companion is a Spaniard, but you are not. Are you one of the English ambassadors?"

"I was sent by King Henry of England to speak with

Queen Isabel and King Fernando on matters concerning the marriage of their daughter, Catherine, who I know well. But I am no ambassador. You are sure you never saw this cupman?"

"I have already told you I did not. I put aside wine of the best quality for the royal table, but it was never taken to the hall. If a bottle contained poison it was not one I provided. Now, if you have finished, I have much work to do."

As they ascended the stone steps, Thomas turned aside from the way to the kitchens and finally took a door leading to the yard at the rear of the palace. He had been here only once before, many years ago, but it had not changed. Why would it? It was a yard for the fetching and carrying of goods for the palace, a place unknown to the exalted who lived within its walls.

"Do you think that is the cart the vintner spoke of?" asked Jorge, pointing to where a two-wheeled handcart sat in one corner.

"I see no other." Thomas started towards it. As he approached, he held up a hand. When Thomas was sure Jorge had stopped, he started again. He had seen something on the far side of the cart and did not want Jorge to witness it. As he passed the cart he glanced at the small bed, which contained a dozen wooden crates. One was open, two bottles missing from the six it had contained. But it was what lay beyond the cart that drew him. He had been unsure until he reached the far side, then there could be no doubt.

A man lay on his back, the stones beneath him dark with blood. Beside him lay a bottle of wine, pot-bellied, fashioned of thick, dark glass. Thomas knelt and turned the man's head one way then the other. A depression in his skull showed where the bottle had been used. The slash across his throat was a precaution, in case the blow had not killed him. Though, looking at the indentation and feeling its softness beneath his fingers, Thomas did not doubt it would have done the job on its own.

He rose to his feet. "Jorge, go fetch Diego Serrano if you can find him."

"Is it the cupman?" asked Jorge.

"I believe so. Diego may recognise him, but if not, we can fetch the vintner."

Thomas waited until Jorge had run off, then looked around. He did not want to disturb the body until Diego had a chance to see it. He walked a circle around the cart, studying the ground but seeing nothing. Someone must have been here but had left no trace. It was not surprising. The stone slabs meant there would be no footprints. Thomas looked around, waiting, but no one crossed the yard. This was a place for taking deliveries, and no doubt remained empty the rest of the time. Thomas suspected there would be no witnesses to what happened here. To the murder of yet one more man.

SIX

Thomas watched the passage of the cart's shadow cross the stone slabs, marking the passage of the lowering sun through the sky. Flies buzzed around the man's spilled blood. He considered covering the face to keep them off but knew there was little point. Nothing kept flies away once they scented death.

He wondered where Jorge was but knew he would be doing the best he could. Thomas would allow another quarter hour before deciding on another approach.

The time was almost up when Jorge returned. He was alone.

"Diego refused to come but said he would send someone as soon as he can. He pointed out they were busy investigating Don Alejandro's death." Jorge came closer and glanced down at the body. His face paled and he stepped back. "How can you stand so close to it?"

"I have seen worse," Thomas said.

"So have I, thanks to you, but it gets no easier."

"Who is Diego sending?"

"He did not say. Is it important?"

"Probably not. At least he cannot pretend this man was not murdered."

Jorge smiled. "You would be surprised how devious people can be."

"No, I would not." Thomas might have said more but at that moment a young man dressed in the uniform of a palace guard entered the yard and approached.

"I have been sent to look at something." He stood beside Jorge, so the body was out of sight.

"That something is here." Thomas stepped aside.

The man approached, then gagged. He turned aside and threw up against the wall. When he was done, his gaze avoided what lay on the ground.

"What happened to him?"

"I thought it obvious," Thomas said. "He was killed by a blow to the head, and then his throat cut. Do you think your master should see the body?"

"I will report back, sir, but..." His gaze took in Jorge, then Thomas, ensuring he kept it high enough not to see the body again. "Should I not arrest you both for questioning? I have been told that is normal in such circumstances."

"It was us who sent for you," Thomas said. "Is that the action of a murderer?"

"I do not know, sir. I have never been involved in a murder before. Most of us do little other than stand around looking threatening if anyone tries to enter the palace."

Thomas decided he might like the lad, for lad he was. His uniform was too big for him and showed his skinny neck, and the sleeves and hose had been rolled up to shorten them.

"You are sure your master will not attend?" Thomas asked.

"I believe he will not, sir, but will tell him what you have found." The lad almost glanced down, then averted his gaze and swallowed hard. "Someone should take care of the body." It was clear he did not believe it his job.

"I will do that," Thomas said. "Now return to your master and tell him what you have seen, and that it is proof Don Alejandro Dominguez was murdered. Also bring another man and take the cases of wine from this cart. Put them in a safe place and tell no one is to touch them, on pain of death." *Literally on pain of death,* Thomas thought.

"Did you mean what you said about taking care of the body?" asked Jorge, once the lad had run off as fast as his legs would carry him.

"You do not have to help, but I would like you to go and see if you can find something to cover the body with once I get it on the back of the cart. We will–" Thomas stopped himself. "I will return it to Don Alejandro's house. Someone there will almost certainly recognise who the man is. So you need to find out where he lived."

Once Jorge had gone, Thomas stripped out of his fine jacket and lifted the body onto the back of the cart. It was heavy enough to remind him he was not as young, or strong, as he had once been. He spent some time trying to manipulate the limbs, but they were already starting to stiffen.

When Jorge arrived with an oiled sheet, Thomas wrapped it around the body, shaking his head when he looked at his handiwork. It clearly covered a body, but there was nothing to be done because that is what it was. He retrieved the bottle used to kill the man and slipped it inside the oiled sheet. He wanted to know if anyone could tell him where it came from.

"I will come with you," said Jorge, "in case you run into trouble. I have been told the name of his wife, and you will need me to show you where she lives."

Thomas suppressed a smile. "That is a good idea."

"Do you think anyone has thought to inform Don Alejandro's wife of his death yet?" asked Jorge, as Thomas led the cart through Sevilla's narrow streets and alleys. Most people they passed showed little curiosity. Those that did looked away quickly.

"I would think so. The man was important, which makes his family important. I am sure Don Rodrigo gave instructions for them to be told."

"Good," said Jorge. "I dislike being the bearer of bad news. The house is here."

They entered a fine square south of the palace, with water at its centre and trees lining the sides. The house Jorge pointed to was wide and tall, rising to three stories beneath a steep tiled roof. A small courtyard fronted it, the rear giving on to the river. Sunlight caught at the windows to reflect brightly across the square.

Thomas climbed three stone steps and rapped on the door. It was opened by a short man dressed in dark clothing. He glanced at the cart and assumed they were peddlers.

"Go away," he said.

"I have news for Doña Carlita Dominguez, the kind

that should be delivered in person. And I need someone to identify a body. I have it in the cart, but it is not a pretty sight."

The man stared at Thomas, then switched to Jorge before returning. A shadow passed across his brow.

"Why do you bring a dead body here?"

"Has anyone else called with news for you today?"

"All deliveries are made to the side of the house." The man nodded to his right. "Along that alley there. Which, if you only knew, is where you should be."

What Thomas did know was if he wanted to make any progress, he would have to reveal what had happened at the palace.

"I was at the banquet with Don Alejandro when he became unwell and died."

This time the stare lasted longer, and a range of expressions passed across the man's face. Surprise, which was good, and told Thomas something. Anger, which was less clear. And then, relief, which confused him.

Eventually the man said, "Is that the body of Don Alejandro? He was in rude health when he left this house."

"I am sure he was, but no, this is not his body. That remains at the palace. I think. This is the body of the man I believe administered poison to your master. Which is why I want to know if anyone here recognises him."

From within the house someone called out and the man half-turned. "Tell the mistress it is no one of importance. I am dealing with it." He descended the first step and closed the door behind him. "Not here. Let us do it in the alley." He brushed past Thomas and led the way.

They eased their way along the narrow alley until it let

them out onto a wide terrace above the river. The house was set far enough downstream not to be directly disturbed by the commerce of the docks.

The man stopped.

Thomas looked at him until he offered a nod, then drew back the cover. He expected a reaction, but none came.

"I have never seen him before."

"Are you sure? His injuries are severe, I admit."

The man moved closer, leaned in. He showed no disgust before shaking his head.

"No, never seen him. Who is he?"

"That is what I would like to know," Thomas said. "I believe he may be connected to the wine trade. Does the house have a vintner?"

"I pass for that as well as mayordomo," said the man. "We are a small household, despite the master's position. If this man has something to do with wine, he has never dealt with me. And he would have had to. So I cannot help you, sir."

As the man started to turn away, Thomas said, "I would like to speak with your mistress."

"Doña Carlita only sees visitors with an appointment. She is a very private person."

"I must insist," Thomas said. He was wondering what to do with the body now but knew that speaking with Don Alejandro's wife must come first. It annoyed him that no one had come to inform the house of his death. Over two hours had passed, which was too long. Thomas wondered if everyone continued to feast, or had the gathering broken up.

"I am not sure you are someone who can insist, sir," said the man.

Thomas pulled himself up to his full height and searched for the voice he once used when he ruled Granada. "I am Thomas Berrington, Duque of Granada, and friend to King Fernando and Queen Isabel, who has tasked me with discovering who killed your master, and why. Speaking with his wife is but the start of that process. Inform her she has visitors." He glanced at the cart. "I will leave this here in the shade for the moment." Thomas waited until, as expected, the man turned away. Instead of taking the alley, he crossed the terrace and entered through another door.

SEVEN

"He did not seem impressed by your title," said Jorge.

"I agree. Most likely it was mention of the King and Queen that tipped the balance."

"Indeed." Jorge glanced at the cart without seeing the contents. "Will this be safe here?"

Thomas laughed. "With good fortune someone will steal it, then it will no longer be our responsibility."

"Your responsibility," said Jorge.

"Is that not what I said?"

The mayordomo returned from the way he had left and beckoned them to him.

"You are fortunate. My mistress has agreed to see you."

"Did you tell her about her husband?"

The man looked appalled at the idea. "I considered it better coming from you."

They entered through a rear door almost as ornate as that at the front, then along a wide hallway adorned with paintings and drapes depicting, in the main, the female form. In quite some detail.

The man stopped outside a gilded door and held his hand up. "Stay here."

"I hope he has not gone to tell her the news after all," said Jorge. "It will be better coming from me."

"I agree. What do you make of his reaction to the body?"

"As far as I can tell he truly did not know the man. The news of his master's death shocked him, which tells us he had no hand in it. Also, he disliked his master, hence the show of relief."

"And the anger?"

"That I do not know. Perhaps he fears for his post. We might know more if we are ever admitted to Doña Carlita."

Which they were within a few minutes, though even a few seemed too many to Thomas.

The mayordomo held the door open. "These are the men who want to see you, Doña."

Doña Carlita was younger than Thomas expected, barely into her twenties. She was tall for a woman, slim, and achingly beautiful, with long dark hair tied into bunches on either side, dark eyes and a full mouth. Her clothes were designed to show her figure to its best, which was good indeed. Her eyes tracked Thomas then moved to Jorge. She smiled.

"Manuel tells me you bring news. Please, let us sit. You can leave us, Manuel, but ask for wine to be brought. One of the good bottles."

"I should stay, Doña. These men are strangers."

"Indeed they are, but not for long." Her gaze returned to Jorge. "Tell me your names, gentlemen."

Jorge spoke, as he had been asked to. "My companion is

Thomas Berrington, Duque of Granada, and I am Jorge Olmos and lack any title."

Once more she smiled. "I would judge you do not need a title, Jorge Olmos." Her attention returned to her mayordomo. "See, Manuel, now they are no longer strangers, and no doubt thirsty." She waved a delicate hand and the man turned and left the room. He left the door open.

"He still does not trust you," she said. "Now, what brings you here? Not that visitors are unwelcome." She gave Thomas barely any attention.

"We come with grave news, sweet lady," said Jorge. "I am afraid your husband is dead."

Doña Carlita seemed unperturbed.

"How did he die? Was there much pain?" She showed nothing of grief, which made Thomas believe her marriage to Don Alejandro one of convenience, most likely for both of them. He wondered if she had wanted him dead.

"No pain, Doña," he lied. "I was with him at the end and he spoke your name."

Finally, her gaze reached Thomas but fluttered there like an escaped bird, ready to fly back to Jorge. "I doubt very much he did," she said, "unless his wits were addled."

"He was poisoned, so that is possible."

"Thomas is a physician," said Jorge. "Rest assured, he did everything he could to save your husband. I understand he has several children. Do they live here?"

"None of them. They have families and lives of their own and rarely visit. Alejandro was not an easy man to love. Or even like. I am not his first wife, but it appears I will be his last." She looked around the room, which was well furnished, the drapes on the walls depicting maritime scenes. Dark wooden furniture filled the room, and expensive paintings hung on the walls. Two showed Don Alejandro, one in his clothes of state, the other dressed less formally. Three others showed women, presumably his earlier wives. In an alcove, two depicted Carlita. One in particular was blatant. She lay on a chaise longue, her clothing dishevelled to reveal one breast and a length of thigh. The expression on her face was of pure lust.

"Do you like it?" asked Carlita. "The painting was commissioned by Alejandro shortly after we married. He liked to show it off to his friends." Her voice showed nothing, and Thomas wondered if Alejandro liked to show her off as well. He had thought it might have been a marriage of convenience for her, but now it did not appear to be so.

"Will his children expect to inherit?" Thomas asked. "I am sorry, I should have asked before leaving the palace, but was your husband wealthy?"

"Of course he was." A trace of spite coloured her words. "And yes, the children will expect their share, as the law states. But half will come to me as the surviving spouse. And the house is in my name. Alejandro knew he was no longer young and wanted me taken care of, so he transferred funds and this house to me, so his children have no call on it."

"It is unusual for a woman to be named," Thomas said.

"I am no ordinary woman, as I hope you can tell." For a moment her eyes went to the painting of herself.

"Indeed I can."

Carlita's gaze drifted towards Jorge again, who sat comfortably, one lean leg crossed over the other, a benign expression on his face as was his usual manner.

“I will look for a new husband eventually but am in no rush to tie myself to one man again.”

“Love is infinite, yes?” said Jorge.

Carlita smiled. “I see you understand love. Do you understand me as well, Jorge Olmos?”

“I understand most women, yes. Their needs, their wants, their obsessions, desires and fears.” Jorge’s voice was soft, lacking any judgement.

Thomas watched as Carlita fell under his spell. It was not the first time it had happened with a woman and would not be the last. He knew she would submit to him in a moment, even now so soon after the death of her husband. Still, it was soon for her to offer herself so quickly, though Thomas had seen her being careful not to be blatant about it. Some men would miss the signals altogether. Jorge was not some men.

Thomas leaned forward, arms draped across his knees. “Can you think of anyone who might have wanted your husband dead?”

“How long do we have, sir?” Carlita’s gaze did not stray from Jorge. A rosy glow showed on her throat and cheeks.

“Do you think you could produce a list for me? Not now, of course. Tomorrow morning will suffice.”

“You said it was poison. From what you say, it was deliberate and not accidental. Alejandro had a friend recently who died from the wrong kind of mushrooms. It is uncommon but happens.”

“I am aware it does. I am convinced what happened to your husband was deliberate. Do you think you will be able to produce that list for me?”

Carlita sighed heavily, her gaze finally leaving Jorge. “I

will see what I can do, but the hour is growing late, and I have plans for the rest of the evening." She smiled at Jorge. "Unless your friend would like me to change them?"

Jorge rose. "It is most tempting, my dear." He bowed and took her hand, kissed the back of it softly then turned it over and did the same to her palm. "Unfortunately, we have more work to do yet. If I was to call around noon tomorrow do you think you might have the list of names for Thomas?"

"I will do it for you. I will have Manuel draw it up and then add anyone he misses. He knows who Alejandro crossed in business as well as anyone, most likely more than I do." She looked at Jorge. "Are you sure you cannot stay, even for an hour?"

Jorge kissed her hand again. "You are a woman who deserves longer than a mere hour. We must take our leave, but I will see you tomorrow."

"At noon."

Jorge smiled. "Yes. At noon."

Thomas rose and turned away. It took Jorge longer to join him. In the hallway, Manuel waited to take them to the rear door to retrieve the cart and its contents.

"Is my mistress upset, sir?"

"How long have they been married?" Thomas asked.

Manuel looked aside as he recalled his answer, then said, "A little over two years."

"She is his third wife?"

"She is."

"What happened to the other two?"

"Both died in childbirth. The child with them." He

spoke without emotion. Such events were common enough to be an accepted part of life and death.

"Have you worked for Don Alejandro long?"

"Fifteen years. There was another mayordomo before me, but he too died, even though I believe he was quite young. Such things happen."

"Yes, they do."

"I am sorry I could not help identify the dead man you brought, but you may have more luck at the *Casa de Contratación*. It takes up half the dockside and grows bigger almost day by day. Ask for Luisa Mercado and tell her Miguel Romero sent you."

As Thomas took the stays of the cart again and drew it into the square he said to Jorge, "I thought you were about to seduce Doña Carlita there and then."

Jorge laughed. "Oh, she wanted me to, but you know there is only one woman for me. Even so, I admit to growing a little aroused at the thought of what she offered." Jorge smiled. "Is the thought the same as infidelity?"

"You are asking the wrong man."

"I suspect I am, but no mind. I take it you saw she was hiding something?"

"Not her breasts, that was certain," Thomas said. "And of course she was hiding something. No doubt where most of Don Alejandro's wealth lies. I suspect she has been busy hiding as much as she can of it away so it cannot be passed down to his children."

"Yes, that might be it," said Jorge. "I take it you are certain he was murdered, and it was not an accident?"

"It is possible the goblet he drank from was tainted, but how to tell is another matter," Thomas said. "If we ever find out who this man I am pulling along is it might offer some hint as to how and why he died."

"Do you think Miguel involved?"

"I did not like the man, but that is no reason to accuse him of murder. And he did offer us somewhere else to try."

"Did you see the way his eyes stayed on Doña Carlita?"

"I did not but trust you to notice such things. Was it love or hatred?"

"Oh, love certainly, and lust."

"To which she would never respond."

When Jorge said nothing, Thomas asked, "Would she?"

Jorge drew the attention of a passing couple when he laughed. The woman kept her head turned and almost tripped on a loose flagstone.

"No, she would not. The woman is sensual, but not foolish. At least I do not think so. It is fortunate we have nothing better to do. We have been here barely a week, and already I saw you were growing bored. Now you have a murder to investigate." Jorge rubbed his hands together. "You are not a man who takes kindly to leisure."

"Whereas you, my friend, enjoy nothing better. But you are right, I need something to occupy me. I must speak with Isabel soon, but it is as if she deliberately ignores me."

"She is protecting herself from her own emotions. As are you."

"What we had, what we did, was but one short afternoon, nothing more. I have no expectation of anything else, and I am sure neither does she."

"The heart cannot be reasoned with, Thomas. You have known great love and grief. I think the latter changed you.

There is no woman for you now, but I also know it does not bother you, does it?"

"It does not. But I like to think that if the right woman came along, I would still be able to respond."

"To rise to the occasion?" This time when Jorge laughed Thomas joined in.

"Yes, that too. Now, we are almost at the dockside. You spoke with Luisa Mercado at the banquet, so I hope we can discover who this man is and unburden ourselves of the cart and him both. I would not ask her to view the body, but she will be able to ask someone else to."

"She did not strike me as a woman to delegate unsavoury tasks to someone else. I thought her strong and determined. But you are right, it will be good to get rid of him."

EIGHT

Emerging with the cart onto a wide dockside Thomas saw much work taking place to enlarge the buildings around it. One remained under construction, only part of the roof tiled. Many people milled around outside, carrying stone, wood, plaster. Some workmen erected elements of the building, others were traders and sailors. Two ships were docked, gangplanks lowered from one so goods could be brought off, supplies being loaded onto the other. In the river beyond, half a dozen ships lay at anchor. It was a scene of almost total chaos, but somehow everyone knew their place and what they were meant to do.

Two men stood on a raised platform of wooden boards. They held sheaves of paper which they consulted, ticking some items off, putting crosses against others. Thomas made his way in their direction, Jorge at his side. They pushed and twisted their way through the crowd, receiving complaints about the cart, but Thomas saw it was not the only one being used. Loud voices and shouts made conversation impossible unless they were shouted above it all, which was not what either Thomas or Jorge would do. When they reached the men, Thomas raised a hand, which was ignored. Thomas tried again, tugging at the leg of one of the men's hose, only to be kicked at.

"We might have better luck over there," said Jorge, pointing to where a familiar figure passed unhindered through the crowd, which parted before him.

"It seems Don Rodrigo has influence here," Thomas said.

"The man will have influence everywhere. He has settled into his new position next to the King and Queen as if he has always held it." Jorge smiled. "I noticed the serving girls were a little flustered by him."

"More so than you?" Thomas asked, surprised.

"Oh, I believe they sense I am not a whole man."

"You may not be a whole man," Thomas said, "but I managed to leave you with half the equipment. Probably the most important part."

"Probably. I would have liked to father children myself rather than having to ask you, though I admit it has made us closer than friends."

Thomas made no reply. Lying with Belia, Jorge's woman, made him feel awkward, pleasurable though the experience had been, and made easier by Jorge asking him to do so. But it was in the past now and would never happen again. They had almost reached Don Rodrigo by following him and making use of the way the crowd parted to allow him to pass. The man reached a makeshift entrance to the wooden structure that appeared to be temporary, because workmen were laying stones on one corner, removing planks and beams as they worked inward. The side next to the river appeared complete, rising two storeys with a wide opening at the base. It was testament to how important this House of Trade was for the work to have started so soon. Don Rodrigo stopped at the entrance and turned back.

"Did you think me unaware of your presence, Thomas? Do you want something?"

"I am here to make enquiries regarding the death of Don Alejandro. I was told it would be worth my time coming here. Now I have, I am at a loss how to proceed. Do you know how I can find Luisa Mercado?"

Don Rodrigo smiled. "Keep close. Inside will be even more chaotic than here. I suggest you leave the cart outside."

Thomas looked at the cart.

"Jorge, stay here and make sure no one interferes with the cart."

Without waiting for a reply, Thomas turned and put his hand on Don Rodrigo's shoulder, feeling the strength of lean muscle. The crowd inside was even thicker. Part of the reason was caused by stalls set out which almost completely filled the interior. Thomas knew it would have been impossible to negotiate the cart through this space. Men, women and children stood beside each stall. The rich scent of spices, some unfamiliar, filled the air. So did the stink of fish, meat, animal dung from cattle, sheep, pigs and fowl penned to await a butcher's knife. The noises of animals filled the air, competing with the shouts of the vendors. Even Don Rodrigo had to push his way through to make progress. Thomas was jostled as he fought to stay with him.

And then, as if by some miracle, the crowd was behind them.

Thomas released his hold. They stood in a small area in front of what looked like a smaller building within the larger building. It was fashioned of stone and small Moorish bricks, and Thomas realised this must be the original market, built centuries before when the Moors ruled Sevilla. This is what he had seen from outside. Not a new building, but one that already existed. It stood hard against the stone dock on one side, linked on the other to the wall surrounding the Alcazar palace. Its proximity to the mighty Guadalquivir was important, the river used to transport goods both upstream and down. Now, with the discoveries being made in the new world, its position had become even more important. Hence this new building: *Casa de Contratación*.

"You will find Luisa Mercado inside," said Don Rodrigo. "I would accompany you, but she would not welcome my presence. Besides, I have other matters to attend to." The man turned away and disappeared into the crowd.

Thomas wondered what had brought Don Rodrigo to this place but suspected the man would need to keep his attention on many parts of the city. This one, so close to the palace, seemingly thriving and becoming more important, would be but one of them.

Thomas approached the entrance to the stone house. It reminded him a little of the one he had left behind in Granada. Only two stories and squat to the ground, it would have stood here long before the discovery of the new world across the great ocean.

In the first room scribes stood at tall desks. One or two glanced at Thomas then returned to their work, incurious. The tall woman Jorge had pointed out to him at the banquet appeared from a room beyond the desks, hands on hips. She had changed since and was now dressed for practicality in brown breeches topped with a dark grey shirt. From what Don Rodrigo and Jorge had said, despite her appearance, and being female in a man's world, she was an important figure.

She stared at Thomas without expression as he approached. "As you can see, we are busy. What do you want?"

"I need for someone to identify a dead body."

The woman scowled. "I have already heard of Don Alejandro's death, and doubt there is any need to identify him. What interest is it to you?"

"As you know, I was at the banquet when he died, and the Queen has asked me to investigate his death. Which was murder."

"That I did not hear," said Luisa. "You said you wanted a body identified. I take it this is someone else." She waved a hand. "Come into my office. It is best no one else hears what we discuss."

Thomas followed her, trying to make up his mind whether she would help or not. Her manner was stiff and harsh, which surprised him after what Jorge had said. Perhaps it was the face she displayed to this world she worked in. The position she held here would need to be held hard to.

Inside, a wide desk covered with papers filled half the space. The rest was covered in shelves holding stacks of more papers, their edges curling. A wide unglazed opening in the far wall looked directly out to the river, where a cutter made its way in search of a mooring.

"Tell me what I need to know," said Luisa.

Thomas took a moment to settle his thoughts so he would not say more than needed.

"I saw a cupman fill Don Alejandro's goblet with wine. Almost as soon as he drank, he stumbled and fell. I trained as a surgeon, so went to him, but by the time I reached him he was dead. I tasted the wine, but could not tell if it was tainted or not."

"You would recognise if it was? Your friend told me you were a physic."

It surprised Thomas she asked because it meant she accepted everything else he had said.

"It was definitely not the fine wine it was meant to be. When I went outside to the palace yard in search of the cupman I found him, but he was also dead. His head had been caved in and his throat cut for good measure." Thomas watched Luisa's face for any reaction, but none came. He sighed, knowing more explanation would be needed. "Don Alejandro's mayordomo did not recognise the man but told me someone here might."

"You brought this dead man with you?"

"He is outside in a cart, covered with an oiled cloth. He has been dead a while now, so might be starting to smell."

"If he is still there. A cart, you say? Leaving a cart unattended around here is asking for the cart, and whatever is in it, to be stolen."

"The thieves would be most disappointed, I am sure, but my companion is looking over it."

"If he is the man I spoke with, I would say he does not look dangerous enough. I hope he does not get his pretty head caved in too."

"He is tall, and when he scowls can make a show of looking dangerous," Thomas said. "Do you think you might recognise the dead man?"

Luisa Mercado jerked one narrow shoulder. "It is true I know many of those who come to this place, so perhaps. Do you want me to see him?"

"Only if it will not upset you. He is starting to turn colour already, and the flies have been at him."

"Then it is fortunate I have a strong disposition. Here, we will leave this way. It is quicker than passing through the marketplace." She turned and stepped through an opening in the wall. When Thomas followed, he found a narrow walkway with the river almost lapping against it. Luisa was already at the corner of the building, and he followed as she disappeared around it. The walkway extended along the large market building, and they came out near the entrance.

Luisa saw the cart and strode to it, reached in and pulled the canvas back. She stared at the body, which had indeed turned a dark blue in places, flies crawling over its eyes.

"It is hard to tell with him in this state," said Luisa, "but it is possible he is one of Mateo Salto's men. He has the look of a Portuguese, and Mateo deals in wines as well as other items from that country – most of it contraband. He did bring someone here to discuss the import of wine some time ago. It is possible this is the same man." She looked at Jorge for a moment, then turned to Thomas. "Do you need to know anything else?"

"Where can I find this Mateo Salto?"

What might have passed for a smile crossed Luisa's face. "You do not want to find him. In fact, I would recommend you have nothing to do with the man." She glanced again at the corpse. "Before you end up the same way as this poor soul."

"I am more resourceful than I might look," Thomas said.

"You would have to be." Her eyes tracked his face, taking their time. "Are you committed to this course of action?"

"I am."

"That is a shame, for I would have liked to know you better. At least when Mateo kills you I can say I briefly met the famous Thomas Berrington, though it turned out he was not as fearsome as his reputation."

Thomas smiled. He liked this woman but doubted she would ever like him. Even so, he said, "I see you know my name, and my companion is Jorge Olmos."

"I know who you are; the Englishman who lived in Moorish Spain and went native. And I know who your friend is, he told me at the banquet. He is Spanish, and you are not. What business is this of yours?"

"I told you, the Queen has tasked me with finding Don Alejandro's killer, and that of this man if they are one and the same."

Luisa surprised him when she laughed. "After you have discovered who wanted Don Alejandro dead – and if it is Mateo I doubt anything can be done about it – come and find me again. I would welcome hearing stories of your years in Granada. My own father was a Moor, but he never told me much about his life."

Thomas studied her a moment. "Yes, I can see it in your features," he said, "but suspect most would take you for Spanish."

"Of course they do, and you must forget I ever spoke those words. I have a position here and would not put it in danger." She shook her head. "I have no idea why I told you what I did. If you continue with your foolishness, and want to know more about Mateo, speak with Rosa Martinez." Luisa raised a hand and pointed across the market square to a row of low buildings, most of which had shades over stalls set outside. "She sells herbs and potions, some from the new world. She has dealings with Mateo among others. Perhaps she will have more luck in persuading you to leave this matter alone." She gave a final glance at the body. "He needs to be buried before he stinks the entire city up." With that she strode away.

"She is magnificent," said Jorge. "You should pursue her, for she shows interest in you."

"You are sure, are you?" Thomas said.

"Almost sure."

"We cannot bury this man until we know who he is and who he works for. Let us try this Rosa Martinez." Thomas glanced at the sky. "The hours are passing and I would have him in the ground before morning. Luisa is right, he is starting to stink."

"I can think of better means of seduction than carting a dead body around," said Jorge, "but you seemed to make an impression on Luisa. Let us see if you can do the same with this Rosa."

NINE

As they approached the house Luisa had pointed out, Thomas caught sight of a short, pretty woman in her thirties. The sunlight caught the woman's light brown hair, turning it golden. She glanced at the cart, but the smell of it was masked by a breeze which had turned as the day moved towards its end.

"What can I do for you gentlemen?" she asked. "Is it herbs you want? Something to help you rise to the occasion with your wife or lover?" Her eyes settled on Jorge. "Though you do not look as if you need much help for that, sir."

Thomas was aware age had crept up on him with a quiet stealth he had not seen coming. His hair remained full, but now showed grey at the temples, and he had lines around his eyes that had not been there a few years before. In himself, he felt little different to the lad of thirteen who had left England, but experience told him he was. He could not fight like once he did, though he was grateful his mind remained as sharp as ever. There were aches in his bones that made getting out of bed a slower process than it had been. Now and again, he envied the easy power of his son, Will, and the suppleness of his daughter, Amal.

"I am afraid we do not need any of your produce, excellent as it looks. We have a less pleasant question to ask."

The woman frowned. "I do not understand. Who are you, sir?" Her attention was now on Thomas. Older and less handsome he might be, but he carried a sense of power Jorge could never emulate.

"I am Thomas Berrington, and my companion is–"

"*The* Thomas Berrington?" The woman interrupted. "The physician who lived among the Moors before growing close to Queen Isabel?"

Thomas thought it interesting she made no mention of King Fernando. It told him she truly knew who he was, and also of the enmity of the King for him.

"I am he," Thomas said. "How do you know of me?"

She gave a brief laugh. "In my profession your name is well known." She glanced at Jorge. "And you are the eunuch, yes? Belia trained me in Cordoba when I was but a child."

"I do not recall you," said Jorge.

"I was little more than a waif, but I remember you."

Jorge smiled. "Looking at you now, you would have been a pretty waif, and I never forget a pretty face, however young or old it might be."

"Belia told me you possessed a golden tongue. I see now she was right. Is she with you?"

"She remains in England," said Jorge. "Together with our three children. Hopefully soon to be four."

Rosa Martinez frowned. "Handsome as you are, Jorge, I

know well enough what you are and that you are incapable of fathering children."

"I have a friend who helped."

Rosa glanced at Thomas. "I see." She shook her head. "No mind. You said you wanted to ask me something."

"I want to show you something, but it is not a pleasant sight."

Rosa made her eyes wide as if in shock before breaking into laughter. "I have seen many unpleasant sights, Thomas Berrington. What can you have for me I have not seen a dozen times before?"

"There is a dead man in the back of the cart, and I need to know who he is. Luisa Mercado told me you might know."

"How dead?" asked Rosa.

"Just after noon today."

"So he may not smell too bad yet. Show me, though I make no promise."

Thomas pulled the cart closer and turned it so only Rosa could see when he drew the oilskin back. She stared at the body, tilted her head, then said, "I do not know a name, but I recognise him. As much as I can with his head caved in." She leaned close and waved her hand so flies rose from the body to buzz through the air. Rosa nodded. "Yes, I have seen him, but..." She looked up at Thomas. "I saw him once with a man by the name of Mateo Salto, who is someone you do not want to meet."

"Luisa Mercado told me the same thing, but I may have to speak with him. Where did you see them?"

"They came to the *Casa de Contratación* on business. I believe it was when he was introduced to Luisa."

"She said he was familiar but knew no name."

"Luisa meets many people, and unless they make an impression she discards all memory of them. We can take him to Mateo if you insist on knowing more, but I will need to prepare the body or there will be little of him left by the time we get to Cantillano. It is half a day's walk, perhaps a little more as you are old."

"You said we," Thomas said. "I would not impose on you. And would not horseback be swifter?"

"If Mateo sees a rider approaching, he will put an arrow through them before they can state their business. He knows me, so it is best I am with you. He does not take to strangers. Bring the cart around the back – there is an alley at the side that runs behind the houses. I will open my workshop door. You were a surgeon, yes?"

"I expect I still am if called upon."

"Then you know what must be done. I have the herbs and oils to keep him sweet for the time it will take to return him to Mateo, but he will last better for the removal of his lights."

"I can do that," Thomas said, before turning to Jorge. "I will not trouble you with any of this, my friend. Return to our lodgings. I will see you there when we are finished, but it may be late."

Thomas waited until Jorge had gone before taking the stays of the cart and pulling it down the promised alleyway, where Rosa Martinez was waiting for him. He hefted the now stiff body from the cart and laid it on a stained table.

"This is not the first time you have done this work, is it?" he said.

"It is not something many are willing to do, so no. It

pays well enough, and I have everything needed to keep a body smelling sweet for a week. Longer than that and they would need someone with more skill." She smiled softly. "I expect Belia still has those skills."

"She does. And I am happy to pay you."

"As well you should be. But tell me, how is Belia?"

"Well and happy. We live in England now."

"Do you not miss Spain?" Rosa handed Thomas a sharp blade and a curved metal implement he was familiar with.

"I thought perhaps I might until we returned, but my home is no longer here." Thomas opened the man along his entire front, ignoring the stink, as he was always able to. Rosa's expression told him she too could do the same. He reached in, cut, lifted, and dropped each organ into the first of the buckets Rosa had set for that purpose.

"What do we do with these when we are done?" Thomas asked. "Burn them?"

"I usually wait until full dark and toss them into the river. The fish and birds can grow fat."

Thomas tried not to show his disgust, but it made him aware Rosa was harder than her soft appearance suggested. Once the internal organs were removed, he spooned the brain matter from the broken skull.

He stood back, holding his blood-stained hands up. "He is all yours now. You say you can keep him sweet a week. Is that long enough to return him to this man you say may be his master?"

"We will leave as soon as the sun rises on the morrow and reach there before noon."

Rosa washed inside the body, then gathered herbs, roots, oils and salves and began to fill the empty space.

"You must know this Mateo Salto well." Thomas meant nothing by the comment, but Rosa gave him a harsh look.

"Our relationship is purely trade, nothing more."

"I did not–" Thomas stopped, thinking how Jorge might deal with a response. He started again. "I meant if he knows you, you will be able to introduce me."

"Mateo does not take to being questioned. You have still not told me what this man has done, or why he died."

Thomas realised she spoke the truth, so while Rosa worked, he explained what had happened at the banquet in the palace. He enjoyed watching the skill with which she worked. The way her hands selected and laid items out. The way her slim body swayed. The way she pushed hair back from her face with her forearms when it fell forward.

After a while, she said, "You are staring at me. Take his lights and toss them in the river. It should be dark enough by now but try not to let anyone see what you are doing."

Thomas set the buckets on the back of the cart and trundled it away. He passed a few people, but they ignored him. He was just one more trader moving goods. At the riverside, he descended stone steps until the water washed against his boots and emptied the buckets into the water. When he was done, he knelt and washed them out, then returned to Rosa.

When he stood beside her once more, she had finished and the body now lay wrapped in a white linen sheet, his clothes neatly folded beside him.

"You are sure this man murdered Don Alejandro Dominguez?"

"I watched him pour wine from the same bottle used to break his skull. I tasted a little and it was acrid."

"Which means, if he works for Mateo, he has a hand in it. One of his men would not do such work without his say-so. It might be better if you do not accompany me. If you have questions tell them to me and I will ask them if I can."

"No. I come with you."

"Mateo will have you killed."

"Others have tried over the years, and I am still alive." He held his arms out in demonstration.

Rosa snuffled a laugh. "I suspect none of those others were like Mateo. He is the Devil himself, even though if you meet him you would not know at first. He is easy to like. Polite, and a good host, but then I suspect the Devil would act the same until he dragged you into the flames of Hell."

"I still want to come."

Rosa took a breath, released it. "Then return here at dawn. You can drag the cart. And explain to your friend that if you are killed it is not my fault."

"Jorge will understand. He knows me better than I know myself."

Rosa looked into Thomas's eyes, the moment drawing out. "I do not think that would be hard to do. I know you are clever, but do you truly know who you are?"

Thomas made no response because he did not think one necessary. He believed Rosa was wrong but there was no point in arguing.

"How much do I owe you for the work?"

She looked around, at the wrapped body, the materials she had used, and told him a price. He did not know if it was too much or too little, only that it did not matter.

"I will bring payment at dawn."

He turned and walked away, not looking back, even though he was curious if Rosa might still be watching him.

At their lodgings, Thomas drew water, undressed and washed his entire body. When he went upstairs, Jorge was already asleep. Thomas thought to wake him and ask what he had found out but decided to let him rest. He lay on his own bed, staring through the open window at the dense black of the night punctured by bright stars. Eventually, sleep came, but it was filled with dreams of fighting for his life.

TEN

Thomas left Jorge snoring softly and tiptoed from the room, pulled on his boots and left the house. When he arrived at Rosa's stall he expected to have to knock, but she waited outside, dressed in breeches and a leather jerkin almost the same as Luisa Mercado had worn the day before. Her hair was tied on top of her head, captured beneath a wide-brimmed hat. The cart stood at the head of the alley. There were only a few people about, and none showed curiosity.

"I managed to get some blocks of ice and put them around him," she said. "I also arranged for a boat to take us and the cart across the river. Come, before the man thinks I have forgotten."

She strode off and Thomas followed. The boat was sufficient for their needs, the river almost still and shrouded in drifting morning mist. As they stepped out on the far bank, light was starting to show at their backs, but not enough to throw shadows. Thomas hefted the stays of the cart and they started off.

"I need to talk to you of poisons," he said, after they had gone a hundred paces.

Rosa laughed. "You should consult your friend on the art of wooing a woman, Thomas. What do you want to know?"

"I am not unfamiliar with poisons, but I do not know what this one might be," he said.

"Nor do I, unless you can describe it better than you have. You said you tasted it – which I would never have done, but I assume you know the dangers. Tell me what you tasted."

"Wine, nothing else."

Rosa was silent for a while. They started to climb a slope and Thomas's breath grew short from pulling his burden.

"I assume you are familiar with many poisons, both here and in England."

"And elsewhere. I lived among the Moors and there are many Arabic poisons we knew nothing of before they came here. I made an extensive study of them."

"In that case, it is possible this poison was brought from the new world across the great ocean. I have had to learn about many new herbs and plants, but there are even more I know nothing of. This could be one of them, but I know of someone who may be able to help you."

"This Mateo?"

Rosa laughed. "No. Someone even more dangerous."

Thomas shook his head. "I wish I knew why these problems fall into my lap instead of someone else's."

"It is because the problems know you can deal with them," said Rosa. "Most others would hide away and ignore the danger. You are not that manner of man, are you."

"No, I expect I am not. Who is this other man, one of Mateo's men? Is that why you said he was dangerous?"

Rosa laughed. "No, his name is Baracoa Caguas, and he likes no one. He feels violated and blames the entire world for it. He was torn from his homeland and abandoned in this one."

"If he is from across the ocean I would be interested to hear his story. He must have many tales to tell."

"If so he tells none to me, and I consider myself as close to him as anyone in this land."

"You have become a friend to him, yes? I can see why, for you are easy to like."

Rosa offered Thomas a dismissive look. "He puts up with me, and friend is too simple a word to describe our relationship."

Thomas might have asked Rosa what the right word might be, but at that moment they crested the ridge and nestled in the valley below was an extensive single-story house, set close to a small town on the western bank of the Guadalquivir river. Beyond the town, higher hills rose, a steep-sided valley cutting through them. It made a good location, with access to trade both upstream and down.

"Is this the track people use who deal with the man we are going to meet? I notice it is well used."

"For goods, most people use the river, even though it takes longer, but yes, it is well used." Rosa inclined her head towards the house. "They will have seen us as soon as we crossed the ridge. There will be people waiting. We will see them as we approach. They will look threatening, but you should be safe with me."

Thomas suppressed a smile. "I have dealt with violent men before. You do not need to be concerned for me."

"You do not strike me as a man who believes in fear. Perhaps you should learn to do so."

They spoke more about poisons, and Baracoa, as they descended the slope. Rosa told Thomas they would have to go to where he lived if he wanted to know more, but that he may refuse to answer his questions.

"You must prepare yourself for that," she said.

"I have a friend who can be most persuasive," Thomas said.

"The eunuch? Yes, I gathered that about him. He is uncommonly handsome and must have women prostrate themselves at his feet. I suspect all will be disappointed, will they not?"

"Why do you say that?" Thomas asked.

"Because he is a eunuch."

"Who I made that way to save his life. I was as kind as I could be."

Rosa's eyes widened, and Thomas wondered if he had changed her opinion of Jorge.

"I prefer my men with more sharp edges," she said.

Below them, men appeared at the house. Three walked forwards. *Only three,* Thomas thought. But then, for most visitors, three would no doubt be more than enough.

The men stopped and waited for the approaching pair. When they were close one of them grinned and walked forwards.

"Rosa, it is good to see you again." He embraced her

and kissed both cheeks before turning to Thomas. "Who is your friend? Does he want to purchase something? I have much to offer an older man." He held a hand out and Thomas shook it, making sure he did not let the man's grip crush his fingers. It seemed he passed the test because the man offered a nod of respect. "Or perhaps he has something to sell in that cart. Who is he?" The man's eyes tracked Thomas and came away less than impressed.

"His name is Thomas Berrington, Mateo. A friend to both the King and Queen, and he has a question for you."

"Does he? Only one?" The man's eyes remained on Thomas. They were dark brown, sharp with intelligence. He stood three inches shorter than Thomas, narrower across the shoulders, but lithe and strong, as evidenced by his grip. "I hope his questions are appropriate, otherwise I may need to chastise you, my dear." He glanced at the sky, where the sun had not yet reached its zenith. "What is this question? Though I make no promise to answer."

Thomas turned to the cart and drew back the cloth to reveal the body. Most of the blocks of ice had melted but had done their work.

"Do you recognise this man?"

Mateo showed no surprise at the body, nor revulsion. He moved closer and stared at it. Rosa had made the man's face presentable and wrapped cloths around his head to hide the gaping hole in his skull.

"What happened to him?" asked Mateo.

"He was attacked after he poisoned a man close to the King and Queen."

Mateo frowned. "This sounds as if it may take some

time. Come, let us go to the house. It is almost time to eat, and you have had a long journey."

"Do you know him?" Thomas asked.

Mateo glanced once more at the body. "He is familiar, but I do not know his name."

"Is he one of your men?"

"I do not believe so, but I do not know them all. Bring him down and I will have others look at him. Someone may know who he is and what he has been doing." Mateo started to turn away, then stopped. "Know that whatever he has done is nothing to do with me. I have ordered no one killed for several weeks."

Thomas thought it best not to question the claim.

"Do you intend to stay the night?" Mateo asked. "And if so, will you want one room or two?"

"Our business should not take that long," said Rosa.

"That is a shame. I have people calling this evening with a new supply of wine, and the best goods from across the sea. Items they claim no one else has seen. I thought they might be of interest to you, but..." He raised a shoulder and held a hand out to Rosa. "Let us walk to the house. I will ask for something delicate for us to eat and drink. I have a wonderful pale wine from the north of Portugal that is exquisite."

Rosa placed her hand in his. She offered an apologetic smile at Thomas as they descended the remains of the slope. Close to, the house was even more impressive, despite its lack of height. Doors and windows were fashioned in Moorish style, the walls built using small bricks. Arches fronted the terrace, which looked across the river and a wide sand shore. It was shallow enough that a person with knowledge might be able to wade across. To one side sat a warehouse with open doors which showed half a dozen men working within. The small town was near, but the land hid it from view so someone coming across Mateo's estate from the south would never know it was there. One of the men who had come to watch them turned and went beneath an arch, so he was almost concealed in the shade. Before he disappeared, Thomas noted he was dressed differently to the others and might be taken for a gentleman. Perhaps he was one of the claimed guests who had arrived early and did not want to be involved in Mateo's business.

When Mateo released Rosa's hand, she took a step aside so she was closer to Thomas.

"I will have the food brought," said Mateo. "Do you want to try some of the exquisite wine, or would you prefer ale?"

Thomas glanced at Rosa for an answer.

"Wine," she said.

After Mateo entered the house, they sat side by side at a fine table. Men remained nearby, but far enough away not to overhear their conversation.

"Mateo would bed me in an instant if I showed him any favour," said Rosa, "which I take care never to do. He beds many women. Some because they like him, others because he is rich and his wealth attracts them. Also, some like dangerous men."

"But not you," Thomas said.

"No, not me."

"I like his house." Thomas was unsure why Rosa was being so honest with him. He stared at her as she turned away to gaze at the river, reflections from the water touching her face. Her skin was darker than most Spaniard's, but not unusually so. Most of the Moors might have been expelled from this land, but they had left their mark on its people. Those who lived in the south were a mix of bloodlines. Thomas liked the fact. It pleased him to see such a mixture living together. Defeat of the Moors was still recent, and hatred of them common, but that did not seem to include those who clearly had Moorish blood running through them.

"We could stay the night here if you want," said Rosa. "I am sure Mateo will find us two rooms if we ask. He has enough of them." She looked away, as if something fascinated her out there. All Thomas saw was water and the hill they had crossed. To their left, the valley curved away with more hills beyond, a higher peak climbing from a deep gulley. This was silent country. Isolated. No doubt that was why Mateo had built his business here, where no one could witness what he did.

"I assume you have seen he already has a guest." Thomas said. He had looked for the shy man since sitting but not seen him. "I imagine many of Mateo's guests might prefer to skulk in the shadows. And as for rooms, let us see what happens." He looked at Rosa. "I take it Mateo is not an honest man?"

She laughed. "That depends on how you define honesty. He is not a wicked man, but operates by his own rules."

"Is he violent?"

"I have heard he can be, but never with me. He wants me, I know, but has never used force. Beneath the outer shell he has a soft soul. Like you, Thomas." She reached out and briefly covered his hand with hers, withdrawing it as Mateo approached.

"Food and wine are on the way," he said as he sat across the table from them. "Now, why are you here, Thomas Berrington? And there is no need to introduce yourself, I know who you are." He smiled. "I have informants in the palace and know all about you, though it surprises me to find you here. I heard you had abandoned Spain and returned to England where you were born."

"It is a long story," Thomas said.

"We are not short of time."

"Perhaps we are. Or I am. I need to know who the dead man is and whether you sent him to kill Don Alejandro." From the corner of his eye, Thomas saw Rosa wince, but Mateo only smiled.

He held up a hand and clicked his fingers. A man came across.

"Has everybody seen it?" Mateo asked the man, who stood as if at attention in front of him.

"They have, *jefe*."

"And is he known to anyone?"

The man gave a shake of his head. "No one."

"You oversaw it all?" asked Mateo.

"It is what you asked me to do."

"Was anyone lying?"

"If they were I did not see it, and as you know I usually would."

Mateo looked at Thomas. "He would. So you have brought a corpse here for no purpose and will have to take it away again." He looked at his man. "Does it stink?"

"Not so much, *jefe*. Someone has done a good job on him."

"Was that you, Rosa?"

Her reply was a faint nod.

"Did you also tell Thomas I was capable of having a man killed?" Mateo's voice turned cold. He called the man closer to him and waited as some information was whispered into his ear, then waved a hand to dismiss him.

Two lithe, dark-skinned women emerged carrying trays. They set small plates of food on the table, a bottle of wine, and three glasses before moving away.

"They are from Africa?" Thomas asked.

"They are. I have many contacts there, and trade is good. They work for me of their own free will, and I pay them the same as everyone else, which is well. Let us eat our food. I think you will like it. I asked for Moorish food, which the girls know how to prepare." Mateo's easy manner drained away like water down an open drain. "And when we are finished, you can tell me why you are truly here, and I will decide whether I must kill you or not."

ELEVEN

Rosa laughed, as though Mateo's words were spoken in jest, but the sound was brittle. Staring into the man's eyes, Thomas saw he meant his words. The stare was unblinkingly returned, Mateo determined to show his strength. Thomas held the gaze, the world around them fading away. Rosa gone. The table gone. Only the soft sound of the river running over shallows remained, as if to remind them there were greater things in this world than men and their petty arguments.

The battle of wills continued, until Mateo blinked and looked away with a deep laugh.

"I see you make a good pretence at being brave, Thomas Berrington. I like men who are brave but not foolish. You do not yet know how dangerous I can be, and I do not yet know how brave or foolish you are. Perhaps we can be friends. Perhaps not. I will decide once you tell me why you are here." He reached out and speared a sliver of spiced pork covered in sauce.

Thomas let his breath out, feeling as if he had held it for

an hour. The world returned, and he glanced at Rosa to see how she had taken their small battle of wills. She had paled, which told him she knew that Mateo meant what he had said. So be it.

"Tell me the truth about the dead man," Thomas said. "He was one of yours, yes?"

"Not one of mine, no." And when Thomas shook his head, Mateo continued, "I admit he is known to me, but is not in my employ. He arrived here with another man."

"So why all the pretence of having your men look at the body and not admit it when I asked?"

Mateo's expression did not change, but there was nothing of friendship in it now, if there ever had been.

"I do not know you, and for all Rosa vouches for you I prefer to make my own judgement regarding someone's nature. Are you a fighting man?"

"I have been known to fight in the past."

Mateo laughed without humour. "How far in the past? You are not a young man."

Thomas made a pretence of having to dredge up a distant memory. "A little over a month, though I also had to fight off brigands as we passed through the Pyrenaeus mountains. I decided not to kill those men."

"How many were they?" asked Mateo.

"Is that relevant to our conversation?" Thomas asked.

"I think so. How many?"

"Four."

"You were alone?"

"My companion Jorge Olmos was with me."

"So two men against four."

"Jorge likes to think he is a fighting man, but he is not. So it was one against four."

"And you killed them all?"

"I said I did not. I injured two, the other two saw sense and rode away with their companions. They were men who preyed on those travelling through the mountain passes and thought we would be easy prey. When they discovered we were not they fled."

"And before that?"

Thomas sighed. "Before that I fought several men in London who also wanted me dead, but I am still here. Can we discuss the dead man now?"

"Not yet. I need you to prove yourself."

"Has Rosa not already vouched for me? Do you want a note from Queen Isabel as well?"

"Women both. You and I know there is only one way a man can prove his worth. With actions, not words." Mateo raised a hand and clicked his fingers. When one of the women appeared at his side he said, "Tell Salazar to come here."

"No," said Rosa. "Thomas does not need to fight." She reached out for his hand. "Let us leave now, while we can."

"You, my dear, are perfectly safe," said Mateo. "You know you are. And I will tell Salazar not to kill your friend. All I need is proof of what he claims. A man's words must be backed by action."

"Salazar is a beast," said Rosa. "You cannot allow this."

"Yes, he is a beast," said Mateo. "But Thomas has told me he defeated four men. Surely he can defeat one, even if that man is a beast."

Before Rosa could continue to argue, a giant of a man

appeared. He topped Thomas, who was not short, by a quarter foot, and was a third again as wide. His head was bald, and he wore no shirt, the better to display the muscles in his chest and belly. Thomas studied him, comparing the man to another giant he knew. Olaf Torvaldsson was slimmer, but as tall as Salazar, and Thomas knew this man would not have defeated Olaf in his prime. His own son, Will, was equally tall, fast, and almost as strong. Thomas wished he stood at his side now. But he had fought tall, strong men before and triumphed. And Mateo had said this was not a fight to the death. If his word could be trusted, which was something Thomas had seen no sign of yet.

"Weapons?" he asked.

"No weapons. I truly do not wish you dead. Not today, in any case."

Thomas sighed and got to his feet. He stripped off his own shirt and shook the tension out of his arms and legs. A group of Mateo's men had gathered to witness the fight, and he saw them making wagers. Not on the winner, because they knew there would be only one victor, but on how long Thomas might last before being knocked out. The men formed a rough circle into which Salazar stepped. Thomas watched his walk, judging the best approach, before doing the same. There was no dropped flag, no word to start the fight. Salazar came at Thomas at once, a lumbering giant with hands the size of platters. He swung and Thomas ducked aside. He hit out with his own blow, but it was like punching a rock, and he danced away to avoid being knocked cold by the next swing.

Salazar's entire plan was brawn above all else. He kept coming, turning only when Thomas moved around him.

Each of his moves was obvious to Thomas, who had fought many men and defeated most. He landed a few blows, each of which would have put a lesser man on his back. When Thomas managed to strike out, which was only occasionally, the results were the same each time. He watched Salazar smile because he had not been hurt. Except Thomas had been testing the man, searching for weaknesses. Most of Salazar's opponents would not last long enough for him to reveal them. Thomas was too fast, still lithe despite his age. After one particularly brutal swing he stepped in close and stamped on Salazar's foot, then punched his stiffened fingers into the angle of the man's throat.

Salazar stepped back, a look of surprise on his face, but he remained on his feet. Thomas knew any other man would lie flat on their back, staring at the pale sky without seeing it. When Salazar came again, he was slower and stumbled on his approach. Thomas allowed him to swing several more times before doing the same again. This time he hit out with every ounce of his strength, the aim of his blow better than the first time, and it worked.

Salazar stumbled backwards, shaking his head. His arms hung slack at his sides.

Thomas got close a third time and hit him hard behind the ear. The big man fell sideways and lay still. Thomas looked around to judge how Mateo's men would react. Instead of the expected attack, most of them laughed and shook their heads. And then Rosa went among them, taking her winnings.

Mateo came to Thomas and took his wrist, raised his arm in the air.

"It was a fair fight, and Thomas Berrington is the victor. He is my guest and not to be harmed."

Thomas picked up his shirt and slipped it on, then knelt beside Salazar and felt his throat.

"What are you doing?" asked Mateo.

"I want to make sure I did not hit him too hard, but he is only unconscious and will wake soon."

Mateo shook his head. "How did you defeat him?"

"Experience," Thomas said. "I told you, I have fought many men and defeated most. Salazar is big, but slow, and all men, however strong they are, have the same points of weakness. I simply made use of them. Now, can we talk?"

Mateo returned to the table, sat and speared another small delicacy as if nothing had taken place.

"You impressed me," said Mateo, when Thomas sat. "So I will answer you with the truth. Yes, as I said, I recognise the man." Mateo studied Thomas. "Do you think he might have killed Don Alejandro?"

"That is what I am trying to find out," Thomas said. "Do you think he might have had a hand in his death?"

Mateo sighed. "I have had dealings with Don Alejandro over many years. I am sure Rosa told you enough about me, so you know my dealings are generally beyond the law, as it was this time. Don Alejandro wanted the finest wine of Portugal brought here. He did not tell me why, and I did not ask. Portuguese wine, as almost all produce from that country, is considered contraband in Spain, but I have contacts. This man was not one of them but was sent by someone I know with the wine. I sent him on to Don Alejandro after I paid him."

“I hope you received payment from Don Alejandro first.”

Mateo smiled. “Of course.”

“Do you know this person from Portugal you said the dead man arrived with?” Thomas asked.

“I do. The important thing for you to know is the man you brought to me was not working under my orders. I did not want Don Alejandro dead. Now he is I will be worse off. He had a position he could make use of and I, in turn, made use of that. I will need to replace him, of course, but he has a son I have already been introduced to. I assume he will take his father’s position.”

“Don Rodrigo Vargas has already been offered it,” Thomas said. “Do you know him?”

Mateo briefly scowled. “He is of no use to me. He is as straight as an iron rod and twice as unbending.”

Thomas glanced around. “Are you able to tell me what it is you do here?”

Mateo laughed. “Rosa can tell you later. She knows all about me. I have access to items she needs and can get nowhere else. I have men in place at the House of Trade who know everything that passes through there. Many goods, not all of which are accurately counted. If a few go missing, who suffers?”

Thomas did not approve of Mateo’s approach but understood it. He needed to know more about him and his connection with the dead man. He picked up a chicken thigh and bit the thick meat from it.

“Are we drinking this Portuguese wine now?” he asked.

“This?” Mateo laughed. “No, this is Spanish wine. I rarely import wine from across the border because everyone knows Spain makes the finest wine in the world, but Alejandro was insistent. He had heard from someone that it was of exquisite quality, and he wanted to impress the King."

"Only the King?"

Mateo smiled. "Alejandro told me the Queen rarely drinks wine these days. She complains of stomach pains. Whether he was meant to tell me such a thing is another matter. How does she seem to you, Thomas? I understand the two of you were once close before you abandoned Spain."

"She seems no different to the last time I saw her, which was a little over two years ago. We all age. All carry aches and pains we never knew before."

"I am as strong as I have ever been."

"Good for you. Now, this wine. Have you dealt with the seller before?"

"You are most insistent," said Mateo. "In another situation it might be something to admire."

"Were they the producer, or a middleman?"

"The producer himself. I do not deal with middlemen for anything of importance. If you truly need a name you will have to offer something in return."

"I have little to give."

Mateo's gaze flicked from Thomas to Rosa before returning. "Let me be the judge of that. Are you willing to trade?"

Thomas stood, aware Mateo had no intention of revealing who the dead man's master was. "It was interesting to meet you, Don Mateo, but we must go now."

"You cannot expect that stinking corpse to become my

responsibility," said Mateo. "I am starting to tire of this game now, so will tell you the name of the man he arrived with. The Infante Duarte de Beja. He is the nephew of the king of Portugal. Why he accompanied the man in that cart I do not know. To discover that, you would have to speak with him yourself. He is staying with me at the moment. Wait here, I will fetch him."

Thomas glanced at Rosa. "Do you know the Infante Duarte?"

She shook her head. Said nothing.

"It surprises me he is here. I saw him at the banquet to welcome the English ambassadors. The boy struck me as younger than his eighteen years and spoiled."

"He is royal?" asked Rosa.

"He is."

"Then it is to be expected he will be spoiled. He will prefer to call it his right to be bowed down to. Word is you have a title, Thomas, but you are not like that."

Thomas only laughed as he saw Mateo lead the Infante Duarte from the house. It was unclear whether he came willingly or not.

Thomas rose. "We meet again, Your Grace. I am surprised to find you a guest of this man."

"What happened to your face?" The boy's voice was weak, as if to speak too loudly might wear it out.

"I fought a man and won."

"If I won a fight I would not expect to be scarred."

"We can fight if you wish, Your Grace, and see the truth of your claim."

The boy paled and held his hands up. "There is no need to prove myself. I in turn am surprised to see you here,

Duque Berrington. Have you given any thought to our conversation regarding Princess Catherine?"

"No more than it deserves. Mateo tells me you came to Spain with this man I have in the cart. What is his name, and who does he work for?"

The Infante did not even glance at it, the scent of decay on the light breeze would have told him what it contained.

"I know no name, and he was but one of many I travelled with. A descendent of Charlemagne is not expected to travel alone." The boy turned and strode into the house but tripped as he reached the terrace and almost fell.

Thomas turned to Rosa. "I believe it is gone time for us to leave." He held his hand out and she took it, which brought a frown to Mateo's face. They walked away without looking back, but Mateo called out to him.

"Don Thomas!"

Thomas slowed, turned back.

"Cross me and I will have you killed."

"Like Don Alejandro was killed?" Thomas watched Mateo for any indication of guilt but saw none.

"That was nothing to do with me. Don Alejandro had his uses, and I would have seen him live longer. Not that he was likely to. He was old and indulged in too many vices." Mateo waved a hand. "Now go, before I change my mind."

TWELVE

Neither Thomas nor Rosa spoke as they moved away from Mateo's estate. Thomas wanted to look back but forced himself not to.

Eventually, Rosa said, "I am surprised Mateo did not insist you take that man's body with you."

"What will he do with it?"

Rosa shrugged. "Most likely toss it into the river, or have his men burn it. He will not want it found, even though I doubt he had any hand in Don Alejandro's death. Mateo takes great care not to cross those in power, and as he said, Don Alejandro was useful to him."

Thomas smiled. "And Don Rodrigo is not."

Rosa returned the smile. "That will sore vex him."

Thomas noticed they were travelling in the wrong direction to return to Sevilla.

"Where are you taking me?"

"To see my friend, Baracoa. You did say you wanted to meet him, did you not?"

"I had not expected it to be today."

"He has knowledge that might prove useful to you. Exactly what, and how, I have to leave up to you to discover." Rosa slowed, stopped. "The path to Baracoa's holding is steep and narrow. It will be a hard climb." Rosa faced him, the sun behind her making a halo of her hair.

"How far is Baracoa's place?" Thomas was thinking if he could spare the time, but if this man knew something that might prove useful it could be worthwhile.

"It is up there." Rosa pointed along a steep, narrow ridge that climbed along one side of an equally steep valley. "It will take all afternoon. Tell me know if you do not want us to go."

"I do."

Rosa led the way, her steps sure on the rough ground. There was no path that Thomas could see, but Rosa knew the way. Thomas sweated until his shirt was as wet as if he had swum the river. They went higher, then higher still.

After a while, Thomas asked, "Is Mateo always so welcoming?"

Rosa smiled. "I have never seen him as difficult as he was today. He is a proud man and feels you insulted him in some way known only to him. He had no choice but to challenge you."

"I did nothing but ask a few questions."

"I suspect you were not meek enough, but that is not in your nature, is it? It is my fault, I should have warned you. Mateo does not take to those who fail to bend the knee before him. As for what happened, why be as wealthy as Mateo if you have to fight your own battles?"

"It is not your fault. Whether you warned me about

him or not I would have acted the same way. It is what I do. Who I am."

Rosa looked at him, her expression unreadable. "You are not a man like Mateo. You have a heart and soul. He saw that, which is why he took against you."

"I expect I can never return to his house now to find out about this trader from Portugal, or discover why that weak boy was with him," Thomas said. "Do you have dealings with Portuguese traders?"

Rosa kept her eyes ahead as she answered. "I know several, but none I would suspect of wanting murder done. You speak as if I am your partner in this matter. I am assisting you, that is all. When we have visited Baracoa, our relationship will come to an end."

Rosa's gaze lay straight ahead and distant. Thomas wondered if he had done something to upset her but could think of nothing. Unless it was the fight with Salazar.

"How much did you win with your wager on me?" he asked. "And how could you know I would be the victor?"

Fortunately, he saw her smile before trying to mask it. "More than enough. And you have a reputation as a fighting man. I asked around, and it is said you are a hard man to defeat. Even then I was unsure, but it was a risk that paid off handsomely."

"For you," Thomas said.

Rosa laughed. "Oh, Mateo will forget. Or if not forget, then forgive. He was testing you. He expected his man to beat you easily. To leave you bruised and blooded, perhaps with a broken limb or two. What he did not contemplate was that you would best his champion. I do not think anyone has ever done that before. But..."

Thomas waited. Eventually he asked, "But what, Rosa?"

She turned to him. "Nothing. I do not know how Mateo will react. He might hold an eternal hatred against you, but most likely he will forget all about it within a few days. I have not known him hold a grudge for long."

"Except I am not you. He does not want me in his bed." Thomas laughed. "At least I hope he does not."

"You will have to fight him again if he does, but no, he does not. And he does not really want me, either. It is a game we play, nothing more. Now, we must get on or we will be caught by the dark. This is a path that needs to be taken in daylight."

Thomas glanced into the steep-sided valley, wishing the path ran further away from the drop.

"Why is it you are not married?" he asked Rosa as he trudged onward and upward. Even as the words came out he wanted to take them back, but she did not seem to mind.

"How do you know I have not been? Or am married even now?"

"I saw no sign of anyone at your house," Thomas said. "Forget I even asked. It is not my business. I was making conversation."

"Are you sure?"

"Yes, I am sure." Thomas was aware his words sounded harsher than her question deserved, but again Rosa let them flow around her without reacting.

"I have never been married, nor ever want to be. Most men want only a slave to wash and cook, to flatter and bear them children. I will not be that." Rosa glanced at him, her eyes sharp. "But I suspect you are not that kind of man, are you?"

"I try not to be," Thomas said.

"Your answer shows you are not," said Rosa. "I have been with men, but always on my own terms." She smiled. "Both myself and Luisa are cut from the same cloth, though she is hungrier for the physical side of love than me." She offered Thomas another glance. "Am I being too honest with you?"

"I am honoured you feel you can be. How well did you know Don Alejandro?" he asked.

Rosa gave him a look, together with a frown. "Why do you ask?"

"Because the man we dragged around half of Spain in that cart might have killed him, but it would be on someone else's orders. I want to know who his enemies were and whether he was well-liked or not."

"Not."

Rosa's tone of voice brought a new question.

"Did he touch you? Try to force himself on you? Or on others?"

"Don Alejandro was a man of position, which carried an expectation his advances would not be rejected. So yes, he tried to bed me once, but once only. I put him in his place. As did Luisa. She told me she even struck him." Rosa laughed. "That sounds like Luisa."

"How did he take it?"

"Badly, of course, because he was not used to it. He even tried to remove her from her position, but she is too well respected in her post. She also knows the weaknesses of those she deals with." Rosa's face was set as she strode across the pale ground and Thomas had to walk faster to keep up.

"Did it upset you he tried to seduce you?"

Rosa slowed. "Of course it upset me. I knew his reputation, but until then he had been a perfect gentleman. Afterwards, he sent others if he needed anything – and he did need special preparations." She looked at Thomas. "You must know of herbs and tinctures that can make a man hard."

"I have never had the need, but yes, I know how to prepare them for others."

Rosa smiled. "Don Alejandro could have used someone else, but my potions are considered the best in Sevilla."

"You said it was a common thing for him to force himself on women. Do you think it might have been enough for someone to want him dead?"

"Perhaps. Some of the women welcomed his advances because he was a powerful man and they believed some of that power might reflect upon them. In other cases, husbands would be angered at the liberties he took with their wives. But again, Don Alejandro's position offered him much protection."

Thomas thought about what Rosa had said and it did not please him. It meant there could be a myriad of suspects who wanted the man dead. There were many questions, but Rosa had answered what he had asked, and the others would have to wait until he returned to Sevilla.

They spoke of less problematic matters. Thomas learned that Rosa's father was a clever man. A surgeon, like Thomas, and a good one. Her mother knew herbs and taught Rosa all she knew of them. In return, Thomas told her some of his past, aware to tell it all might take several days.

"How much further?" he gasped, wondering how much longer he could go on.

"Almost there," said Rosa. "You can rest here and wait for me – I will go to Baracoa and ask for his help."

Thomas stopped. "You told me he does not welcome strangers."

"I am far from a stranger to him."

Before Thomas could say anything, Rosa turned and strode along the slope at pace now she was no longer held back by him. Thomas went on more slowly, pacing himself on the steep slope. He should be asking questions in Sevilla, where Don Alejandro was murdered. His mind conjured possibilities which he followed. Only when his downcast gaze caught sight of a pair of bare, browned legs did he look up.

A short man stood next to Rosa.

"Rosa tells me you need help," said the man.

THIRTEEN

As Thomas crested the ridge a shack came into view. It sat on a narrow, rock-scattered plateau with a view beyond into the distance where mountains faded into a haze. It stood hard against the slope, which formed one of the four sides. The other three consisted of little more than woven walls and a roof of bamboo canes covered with reeds. When heavy rain came, which it would do over the winter months, it would offer little shelter. In front of the shack lay a good-sized plot of flat land where animals wandered. Chickens pecked at the ground. A small herd of goats negotiated the steep slope to one side in search of dried stalks or better. Unfamiliar vegetables grew in a patch of cultivated ground. Tall plants stood higher than a man, their tassled heads bobbing. Greenery staked with canes where dark red fruit hung from the stems. A patch of leaves dying back which showed nothing edible above ground. Thomas recognised none of them. To one side, an ancient oak tree, gnarled and lightning struck, carried enough leaves to keep it alive. Tatters of coloured cloth and eagle feathers on strings swayed from the lower branches.

Baracoa stopped near the shack and turned to watch Rosa and Thomas approach. His strangeness was plain to see. He was shorter than most Spaniards – though Thomas accepted that he was tall himself, so often found relative heights difficult to judge. Baracoa's hair hung in a thick plait along his back, the end almost touching the ground. His eyes were hooded and dark, with no colour showing around the pupils. A single loose item of clothing was caught at his waist by a knotted hemp rope. He wore no shoes. His feet were broad, the toes splayed to show this was his normal state. The air was chill, but he showed no discomfort.

Thomas held back as Rosa approached. Baracoa's eyes stayed on her, briefly flickered to Thomas, then returned. They spoke, but he could not hear their words. Baracoa's gaze returned to him. Thomas stood erect and still, allowing the man time to study him. He held his hands loose at his side to show he was no threat. Except he had no idea what this man might regard as a threat. He was from a far-distant land, whose culture would differ from that of Spain or England. He had almost certainly been brought here as a captive but seemed no longer to be so. It was a question Thomas would like to ask but was unsure it would be welcome.

After some time, Rosa turned and waved him closer.

As he approached, Thomas wondered what the protocol should be. An offering of the hand? An embrace? He had noted Baracoa offered neither to Rosa.

Thomas stopped six paces from them. Baracoa's eyes

gave him a sharp study, then he came closer. Thomas's right arm twitched but he managed to keep it at his side as Baracoa came closer still. He leaned in and sniffed. He moved around Thomas, raising himself up, half-kneeling, his nose doing all the work. Then he ran his fingers through Thomas's hair, lifting and parting it. Finally, he stepped away.

"He does not smell like a Spaniard." His accent was lyrical, unlike anything Thomas had heard before.

"Because he is not," said Rosa. "He is from England."

"Which is where?"

"Far to the north. It is wet and cold."

"I see," said Baracoa. "It is why he came here?"

"Thomas is an important man. He has come to negotiate a royal marriage."

Baracoa shook his head. "I do not understand what that is. It is cold and will get colder still." He pointed to a pile of boulders that surrounded a small open space. "The man will fetch wood. There is much beyond the stones. And he smells of death, so good if he works it off. Who died?"

Rosa looked at Thomas, waiting for him to respond.

"A man in Sevilla. His skull was caved in and his throat cut for good measure."

"What business was it of yours?" asked Baracoa.

"Another man also died. I was asked to find out who killed him."

"Same man killed both?"

Thomas smiled. "That I do not know but intend to find out."

"Why?"

"Because I was asked."

"How did the other man die?"

"I do not know that either. Poison, I think. Most likely poisoned wine delivered by the dead man you smelled on me, in spite of Rosa's efforts to mask the stink of him."

"Yes, she is good at her work. Tell me how the other man died."

Thomas explained about the banquet, the royal table, the cupman, the wine, how Don Alejandro had died gasping for breath. "Do you know what might have killed him?" Thomas knew Rosa had brought him to Baracoa for some reason. So far it was not clear what that reason might be.

"The wine did not kill him."

"Are you going to tell me what did?"

"Not until I have thought on it more and decided whether I trust you or not. Now go, fetch wood."

Thomas followed the direction he had been given. There were scraps of wood here and there, then as he went further, he found a small copse of trees where branches had fallen. He took one under each arm and dragged them back to Baracoa's camp, where a small fire had already been lit. Rosa came and stood near to Thomas as he used a curved blade to chop up the wood.

"Have you ever taken the mushrooms that bring visions?" she asked.

The question was unexpected. "I have, but not for some time."

"So have I, and more recently. Baracoa will offer us something soon that is the same but different. He has done so with me twice before. I learned a great deal about myself. You can refuse to join us, but I intend to drink his liquor, and you should too if you want him to trust you. Unless you are afraid."

Thomas thought about what it might mean.

"If I do not he will refuse to help?"

"He only trusts those who share the visions with him, so yes, he will refuse."

Thomas nodded and started back to where Baracoa sat grinding roots into a metal pot which sat next to the fire. He muttered words in a strange language, all his concentration on his work.

How bad could it be, Thomas thought. No worse than he had experienced before. If he refused, he would be cutting himself off from whatever information this man might possess. Baracoa was the reason Rosa had brought him up this hillside. He did not yet know if the journey might prove useful or not but would never know if he did not hear more.

He recalled other experiences with visions brought on by mushrooms or an excess of hashish. Most had been good, but a few had gifted him nightmares. He had survived them all. He would survive this.

The ceremony – and that was what it was – of creating the liquor took time. Thomas and Rosa sat cross-legged, side by side, and watched. Smoke from the fire drifted across them. Darkness fell and the moon rose from behind the surrounding hills, its light touching distant clouds. Eventually, Baracoa used two sticks to work the metal pot from the fire and set it to cool. He rose and slipped off the single garment covering him and stood naked, staring at the sky.

“I should have warned you of this,” said Rosa. “It is part of the ceremony.”

“Am I expected to do the same?” asked Thomas.

“It is part of the ceremony,” repeated Rosa. “So yes, you must be naked, as I will be. It is for your safety, not sex, but something else. Sometimes the visions make you writhe about, and you might strangle yourself. That strange scarf you wear would be most dangerous.”

Baracoa sat, as if unaware of his own nakedness, and waited.

Rosa rose and removed her clothes. Thomas tried not to look. The time had come for him to make a decision, but he knew there was only one he could make. So he did the same, piling his clothes to one side, then sat further from Rosa than before.

Baracoa picked up the metal pot and offered it first to Thomas.

He took it.

“How much?”

“As much as you want.” said Baracoa. “Leave enough for us.”

Thomas took a sip. The liquid was sharply bitter, but not impossibly so. He took a deeper draught and handed the bowl to Rosa, who did the same. Baracoa took it back and drained the remaining contents, taking the biggest share.

“Now we wait,” he said. “If you grow afraid, cry out and I will help you, but the visions come to guide you. Do not fear them.”

The moon rose higher. The brightest stars sparked the sky. The air cooled, but Thomas barely noticed. His attention was turned inward, waiting for any change in himself, but he found none. Baracoa reached for a small drum and began to beat it softly with his palm. The sound was soothing, and after a time Thomas felt his heart slow to match the rhythm. An owl flew low overhead, unafraid. The sound of its wings whispered through the night air.

Nothing happened.

FOURTEEN

Thomas came awake in starts, sank back into dreams, deeper still into endless oblivion. Then he rose again into awareness. Except there was little difference between each state. There were times he dreamt he was awake, and times when awake he was sure everything was a dream. Memories assaulted him, both good and bad. His father on the battlefield at Castillon, a thirteen-year-old Thomas finding him among the dead, except his father was not dead. He screamed in agony and did not recognise his son. And then the memory, the horror of battle, was gone. What he had done faded to be replaced by an image of Bel Brickenden before he left for France. Of lying with her for the first time. There would be other women – including times he was not proud of – but Bel was, and always would be, the first. There had been others he had loved, though none as much as Lubna.

And then the visions faded, and Thomas's mind became crystal clear. He lay on his back, cool night air caressing his skin, and stared at the sky as he tried to work out how much time had passed since he drank Baracoa's liquor. Each star was unique, separate, and there seemed to be more than usual. The moon had crossed the sky and was about to set behind a hill. Thomas turned his head to look for Rosa but could not find her. When he looked the other way Baracoa was not where he had been. Thomas was alone. He heard animals scuttling through the dry brush. Further away, larger creatures hunted the small. His mind was sharp despite the visions. He conjured a memory of the banquet. Of Don Alejandro moving through the room, a touch here, a touch there, speaking to many people. Some Thomas knew, others were strangers. He did not know what was being said, but the way each reacted told him something. He recalled the moment when Don Alejandro slapped at his neck as if stung by an insect. Thomas had taken little notice of it at the time and wondered why it came to him now. Was it Baracoa's gift to him, offered through the potent liquor?

A giant bird flew overhead, its wingtips almost touching him, but whether it was real or a vision he could not tell. It reminded him of the peacocks that stalked the gardens of the palace. He thought of Rosa, then of Queen Isabel. He thought of the dead man they had abandoned with Mateo.

With a jerk, Thomas sat up, the world spinning for a moment. Visions crowded in, but he had been in this place before and knew he could accommodate both their madness, their horror, and their beauty.

Embers of the fire glowed with a soft amber light.

"Who were you?" Thomas did not know if he spoke aloud or not. He supposed it did not matter. It was not as if he expected an answer. Except he did. There was no voice, but words formed in his mind in response to the question.

No one. An empty vessel when I lived. An empty vessel now.

"Who sent you?"

All men have masters. If you want answers seek mine.

"Where do I seek them?"

No reply came, only a recent memory, though it seemed he had heard it an age before. Portugal, Mateo had said. The dead man he would not name had been sent from Portugal. As had the Infante Duarte. Were the two linked, or was their presence a coincidence? Thomas did not believe so. He wanted to speak with Rosa but could not see her.

He rose and walked to the ridge. From the crest he could see forever. In the far distance, a faint glimmer of lamps showed where Sevilla lay. In other directions towns and hamlets lay scattered like embers in the darkness. He turned a full circle, searching for dawn, but there was no promise of it. He started back down the slope, then stopped. Two figures stood close together near the distant fire. Baracoa and Rosa embraced each other. Had they always been there and he had not seen? Thomas's vision narrowed until everything else faded into a writhing wash of unreality as the two of them melded into one.

Is this real or not? he thought, then, *No, on this night, nothing is real.*

He sat naked on the ridge and let the velvet dark take him once more.

When Thomas woke the sun was in his eyes and he had returned to his body. The memory of what he had seen and experienced became dreamlike. He stood and looked around to find he was still on the ridge, but the city, towns and hamlets he had seen – or thought he had seen – in the night were now invisible, obscured by a faint pink haze that hung in the air like mist. He tasted desert dust on his tongue, and it brought back memories. He started down the slope without concern at his nakedness. When he reached Baracoa's hut both he and Rosa were clothed. Thomas dressed before sitting. Baracoa passed him a bowl of clear liquid, which Thomas looked into with suspicion.

"It is clean spring water," said Rosa. "Drink, you will be dry."

Thomas drained the bowl's contents then held it out for more. Baracoa refilled it.

"Is your head clear?" he asked.

"It is." Thomas drained the bowl again and set it down between them. Each sat on the corners of a triangle. He studied them, looking for any signs of distress but finding none. Baracoa, no doubt, was used to what they had gone through. Was Rosa the same? How often did she come here to visit the shaman? For that is what the man was – a shaman. There were few in Spain anymore. The Moors had not approved of them, but Thomas had met a few over the years and admired their view of the world. They also possessed deep knowledge of herbs, spices and plants that others knew little of.

"Rosa tells me you are a clever man," said Baracoa. Each word came out as if it required rolling around in his mouth to taste its true meaning before it emerged. Each time he spoke it took Thomas a moment to work out what had been said.

"It is not for me to say."

"But it is. Who else knows you as well as you know yourself? I do not trouble myself with stupid people, so tell me if I should dismiss you as unworthy."

Thomas took a breath. "Yes, I am clever. I know a great deal about many things. But you are also clever, yes?"

Baracoa simply inclined his head in agreement.

"Did Rosa tell you why I want to speak with you?"

"A death. You mentioned there were two. My gift to you was the visions. They may help you to see what you have not seen before."

"An important man died." Thomas glanced at Rosa to see if she had anything to offer, but she sat cross-legged, an expression of complete relaxation on her face.

"No doubt he thought himself important," said Baracoa, "but we are all of us only men and women, none better than other. Some are clever. Some are not. Some can create objects. Others cannot. Life is a weave of skill and knowledge. Did this man possess a skill that made his life important?"

"I did not know him well enough to judge," Thomas said. "He had an elevated position in the Spanish court, so no doubt he did." Thomas glanced at Rosa again. "Does he know of the court?"

Before Rosa could reply, Baracoa said, "I was a chattel of the court when I first arrived in this land. A gift to their majesties, though what is majestic about them I could not see. I was prodded and poked and made to perform silly tricks, to talk in my native tongue, which made them laugh."

"Do you still remember it?" Thomas asked, curious.

"Do you remember yours?" asked Baracoa. "Rosa told me you are from a land far to the north where they speak a different language. And that you used to live in a part of Spain where yet another tongue was used."

"I speak my own language still, as well as the one we use now. Also Arabic, some French, Latin and a little Greek."

"That is more tongues than a man might need. And yes, I remember my own." Baracoa's speech changed at once and he ran off a flurry of words. To Thomas they sounded both soft and hard, with extended vowels punctuated by sharp endings. When it was done, Baracoa said, "I invited you and Rosa to eat with me. Did you hear your names in what I said?"

Thomas considered the question before shaking his head. "No. Can you repeat it?"

Baracoa's mouth twitched, but he did not smile. He spoke again. This time, Thomas listened for the sounds of their names and thought he caught them, but the pronunciation was so different it was difficult. More so with his name than Rosa's.

Thomas responded in English, and then Arabic, before returning to Spanish to say, "My thanks, I would be honoured to eat with you."

This time Baracoa's smile reached the surface. "You spoke two other languages, yes?"

"Yes."

"One was fluid, the other not. Which was which?"

"My own native language is not fluid," Thomas said.

"For a long time, I came to consider the language spoken by the Moors in Spain to be my own tongue and almost forgot where I came from. Unfortunately, it had not forgotten me."

Baracoa nodded. "Your story sounds like mine." He rose to his feet. "Come, walk with me. Let us talk while we gather food for our meal. You too if you wish, Rosa."

As they walked, Thomas questioned Baracoa. When he began, he was unsure of the response he might get, but as they continued, stopping now and again to pick some fungus, plant, or insect, Baracoa showed no reluctance to offer answers. Rosa remained quiet, staying close to Baracoa's side, her hand occasionally brushing against his. The gathered food was not what Thomas might have chosen, but he was determined he would eat with Baracoa, trusting him not to poison him. He did not raise the subject of why he came but knew he could do so later if he managed to prove himself. Which he was trying to do now.

The collection of food took several hours, and at the end as they walked back to the shack nestling on the side of the barren-looking hillside, it was Baracoa who raised the reason for Thomas's visit.

"Rosa tells me you are a man who puts matters right."

"She seems to have told you a great deal about me."

"She did. I too am a man who rights wrongs. At least I was before I was captured and brought across the sea."

"How did you escape from the palace?" Thomas asked.

"I had no need to escape. The Queen offered me my freedom."

"Isabel?"

"I believe that is her name, but I was told only ever to call her 'Your Grace'. You are familiar with her?"

"I am." Thomas did not wish to share how familiar. "Why did she release you?"

"She saw I was a clever man, and she disliked the way others at her court treated me. There was one there who acted the fool and wore silly clothes. He beat the furniture and people with sticks and other items. It amused the King greatly, but I could see the Queen did not like it. I made no complaint, but she must have known. And then, one of her daughters fell sick. I suggested a cure. She told me she could not be seen to use it, but found a way. She said she knew another man who offered unusual cures and trusted him a great deal. Was that man you, Thomas?"

"I suspect it was. I can think of no one else it might be. I helped her son, who is now dead, to walk again when he had but seven years. His leg was badly broken and badly healed by her own physicians. I was sent for."

"And you fixed it?"

"As well as I could, which was good enough. He always walked with a limp, but at least he walked."

"We are not so different, then," said Baracoa. "Come, I will prepare the food, and you can ask me what is really on your mind."

It took some time, partly because Baracoa wanted to show them how to prepare what they had gathered, but he also asked many questions about how Don Alejandro had died.

"How long did it take him to die?" asked Baracoa as he scattered the insects across a heated stone.

"To the count of fifty, no longer."

"He was in pain?"

"I would say so. He could not catch his breath, hard as he tried."

"I understand."

"I thought he had food stuck in his gullet, but it was not that."

"No, it would not be."

"You said it was not poisoned wine that killed him. Do you know what did?"

The food appeared to be ready. Baracoa walked outside and laid it on another flat stone so they could each pick at what they wanted. Thomas tried a little of everything, as he knew he must.

"I know what could have killed him, but do not think it was the man who served him wine. Did you examine this important man's body after he died?"

"I had no chance for a detailed examination. I made enquiries at the palace, and when I returned Don Alejandro had been taken away. He was buried the following morning."

"It is not good you could not see him again. Do you have any other information, or know of anyone else who died?"

"People die all the time in a city as big as Sevilla, but I have heard of nothing suspicious."

"I think I know what killed this man, but do not know of anyone in this land, other than me, who might have the knowledge, the skill, or the ingredients to produce what killed him. But there must be someone, for I did not do it." Baracoa gazed into Thomas's eyes. "What I do not understand is, if it was what I think was used, it is not fatal when eaten or drunk, only when the skin is pierced and it enters a person's blood. Did you find any mark on him to show this had happened?"

Thomas frowned as the memory from his vision returned to him. "Before he took his place at the table he slapped at his neck as if bitten by an insect. I barely took notice of it at the time, but during the night it came back to me."

"Which is what happens if you accept the knowledge as well as the madness. Did this mark bleed?"

"I did not check. As I said, I dismissed what I saw. I believed the wine poisoned him."

"If I am right, it will not matter if you looked or not. Once the poison enters the blood death cannot be avoided, and it comes fast." Baracoa leaned forwards. "I will come to Sevilla in a day or two and tell you more."

"Not now?"

"I need to show you how the poison affects a body, which means I have to prepare it."

"I hope you do not intend to kill someone."

Baracoa smiled. "We both know there are people who would be better off dead, but no." He rose. "I have much to do. Thank you both for coming, and for joining me in opening our hearts and minds. And you, Thomas, for trusting me." He turned away and strode up the hill where his goat had moved higher. Dried grass was in short supply.

FIFTEEN

Rosa was silent as she and Thomas started their return to Sevilla; only occasionally did she raise her hand to point the way. As they skirted the ridge Thomas had spent half the night on, the city appeared in the far distance, smoke from fires drifting across tiled rooftops. Thomas wanted to speak to her of his experience but found it difficult to know where to start.

"What?" said Rosa, her first words since they started out.

"Nothing."

It seemed a one-word question and answer was enough to open the floodgates.

"It does not seem like nothing. Tell me what your visions were like."

"You said you have partaken of Baracoa's gift before?"

She walked two score paces before replying. "I have, and each time it was different, as was last night. You said you have used the mushrooms that bring visions. How different was this?"

"A great deal. My mind was both clear and chaotic."

"That is a good description. Where did you go?"

"You and Baracoa are lovers, yes?" Thomas asked, relieved to have finally put his thoughts to her. Jorge, he knew, would have done a better job of it, but he thought it was good enough.

Except Rosa said, "What makes you think that?"

"In the night I saw you together, at the fireside."

Rosa stopped and turned to him, anger flaring in her eyes. "You did what?"

Thomas held his hands up. "I did not sneak up on you. I was on the hillside, and you were both near the fire. I could not help but see what you did."

Rosa was silent as they walked on, her eyes fixed in the distance. Eventually she said, "Baracoa and I have been lovers for half a year." She glanced at Thomas. "Does it shock you that I would lie with a man from across the great ocean?"

"It does not."

She made no reply. When she increased her pace Thomas did the same.

At the dockside, Rosa told him she would send a message if Baracoa came and wanted to see him. He watched as she unlocked her house and went inside without looking back.

As he made his way towards his lodgings, wondering if it was too soon to collapse into his bed, Thomas saw Jorge sitting at a small table, food and wine in front of him. The sun already approached the eastern hills so the table sat in shade, a lamp burning beyond it.

"Where have you been for two days?" asked Jorge as

Thomas sat on the chair he pushed out for him. A sylph of a girl appeared and stood too close to Jorge, who said, "My sour-faced friend will have the same as me."

The girl nodded and ran off.

"I have been meeting interesting people." Thomas did not want to reveal everything he had done while away with Rosa. He barely understood some of it himself. "Have you been beguiling waifs while I have been putting myself in danger?"

"I have been talking to people. As for the waifs, I offer no encouragement, yet still they come to offer adoration. Do you want to know what I have found out?"

"Is it worth hearing?" Thomas watched as Jorge's expression changed. His usual benign visage melted away to be replaced by something Thomas did not recognise.

"What is wrong with you?" Jorge asked, an unusual touch of impatience in his voice.

Thomas hesitated. How much to reveal? And then, he thought, why not everything? He wondered what had changed in him, and whether it was a result of what he had experienced with Baracoa and Rosa. What he believed he had seen in the night. Both of them lying together, naked, skin against skin, reminding him of what he had lost many years before.

"Why are you shaking your head?" asked Jorge. "Do you intend to tell me nothing?"

As Thomas opened his mouth to reply the waif returned and set a plate none too gently in front of him. He looked at it but made no move to eat.

"I apologise. I am not myself. I..."

Jorge waited, then said, "Is this something to do with Rosa?"

"There is nothing between us, nor do I want anything of her. I am too old for her."

"To hear your words, you are on death's door, and we both know that is not the case."

"This is nothing to do with Rosa. I met two men, one evil, the other who confused me. The latter claims he may know how Don Alejandro was killed. He promises to come to the city in a few days and demonstrate for me. Also..." Thomas's voice trailed off, unsure how much to reveal.

"Also what?" asked Jorge.

"I met a man by the name of Mateo Salto, who is a rogue, but might prove a useful rogue. He ordered one of his men to challenge me. To test me."

Jorge laughed. "I hope he was a big man." He leaned closer before shaking his head. "He must have not been so big, you have only one small bruise." He reached out and touched Thomas's brow. "Here."

"He was a big enough man, and wide, which made him slow. I have fought harder opponents."

"And this Mateo allowed you to leave when you beat his champion?"

"He respected me the more for it, which came as a surprise."

"How useful is he?" asked Jorge.

"That I do not know. He said the dead man was familiar but offered no name. However, he did say the man was employed by a Portuguese, though he would not tell any name for him. I believe it might be the Infante Duarte. The boy was also there."

"Is he the other person you spoke of?" asked Jorge. "I feel as if I am being told only half a tale. Whatever it is I hope you left both the cart and the body wherever you went."

"We did, though Mateo Salto was not pleased," Thomas said. Then he told Jorge about Baracoa, trying to pull together his own feelings about the man. He also told of the visions he experienced.

"Did these visions tell you anything new?"

"I still need to work through what they were about, if anything. It was a madness without real knowledge, but useful all the same. I feel clear-headed today. For that alone it was worthwhile." Thomas took a breath. "Enough about me. Tell me what, if anything, you have found out. Who have you spoken with?"

"I returned to the palace," said Jorge. "I asked no permission in case it was refused and used the entrance from the courtyard where we found the dead man. From there I gained access to the kitchens. I chose a time in the evening when I knew they would not be so busy. I was made most welcome."

Thomas smiled. "I expect you were. Did you learn anything useful?" He tried some of the food set in front of him and found it good.

"I learned things we did not know before," said Jorge, "but whether they are useful or not I will leave up to you to decide. Much of it involves palace politics." Jorge shook his head. "I am glad not to be involved in such things. I do not know how you can put up with it."

"I never intended it to be something I had to contend with," Thomas said, "but as with so much else it seems to seek me out. How much of what you learned involves Don Alejandro?"

"Bear in mind much of what I was told might be little more than gossip. You know how places such as kitchens work. They chat away, sometimes with little regard for the truth. And yes, some of it involves Don Alejandro. He was, as you know, old and grossly overweight. There were times he had to be helped upstairs to visit the King and Queen. According to the head cook, Rosita – do you remember her?"

"Of course I do. It was three days ago, not three months. Go on."

"Rosita told me there was talk of wanting to oust Don Alejandro from his position. He was no longer effective but had much power and it would be difficult. She also hinted he was diverting funds he had control over into his own pocket."

"What credence do you give the rumours?" Thomas asked.

"Rosita believed many to be true. She also told me that a few years ago Don Alejandro had expectations of many of the female staff. Do you need me to give you details?"

Thomas smiled. "I prefer not to hear them. When did these expectations stop?"

"Around two years ago. I think Don Alejandro was unable to rise to the occasion anymore, though his hands continued to wander. I also visited his house today, intending to speak with his wife again, but was turned away by the mayordomo, Manuel. A man in your position might have better luck."

"If I had a position. If necessary I will try tomorrow."

"No need. I managed to find a way in through a back door. Rosita and several of the girls spoke of Don Rodrigo Vargas. A man they would not have refused the advances of if he made them. Which he never has. He is always perfectly correct, which is unusual enough for them to make a point of telling me."

"There are always expectations among men of status, we both know that. Did Rodrigo expect to take Don Alejandro's position? Did you ask anyone about that?"

Jorge stared at Thomas before shaking his head. "I am sorry, it did not occur to me. It is why you may need to speak with Rosita yourself. Your mind conjures far more devious plots than mine. However, what I did learn was that Don Rodrigo and Diego Serrano are close."

"Explain close," Thomas said.

"They are often seen with their heads together, as if they are plotting something, but Rosita told me Diego is strongly loyal to the King."

"And Isabel?"

"She did not mention any feelings either man may have about her. King Fernando has grown in stature in their marriage since the fall of Granada. He is the general who fights battles. Isabel has lost some of the glitter that once touched her. I know how you feel about her, Thomas, but even you must see it."

"It is true she does not look well. It concerns me."

"As well it might, but there is nothing you can do. It would not be allowed."

"I know. So tell me, might Don Rodrigo have been involved in Don Alejandro's death so he could usurp his position?"

Jorge raised a shoulder. "It is possible, but I consider it unlikely. The entire palace knew Don Alejandro was not long for this world. Even if he did not die from over-indulgence, he would have been set aside within months. Spain is in the ascendancy in the world and needs men with sharp minds managing its affairs. Don Alejandro was not that man. Don Rodrigo is. All of which is to say, he would not risk his position by murdering the man he wants to replace."

"He may not have had a hand in the deed himself, but he could have arranged for someone else to do it."

"See, that is what I mean. You have a suspicious mind. Everyone in the palace likes Don Rodrigo. He is unusual in being a man of power who does not abuse his position. He is also regarded as intelligent and courteous. So no, I do not think he would be involved when all he has to do is wait."

"Is he married?"

"It is expected for a man of his position, though his family do not live with him. He has a house somewhere near where he was born, so no one has seen them. Rosita tells me he has three children, all girls. Sometimes it happens that way, but word is he loves each of them."

"I need to speak with Don Rodrigo in the morning to confirm what you tell me."

"Do you want me to accompany you?"

"I would rather speak without distraction. Man to man."

Jorge smiled. "Am I not a man?" He hesitated. "I almost forgot, I have a message for you from the Queen." He reached into his jacket and pulled out a sealed note.

"More likely from one of her scribes." Thomas snapped

the seal and read the note. "She wants me to attend a meeting in the palace tomorrow morning. It involves the English ambassadors, which is a waste of time, but I will have to attend to ensure they speak the truth. It is the reason Henry sent me. I want to go to the *Casa de Contrat-ación* before I go to our lodgings and ask Luisa Mercado what she knows of a man by the name of Mateo Salto. Also to ask about Baracoa. He fascinates me, and I would like to know more of him from someone other than Rosa."

"I am sure Luisa would welcome you with open arms." Jorge smiled. "Or do you not trust yourself in her presence?"

Thomas picked up a piece of pork from his plate and threw it at Jorge. He missed.

SIXTEEN

When Thomas opened his eyes he knew he was late. Sleep had dragged him deep the previous night as soon as his head touched the thin pillow. Now, dressed uncomfortably as a gentleman, he asked one of the guards where he might find Don Rodrigo and was directed to a far corner of the palace gardens. So distant that when he turned to look back at the palace it was no longer in sight, and all sound from the city had fallen away. Surrounded by shrubs, trees and foliage, he might have been miles from the bustle of the streets. Only as he proceeded and the high stone walls met in a corner, rising to five times his height, did it once more feel like a royal garden. Don Rodrigo was on his knees, a small scattering of hand-tools on the ground beside him as he used his fingers to bed in a row of plants. He was unaware of Thomas's approach.

"Don Rodrigo," Thomas said, soft enough not to startle the man. Even so he turned sharply, a hand reaching for a knife at his side until he saw who it was and rose.

"Thomas Berrington. How did you know where to find me?"

"I asked."

"Ah yes, that often works. Where is your handsome companion?"

"Making a nuisance of himself, I hope." Thomas did not want to reveal too much to this man yet.

Don Rodrigo smiled. "Alone, or with company?"

"Oh, usually alone."

"Are you and he lovers?" asked Don Rodrigo, which made Thomas laugh.

"I am sorry if we give that impression, but we are not. Both of us prefer the company of women, though I admit there are times it feels as if we are closer than lovers." Thomas surveyed the series of neat beds which ran hard beneath the south facing corner. "Is this your own doing, or do you have help?"

"All mine." Don Rodrigo turned to look across the large plot where trees, shrubs and plants grew. His expression softened, as though he was looking at his own children. "Does it surprise you?"

"There is little in this world that surprises me anymore, but yes, it does. You are a man of stature, yet I discover you doing the work of a serf with your fingers in the soil."

Don Rodrigo smiled. "My father worked the soil. He taught me how, but now I am a self-made man. I suspect you might approve of what I do here, for much is a matter of science rather than tillage. Most of what you see is not native to Spain, nor of any land this side of the wide sea."

"They are plants from the newly discovered lands?" Thomas recognised some from those cultivated by Baracoa.

Others were unfamiliar. The thought these were from across the sea sent an excitement through him. What wonders lay within them? What cures? What beauty?

"Almost all, yes. Seafarers and explorers find and return seeds to me, for which I pay them well. Perhaps it is my father I get the interest from, but more likely he has nothing to do with it. I am curious by nature, as I believe you are, Thomas Berrington. Is it true you studied medicine in the infirmaries of Moorish Spain?"

"In Malaga, under the Moors, yes. Do you disapprove? Most Spaniards would. They see Moorish science as ungodly so give it no credence."

"Knowledge is knowledge, Thomas. I may call you Thomas? And you must call me Rodrigo. I despise the use of honorifics among men of equal standing. Unless you wish me to call you Duque."

Thomas laughed. "I would prefer not to ever be called that again. Do all the seeds brought back grow?"

Rodrigo shook his head. "Little more than half. I have tried everything I know. Ice to freeze seeds as we sometimes need to before they will germinate. Different mixes of soil. Glass frames over some to warm them. Some seeds take, others do not, but I will not give up."

"Have you ever had your explorers bring back a sample of the soil from the land the seeds come from?"

Rodrigo stared at Thomas with a serious expression. "I have not, but that is an excellent idea. I will ask next time a ship leaves." He clapped Thomas on the shoulder. "My thanks. I should have thought of it myself. It might be what I need. There are many different soils in Spain. If I have a sample from across the wide sea, I may be able to match it.

Of course, I could always consult the natives, of which there are several in the palace, but I doubt any speak our language well enough to be useful."

"I may know of one who does," Thomas said. "Rosa Martinez introduced me to a man by the name of Baracoa Caguas."

Rodrigo stared at Thomas for a moment. "When was this?"

"Yesterday. I was trying to find out who the dead man in the courtyard was, and whether he was involved in the death of Don Alejandro."

"And did you?" asked Rodrigo after a moment.

"Rosa also introduced me to a man called Mateo Salto–"

Rodrigo held a hand up to stop Thomas. "She did what? That man is dangerous."

"As I found out. He had one of his men challenge me."

Rodrigo looked Thomas up and down. "I see no broken bones. That does not mean Salto will forget about you. Take care, Thomas, the man is a devil."

"Who may prove useful. He did not know who the dead man was and told me what he knew of him." Thomas was not yet ready to reveal the dead man and the Infante Duarte were known to each other.

Rodrigo snorted. "Believe nothing Salto tells you. Where is this man's body now?"

"Disposed of. Buried." Thomas considered it wise not to say what had happened after that.

"So no one will be able to identify him now," said Rodrigo.

"I can describe him well enough and have not yet

finished making enquiries in Sevilla. Jorge has spoken with several of the palace staff, and they are people who notice a lot but say little." Thomas smiled. "Unless you are a man such as Jorge."

"I want you to report anything you discover to me," said Rodrigo. "The death of Don Alejandro cannot go unpunished."

"Of course. You mentioned there are natives of this distant land in the palace. I saw they were serving food at the banquet and would like to speak with them, either myself or Jorge. Do we need your permission?"

"You are meant to ask it, of course. I will have a note prepared giving you both free access. Not that I expect you will need it. Everyone knows you are a favourite of the Queen."

Thomas smiled. "But not the King."

"I expect he gives you no thought at all," said Rodrigo. "He has a great many calls on his attention. Spain is strong, but it has many enemies, not least of which is Portugal. Fernando cannot let himself be distracted. No doubt he considers you no more than a minor irritation. He is the power in this land now the Moors have been defeated. Why do you want to speak with these natives? Not that I expect you will get anything useful from them. They are not intelligent like you or I."

"Has anyone ever tried to learn their language?" Thomas knew Baracoa possessed a reasonable grasp of Spanish and suspected some of the others would also.

"Why ever would someone want to do that? This is Spain, not some fetid land across the ocean. If you are interested, you should speak with one of the priests who has been there and returned. I believe a few learned a word or two of theirs, but I also hear that every island speaks a different tongue. They will learn to converse in Spanish or suffer the consequences."

Thomas had started to warm to Rodrigo but now his opinion changed. He knew he was out of touch with Spain, but England was no better, nor any other land east of the wide ocean. He took a breath, knowing he must let the moment of annoyance pass. He surveyed Rodrigo's garden and decided to change the subject.

"Are you settling into your new position?" he asked, which brought a scowl to Rodrigo's face.

"Such as it is. I am unsure exactly what my responsibilities are meant to be. Don Alejandro had allowed many matters to slide. I have people trying to work their way through palace records to discover what he did and what he spent funds on, as well as find out the names of those he dealt with." Rodrigo shook his head. "I do not even know if it is worthwhile, as my position has not yet been made official."

"An oversight, I am sure," Thomas said. "You are best qualified for the work, are you not?"

Rodrigo offered a brief laugh. "I believe so, but already others are circling. Alejandro's son shows an interest, but lacks the skills needed." Rodrigo laughed again. "But then so did Alejandro himself."

"How long had he held the post?" Thomas asked.

"More than fifteen years. He must have been suited to the position when appointed, but I saw no evidence of it in all the time I knew him. Enough of the dead. Let me show you what I have done here. Some of the plants are most interesting."

Thomas knelt as Rodrigo began to explain the names he had given each plant and what it was used for. Some could be eaten, some used for spicing food, others merely decorative, and yet others Rodrigo was still looking for uses for. An hour passed, and more might have done so, but they were both startled when a peacock landed on the plot in a loud flurry of wingbeats, tail-feathers and a loud call.

"Damn it," said Rodrigo. "That creature keeps digging in my garden. I should bring a sword and take its head the next time it tries."

Both men got to their feet, using each other as they rose. Rodrigo called out and ran at the peacock, which took off again, flying a short distance before coming down along the path.

"I hear Queen Isabel likes the birds," Thomas said, "so perhaps best you leave its head on."

Rodrigo smiled. "Yes, perhaps. Though I could do it and blame one of the gardeners." He glanced at the sky, judging the passage of time. "I had best change my clothes. The English ambassadors are due to meet with the King and Queen at noon. I assume you are also attending?"

"In the capacity of an observer. Also, I find there are times those translating do not do so accurately. They often say what they believe Isabel and Fernando want to hear, not what has been said."

SEVENTEEN

Don Rodrigo was resplendent in his official robes as he met Thomas, who waited for him at the entrance to the inner palace.

"I assume the English ambassadors know who you are?" he asked.

"One of them, certainly, most likely all. Whether they know I have been sent by King Henry is another matter. It will be interesting to see their reaction."

Rodrigo led the way to the room where the meeting was to take place. A grand chamber rich with wall hangings, paintings, fine furniture and ornate carpets brought from the east. Gold items dotted the surfaces. Fine crystal glasses awaited the pouring of wine, which would be of the best quality. A wide terrace lay to one side, and it was there Isabel and Fernando stood, flanked by two guards on either side. At the end of the terrace, Diego Serrano stood watch over King and Queen, also ensuring his men acted properly by never meeting their gaze and not standing too close. It was unlikely either would be attacked here, but it pleased Thomas that Diego took his responsibilities seriously.

Fernando shook Rodrigo's hand before approaching Thomas, no welcome on his face. He leaned close and said, "Let it be known, Berrington, that your presence at this meeting is against my advice, but I have been overruled."

With that he strode to the end of the terrace and disappeared towards the meeting room.

"You must have annoyed the King something fierce in the past," said Rodrigo.

Thomas smiled. "More than once, I suspect."

"He is not a hard man to cross, but Spain needs a general now more than ever. France threatens, Portugal tries to best us on the sea, and Naples continues to be a constant thorn in our side. However, the Queen still holds your friendship close. She asked that she speak with you alone before this meeting. I advised against it, of course, but she can also be stubborn. A guard will remain with you, but she has spoken to me of the assistance you have offered the crown in the past, so his presence is a formality. When you finish, I would also welcome a conversation with you to find out what you intend to do about Don Alejandro's death."

"There is little to report," Thomas said. "Jorge and I went to his house to inform his wife of what happened. She did not appear upset."

"I doubt she would; it was a marriage of convenience, for them both. I was going to send Diego today but will not do so now. Even so, come and find me when we finish and bring me up to date on anything you have found out. I will most probably be in the garden again."

Don Rodrigo offered his hand, then left to join the meeting.

When Thomas cast his gaze along the terrace, he saw Isabel watching him, hands clasped in front of her. As he passed the guard and approached, her eyes remained on him. He had forgotten how small she was, and it surprised him. In his memory she was always a larger-than-life figure.

He bowed, took her offered hand, and kissed the back of it, holding her fingers a moment longer than protocol allowed. She smiled.

"I see you are still pushing matters, Thomas. You have not changed much. There is more grey in your hair these days, and lines around your eyes, but you are as strong and handsome as ever."

"And you still as beautiful, Your Grace."

She waved a hand. "Do not try to flatter. I know these last years have been hard on me, and my body aches in places it never has before."

"Have you consulted a physician?"

"I have, but none are as skilled as you."

"Except I would not be allowed to examine you, Isabel." Thomas could not continue to Your Grace her.

"And yet you have seen more of me than any of my doctors."

"That was long ago, and wrong of me."

"Was it? I wanted that moment as much as you. We both knew it could never happen again, but the memory remains." She tapped the side of her head. "Does it for you?"

"Of course. It was magical and illicit, so perhaps that is why. But you know the reason I am here, and it is not to recollect old times, perfect as they were. What is your opinion of Henry's ambassadors?"

"They demand too much, which my husband is determined to reject. But I suspect King Henry has sent you to persuade us otherwise."

"He told me only one thing, and that is what his true terms are to settle this matter."

She touched his arm, glanced beyond him at the guard, then left her hand where it was.

"Are they terms we can accept?"

"I believe so."

"Then you can bore me with the details later. Now, I wish to hear of Catherine. How she bears up, but also of her marriage to Arthur." Isabel made a small scowl of distaste. "That could have ended better. I assume you were there at the end?"

Thomas nodded.

"And you could not save him?"

"You know I would have if I could. But I did save Catherine, with the help of Amal and Belia."

"For which I am eternally grateful. I would bestow more honours on you but know you value them not at all. Perhaps, when we are truly alone, a kiss will do."

"More than any honour," Thomas said.

He told Isabel of Catherine's brief marriage to Arthur, Prince of Wales, the youth who was meant to be king. He made her laugh at some of the things they did, and cry at others.

In the end she said, "She was happy? No – *they* were happy?"

"As any man and woman in love could be."

She looked into his eyes for longer than was comfortable, but Thomas met her gaze and waited.

"One item of information told to us was that the marriage was never consummated. It appears that fact is important if Catherine is to marry this new prince."

"That is the official position, yes, but I know they enjoyed a full marriage." Thomas smiled. "Enjoyed it a great deal, and often."

Isabel laughed. "That sounds more like the Catherine I knew in your house rather than mine, where she was always careful of appearances. I used to love coming to visit you and seeing her enjoyment at being with your children, dangerous as that might have been."

"My son would never act out of place. You know he would not."

"There were times I think Catherine wanted him to. Will is handsome, and a strong protector, like you."

"He still protects her whenever he can," Thomas said.

"And your daughter, Amal. How is she?"

Thomas smiled. "Far cleverer than I am, and as beautiful as the sunrise and sunset."

"Is she married? She must be of an age."

"She has sixteen years, so yes, more than old enough, but I suspect Amal will never marry. I cannot see her submitting to any man."

"Then she must find one who is content with a strong wife. A man who respects women and allows them to be themselves, like her father would. Is there someone new in your life, Thomas?"

"I thought so for a time, but it was not right. We are both content with the situation. I will never marry again. It is unlikely I will ever be with a woman again. I am growing old and like you carry aches and pains."

"No, Thomas, you are still strong. You will live forever. And you must find another woman. You are too much of a man to waste yourself in celibacy." Isabel sighed. "Enjoyable as this is we have much to decide. You say Catherine and her husband enjoyed a full marriage, but if she is to marry the brother that will not be sanctioned."

"Unless people lie."

"You cannot lie. I know you well enough to say that."

"For Catherine I will lie. So will others who were there. Doña Elvira will also state the words we want to hear, and you know how flint-like she is."

"Then it can be done. This boy, Henry, what is he like? Will he make a good husband? Is he clever?"

"They call him Harry most of the time, as do I, and Will."

Isabel smiled. "Why does that not surprise me."

"Harry likes Will better than he likes me. He is clever but hates studying. His tutors are good and make him learn the classics. Greek, Latin, numbers, other skills he will need to rule when the time comes. He likes to ride, to hunt, to fight. He thinks that will make him a good king. He has a wild side at times, which I think comes from youthful excitement. It will fade as he grows older and needs to make decisions."

"He is younger than Catherine, yes?"

"By almost four years, which means any marriage will not be for some time."

"But it will come?"

Thomas nodded. "Yes, it will come."

"She has met him?"

"With a chaperone. I spoke with her not long before I left England and she is content with the choice being made for her. She loved Arthur, and I believe in time she will come to love Harry. He is more handsome than his brother and, I suspect, more able to make a woman happy."

Isabel stared into Thomas's eyes before saying, "Love is not always expected or essential in a royal marriage, as well I know. As for what else you do not speak of..." She held a hand up. "No, do not argue, Thomas. You are aware of my husband's nature and his infidelities. But he is a good king, which is all that matters. And this Harry will be a good king as well, and we both know Catherine will be an excellent queen beside him." She leaned close, too close, and Thomas saw the equerry start to move towards them. "Stay near her for me, Thomas. Always." By the time the equerry approached, the distance between them had been restored.

"I am old, and Catherine is young, but I will protect her for as long as I can, and when I cannot my son will take my place." Thomas smiled at the expression on Isabel's face. "All will be well. Will knows how to behave himself, and so does your daughter. Catherine will be a willing and loyal wife to Harry."

Isabel wanted to walk, so they followed the balcony, the equerry a dozen paces behind.

"I assume you are looking into Don Alejandro's death. Are you making progress?"

"Only that I now have more questions than answers, but that is the nature of it. I visited his wife, and it is fortunate I did, for no one else had been to tell her of his fate."

"She must have been upset." They stood side by side,

close enough to reach out if they had wanted to. The equerry stood nearby, his gaze averted.

"Less than I expected. She is a lot younger than him. And..."

"And what, Thomas?" As though by accident, the back of her hand brushed against his. A moment's contact, no more.

"Doña Carlita tried to seduce Jorge," he said.

Isabel laughed. "I suspect many women have tried to do the same. He is remarkably handsome and has a life force like no one else."

"And has been loyal to the same woman for many years now. He played a little with Doña Carlita. It is what he does. And her responses showed there was nothing of love in her marriage."

"That does not surprise me. I have never met her but have heard rumours. It is said she takes lovers and discards them like others pluck fruit and toss away the core once satisfied. I expect she will be well provided for now."

"Most of his wealth should by law go to his eldest son, but she made clear that will not be the case. Some will reach him, but she wants the bulk to remain with her."

"Do you think she had anything to do with his death, Thomas?" Another accidental brush of the hand.

"I suspect I know who killed Don Alejandro, but that man is also now dead. What I do not know is whose orders he worked under. It could be Doña Carlita, but I would say not. She is rid of a husband she did not want, though he made no demands of her and allowed her to do as she wished. His death does not benefit her. I have not been idle, and made several contacts, one of whom promises to tell me of a poison that could have been used. He is a native of this new world Columb discovered."

"What makes you think the poison is not native to Spain? I assume you are familiar with those."

"I am, but I am also familiar with their actions and none that come to mind would have killed Don Alejandro so swiftly. It is possible he had ingested it before arriving at the banquet, but even then, he would have shown signs, and I saw none until the moment he stepped back from your table. I do not dismiss the idea, but I made contact with a native of the new world who told me of a poison from those lands that would have acted as quickly as this one did."

Isabel smiled. "I remember you leading Columb into Alhambra the day after it fell and persuading us to fund his journey. Yet you often told me you believed him mistaken."

"I changed my mind," Thomas said. "Though I believe Columb still thinks he has found a new group of islands off the coast of the Indies."

"You do not?"

"I have no opinion, but it would please me to believe what lies there truly is a new world. A world of immense wonders, where poisons we do not know of can be fashioned, but also cures we know nothing of. Where much remains to be discovered."

"Don Rodrigo has made a study of these plants of the new world. I suspect that is where he is going after we finish here. He has made a plot of ground his own, a sunny corner where he grows seeds brought back by returning mariners. He has told me he tastes most of them himself, so there will be no poisons there."

"I have seen his garden," Thomas said. "We had a long conversation only this morning."

"I would prefer to stay longer and learn of all you have done in England but cannot. I have kept the English ambassadors waiting long enough." Isabel smiled. "You will enter when I do because it will annoy them."

"They certainly will not want me there, I agree. I know both men, and their hangers-on. They believe me an interloper and do not respect my skills, my knowledge, nor my position."

"Then they are fools – which I already know. They are full of their own importance and spend most of their time bickering over tiny points of protocol. They forget we want the marriage as much as they do. It should be so easy but is not."

"Take care, Isabel, for they are not fools but clever men. Henry also wants this marriage, but he also wants the balance of her dowry for the first one. Offer that and he will be content."

"The ambassadors are asking for a second dowry for the new marriage."

"Then that is their own idea. I know Henry will be satisfied with the half he has not yet received."

"That is useful information, Thomas. My thanks. Make time after the meeting is finished and tell me what they really say amongst themselves. And we can talk more of your new life. I would hear all about it and be content to know you are happy there."

EIGHTEEN

As Thomas left the palace and crossed the gardens to the nearest gate that would let him out onto the surrounding square, where the two-hundred-year-old cathedral projected the power of both Crown and Church across the city, the peacock he had seen earlier, or *a* peacock, almost flew into him. He stepped back, waving his hands. The bird landed two yards away and Thomas watched it, the iridescent wings, the ridiculously long tail feathers that allowed such a large bird to fly. Not far, it had to be admitted, but fly it could, as it had just evidenced. The bird staggered away, weaving from side to side, and Thomas frowned. He was not familiar with the birds, though he knew King Henry kept a small number to enhance his position. The peacock sat, then staggered on. Thomas followed, curious. He wondered if it was sick, though he knew nothing of diseases that might affect birds other than chickens, which Amal and Belia took care of back at his house in Ludlow.

The bird hopped into a flowerbed, then tried to fly again but failed. It came down hard and lay on its side, breathing fast, wingtips fluttering. Thomas moved closer, taking care it did not leap up again, but as he approached, he saw it was beyond doing such. Thomas knelt, wanting to do something, but there was nothing to be done. He waited until the bird breathed its last, then carefully picked it up by its heels before wondering what he was doing. Where would he take it to? What could he do with it? The bird was dead.

Thomas looked around for somewhere to dispose of its body. He did not want to leave it to rot here on the path. In the distance, he saw a pile of cut grass and leaves, set aside to rot down. He carried the peacock there and tossed it onto the heap before covering it over. He rubbed his hands together, knowing he would have to wash well before touching anything else.

As he returned to pass through the gate it came to him, he had no idea what to do next, or where he should go. Return to the house and talk through his morning with Jorge? Walk the streets of Sevilla randomly, trying to find clues to the death of Don Alejandro? He felt cut adrift, at the mercy of others while he waited for them to provide information. He expected nothing from Mateo but held out some hope Baracoa might bring some enlightenment. Thomas was at a loss as to why his mind was not working as well as it usually did. Perhaps the journey on foot and his night of visions had tired him more than they would have done a few years before.

He sat on a wall in a patch of shade surrounding a single tree that grew tall. He drew his cloak around himself because the air was chill, and tried to make himself think clearly. He had drunk no wine at the meeting, so it was not that. More likely it was a remnant of the liquor Baracoa had given him. It had brought visions stronger than any he had experienced before. He knew he needed to do something that might spark his mind into clarity. So he stood and made his way back to Don Alejandro's house, where Jorge had promised to visit again. On his arrival he was informed that Doña Carlita was not at home, but Jorge was inside with the cook. When Thomas was taken to the kitchen, he discovered them sitting together, the cook's hands wrapped in Jorge's, a flush on her face. Jorge had seduced her soul and no doubt she wished he might seduce her body as well. Thomas held back until Jorge noticed and nodded for him to approach. As he did the expression on the cook's face soured. She stood abruptly and turned to her work.

"Outside?" Thomas asked.

"There is a place here I can use," said Jorge. He turned and led the way from the kitchen to the ground floor. He opened a door into a pleasant room which looked across the square. It was furnished with comfortable chairs, a wide desk fashioned of oak, and wall-hangings which showed not only the usual hunting scenes, but also several of women reclining with little in the way of clothing.

"This is Don Alejandro's study, or was," said Jorge. "I understand his wife never entered, which meant he could satisfy his interests without fear of discovery."

"Someone must have cleaned in here," Thomas said, looking around.

"Servants. There is an expectation they will not mention what they might see. Nor speak of it outside their own kind. He has books on the shelves even more explicit if you are interested."

Thomas laughed. “I have had more than enough of bawdy tales to last me a lifetime.”

“Ah, but how long might that be? You are an old man now.”

Thomas swatted at Jorge, lightly slapping his cheek to demonstrate he was still fast enough if needs be.

“There are drawings on their pages if your eyes are not up to reading the text.”

Thomas took a seat. “Tell me what you have learned. At least what might be useful to me, for I am sure you teased out every wish and want that poor woman holds, as well as her entire history.”

“Of course, and she will go away content with the thought I might, at some time, weaken and seek her ample charms.”

“I was told Doña Carlita was not home,” Thomas said.

“She has gone to their house in Malaga. If you want to visit, I can find out exactly where it is.”

“Malaga is three days’ ride, so not unless we have to. What else have you discovered?”

Jorge fumbled inside his jacket and pulled out a sheet of paper. “This is the list of names you asked Doña Carlita to produce. She did not do so, of course, and neither did Manuel. But one of the kitchen girls could write and gave me this. These are the people the staff know of who have had arguments with Don Alejandro.“

Thomas laid the paper on the table and read through the list.

“There are a great many names here,” he said when he finished. “Was there any indication which might be the most important?”

Jorge shrugged. "She did not have any opinion on that. Perhaps the kitchen staff believe it is your job." He smiled. "It usually is."

Thomas looked around until he found what he needed. A quill and ink pot, as well as several sheets of paper, but he only needed one. He set them in front of him and went down Jorge's list again, putting marks against names he wanted to deal with first.

"This one says only 'Portuguese man' and nothing more."

"That is all they knew. It was someone Don Alejandro dealt with directly."

"Perhaps we should speak with Manuel and see if he knows more. Mateo Salto told me the dead man in the courtyard worked for a Portuguese."

"Manuel accompanied Doña Carlita to Malaga, as well as over half the staff from here. I was given the impression they would be away some time. They told me Sevilla grows cold over winter, and Doña Carlita likes the little warmth the sea provides."

"Should I wonder why she abandons the city so soon after her husband is murdered?"

"Malaga might be far, but we could follow her," said Jorge. "I like the city."

"We could, but we have a list of names to speak with here first. You spent time with her, what do you think? Might she have had her husband killed?"

Jorge smiled. "As you know, I was able to read her soul, but in matters of murder I prefer not to be involved in the details. Doña Carlita is sensual and takes many lovers, almost all of them are young, handsome men. There have been a few older ones, but those had influence, like Don Rodrigo."

Thomas scanned the list again before shaking his head. "I do not see his name here."

"Turn it over," said Jorge.

When Thomas did, he saw another dozen names, including that of Don Rodrigo.

"When was this?" he asked.

Jorge shrugged. "Less than a year ago, more than three months. The girls were unsure. I think she took so many men into her bed they found it difficult to identify them all."

"Too many to investigate, then." Thomas stared into the distance, a strange reluctance filling him he had rarely experienced before. He was starting to wonder if he cared who had killed Don Alejandro or not. Everything he heard about the man told him he was inept and corrupt. Don Rodrigo had taken his place and appeared far more suited to the position. Thomas thought of all the times he had taken on tasks others had turned away from and often wondered why he had done so. He had been told many times they were not his responsibility but had been unable to turn aside. And now...?

He tried to think what had changed to make him doubt himself. Had the drive for justice left him? Perhaps so, because over the years he had pursued it he always discovered there could never be true justice. Evil would always exist. Men like Mateo Salto, who lived on the edges and took what they wanted, would thrive. Those in power abused their positions, as Don Alejandro had, seducing women who had no power to say no.

"Do we start on the list of names today?" asked Jorge, drawing Thomas from his dark thoughts. "You look tired, so it can wait until the morning."

"Or not at all," Thomas said.

Jorge stared at him without expression.

"This is not like you," he eventually said.

Thomas ran a hand across his face. "No, it is not like me. Perhaps you are right after all and I grow old and no longer care."

Jorge surprised Thomas when he laughed. "You? Not care?" Jorge shook his head. "Has the sun stopped rising and setting, and the moon fallen into the great ocean? You are tired, nothing more. We will find somewhere to eat fine food and drink fine wine and then, if you have any wits left in that clever head of yours, you will go to Luisa Mercado and let her seduce you. I hope you know she wants you to."

"You see that, do you?"

"Of course I see it. I am only surprised you do not."

"I am not as blind as you pretend, my friend," Thomas said. "I admit the thought is tempting, but..."

Jorge waited, but when Thomas said no more, he said, "Why not? You have no one else anymore. And she would make no claim over you. I sense she is not that kind of woman. But if you submit you will enjoy the experience, I am sure. And I expect so will she. Belia tells me you are a considerate lover. But do what you wish. You right wrongs and fight evil men. I see into the souls of people. It is why we are still friends, because we make each other whole. Now, let us at least eat, for I have much hunger and thirst."

NINETEEN

The fine food and wine would have to wait. Thomas and Jorge ate bread and some kind of meat neither could identify while they stood at a stall on the edge of the dock. Thomas drew out the list of names and addresses. He wiped the grease from his fingers on his best jacket before unfolding the paper. He had set his reluctance aside with difficulty but set it aside he had. There was work to do. People to question. Information to gather. He had marked the most important names, and they would start with those.

"Six names, six households," he said. "Too many to cover today."

"Are you confident we can dismiss the others for now?" asked Jorge.

"No, but it will take several days to speak to everyone. We start with Don Alejandro's eldest son."

"Let us go then." Jorge tossed his almost untouched food into the river and walked away.

"Do you know where you are going?" Thomas called after him.

"I am sure you will tell me if I go wrong."

Thomas threw his own food after Jorge's and ran to catch him up.

"What is the matter with you today?" Thomas wondered if Jorge was experiencing the same feelings as himself.

"Our life is no longer in Spain. I miss my family. I also miss your family." Jorge shook his head. "No, we are all one family, and I miss them."

Thomas knew he spoke the truth. He had not seen it himself, too enamoured at the thought of seeing Isabel again. Except now everything was different. She was different. He was different. He became aware of how much he had changed since returning to England, surprised at the effect his homeland had had on him.

He tried to push his unease aside. They had work to do.

"Don Gabriel's houses is nearby. We go there first."

"Good. And later we will find that fine place you promised me and eat good food, drink rich red wine, and watch beautiful women dance."

"Some of that, I am sure."

Thomas led the way along the riverside, then right into a narrow alley which in turn led to a small, tree-lined square. A water feature sat at its centre, a remnant of the time the city was ruled by the Moors. Almost all the water features in the city had been built by them, but few who now lived here were aware of their history.

They were admitted easily enough to the first house. Jorge remained talking with the doorman while Thomas was led to a study which looked across the square. A squat, wide man with thinning hair sat behind a desk, his similarity to Don Alejandro obvious. He rose and offered his hand, but there was nothing of greeting in his expression.

"My man tells me you have questions about my father's death. I was at the banquet and witnessed it."

"As did I," Thomas said.

The man looked at him, head to one side. "Yes, you were." His lips thinned. "Seated close to the King and Queen. You have the advantage of me, sir."

"My name is Thomas Berrington. I returned to Spain from my homeland of England."

"Berrington ... you were, or perhaps still are, Duque of Granada, yes?"

"I expect I am, since no one has informed me otherwise. I do not recall seeing you at the banquet."

"I was seated across from you but at the far end of the table, so some distance away. I could see little of the royal party, like many others. I expected a better position, as I frequently hunt with King Fernando. I would call him a friend."

"The King has many calls on his time and, I expect, many friends."

"People are asking who benefits most from my father's death," said Don Gabriel. "Many claim Don Rodrigo Vargas is too young and too inexperienced for the position."

Thomas recalled the argument at the banquet when Don Rodrigo was offered Don Alejandro's position.

"People are bound to talk," he said. "How has Don Rodrigo performed so far? Can he step up to the position, or not?"

"He comes from a poor family with no wealth. He even boasts of how his father barely scratched a living from the soil to show how he has bettered himself. The entire city knows this, which is why they talk."

Thomas saw the reason for the accusation. Rodrigo was an interloper who had worked his way into a position of power. A position Don Gabriel might have been expecting for himself, for was he not a person of importance, rather than the son of a poor farmer? He suspected it would not be the last time he would hear such accusations against Don Rodrigo. Jealousy could so easily be cast as such, rather than admitted to.

"Tell me," Thomas said, "What interest did you have in your father's business dealings?"

"Sevilla is a large city, but those who run it and those who trade here are few in number. Of course I had business with my father at one time, but not recently."

"What manner of business?"

"Several matters, none of which are of interest to you, I am sure."

"Would the sale of wine be one of them?" Thomas asked.

"I deal in wine, yes, and have a reputation for providing the highest quality, but there are others who do the same. Competitors, you might call them. Trade can be a cutthroat undertaking, especially here where everything changes so quickly." If Don Rodrigo realised what he had said he showed no sign of it. Don Alejandro had not had his throat cut, but the man in the courtyard had.

"What about these others you speak of?" Thomas

asked. "Would any of them be pleased to see Don Alejandro dead?"

"They may, but if you think I am the kind of man to provide you with a list of their names then you can think again."

Of which, Thomas thought, there would be many. Don Gabriel was not an easy man to like, and Thomas was not yet sure whether he had persuaded him he had nothing to do with his father's death. Listening to the man, he grew aware of how things were in Sevilla. He had been here a matter of days and was remiss in not recognising how much the city had changed. Not the buildings, but the people and, in particular, commerce. The opening up of new trade routes had brought great wealth, but that was only the start of it. Thomas knew he had been too concerned with the fate of Catherine and meeting Isabel to worry about how much Spain had changed even in the three years he had been away. Why would it be his concern? Until Don Alejandro was murdered, there had been no need for him to be involved in such matters. He did not welcome being involved in them now. Even so, he had one last difficult question to ask Don Gabriel.

"Members of Don Alejandro's household told me you and he were once close but had a falling out a year ago."

"Who are these people? Whatever they say is a lie."

"They claim you sold your father a tract of land for a great deal of money. The land turned out to consist almost entirely of rocks too large to move. When he confronted you and asked for the return of his money you refused."

"Then he was a fool not to send someone to look at this land before purchasing it."

"You knew what it was like?"

"Of course I did."

"So you lied to your own father? You took his money and refused to make good on the transaction. Is that how families behave in Sevilla?"

"It is only what he would have done if the tables were turned. How do you think he became so wealthy?"

"Doña Carlita seems to think the house and all land and money will come to her. She says she has documents to prove it. She also claims there was bad blood between you and Don Alejandro and that it is possible you had him killed. Not by your own hand, but it would be a simple enough task to have someone slip poison into his food or drink." Thomas's words were untrue, but he wanted to see how Don Gabriel reacted.

What he did was surge to his feet and come around the desk to stand as close to Thomas as he could. When Thomas rose, he stood a foot taller than the man.

"You accuse me of murder?" Spittle flew from the man's mouth. "How dare you! The King will hear of this, and when he does, not even the Queen will be able to save you. Yes, I know you think yourself close to her. The whole of the city knows it and fails to understand why she has time for someone such as you. A stranger. An *Englishman!* An accusation such as this will not go unpunished."

The man punched Thomas on the chest. It was a hard enough blow, but Thomas had been hit far harder. He did not respond. As if taking that as a sign of cowardice, Don Gabriel hit him again, but still not hard enough. When he struck out a third time Thomas gripped his wrist and held it, squeezed.

"I usually find someone who carries a measure of guilt often responds by attacking their accuser. What are you hiding?"

"Release me now or I will call for help."

Thomas squeezed the wrist harder and twisted. Don Gabriel winced and tried to step away but was held tight.

Thomas leaned close and spoke coldly. "How much guilt do you carry, sir? Do you believe that now Don Alejandro is dead you will benefit?"

Don Gabriel pulled his wrist free and stepped back. "As you are no doubt aware, I have not yet benefited, but expect to. And despite our falling out, I am sorry he is dead. I am not the only one to fall out with him. He conducted trade with an eye always to winning by any means. Ask and you will find reasons why many men might want him dead. But I am not one of them."

Thomas believed he had pushed the man far enough for now, but that his name should remain on the list of suspects. He could return when he had asked questions of others and, if he did, would press the man harder.

Thomas saw himself out of the room. He found Jorge waiting for him on the street.

"Have you been speaking with the staff?" Thomas asked. "Did you learn anything?"

"They were remarkably private. I believe they are afraid of their master. In particular, the younger females. Before we leave, you should visit his wife. She complains of being unwell."

"Am I to treat the entire city?" Thomas asked.

Jorge smiled. "Only this woman for now. I think you might be interested in what she has to say."

TWENTY

It was, of course, impossible for two men to be alone with Doña Sarita, so the housemaid who had told Jorge about her mistress's maladies accompanied them.

Doña Sarita sat in a comfortable chair set beside a window, which offered a view across the square. From there she could watch the comings and goings. She was a short woman, with dark hair tied in an ornate knot atop her head. She was dressed in fine silks, which covered a body that might once have been enviable had it not outgrown the skin she now wore. She was handsome enough to hint at the beauty she had once possessed.

She did not rise but offered the back of her hand. Thomas took it and pressed his lips against it, taking the opportunity to judge her temperature, which was normal. When Jorge did the same, Doña Sarita's pale face blushed. The housemaid stood to one side, trying not to appear to be watching or listening, and failing.

"My companion tells me you have been unwell," Thomas said.

"For some time, yes. Your companion told my maid you were perhaps the best physician in the whole of Spain, so I thought, as you are here, perhaps we should talk." Her neutral expression changed to one of distaste. "Have you finished with my husband?"

"For now. Tell me what ails you. Where is your pain?"

"Do you suspect my husband of murder? It would not surprise me. Nothing about that man surprises me."

Her words interested Thomas, not only for their meaning, but the spite with which she spoke them. Clearly their marriage had reached the stage of hate rather than love.

"I cannot discuss what was said between us, madam. I am here because you complained of sickness."

She waved a hand as if in dismissal. "The usual aches and pains a woman has to put up with as she grows older. Nothing a young lover would not fix." Her gaze took in Jorge and stayed on him. He smiled at her, always willing to offer a promise he would never make good on.

"Are there Moorish physicians in Sevilla?" Thomas asked, drawing her attention back to him.

"Of course. All others of their kind have been expelled or executed, but Spain knows to keep those useful to it. We have two we call on. They are more skilled than my countrymen."

"If you give me their names I will speak to them and arrange for treatment." Thomas knelt in front of the woman and took her hand again. This time the touch felt more sensual. He was sure she would have preferred Jorge to be doing it, but Jorge would not know what to check for.

Thomas laid his finger along her wrist until he found

the faint pulse there. It ran a little fast, but that could be caused by their presence.

"If you would allow me to ask you some delicate questions?" he continued, looking into her eyes. He saw the woman she had once been and felt a faint attraction he was surprised by.

"If your friend would hold my other hand," she said. "Carmelita, you can leave us."

Thomas glanced at the maid. "Please, stay. It would be improper for us to be alone with your mistress."

"I trust you both," said Sarita.

"But my sweet, we may not trust ourselves," said Jorge, which brought another flush to her cheeks, and Thomas felt her pulse increase.

"Then let her stay." Sarita spoke curtly. "Ask me what you will, sir. I have no secrets."

So Thomas did, as delicately as he could, and when they were done, he knew more about the rivals to her husband, and why she believed they might want his father dead. Thomas's problem was there were too many rivals and too many reasons, too many men to speak with and it would take a year to visit them all. Many had been in debt to Don Alejandro. Others had been cheated by him. Wives had been seduced, both recently and many years before. And, of course, there was his position, close to the King and Queen. Half of Sevilla envied him that.

The sun was edging towards the eastern hills Thomas had walked over the day before as they crossed the square and Jorge said once more he had much hunger.

"You always have hunger," Thomas said, "yet you are as

slim as ever. Perhaps I should examine you as well – you may have a worm."

Jorge smiled. "Ah, I would welcome such an intimate examination."

Thomas swatted him with the back of his hand. "I thought she might accost you there and then and I would have to protect your honour. I judge she suffers the same as most women her age. A good Moorish physic would be able to create a potion to help. We will seek one out and inform him of her needs."

"Oh, she has needs, perhaps too many, and that is part of her ailment," said Jorge. "She clearly detests her husband. It was interesting what she told us about why the son might might want the father dead."

"It was, but not unusual. Lust is a great driver of men. More than with women, I think."

Jorge laughed. "That is because of who you are, Thomas. Having lived many years in the harem of al-Hamra, I have a more intimate knowledge of the lusts of women. It is why I am able to enchant them. That, and my unusual beauty, of course."

"Of course, how could I forget? Doña Sarita accused her husband of having lust for Don Alejandro's wife."

"It would not surprise me," said Jorge "Don Alejandro was old and would have difficulty satisfying a woman such as Doña Carlita, and we know already she sought pleasure outside her marriage. Such infidelity would cause friction Possibly even within her own household. It may be worth asking about footmen, stable hands, gardeners who came and stayed but a short time. Having used them, Carlita would have ensured they were dismissed before they grew ideas above their station. Most likely she would also have seduced the husbands of other women. On many occasions."

Thomas shook his head, aware he was in many ways far too innocent for a man his age. He had been with many women, though not so many of late, but the innocence lay in his mind rather than his body. He believed it was this innocence that had led him into several unfortunate liaisons with beautiful women who wanted to do him harm.

When he looked up, he discovered they had returned to the *Casa de Contratación* and recalled one of the Moorish physicians could be found nearby.

"Can you wait a short while before eating?"

"You intend to visit the Moor she told us of? If so, I will find somewhere to eat myself, because once you start talking you will be an hour at least."

"I will not."

Jorge only looked at Thomas and shook his head. He pointed. "There is a stall over there selling what appears to be fresh food, and it has a brazier against the chill, together with tables and chairs along the riverside. I will sit and wait for you there."

"And if I am an hour?" Thomas asked.

"I will still be there, watching the industry going on around me and taking solace that it is not me who has to do it. I have learned to enjoy a life of leisure."

"You have always enjoyed a life of leisure." Thomas raised a hand. "I apologise, I forget myself."

Jorge smiled. "I forgive you. It was long ago since you made me what I am, and I barely remember the life I lived before then."

When Thomas returned, Jorge remained at the small table, the wide river behind him and the last rays of the sun on his face. The remnant of a meal lay before him.

"Is the food worth bothering with?" Thomas asked as he pulled out a chair and sat.

"It is excellent, and I suspect much to your taste. There are items here from the world across the sea, which I have never tasted the like of. You will find them interesting."

"Will I?"

Jorge raised a hand to attract the vendor. When he had requested the food he said, "I saw Luisa Mercado again, and she saw me. She came across and sat where you are. She is curious about you. She has made enquiries, and knows much of what you do, and have done in the past. I think she may even be a little impressed."

"But only a little, I suspect."

"Of course, only a little. You should talk with her. She knows everyone, and no doubt their secrets. She might help you discover who killed Don Alejandro."

"Then perhaps I should talk with her," Thomas said with a smile. "We certainly got nothing of help from Don Gabriel or his wife. I am starting to think we will not discover who killed Don Alejandro."

"Then talk to her, and more if you wish, for I am sure it is her wish. She is most handsome, not that she allows people to see it. She keeps her face set hard most of the time, but she revealed her true self to me as we spoke."

"Because it was you," Thomas said. "Women respond to you."

"It is not me she wants. She needs someone with a harder edge than I possess."

"Then that is not me, either. Besides, I am not looking for any liaison. We will be here a month, two at most, and then we return home."

"It was a long journey for such a short stay," said Jorge. "Do you not want to return home?"

"I want to see Belia and my children again, of course, and Will and Amal and everyone else. But you know we all went to England from Spain and could as readily return here. Where the sun shines more often and the women are more beautiful."

"Is that what you want?" Thomas leaned aside as a girl set plates of food in front of them. "I thought you had already eaten."

Jorge patted his belly. "You told me I was too skinny, so I thought more food would be a cure for that. And no, I am not suggesting we return to live in Spain, but is it not a thought worth considering?"

"Our life is in England now."

Except, as Thomas tasted what was indeed excellent food, he wondered if he spoke the truth. He was quiet as he ate and, much to his surprise, so was Jorge. Perhaps they shared the same thoughts, the same uncertainties.

And then Luisa Mercado crossed the dockside again and sat beside him, pulling her chair close.

"We need to talk," she said. "Not out here. In my office." She turned and strode away, slim backed, long legged. The throng around the *Casa de Contratación* parted to let her pass.

TWENTY-ONE

Thomas rose and followed Luisa. For most people, pleasantries would have been exchanged as they eased towards the heart of what she wanted to discuss, but neither Luisa nor Thomas was that kind of person.

"What do you want of me?" Thomas asked as they crossed towards the *Casa de Contratación*.

"Two things," said Luisa. "I have information for you on the wine that was supplied for the banquet. In particular, the wine that was sent to Don Alejandro at his specific request. And Rosa says she wants to see you." Luisa stared at Thomas, her expression showing something only Jorge might have understood. Thomas certainly did not.

"Does she have new information about the murder?"

Luisa shrugged. "I have no idea, only that she wanted to see you. Have you forgotten how to find her?"

They reached the building where work continued apace. From the dockside, Thomas saw it would soon be a substantial edifice, to reflect the new wealth of Spain and this city. Thomas followed Luisa into the interior, where men were removing sections of the roof.

"What will stand here when the work is complete?" he asked.

"A building fit for its purpose." Luisa smiled, an expression unusual enough to surprise Thomas. "Which is mostly to impress. It will lie as close to the palace wall as allowed, with a larger area in the centre for conducting trade and recording transactions. Around all four sides will be rooms three storeys high, with a balcony in the same style as the palace." She entered her office and closed the door behind them.

"Moorish, then," Thomas said.

"I hear you lived with them for many years."

"Almost forty."

"You went native?" Luisa appeared genuinely interested.

It was a question Thomas was unsure if he had an answer for.

"I lived among them, dressed like them, spoke their language, but did I become one of them?" He shook his head. "Even over all those years, I do not think such is possible. You are born into that culture. You cannot become it from outside."

"Did you convert to their religion?"

"No." Thomas considered this answer enough. He felt no need to tell Luisa that he possessed no religion and no belief in any God. "Pleasant as this conversation is, what have you to tell me of this wine?"

"You will need to speak with the merchant to confirm what I am about to tell you, but I heard that the wine used at the banquet was imported by special request of Don Alejandro and was obtained through a contact of Mateo Salto's."

"He told me a Portuguese trader, but no name."

"A man called Salvador Flores. Mateo has used him before, and I have met him. He is a trader, nothing more."

The name was unfamiliar to Thomas. "I would speak with him."

Luisa stared at Thomas, almost a smile playing on her lips which she would not allow to escape. "It is unusual to find a man as sparse with words as myself. Are you this way in all your actions?"

"I have been told I can be."

"Flores comes every two or three weeks," said Luisa. "His main business is based in Cadiz, but he does not live there. He has a place in the hills. Are you and Rosa lovers?"

The last took Thomas by surprise.

"No. She is with Baracoa," he said.

The answer seemed to surprise Luisa. "Good. I would like to share my bed with you. Few men spark my interest, and you are one such."

Thomas showed nothing. He needed Luisa's knowledge and contacts. He was attracted to her, but she also scared him. She made no pretence. She wanted him, so why not state it? He decided to ignore her question as if it had never been asked.

"When do you expect this merchant again?"

Luisa too seemed unconcerned at his lack of response.

"Tomorrow, perhaps. I expected him today, but it is too late now. You can return first thing or remain here. My rooms are above where I work."

"Is it not unusual for wine to be imported from Portugal into Spain?"

"Some consider it more exotic than our own. They are fools, but there are always merchants happy to pander to their foolishness. Do you like wine, Thomas?"

"I have been known to enjoy it." He waited for Luisa to restate her invitation, but he suspected she would ask only the once. Thomas tried to tell himself not to be disappointed.

"Come early in the morning then, if you want to speak with him," she said, and turned away.

Thomas pushed his way back through the traders, confused. He needed to speak with Jorge, except he knew what he would say. He would call him a fool for not accepting Luisa's blatant invitation, and Thomas still might. There was something about her that called to him. Her toughness. Her sharpness of mind. The fact she would not want to tie him down to a long-term relationship, and they would part on good terms.

Before he left the building he stopped and looked back, but Luisa had gone.

On the far side of the dockside, Thomas approached Rosa as she stood behind her stall.

"Luisa said you wanted to see me."

"Baracoa is inside finishing his preparations. It is he who wants to see you, Thomas. Go in."

Thomas went past her, still working through his conversation with Luisa. Had he given the impression he and Rosa were lovers? He did not know how, but then he was aware he never did. More than ever he needed an hour with Jorge to settle his mind on matters of love and lust, on the difference between attraction and beauty.

He found Baracoa inside, sitting cross-legged on the floor with a metal pot in front of him balanced on a small brazier. He glanced up and nodded.

"This is what killed your man," he said. "It will be ready in a small while. Then I will show you how dangerous it is. But we must go beyond the city to do it. I would have no one see what I do. You will come with me?"

Thomas knew there were many calls on his time, the list of names of people he still needed to speak to, the demand of the negotiation regarding Catherine's marriage, as well as the confusion over his personal life. But he believed what Baracoa wanted to show him was important.

"Yes, I will come. To where?"

"Out of the city," Baracoa said again. "Somewhere we might find boar. Do you know of such a place?"

Thomas frowned. "I do not, but why boar?"

"We need an animal as heavy as a man. Unless you want us to try it on a man?"

Thomas laughed. "No, a boar it is. I may know someone who can help. Do not leave until I return."

Thomas ran across to the palace and entered. He asked the first guard he met where he could find Diego Serrano and was told he was in the gatehouse the last time the man knew of.

Thomas entered without knocking to find Diego in conversation with Don Rodrigo. Both men turned at the interruption.

"Ah, Thomas," said Rodrigo, "we were discussing Don

Alejandro's death. Diego has some ideas about who might have wanted him dead. I told him to speak to you."

Thomas looked at Diego, who appeared annoyed at the news.

"I will find you again soon," Thomas said. "At the moment I have a simple question. If a man wanted to hunt boar, where is the closest place to find them?"

"When you say a man, Thomas, do you mean yourself? I ask because there are boar close to the city, but they roam the King's hunting grounds and it is against the law for anyone but him or his guests to kill one. I am sure for you he would make an exception. Do you have many mouths to feed?"

"It is Jorge's idea," Thomas said, his mind spinning as he tried to come up with a reason without implicating Baracoa, who would definitely not be allowed to hunt the King's ground. "He wants to hold a celebration at the turning of the year. It is a thing he has learned about in England. He has made friends already and intends to invite them all." It was not a good explanation, but Rodrigo laughed.

"I am not surprised. That man makes friends like others gather fleas. Is it not too soon to kill a boar for the turning of the year?"

"It is, but I would look at these boar and pick one the King would find unsuitable. Something old and lame, unworthy of his attention. I would take it closer to when it is needed."

"Yes, there are creatures like that," said Diego, who no doubt rode with the King to offer protection. "I have suggested culling them would be in the best interests of all, animal and hunter alike."

“Will I receive an invitation to this celebration?” Rodrigo asked. “It sounds interesting. And if Jorge is hosting it I expect there will be many pretty women. You must come as well, Diego. You must also invite the King, Thomas. Though you will need to roast this old boar slowly and for a long time if it is to be edible.”

Thomas cursed himself for coming up with such an excuse. He might have to go through with it to avoid suspicion.

“I doubt he would be interested,” Thomas said, but Rodrigo shook his head and laughed.

“If there is meat, wine, and beautiful women, he will be interested. Do you know where these hunting grounds are?”

Thomas shook his head, his gaze moving between them in search of some disbelief, but there was none. He managed to get away from them after descriptions of how to find the best locations were offered. When he reached Rosa’s house Baracoa stood outside, a small pot in one hand, a long bamboo pole in the other. How long he had been waiting Thomas did not know, but Baracoa showed no impatience, as if he could stand there for many more hours yet.

“You know where?” he asked.

“I do. I will take you now.”

“And me,” said Rosa.

“It might be dangerous,” Thomas said. “I know little about the boar in the hunting grounds, how aggressive they are, how protective of their young.”

“Do not look at me as a weak woman, Thomas. I am coming.”

It was easier to agree than argue, so Thomas set out with Baracoa on one side and Rosa on the other. The day was fading, and he wanted to see what Baracoa had in mind while there was still light enough to see. Fortunately, the hunting grounds were less than a mile away. They crossed the river on a boat then set out through a scattering of large houses on the far bank. Soon they moved beyond them. The ground rose, then fell until they stood on a shallow slope looking over a thickly wooded valley where two small streams wound through on their way to empty into the Guadalquivir.

The setting sun crept closer to the hill on the far side of the valley and shadows deepened and crept across the ground.

"There," whispered Rosa, pointing.

Thomas narrowed his eyes but saw nothing. Baracoa did.

"Too much health," he said. He arranged the length of bamboo across his knees and set the pot of dark, oily substance by his side.

A small family of boar appeared, three females, four shoat and a male which took up the rear. Hanging back in the tree cover stood two other males.

"The big one is injured," said Baracoa.

He spoke the truth. The animal came slowly, limping badly on its front leg. Behind it, the two boar came from beneath the trees. They had also seen it move awkwardly and wanted to replace it.

"It is a big beast to kill," Thomas said.

Baracoa only smiled. He reached into a small linen bag

and withdrew a small arrow, tipped with three feathers. The shaft was narrow, the tip lightly barbed.

"Is that what you use?" Thomas asked, pointing at the arrow.

Baracoa nodded as he began to work the tip through the dark, viscid liquid. Thomas thought of the arrow. It was small, and he was interested to see if it was large enough to bring down a boar, which he doubted. It made him think of Don Alejandro slapping at his neck. Thomas had seen no arrow, but he had not been expecting to see one. If it had fallen to the floor, it would be gone now, swept away and discarded.

Baracoa worked it into the bamboo, then pushed a twist of cotton after it.

He started down towards the group of boar.

The dominant injured male saw him and turned, aware of a threat. It started up the slope, preparing to charge. Thomas watched, unease filling him. He drew two knives from sheaths tied to his belt and passed one to Rosa.

"That is a lot of animal to stop with a tiny dart. If it comes at us, do what you can. I will try to cut its throat."

Rosa said nothing, her eyes on Baracoa.

The boar came nearer, but slowly, its front leg clearly painful. When it was close enough Baracoa lifted the bamboo to his lips, took a deep lungful of air then let it out all at once. Thomas did not see the dart. If it hit the boar it showed no effect.

Thomas stood, ready to protect Rosa.

Baracoa lowered the bamboo and remained where he was. The boar lowered its head and attempted to charge, but something was wrong. It came at a trot, then stopped. A moment later it fell sideways. Its chest heaved as it gasped for air, then stopped moving. Everything happened within a count of forty.

In the valley beyond, the two male boar faced up to each other, ready to fight over the females.

Thomas walked down to stand beside Baracoa.

"You killed it?"

Baracoa smiled. "Curare killed it."

"That is the potion you mixed?"

"Yes."

"It acts that fast?"

"Yes," said Baracoa again.

"How many people in Spain know how to prepare it?"

"I believe only one. Me. But I did not kill anyone. Not here."

"There are others like you in the palace," Thomas said. "Might one of them know how?"

"They are – how do you say it – idiots? Only a strong shaman can create curare."

"So if it was not you there must be another." Thomas looked at the dead beast. He did not see the arrow embedded in its flesh, nor any sign of where it had hit it. "Where is the arrow?" he asked Baracoa.

"They fall out. It will be here somewhere if you look, but there is no need."

Thomas considered the idea. "And if someone should come across it and pick it up, might it kill them?"

Baracoa gave the question some thought. "It is possible but would need the right circumstances." He glanced at the sky. "It may rain, in which case the curare will be thinned. It may be trodden into the dirt, so safe. But look if you wish."

Thomas looked around, realising the futility of a search. "It is a shame the meat is spoiled," he said, "but it would have died soon anyway."

"Not spoiled," said Baracoa. "The meat can be eaten. Even if the liquid is swallowed it will not kill. Only in the blood does it kill. I picked a good spot. Sometimes it takes longer, but once the dart hits a beast it is dead. I will take some of the meat, salt and dry it. I will eat well for a month."

Thomas went back to where Rosa waited. He stood beside her without speaking.

"Are we going back now?" she asked.

"I want to wait until Baracoa is finished. I would examine the animal's organs. And I need to talk with him again. Is he staying with you tonight?"

She shrugged, turned and walked away.

Thomas sat on the ground and waited. When Baracoa had cut several pieces of meat and wrapped them in cloth, he climbed to Thomas.

"Rosa says you can stay with her tonight if you wish."

"I thank her, but I go."

"I need to ask you some more about this poison you used."

"Then ask as we walk."

"I want to get rid of the boar before someone finds it. This ground belongs to the King, and for all I was told I could hunt one boar here I prefer no one knows exactly how it was done."

“Rosa says you are a friend of the Queen.”

“But not the King. You can go. I will drag the carcass to the river.”

Baracoa started down the slope he had come from. “It is quicker with two. We can talk while we do it.”

TWENTY-TWO

Thomas found Jorge sitting in a comfortable chair when he reached their house. He was turned so he could once more look across the cathedral square. There were no candles or lamps lit so the room lay cloaked in darkness, which allowed Jorge to watch those passing unobserved. Thomas remained at the door, watching his friend.

"I know you are there, Thomas."

Thomas crossed the room and pulled up a smaller chair to sit beside Jorge. "What are you doing?"

"Watching the world pass by. The cathedral bell rang not long since, calling the city to prayer. This is the result."

"Since when have you been so interested in the Church?"

Jorge glanced at Thomas and smiled. "Since we have been looking for a killer."

"You thought you might recognise them by looking?"

Beyond the window, groups of men and women – separate in the main – stood and talked, but already some were breaking off and making their way into the cathedral. Unlike the one in Cordoba, this had been built anew when the Moors had been expelled from the city two centuries before.

"I thought I might notice anyone who looked suspicious." Jorge offered another smile, this one apologetic. "But at least half appear guilty of something or other."

"Which is why they come to worship and attend confession. Their God demands piety, but the Church allows them to purchase indulgences for their sins. For many it is the perfect arrangement."

The square was more than half empty now. Jorge stood and lit a candle, then used it to light two lamps.

"What have you learned I do not know about?" he asked as he retook his seat.

"Baracoa showed me how Don Alejandro was killed with a poisoned dart. I even saw when it happened but did not realise what it was until today. It changes my ideas about his death." Thomas told Jorge about the curare poison, the dart, and the dead boar before stopping, aware Jorge had lost interest.

"Does how he died make a difference?" asked Jorge.

"Of course it does. Baracoa told me he knows of no one else who can make curare."

Jorge smiled without looking away from the window, though the square was now almost empty. "So now you know who killed him. Get Diego Serrano to arrest this Baracoa."

"He says he did not kill Don Alejandro, and I believe him."

Jorge glanced at Thomas then away. "So who did? All

you have done is add one more mystery to what is already an abundance of mysteries."

"Perhaps one of those on our list of people we need to talk to will give us cause for suspicion. Baracoa also said that when he first came to Spain, he was among others from across the sea living in the palaces for the entertainment of people. He left, or was released, to live his own life. But others of his kind remain. We saw some at the banquet, and there will be others. Baracoa claims over a dozen. He says only a shaman would know how to create the poison, and none of those in the palace would be capable."

"So it does not help us," said Jorge. He rose to his feet and stretched. "If you are right you need to find another shaman. Do you intend to do that tonight or in the morning?"

"I want to see if Baracoa is still with Rosa and ask him if he knows of any others in Spain who may be shaman." Thomas was tired but knew now was the best time to ask Baracoa, if he remained in Sevilla. So they went out and walked towards the docks.

As they rounded a sharp turn in the street, Thomas heard a wailing sound and began to move faster, responding to trouble as he always did, by advancing towards it.

Another turn, and he saw a small group of people standing outside a house. When he got close, he saw the door was open, but no one tried to enter.

"What is happening here?" he demanded.

"They are all dead, sir. The entire family." The man who spoke crossed himself and, as if it was a signal, everyone else did the same.

"Who is dead?"

"All of them."

"Who is all of them?" Before Thomas entered the house, he wanted to know who lived there.

"Roberto, his wife, their children. Even their hound." The man shook his head, as if the dog was the worst of the victims.

Thomas doubted he would get any more sense from the man. He turned to Jorge. "Speak with them, find out all you can about those who live here, and who they are as well."

"You are going in?"

Thomas did not think an answer necessary. Jorge knew who he was, and what he did.

The interior of the house was dim, and he took the one candle already burning and used it to light others and three lamps. The illumination showed a single room where the whole family lived. Thin horsehair mattresses were piled into one corner to be laid out for sleep. A single open door showed a small yard at the rear. There was only the one floor. An open fire stood to one side, logs still smoking and giving off heat. A large, black-sooted pot hung from a chain over the logs. A man and woman remained sitting at the table, their upper bodies leaning across it, hands extended so they could clasp each other's.

They knew they were dying, Thomas thought, touched that they wanted a final contact.

Three children had tumbled to the floor. And then there was the dog. It lay in front of the fireplace. All of them had vomited, the sharp stink of it filling the room. On the floor beside the dog lay a leg from a large bird that sat on the table. Thomas stepped closer and examined it, noting the substantial breast had been carved. Vegetables and meat lay on five plates. Each of the meals had been half consumed.

The bird was too large for most fowl, even a goose, and Thomas looked around for a clue to what it was, though as he did so the answer came to him. It was confirmed when he went out to the yard and found a pile of feathers moving loosely in a light breeze that curled over the surrounding wall. Long tail feathers added certainty. The bird was a peacock.

Thomas wondered if it was the same bird he had observed in the palace gardens, running madly around before falling dead. If so, he now knew it had been poisoned. As had this family. His mind conjured possibilities of what could poison both bird and those who ate its flesh. Several came to mind but would have to wait.

He turned and went outside, where Jorge was talking to a lone man, the others having lost interest.

"This gentleman tells me the man's name is Roberto, and he works in the palace gardens," said Jorge.

"Is that where the bird came from?" Thomas asked, speaking to the man.

He nodded. "Roberto promised us all some of the flesh. There was far too much for them. He said he would distribute in the morning. He plucked it and hung it for a day or two first. They are dead, sir, are they not?"

"Yes, they are dead. Poisoned by the flesh of the bird, I believe."

Thomas turned back into the house. He looked for a key to lock the door but found none, only a bar to secure it once inside, which was no use to him, so he went out again.

"No one is to enter here. No people, no animals. Do you understand?"

"I do, sir."

"I want you to stand guard until I return with someone."

The man nodded and firmed his shoulders, pleased to be trusted with such an important task.

As Thomas walked away with Jorge, he realised he needed to find someone in the *hermanos* to take care of what had happened in the house, but first he needed the skill of someone else and hoped he remained in the city.

"Yes," said Rosa from where she stood behind her stall. Two lamps hung on hooks so she could continue her trade. "He is in the back, but I know not what he is doing. He took some of my plants and seeds with him."

Thomas found Baracoa where he had been earlier that day, sitting cross-legged next to a small metal pot over a fire. He looked up at Thomas before returning to whatever he was doing.

"I need your help," Thomas said.

"I gave it today. I am preparing something new for you, in case you ever need it." He stirred the pot, then took it from over the fire, rose and set it on a side table. "It is done now. What do you want?"

"A family is dead, poisoned from eating the flesh of a peacock, which I believe may have been poisoned the same way as Don Alejandro."

"Who is Don Alejandro, and what is a peacock?" said Baracoa.

"Don Alejandro is the man who was killed, the one

who brought me to you. And a peacock is a large bird with bright feathers."

"Ah, yes. I saw them in the palace. The dead family are there?"

"The man worked there, but they are in his house. You will come?"

"Yes, I will come."

Thomas led the way. Rosa and Baracoa fell into step beside him.

"Why is it trouble always seems to find you, Thomas?" asked Rosa.

"I expect I am fortunate that way," he said, pleased when she smiled.

At the house, the man left on guard remained there. Thomas took Baracoa inside, but Rosa remained on the street with Jorge.

Baracoa looked over the bodies, then went into the yard and studied the remains of the butchered bird. He nodded. "I see. Peacock. I will remember the name." He looked at Thomas. "Curare did not do this. I told you it must enter the blood, not the belly." He looked around the small yard, then knelt where the discarded guts of the bird had been thrown. They stank, but Baracoa sliced into them then used the tip of his knife to lift out something from within. He showed it to Thomas.

"This is unfamiliar to me. Do you recognise it?"

Thomas leaned closer, ignoring the stink. He used a stick to stir the contents before nodding.

"I do. It is the root of a mandrake plant and will be what killed the family. It is a powerful poison and can leach into the flesh of whatever it kills. I did not know it grew around here, but the bird lived in the palace garden so there must be some there. I will need to find someone to ask. I saw this bird convulse and die in those gardens."

"How long ago?"

"Three days. Before I came to see you."

"Is that enough time for the poison to move from belly to flesh?" When Thomas nodded Baracoa turned and walked out through the house. When Thomas followed, he found the man already gone, but Rosa and Jorge remained.

"Where are the *hermanos* based these days?" Thomas asked Rosa as they made their way back to her house.

"Where they always have been, on the far side of the river in Santa Ana de Triana. You will need to take the Barca bridge. Do you know where it is?"

"I am afraid I do." Thomas recalled crossing the bridge many times when he was tracking a killer in Sevilla, and how he was taken prisoner himself and held in a dungeon on the far side of the river. Now he nodded his thanks.

"You can return to Baracoa. I would not have you enter that terrible place, or even be near it." They had reached the edge of the docks once more and Thomas left her standing alone.

"You did not flatter her," said Jorge as he walked beside Thomas. "Women like to be flattered."

"Rosa strikes me as a woman, like Luisa, who would not take to flattery. Besides, I have already told you, I am not seeking refuge in anyone's arms."

Jorge grinned. "Not even mine?"

"Especially yours."

They crossed the bridge to discover the building housing the *hermanos* had several new additions, and it took some time before Thomas found anyone willing to listen. Even after he passed on news of the deaths the man seemed uninterested.

"I can always tell the palace guard, or the Queen, that you did not have time to devote to your duties," Thomas said. "Are not all citizens of this city worthy of decent treatment?" He stared at the man. "No mind, the Queen will dispatch her own men." Thomas turned and left, trying to quell his anger. He was aware he grew angry more readily these days and wondered if it was him or the world around him that had changed.

"Do you think he is afraid you might actually tell Isabel what a poor excuse of a soldier he is?" said Jorge as they recrossed the bridge.

"It might persuade him to act."

"Did you mean your threat?"

"Probably not, but it gave me pleasure to let him think I did."

"Can we find somewhere to eat now? My hunger grows by the hour."

"You will have to eat alone tonight. I intend to find Diego Serrano and tell him about the dead family. It involves the palace because the man worked there, and the peacock came from the gardens." Thomas clapped Jorge on the shoulder then moved away before he could object. "Tomorrow I will see if I can find out if mandrake grows there."

TWENTY-THREE

By the time Thomas approached the palace, the square between it and the cathedral had once more filled with people leaving worship. The frequency with which they did so often made him wonder at the degree of sin they suffered from, or was it nothing more than social contact they craved. They gathered in groups, their voices loud. Street vendors wound between the crowd selling roasted almonds and chestnuts, pastries and meat wrapped in buns. As he moved closer to the palace entrance, the crowd thinned. He was admitted without question, his face familiar. The guards knew he was a friend to King and Queen. At least that is what they had been told.

Thomas slowed and asked one of the men, "Do you know if Diego Serrano is here?"

"He should be, sir. The best place to look is the old infirmary."

Thomas frowned. "Is he sick?"

The guard returned the frown, then realised Thomas was unfamiliar with the layout. "It probably was an infirmary at one time, sir, but was replaced with something smaller and more suitable. Now it is where the *hermanos* and palace guards have their offices. It is the building beyond the stables. You cannot get lost."

Thomas thanked the guard and passed beneath the high walls surrounding the inner palace. He managed to confound the guard's words and get lost, but a passing servant sent him the right way. The infirmary, when he reached it, surprised him with its smallness. It was only a little larger than the house he and Jorge were sharing, and only a single storey. Thomas supposed there would have been little use for an infirmary within the palace. Any injury or illness would be treated elsewhere, as he had treated Prince Juan when he repaired the boy's leg to allow him to walk straight again.

Diego Serrano sat outside, a glass of wine on a small table at his side, with food next to it. He watched Thomas's approach with neither sign of welcome nor annoyance at being interrupted.

"If you are here to tell me about the death of one of the gardeners and his family it is already being taken care of. I heard the news some time ago and dispatched men to have the bodies interred. Or more likely burned."

"And to find out who killed them?" Thomas asked.

"I was told that eating the spoiled flesh of a stolen peacock killed them."

"I saw the bird die four days ago, which is not long enough for the flesh to spoil at this time of year. It was poisoned, and the poison that killed it then killed that entire family. The bird had ingested mandrake and must have done so within the palace gardens. I want you to send men to speak to all the gardeners and ask if they know of this plant." Thomas watched Diego as he spoke, unsure if the man wanted to ignore their deaths or truly believed what he had been told. As it was, he saw it was the latter.

"You are sure of this, Thomas?" Diego rose to his feet and pulled at his jacket to draw the creases out of it.

"As sure as I can ever be in such matters. The poison was unusual for these parts. How it came to grow in the gardens is something I intend to find out."

"Is that not a matter for the *hermanos*?"

"I heard you used to be a captain with them," Thomas said, and when Diego nodded, continued, "which means you know well how they will respond. A dead family and bad meat, which is what you were told."

Diego stared at Thomas so long and hard he thought he had pushed the man too far. So was surprised when he spoke.

"You have no position in Spain anymore, but you are right in your judgement of the *hermanos*, which is one reason I sought a post in the palace. It used to be little different here, but I have made changes and matters have improved. But what to do about you, Thomas?"

"I am content to continue as I have so far. I need no position."

"It will make your work easier, so I will come up with something."

"As long as a uniform is not involved," Thomas said, and Diego laughed.

"I had you as a man who likes to dress well."

"You mistake me for my companion," Thomas said.

"Ah, yes, that must be it. I will have my men talk with

the neighbours, and the other gardeners, and see if they know anything. The man worked here in the palace and that is reason enough for me to become involved." Diego looked past Thomas as something caught his attention. "I see Don Rodrigo is coming to see me. You should stay."

Thomas stepped aside and saw Don Rodrigo approaching as if he had something on his mind. Which, as it turned out, was the same thing Thomas had on his own mind, and more.

"I am glad you are here, Thomas. I have heard grave news regarding a man I know well. He works in these gardens and has been found dead. It sounds like the kind of work you are known for."

"I am already looking into the matter," Thomas said. "And Diego wants to grant me a position which will help open doors that would otherwise be closed."

Rodrigo glanced at Diego before smiling. "I believe the position of *alguacil* is currently vacant."

"It is," said Diego, "and has been these last twelve months. It would be perfect for Thomas."

Thomas recognised the term, which indicated something close to a sheriff in England. A not unimportant position, so it surprised him it had stood vacant for a year.

"I will arrange it," said Don Rodrigo. "I am sure the Queen will sign the appointment once I have the document drawn up. Now, Thomas, tell me what you know so far."

"There are many things I have learned, but which are relevant to this death I do not know. Also, I still need to speak with a list of people Jorge has found for me, including Don Alejandro's eldest son."

"Gabriel Ortega-Dominguez can be a difficult person,

full of his own importance. Or what he regards as his own importance. Have you spoken with Doña Carlita again yet?"

"Only on the day Don Alejandro died. She has gone to her house near Malaga. I may have to find out where it is and go there if I make no progress here."

"I can tell you how to find it if you need to. When do you intend to speak with Gabriel? I am known to him and may be able to question him without him losing his temper."

"Would I be able to accompany you?" Thomas asked.

"That might prove difficult. If it can wait a day or two you will have your new position to protect you from his ire."

Thomas did not want to delay speaking to Don Alejandro's heir but decided he also did not want to antagonise Rodrigo, so made a show of agreeing. He would decide what to do in the morning. Tonight, he had other matters to attend to, and was aware that time was passing.

"A day or two suits me fine, Rodrigo. I have one last question. The bird the gardener and his family ate, which killed them, died of mandrake poisoning. Are you aware of any that grows in the palace garden?"

"Mandrake?" said Rodrigo. "It grows in woodland and old olive groves, but I cannot see there would be any in the palace garden. If there is, it is unknown to me. Speak to the gardeners, but I suspect they will tell you the same."

"Diego said he will do that in the morning."

"Then we are done here."

Thomas went directly to Rosa's house, hoping to find Baracoa still there. He was sitting cross-legged on the table in the back room, staring into a darkness unlit by candles or lamps. Thomas almost did not see him.

"What do you want?" asked Baracoa in his soft, accented voice. "Whatever killed that family is not known to me."

"Diego Serrano, captain of the guards, is looking into it, but I believe they died through accident, as did the bird. My mind has returned to Don Alejandro. After your demonstration with the boar, I believe curare may indeed be what killed him. I want you to come with me to speak with the Kalinago in the palace," Thomas said. "Some may speak Spanish, but if not, I need someone who speaks their language. You said you were once one of them."

"I was. Now they do not welcome me."

"Perhaps they want their own freedom."

"Then they should take it, as I did. Also, there is one man there who carries much hatred of me."

"You are afraid of him?"

Baracoa stared at Thomas without expression, before saying, "I am afraid of no man. I will come. Tonight?"

"In the morning. The palace sleeps early and wakes slowly."

"Then I will stay the night here so we can take our time."

TWENTY-FOUR

Thomas woke early and lay in his bed, staring at a bar of light as it crept slowly across the ceiling. He knew he should rise but also knew he had spoken the truth to Baracoa when he said the palace roused only slowly. Eventually he rose, dressed, and shook Jorge awake to ask if he wanted to accompany him to the palace. Jorge mumbled and rolled over, which Thomas took as a refusal.

When he reached Rosa's house Baracoa stood outside, dressed as the day before, except this morning the coarse cloth draped over his body was rust-red, with bold blue and white splashes of colour. He had wrapped his hair around itself, so it hung only half-way along his back. He said nothing as Thomas approached, nor as they walked to the palace gates. The guards nodded at Thomas, but one held a hand up to stop Baracoa.

"He is with me," Thomas said.

"He is not of Spain," said the guard. "I do not care who he is with – he stays outside."

"I need him so I can speak with the other Kalinago. Go ask Diego Serrano or Don Rodrigo, if either are here."

"My place is at this gate. If I leave you will take him inside."

Thomas looked at the other guard, who simply raised a shoulder as if it was none of his business.

Thomas cursed and turned away, Baracoa already ahead of him.

"I am sorry about that," Thomas said. "They do not like strangers."

"It always happens, but there is a way at the back. I will show you."

Baracoa led Thomas along the side of the high wall and beyond. He took an alley on the right, then another, until they emerged at a small door set into the rear wall, which was lower than those surrounding the front of the palace. Baracoa nodded for Thomas to try it, and when he did the door opened and they both stepped through.

"I did not show you this way in," said Baracoa. "If people ask, I came with you."

"Of course, and the guards were happy to admit you."

Baracoa smiled.

"I want to find Diego first and tell him we are here. It will save trouble if we are found without permission."

Baracoa offered no response, which Thomas was growing used to.

Diego was in the same office as the night before and Thomas wondered if he had slept at all. He rose and greeted Thomas, then Baracoa, offering his hand, which was taken.

Seeing the frown on Thomas's face Diego said, "I know

Baracoa of old. He was one of the first of his people to live in the palace. I was a simple guard then. I would not say we became friends, but we grew used to each other."

"No, friends," said Baracoa, and Diego smiled and nodded.

"Yes then, friends. Now, you told me you want to speak with the others. I will accompany you, so nobody will question your presence. Not that any are likely to, because all know the Queen approves of you even if the King does not."

"Are you allowed to say such a thing?" Thomas asked.

"Likely not, but it is said now."

They entered the main body of the palace, which was busy with servants carrying trays of food for the residents to break their fast. No doubt Isabel and Fernando would be doing the same, together with those of their children who remained with them.

"The Kalinago eat apart," said Diego.

"How many are there in the palace?" Thomas asked.

"There were twenty at one time, including Baracoa. The others were brought here on three different voyages. Two died, three ran away, so now there are fourteen. Nine men and five women. The men have an easier time of it than the women."

There was no need for Thomas to ask why. Both would be seen as outsiders, strangers, but the women would be considered both exotic and easy prey, unable to complain. Why would they be believed over the word of a Spaniard?

The group were seated around a table, which surprised Thomas, who knew Baracoa sat on the ground to eat.

Thomas recognised several as those who had served the royal table at the interrupted banquet. Each turned as they entered. One man, a tall native whose hair, unlike the others, had been close-cropped, came forward. Thomas recalled his name as Jayuya, though their contact at the banquet had been brief.

"We are eating." He waved a hand aggressively. "You must leave."

"You know who we are, Jayuya," said Diego. "Don Thomas is friend to both Queen Isabel and King Fernando and has questions to ask you all."

"Later! Or never," said the man, glaring at each in turn. It appeared most of his ire was aimed at Baracoa, who stood passively, ignoring it. "The man spat a single word at him in his own language."

When the man took two more paces towards Baracoa, Diego placed himself between them. Thomas stood to one side, ready to intervene or draw a knife if needs be.

The man pushed at Diego, who pushed back.

One of the men at the table shouted something, repeated by one of the women.

"He is angry," said Baracoa.

"What did he say to you?"

"He called me a traitor."

The pushing between Diego and the man continued, but Thomas saw his help was not required. The man was taller than Diego, broader across the shoulders, but Diego was battle-hardened. Thomas recognised the look, which was mostly in the eyes. The man did not see it, which was his mistake. When he raised a fist, Diego punched him hard in the belly and he staggered back, but only for a moment. The next time he came forward, Diego drew a long, wickedly honed blade.

Jayuya glared at Thomas, at Baracoa, then turned and stormed from the room. Those seated seemed to release a common sigh of relief.

"He is not liked," said Baracoa.

"Is he dangerous?" asked Diego. "Can I allow him to leave this way?"

"Dangerous?" said Baracoa. "You saw him. Not dangerous. But he might creep up on someone."

Diego sighed. "I will send a guard to find him. It might be time he is evicted from the palace. I fear what might happen if he acts this way before the Queen or her daughters. Thomas, stay here and ask your questions. Come find me afterwards."

Thomas watched Diego hurry from the room, then turned to Baracoa. "I want to know if any of them have information about the death of Don Alejandro. Some were in the room with him. All of the women, I think, and perhaps four or five of the men. Ask them what they know of poisons from their land. Will they speak to you?"

"They will. Before I left, I was *cacique,* leader of our small tribe here in the palace. Jayuya wanted to replace me when I lived here, but he is not liked. He is an angry man. He will stamp around outside until he calms down, but Diego is right, he is a danger if he remains within the palace. He should be killed."

"You cannot kill a man because you do not like him."

"He is like a wild animal that cannot be tamed," said

Baracoa. "In my land we would send him away. If he came back unchanged we would kill him. It is the way."

Thomas did not want to get into an argument, though he had met many men, and women, who deserved the same fate Baracoa was proposing. And, Thomas knew, he had sometimes been the bearer of such punishment himself.

"Ask them my questions. I will stand to one side so as not to interfere."

Thomas watched as Baracoa went to the table. He sat with them in the place vacated by Jayuya and picked at the food. Once the others started to eat again Baracoa spoke with them, the sound of their conversation strange but soothing. Thomas picked up on their names, both soft and unusual. The women who spoke most were Yariel, Anacoana, Yaiza and Zoraida. The two men who answered Baracoa's questions were Iacaco and Rocio. The silent ones were no doubt afraid of what Jayuya might do to them if they revealed anything he wanted to remain secret.

It was an hour before Baracoa rose and bowed to each in turn. He shook the hands of the men and embraced the women before returning to Thomas.

"We will speak outside," he said. "Some of them understand Spanish."

They went into the gardens and found a low wall to sit on. The day was bright, the sun warm, but the air carried the chill of winter even in this southerly place. From a distance they heard shouting, but Thomas thought it came from beyond the wall.

"Did they tell you anything useful?"

"You must judge. Those who saw this Don Alejandro die did not think him poisoned. Most said he was old and fat and drank too much. Also, he touched the women in their private places. They were not surprised he died."

Baracoa's simple report seemed too little for such a long conversation.

"You asked about poison?"

"Of course. None claimed to know how to make it, which is as it should be. Only a shaman can make curare."

"This Jayuya could not do it?"

Baracoa shook his head. "Never. He is ... you have a word for it ... a bully?"

"Yes, a bully."

"He is a bully who thinks himself better than all others. Me. You. The King. He may flee now, or may not."

"What else did you speak of?" Thomas asked. "More than what you have told me."

"We spoke of our homeland and how we miss it." Baracoa offered a sad smile. "The mountains, the clear water of the sea and lakes, the white sands, the trees and plants, the animals, the fish, the fowl ... our world." He scowled. "People here call it a new world, but it is not. It is an old world. As old as yours. Perhaps older. There are great cities like you have, but neither the Spanish nor the Portuguese believe we are fit to rule anything. It is why I cannot live near you people." Baracoa's gaze met Thomas's. "You are a good man, Thomas, but still you are one of them. Rosa is a good woman, but she is also one of them."

"If you could, would you return home?" Thomas asked. He had no argument with Baracoa. He did not feel like an oppressor, but knew this good man regarded him as one. Regarded all of them as oppressors.

"In a heartbeat, yes. But it cannot be."

Thomas thought of Columb, who had discovered this new world. A man he had once considered mad but grew slowly to regard as a friend.

"I cannot promise, but it may be possible," he said.

Baracoa said nothing, only looked away through the swaying trees and grasses until someone screamed.

TWENTY-FIVE

Thomas ran in the direction of the scream, but Baracoa was faster, flying across the ground until he was out of sight. When Thomas caught up with him, Baracoa knelt over Don Rodrigo, who lay on his back, arms spread. Diego was several feet away, on his front.

When Thomas started towards Diego, Baracoa said, "That one is dead, but this one not. Give me your knife."

Thomas changed direction and knelt beside Baracoa. He reached out and put a finger against Rodrigo's throat. There was a pulse, but it was too slow.

"He is still alive," he said. "You cannot kill him."

"Not kill," said Baracoa. "Save him. Knife. Now."

Thomas drew his knife and handed it across. When Baracoa laid the honed blade against Rodrigo's shoulder, Thomas saw a dart similar to the one Baracoa had used on the boar embedded in the skin and wondered why he had not removed it. Instead, he sliced into the flesh at an angle, then cut above the dart until he managed to work a chunk of flesh free. He tossed it aside, the dart still embedded. Baracoa leaned close and put his lips over the bleeding wound. He sucked, spat, repeated it three times more, then sat back.

"Now his fate is in the hand of his Gods."

Thomas went to Diego and searched for a pulse, but there was nothing to find. He leaned closer, searching until he found the dart embedded in his neck, directly over a major blood vessel. Was that why he had died, and Rodrigo lived?

Thomas returned to kneel once more beside Baracoa.

"You are safe?" he asked.

Baracoa wiped his mouth. "It kills only in the blood. I told you this. But find me water if you can. I do not welcome the taste of Spanish blood."

"Diego is dead," Thomas said.

"I know. This one moved, so I thought I might save him. He was fortunate the dart punctured the top of his arm where there is little blood. He may still die, but we wait and see. I also need water to wash his wound."

Thomas ran back through the gardens until he found a barrel holding water. He filled the pot sitting beside it and brought it back to Baracoa, who washed Rodrigo's blood from his face, then rinsed his mouth out several times.

Thomas picked up the hunk of flesh and examined it.

"Do not touch the dart," said Baracoa.

"I will not." Thomas examined the flesh, mottled dark around where the dart had broken the skin. Whoever had fired it, and Thomas could think of only one man who could have done so, had missed any blood vessels. But he knew over time the poison would leach into Rodrigo's flesh and kill him. Without Baracoa's knowledge and quick action, the man would likely be dead by now.

"Burn it," said Baracoa.

"I need to fetch someone to deal with Diego's body. Then I have to take Don Rodrigo to the infirmary. I will need to stitch his wound."

"Leave it open for a day. He will wake soon and there will be pain."

"Rosa will have something to help with that."

"Yes, she will. Jayuya did this. I did not believe he could prepare curare. That was my mistake. He has fled, but I will find him and kill him."

"Stay here until I fetch help." Thomas said.

Baracoa shook his head. "I will track Jayuya. These men go nowhere." He rose and walked away.

Thomas hesitated, then did what he knew he must and returned to the palace. He informed Diego's men of what had happened, seeing their suspicion of him. He remained with them while they brought one body and one unconscious man back to the palace and set them in a room which contained two cots. By which time, word had spread, and King Fernando stood waiting as Thomas and the others returned.

"Who did this?" he asked, his face twisted with anger.

"One of the Kalinago housed in the palace, Your Grace," Thomas said. "A man by the name of Jayuya. Don Rodrigo may recover, but Diego Serrano is dead. I will stay with Rodrigo until I know more. I want to question him when, and if, he wakes."

"You are once again involving yourself in matters beyond your concern," said Fernando.

"With Diego dead, his own investigation will have stalled," Thomas said. "I already know a great deal, and am the best person to deal with finding the culprit. I suspect this Jayuya is also the man who killed Don Alejandro. He has fled, but there is a man tracking him."

"I still say it is not your responsibility."

A familiar voice spoke, making Thomas turn.

"And I say let Thomas finish what he has started." Queen Isabel entered the room. She glanced at Diego's body laid on a pallet, at Rodrigo on a narrow cot, his chest rising and falling. His breath came more readily now, and Thomas believed the moment of danger was past and he might wake soon.

"I disagree," said Fernando. "This is not the place to discuss it. Follow me. We will talk privately." He turned and strode from the room.

Isabel hesitated. She glanced at Thomas and spoke so quietly he could not hear her but gathered the meaning from the movement of her lips. "Do what you do." Then she followed her husband from the room.

The four men who had helped bring Diego and Rodrigo from the garden stood uncomfortably, their gazes avoiding Thomas.

"Who is the most senior officer now Diego is dead?" he asked. For a moment he thought none would reply, then one man raised his eyes and took a few steps towards him.

"There is no one, sir. I am the longest serving, but it is not my place to say it is me."

"Your name?"

"Inigo Alvarez, sir. But only Don Rodrigo can elevate me to command."

"Don Rodrigo cannot do that until he wakes, and the more time passes the more easily the man who killed your commander is making his escape. Do you have contacts in the *hermanos*?"

"Of course, sir."

"What would Diego want you to do?"

"My best, sir. Always my best."

"Then send someone to Triana and tell them what happened here. They must look for a tall, strong Kalinago with a shaved head. Are you familiar with those who live within the palace walls?"

"I am. You mentioned the name Jayuya. I know the man. Did he do this?"

"It is possible. He needs to be tracked down and questioned."

"And punished if he killed my master," said Inigo. "There are few Kalinago who walk free in the city. Jayuya will stand out." Inigo turned to one of the other men. "Go across the river and inform the *hermanos*. Tell them we are looking for the man who killed Diego. Describe him as this man said. Go."

Once the man had run off, Inigo approached Thomas and lowered his voice. "I saw what the Queen said to you, sir. 'Do what you do.' What is that?"

"Punish the wicked," Thomas said.

"Until I am told otherwise, I will allow you to continue doing so. I have been present when Diego spoke with you and know he regarded you as an honest man. Tell me what I must do."

"What you are. I need to speak again with the other Kalinago in the palace."

"Do you need someone to show you their rooms?" asked Inigo.

"I only recently came from there, but my thanks."

"I will come with you anyway to see if they have information which may be of use to me regarding Jayuya."

Thomas wondered if he also wanted to keep an eye on him. If so, the man only impressed him the more. It is what he would have done in his place.

Inigo told the two remaining men to keep watch over Don Rodrigo and find him at once if he showed signs of waking. Then he led Thomas through the corridors, into the yard at the back, and then towards a set of what looked to be little more than wooden huts set against the rear wall. There were no doors, but blankets hung over half a dozen openings. Thomas realised this was not where he had met the Kalinago earlier, and was fortunate Inigo was with him.

"I do not speak their language, sir, but a few of them speak Spanish. I should return to check on Don Rodrigo and see what progress is being made."

"I will return there once finished here," Thomas said. "I would speak with Don Rodrigo as soon as he wakes. When he does send for me."

Inigo offered a nod and ran off back into the main palace.

Thomas started at the opening on the left for want of any better plan. He rapped on the side of the opening then entered, too impatient to wait for an invitation. He found three people inside, two men and one woman. The only light came from the doorway and a small hole for the smoke of a fire to rise through at the rear of the room. All three sat on a mattress against the stone wall. Flatbreads cooked on a stone slab laid directly on the coals of the wood fire.

"Who here speaks Spanish?" Thomas asked. He waited, but none of the three responded, so he turned and did the same in the next hut. He tried four more before entering the penultimate hut and found what he was looking for. This time, he was greeted by only two people, both female. The layout was identical to the others, but its occupants had found chairs from somewhere. One sat, while another knelt next to the fire, cooking the same flatbreads he had seen in the first hut. He repeated his questions, and this time one of the women responded.

"I speak a little. You came with Baracoa, yes?"

"I did. I need to know about Jayuya. How well did you know him?"

The seated woman spoke in their own language to the kneeling one, who responded, then said, "We are Jayuya's women."

Thomas recalled their names. Some men would have been unable to distinguish them from each other, but Thomas had lived many years among the Moors. He accepted people of all colours and kinds and saw through the lazy classification of 'other' that did not recognise them as individuals. "You are Yariel and..." he tried to retrieve the name. After a moment it came to him. "...and Anacoana, yes?"

They nodded.

"You are both his women?"

Yariel nodded. She was the younger but carried an easy power. "Yes. Both of us." She showed no expression.

"Was he always angry?"

"Not always. Sometimes he was worse." She drew up the side of her *sayapa* to show a dark bruise along her side. The movement also displayed her breast, but she was unconcerned.

"And your..." Thomas was unsure how to refer to the other woman, "...friend?"

"My wife, though it does not mean the same as in your land," she said with a smile, before speaking in her own language. The kneeling woman rose and showed her own bruises and scars to Thomas. She said something which was translated as, "He hurts us, but what can we do?"

"He is a hunted man," Thomas said, "and when caught will be executed for murder. He will trouble you no more." He watched her face for some reaction, but there was none.

"You will not catch Jayuya." Yariel tapped her head. "He is ... what is your word. Sly? Cunning? He will not be caught."

"If he tries to return to the city he will," Thomas said.

Yariel smiled. "Then we will be safe. I thank you." She spoke to her companion, who rose and came across to embrace Thomas.

"Anacoana also thanks you," said Yariel.

"Do you know how Jayuya made the curare he used to kill with?"

The woman stared at Thomas before saying, "He could not. He is not shaman."

"It was used to attack Diego, who you know, and Don Rodrigo."

"I know both of them. Don Rodrigo likes to chase women like us, but not so often these days. Are they dead?"

"Diego is. Don Rodrigo is not. Baracoa saved his life."

"I see."

"Would Jayuya know where to get curare?"

"Only Baracoa is shaman, and he would never offer it to Jayuya. They hate each other."

"Do you know how it works?" Thomas asked, more for curiosity than information.

Yariel raised her hands as if holding something, pursed her lips and blew hard. She traced the arc of a dart through the air with her finger.

Thomas smiled. "Have you ever used it?"

"In my homeland, yes, when hunting. But I do not know how to make curare, only use it. Everyone here knows how to use it." She cocked her head to one side as she stared at Thomas. "Do not try, sir, it is dangerous."

"As I know well. Is there anything else I should know about Jayuya, or anyone else here? Are others of your men like him?"

She shook her head. "None of them. Our people are peaceful. Jayuya came from another island. Perhaps they are different there. Do you want me to come with you and ask the others if they know anything?"

"Will you?"

"Of course. You are a strong, handsome man, and we have no husband now."

Thomas laughed. Two hours later, he knew nothing more of the murders, but much about the people who had been brought here against their will, to be paraded before the Spanish court and its visitors. He might have stayed longer, content in their company and simple truths, but a guard came to tell him Don Rodrigo was showing signs of waking, and that a woman was waiting for him.

As he walked through the palace it came to him that the Kalinago had not lied, but had they withheld an important truth? They claimed only Baracoa capable of making curare and would never supply it to Jayuya. Either they lied, or someone else possessed the knowledge. If the latter was true, Thomas needed to find out who that was.

TWENTY-SIX

Thomas found Rosa in the makeshift infirmary, standing off to one side of the cot where Don Rodrigo twisted as he came awake.

"I brought hashish and a little poppy," she said, handing a bag to Thomas. "Also, Baracoa told me some time ago of a mix of plants and seeds that, if given in time, can help someone darted with curare. I mixed some up and we should get him to drink the liquor when he can." She set a small pot down on the table beside Rodrigo's cot and moved away.

"Stay until we are sure this is enough," Thomas said. "You are better with herbs than me and will know if there is anything else he may need. Have you seen Baracoa?"

Rosa shook her head. "No. It was a palace guard came to tell me Rodrigo had a bad cut to his arm and had been poisoned with a dart. Where did Baracoa go?"

"Following a Kalinago by the name of Jayuya. He killed Diego and almost killed Rodrigo."

"I know the man," said Rosa, "but not well. You might

ask Luisa. Some of the Kalinago work the docks. The men are slim, but strong. She may know of him."

"I was told he can be a violent man with women."

Rosa laughed. "With other women, perhaps, but Luisa is a match for any man. And she has too many sharp edges for most."

Thomas believed her.

"Do you know when Jayuya came to Spain?"

Rosa stared into space before saying, "He arrived after most. Baracoa came earlier still. Columb brought him back on his first voyage."

"Fourteen ninety-two," Thomas said.

"That was when he left. He returned early the next year." Her eyes scanned Thomas's face. "Jorge told me you lived in Spain then, and for years afterwards. Did you ever meet Columb?"

"At one time I might even have called him a friend but have not seen him in over four years now." He knew they were only making small talk, waiting for Rodrigo to come fully awake, which was about to happen.

Thomas went to the man and unwound the loose bandage he had covered his wound with. He leaned close to check, but as far as he could tell there was no sign of the poison that had knocked him out.

Rosa returned to his side and looked down at Rodrigo, whose eyes fluttered open, closed, then opened again. He stared up at them both with no sign of recognition.

"Where..." His voice faded. He tried to take a deep breath and failed. Thomas touched Rosa's arm and stepped back, taking her with him.

"We should let him wake in his own time," he said.

“Sit him up and give him the liquor I made, it will help him recover more quickly.”

Thomas considered it, then nodded. “Help me. I will lift him. You get the liquor into him.”

They approached the cot again where Rodrigo now lay unmoving, his eyes once more closed. Thomas lifted him into a sitting position. Rosa held his nose until he opened his mouth. She put her fingers inside to keep it open and poured half the bottle she had made between his lips before clamping her hand over them, forcing Rodrigo to swallow. When it was done, Thomas kept him upright until he was sure he was not going to throw it all back up, then laid him down once more.

They stood side by side, watching the man, waiting.

“It would be good if Baracoa was here,” Thomas said. “He would know better than either of us whether Rodrigo will survive or not. But I think he saved his life.”

“Do not tell that to Rodrigo,” said Rosa. “It will anger him to think himself indebted to a Kalinago. Better you tell him you cut the poison from his arm.”

“Baracoa knows the truth.”

“He does, but Rodrigo is unlikely to ever speak to him so your story will never be questioned.”

“Will Baracoa kill Jayuya if he finds him?”

“What would you do, Thomas?”

“If possible, I would bring him back for the authorities to decide his fate.”

“That is not what I have heard about you,” said Rosa. “Word is you are a bringer of death to wicked people.”

Thomas started to form a response, then stopped, because he knew Rosa was right. It was not something he ever wanted but knew he did. He could not turn away from where evil flourished, where wicked men and women took what they wanted and killed those who tried to stop them. He wondered if Rosa thought of him as wicked but was afraid to ask. Afraid of what she might say. So it was fortunate that at that moment Rodrigo suddenly sat bolt upright and vomited.

Thomas reached him first, but Rosa was close behind.

"Baracoa warned me that might happen, but it is a good thing. It is why I only gave him half the liquor. I was told to give him the rest after this happened, if it did. But not yet. I will find something to clean him first."

"Why am I here, Thomas?" asked Rodrigo.

"Do you remember what happened?"

"I recall an argument with Jayuya. He ran off, yes?"

"He did. You went after him."

"Did I? I do not remember doing that." He touched the loose bandage on his arm. "Did I fall? And what is this wound?"

"Jayuya darted you and Diego, like he darted Don Alejandro, then fled. Baracoa saved your life by cutting the poison from your flesh."

Rodrigo shook his head. "I remember nothing after the argument with Jayuya. I will get Diego to send men to scour the city and find him. He will hang, or worse."

"Diego is dead. He had already expired before we found you both. You are a lucky man."

"Yes, it seems I am." Rodrigo started to stand then discovered he was naked beneath the thin sheet, just as Rosa returned with a bucket and mop. She ignored Rodrigo and set to cleaning the floor.

"I take it you have rooms in the palace?" Thomas asked.

"Of course. I will go there and find some clothes." Rodrigo took the sheet and wrapped it around himself. He shook his head. "If I can remember where it is. My head is filled with rocks."

"If he can stand then he can drink the rest of what I made for him before he goes," said Rosa, as she set the mop in the bucket. "It will help."

Thomas offered the half-empty bottle to Rodrigo, who looked at it suspiciously.

"Drink it," Thomas said, and eventually Rodrigo took it and drained the contents. He pulled a face.

"It tastes foul."

"All good medicine does," said Rosa with a smile. "Try to keep it down this time, it will be good for you."

Thomas took Rodrigo's arm to steady him as they left the room. At a parting of the ways, Rodrigo hesitated and stroked his head, then turned left along the narrower way.

"My room is here at the end," he said. "I only use it when there is an early start. Usually when the King goes hunting. He likes to rise and leave before dawn."

"You have a house in Sevilla, yes?"

"Of course, and I still have a home in the countryside, but do not go there often. It is three days ride to the west."

"It is where you were raised?"

Rodrigo smiled. "It is where I was born and lived until I had fifteen years."

"What happened to bring you here?" They reached a doorway at the end of the corridor and Thomas waited for Rodrigo to open it. Inside, there was a bed pushed against one wall and a set of shelves holding folded clothes. A single window offered a view across the gardens which Rodrigo seemed to like so much. Now, the man discarded the sheet and picked out items of clothing, pulling them on.

Thomas sat on the bed so he was out of the way. There was no table or desk, no chair. This room was for sleeping and nothing else.

Dressed, Rodrigo turned to him. His pallor had faded and his face was serious.

"Bandits attacked our farm. They killed my father. Papa told me to run and hide when he saw them coming, which I did. I wanted to fight but know if I had I would also be dead."

"Some life lessons are hard to take," Thomas said. "You came to the city then?"

"No, I followed the bandits to their lair. Then I went to a town large enough to have *hermanos* and told them where it was. I asked to be with them when they went to arrest the men."

"You fought?"

"I had not intended to, but it came to that, yes. I was young, but strong, and fast. Papa had been a soldier and taught me well. The bandits did not surrender, so it came to a fight. Two *hermanos* died, and all the bandits but one. Their leader was taken to the town to be hung on the walls. I watched him for two days until he died. Then I was asked to join the *hermanos*. I came to Sevilla five years later and made my way to the palace. Despite being of low stock in the eyes of many, I rose through the ranks."

"Fernando likes you," Thomas said.

"Yes, he does. And he prefers to be called King Fernando." Rodrigo smiled. "You seem to play fast and loose with royal titles, Thomas."

"I have been told that before. I too am of common stock and have spent time in the employ of both Sultans and Kings, much like yourself."

"I like you, Thomas. We must talk again when there is time. But now I have a killer to find." Rodrigo straightened his back and firmed his shoulders, dressed now in the fine clothes of the important man he had become. The closest advisor to the King and Queen.

"Has Jayuya always been so difficult?" Thomas asked as he followed Rodrigo from the room.

"He has always believed himself better than the others, even Baracoa when he lived within the palace, but this is the first time he has acted as he did today. He has never shown such anger before."

"He beats his wives," Thomas said.

"That is a matter between themselves. I try not to interfere."

Thomas did not agree with the sentiment but kept his opinion to himself. He considered telling Rodrigo that Baracoa was on Jayuya's trail, but something held him back. If he returned with the man as captive, that would be time enough. If Rodrigo sent two dozen *hermanos* out on a search it would make Baracoa's job harder, and they might mistake him for who they sought, unable to tell one Kalinago from another. Safer to say nothing, for now.

TWENTY-SEVEN

It was dark by the time Thomas returned to the small house he and Jorge shared, to find it empty. He considered going into the city to try and find him, then dismissed the idea. He could be anywhere, with anyone. Instead, he stripped and washed himself before falling exhausted into bed. Sleep came fast.

He was woken by the sound of someone climbing the stairs and reached beneath the thin pillow for a knife, slipping it back when Jorge stepped into the room.

Thomas sat up. "Where have you been?"

"Doing your job for you. I have been talking to the people on your list of names." He sat heavily on his own bed. "I did not realise how hard it would be. I like to talk with people, but questioning them about murder? That is the hardest."

"Except you will not have accused them straight out," Thomas said.

"Of course not. We spoke of the city, the weather, children and parents and friends. I listened to their words and looked into their hearts to judge if they spoke true or false. That is why it was hard." Jorge rose again and undressed before slipping into his bed, but he did not seem to be ready for sleep yet.

"Did you speak with Don Alejandro's son again?" Thomas asked. "I assume he still expects to inherit his father's wealth."

"His position, too. He told me that is how matters are handled in Spain. I do not like the man, nor his family. And he may be unlucky in his expectations. I heard that Doña Carlita is still claiming her husband's wealth belongs to her by right." Jorge leaned back into the corner and glanced across at Thomas. "Is she correct or not?"

"In England she would have no claim. I do not know what the law is in Spain, but I expect Rodrigo will. I will ask him once he is recovered, but I am not sure it will help. She can claim what she likes. She knows where Don Alejandro's wealth is and, if I judge her correctly, will have it spirited away so only she knows where to find it. Did any of these conversations point to anyone who might be guilty of his death?"

"You know I am not the person to make such a judgement. I leave such matters to you, Thomas." Jorge frowned. "Did you say, 'when Don Rodrigo is recovered'? Is he unwell?"

As Thomas explained what had happened Jorge's eyes widened.

"This Jayuya," said Jorge, when Thomas finished. "You are sure he is who killed Don Alejandro?"

"I cannot see who else it might be. Baracoa does not know how he managed to create curare, but he must have."

"Why would he kill him?" asked Jorge.

"Perhaps they had a falling out. Jayuya is a man filled with anger, which I witnessed. But he may have been told to kill him by someone else. Which means we must ask more questions and look in new places."

Jorge sat up straighter. "When you find this Jayuya you will have caught the killer. Question him and you will learn why, and if he was put up to it."

"Baracoa is trying to find him. He has many talents, and I expect tracking a man is among them. It would be better if Usaden were here, but he is not."

"It is strange for it to be just the two of us," said Jorge.

"Like old times, yes?"

Jorge smiled. "Whether we want it to be like old times or not is another matter. I have grown used to our house in England, and my place in Ludlow. Does this mean I can stop speaking with people? I do hope so, for they are hard to deal with here."

"Let us see what the morning brings. We will go to Rosa's house and see if Baracoa had returned. They are close to each other."

Jorge smiled. "As in close?"

Thomas laughed. "Yes. As in close."

Jorge turned over. Within minutes, Thomas heard a soft snoring coming from his direction. Unfortunately, he was now wide awake again. He lay on his back and stared into the shadows, thoughts swirling through his head, which helped not at all. He was unaware of falling asleep again, which is the normal state of affairs, only of coming awake. He lay in the dark once more, wondering what had roused him. He glanced to the dark corner to see Jorge still slept. Then he heard a noise from below. There was someone downstairs. The scrape of a chair on the stone floor. Low voices.

Thomas slipped from the bed, wrapped the sheet around his shoulders and softly opened the door. He stood at the head of the stairs, listening.

Two different voices. He descended four steps, enough to see into the room. A single candle was lit, and in its faint glow he watched as the men went through the small array of objects set on shelves against one wall. There was little Thomas and Jorge had brought with them other than clothes, and most of those were in the second upstairs room, which had been empty when they arrived. The men were looking for something, but what he had no idea. Until one of them pulled out a scrap of paper and held it close to the light. Both read it before nodding. One of them folded the paper and slipped it inside his jacket. As he turned away, he caught sight of Thomas on the stairs and reached to his waist.

The other man caught his arm. "No. We have what we came for." He looked up at Thomas. "If you have any sense, you will stay where you are."

The men were strangers who clearly did not know that Thomas rarely chose the sensible option.

He started down the stairs, but his feet caught in the loose folds of the sheet around him and he stumbled. By the time he recovered, the men were through the door. Thomas adjusted the sheet and followed, aware if one of the *hermanos* saw him they might wonder what he was doing.

He caught sight of the men, moving fast as they turned onto the dockside. He followed, the cobbles sharp under his bare feet. When he reached the docks the men had disappeared among others working to load and unload goods from two crayers, one of which had its sails being raised in readiness to depart. He considered asking the *estibadores* if they had seen the fleeing men, but his experience with them was they were truculent most of the time and offered little. Instead, he turned and walked back to the house to find out what had been taken. The candle still burned, wax melting to gather at its base. Thomas stood for a moment, listening, but he heard nothing from the street, nor above where Jorge continued to sleep. He closed and bolted the door, wondering why he bothered, then went to where the men had been. A few books had been tossed to the floor. Some papers were beside them.

Thomas climbed the stairs, but instead of returning to the warmth of his bed, he dressed as quietly as he could. When he reached the door, Jorge said, "What are you doing? I am trying to sleep and you get up, go downstairs, come back, get dressed. I think we need a house each, or at least rooms of our own."

"There is a room next to this one if you want to take your bed there," Thomas said. "I am going out."

"Without me?"

"Do you want to come?" Thomas asked.

"I would like to be asked."

Thomas sighed. "So do you want to come?"

"Are you going to get into trouble again?"

"I do not intend to, no."

"You never do, but it does not stop trouble finding you." Jorge threw back the covers and stood. "I expect I had best come to keep you safe."

"My thanks," Thomas said.

When Jorge descended the stairs, Thomas was staring at the shelves again, a frown on his face. He turned.

"Where did you put the list of names you were given? Or are they somewhere in your clothes?"

"What point would there be me carrying them when I cannot read? I left them over there, pushed between two of your books you insisted on bringing."

There were only two books Thomas had brought, and both were on the floor. He leafed through them but found no list. He checked the shelf and everywhere else to no avail. The men had taken it, but why? And how did they know of it?

"The men took our list," Thomas said.

Jorge smiled. "They might have taken the paper, but the list is still here," he tapped his brow. "I can tell you the names again once the sun is up."

They went out into the dark streets where Thomas told Jorge about the men and their flight. He wanted to know if anyone had seen them running away, and the best place to find answers was the dockside, of course.

TWENTY-EIGHT

A faint promise of dawn showed in the eastern sky as Thomas led Jorge onto the wide cobbled dockside. Lamps remained lit to allow work to continue, and the *Casa de Contratación's* windows showed bright. This was a place that never stopped work, day or night. Boats arrived to be unloaded, loaded again with fresh goods and depart, all in darkness if need be.

"We should split up. It will make things quicker," Thomas said.

"What is it you want me to ask?" said Jorge.

Thomas explained once more about the two men and described them as best he could. "Can you remember all of that?"

"I will do my best," said Jorge, before disappearing among the throng.

Thomas waited a moment then started on the other side of the dock. He did not know how Jorge was faring but soon discovered those he spoke to did not welcome being questioned. It was as he expected. Some simply ignored him. Others pushed him away. These were hard men, made of muscle, sinew and bone. They lifted sacks of food in each hand and carried them onto the boats as if they weighed nothing at all. Still Thomas continued.

"I am looking for two men, normal height, both with dark hair. They were wearing leather jerkins and brown hose and were most likely hurrying." Thomas asked the same question for perhaps the fortieth time. The result was the same.

"Go away."

Most responses were far coarser.

When he stood tall, Thomas saw Jorge in the distance, speaking with a small group of men. He appeared to be having more luck, but then he was Jorge, so it was only to be expected.

Someone tapped him on the shoulder. When he turned, Luisa looked up at him, dressed as always in leather jerkin and men's hose. Thomas realised it was little different to the description he gave of the men he sought, and that of a thousand others.

"You are causing an upset," said Luisa, though she seemed more amused than annoyed.

"I am looking for someone."

"Who?"

When he told her she laughed. "Good luck with that. What has he done?"

"Not here." Thomas glanced around. Most of those nearby were working hard, but that did not mean they would not overhear what was said.

"I am finished for now in any case," said Luisa. "I have been working all night and plan on getting a few hours' sleep. Come to my rooms and we can talk. Is that Jorge over there?" She nodded past Thomas.

"It is."

"Fetch him, too. He is most pleasant to look at." She turned and strode away before stopping and coming back. "When you come, simply ask for me. You will be shown the way."

And then she was gone, disappearing among the crowd. Thomas pushed his way through to Jorge and told him what Luisa had said.

"She wants us both?" asked Jorge.

"That is what she said. She is willing to talk with me. Perhaps she knows the men we seek."

"Or she wants us both to ravish her?"

Thomas stared at Jorge, then snorted a laugh and turned away, assuming his friend would follow, whether it was conversation he sought or ravishment.

When he entered the offices that gave directly on to the river, Luisa was standing on a balcony and waved him to the stairs. Thomas went up and stood beside her until Jorge followed.

"I have sent for wine and food to break our fasts," she said. "This way."

She led them into a wide room, furnished with a table and four chairs, a fireplace where logs glowed, and a bed set to one side where she could lie and look across the river. Beyond the window, the sun was starting to rise and cast bright rays across the water and hillside beyond.

Luisa sat at the table. "Now tell me, Thomas, what you were doing annoying my workers?"

"Are they your workers?" Thomas asked.

"They do as I tell them, so I consider them mine. Their masters pay them, but they take orders from me. If they did not, everything would descend into chaos. Now tell me." She stared at him, her face showing no expression, and he could not work out whether she was annoyed or not. Best, he thought, to assume she was.

"I apologise, but two men invaded our house in the night. They were looking for something and seemed to find what they sought. A list of names provided to us of those we should question in regard to Don Alejandro's death. Not that it will stop us, as Jorge claims to remember them all. But I would know who the men were and where they went."

"Describe them," said Luisa.

Thomas again offered the same description he had given multiple times already.

"That is not much to go on." Luisa rose as a knock came at the door. As she passed Thomas, her fingers brushed his shoulder. It could have been nothing, an accident, or not. She took a tray from the man at the door and set it on the table. Several bottles of dark ruby wine, goblets, bread and slices of meat and cheese. She broke the seal on a bottle and poured for each of them before taking her seat again.

"I do not know who the men you seek are, nor did I see anyone who might be them, but if I had to hazard a guess, I might know who sent them. I suspect so do you. You seem to have annoyed a number of people in a very short time, Thomas Berrington."

"Are you one of them?" asked Jorge, his voice soft.

Luisa glanced at him. "Strangely, I am not." She took a

sliver of fowl and slid it between her lips before following it with a swallow of wine.

"Have you heard about Jayuya?"

Luisa shook her head. "Who?"

"He is a Kalinago from among those living in the palace. I believe he killed Don Alejandro. Earlier today – no, yesterday – he also killed Diego Serrano, and attempted to take the life of Don Rodrigo, but we managed to save him."

"I had not heard." Luisa, for the first time since Thomas had known her, appeared shocked.

"I suspect it is not common knowledge. The palace will want to keep news of it within their walls. Perhaps I should not have told you."

"No, you should have." Luisa reached out and briefly touched his hand. Thomas saw Jorge watch the move, a smile on his face. "Do you think these men who came into your house have something to do with this Jayuya?"

"I do not. I suspect he is still running and will never be seen again. If they were sent by anyone, I would suspect one of the English ambassadors trying to find out what orders the King gave me. Or Mateo Salto, though not for the same reason. Perhaps it is both, one working for the other."

"I have heard Mateo does not like you, Thomas, which is not good. But he does like Rosa, and she vouches for you, so you may be safe. Apart from which, Mateo likes to give the impression he is a hard man and will kill you in an instant, but beneath the bluster he is someone who can be dealt with. If you are fair with him, then the chances are he will be fair with you. And Rosa tells me you have already proven yourself in front of the man. I will make enquiries whether any of Mateo's men have been seen recently. Of course, he might have paid someone else to do his work for him. Both of you wait here while I ask for your request to be spread. It is more likely to bring an answer if it comes from me."

After Luisa had gone, Jorge looked at Thomas without speaking until the tension became too great.

"What?" Thomas said eventually.

"She likes you," said Jorge.

"I know it is unusual for people to like me, but it does happen on occasion."

Jorge smiled. "She likes you as a woman likes a man."

Thomas laughed and shook his head. "Even I know that, but I am too old for her, and she is ... too independent."

"She does not want to marry you, and as for independence, I agree. Would it be so bad to lie in the arms of a handsome woman even if only for a short time?"

"I have a poor record of picking women, or do you forget?"

"Luisa is not like those others. And there were not so many."

"But most of them recent," Thomas said. "Besides, it may be you she wants to lie with, in which case she will be sorely disappointed because you always say you are loyal to but one woman."

"This is not about me, Thomas," said Jorge. "Luisa wants–" But he did not explain what she might want, even though he had already stated it, because she returned.

Luisa sat cross-legged on her bed, eyes bright. "I have news. Mateo sent men to the docks earlier today. Three of them, including that giant of a man."

"Salazar," Thomas said.

"I do not know his name, only his size."

"When I visited Mateo, he had the man challenge me. I think Mateo might have wanted me dead, but when I defeated Salazar he allowed me to leave."

Luisa stared at him, eyes wide. "You defeated the giant?"

Thomas nodded. "I did."

She gave a brief shake of her head, as if barely believing it. "Mateo allowed you to leave because, despite all his faults, his avarice, and wanting to get his own way, he respects strength." Luisa's eyes remained on Thomas, and she leaned slightly forward as if wanting to close the space between them. "The big man is less than half your age."

"Then experience counted that day."

"Yes, it must have. In any case, I have more news, and you distracted me. The big one stayed on the dock, the other two went into the city. When they returned there was a third man with them. A native of the new world. I asked if anyone knew him, but they did not. Most of the workers here know Baracoa, but this man they had never seen."

"Did any say the man looked afraid?" Thomas asked.

"Not afraid," said Luisa, "but agitated. Disturbed."

"Where did he go?"

"With Mateo's men. All three accompanied him. They took the Triana bridge. Beyond there, I do not know where they went, but it makes sense they took him to Mateo's estate."

Thomas stared into empty space, his mind working. The Kalinago had to be Jayuya. The men who took him were Mateo's. Did that mean Jayuya was working under

Mateo's orders? Did the man want Don Rodrigo dead? Thomas did not consider Diego Serrano enough of a threat to someone who lived beyond the city. Diego's responsibilities stopped at Triana. Had Mateo ordered Don Rodrigo to be killed? Was Diego collateral damage? If Jayuya had been caught there would be no link to Mateo. Which made Thomas wonder why the men had come to take him out of the city. They must have known they would be seen. And what were they looking for in Thomas's lodgings? There was nothing there other than the list, but they did not know that, and the list would tell them little.

He glanced around the room, impressed at its homeliness. Vibrant drapes covered some of the walls. The bed Luisa now sprawled on as if her day was ended rather than about to start, had a multi-coloured throw across it. When Thomas raised his eyes, he found her staring at him.

"We should go," he said, rising to his feet, trying to ignore the raw emotion he felt in this woman's presence.

"Stay if you wish, Thomas."

"I have learned what I came to find out," he said.

"Not everything, for I am still a mystery to you. Go if you must but know you are welcome to return at any time. You fascinate me, and I would know you better." Luisa glanced aside. "You also, Jorge, but not in the same way as Thomas."

Jorge shrugged. "My life is filled with disappointment, my sweet."

Luisa smiled.

Outside, Jorge said, "You are a fool, Thomas. She offered herself to you. No strings attached. And I venture she is a wildcat in bed. Why did you not stay?"

Thomas said nothing because he had no answer. Luisa attracted him. She was a different manner of woman to those who had betrayed him over recent years. She was strong and, he believed, honest. She said what she wanted without fear. She was not beautiful, but attracted him strongly.

"Go back to the house," he said. "I will come for you later. We will go to the palace, and I will try to question the ambassadors without raising suspicion."

He turned and retraced his steps. Luisa was waiting for him when he entered her room. She greeted him with a smile.

"I am pleased you saw sense." She threw back the cover to reveal herself, and Thomas went to her.

TWENTY-NINE

When Thomas woke he found himself in Luisa's bed. He lay on his back and stared at the inside of the roof. Raw beams and ochre tiles. No attempt to make it anything it was not. Much like Luisa herself. She made it clear she wanted him in her bed, but it did not mean he had any kind of hold over her, or her over him. It was an itch she needed to scratch. She had laughed when Thomas said, "You make it sound so romantic."

"I do not believe in romance," she had said. I believe in this."

Now, she lay on her side, her body displayed, and stared at him.

"Do you have to leave on important business, Thomas?" she asked.

"Of course, but not as important at what I believe is on your mind."

She laughed and pulled him on top of her.

When they were done, she said, "There are things I need

to tell you, but not now. I have to get them straight in my own mind first. And I must speak with another." She kissed him. "Now go, before I have you ravish me again." She smiled. "If you can."

Thomas gathered his clothes together and dressed before descending the stairs. None of the scribes looked in his direction as he passed their desks. Outside, he saw Rosa on the far side of the dock, arguing with a tall man whose dress and features indicated he had crossed the narrow sea from Africa. Thomas thought briefly of going across in case she needed help, then decided not to. Rosa, like Luisa, was not the kind of person who would ever need help.

When Thomas entered the house Jorge sat at the table, grinning.

"No," Thomas said.

"No what?"

"I will not tell you anything."

"Good." Jorge rose. "Tales of your lovemaking would no doubt disappoint. Are we going to the palace now?"

"I need to wash and change first."

"Indeed. It would not do to stand in front of the Queen smelling like a bordello."

Thomas sniffed under his arm. "I do not smell like a bordello."

"You smell of sex," said Jorge.

"Why does it not surprise me that even from this distance you can tell?"

"I have a sensitive nose." Jorge sat again and picked at the fruit and nuts in front of him. No doubt he would want something more substantial before noon, but would be able to find that from the palace kitchen, where he was now a favourite.

It was still early for the meeting between ambassadors and Isabel and Fernando, so Jorge went to the kitchens and Thomas to the infirmary to check on Don Rodrigo. Except when he got there he found only Rosa, washing down the pallet Rodrigo had lain on. The stone floor was damp, Rosa's face flushed from the work. She straightened and offered a smile that brought a moment of guilt to Thomas, sure she would know what he had done.

"Where is he?" he asked.

"He left at dawn, claiming he was cured. I accompanied him to his house, but he did seem much improved, so I called for a man I know for the best thing to clean a sick-room then returned here. He vomited several times overnight, and soiled himself, but I am used to caring for people and do not mind. Better I clean the room than ask one of the servants."

Thomas almost offered that was what they were there for, then saw the sense in it.

"I am surprised he recovered so quickly," he said. "Were you here the entire night?"

"I could not leave him, could I? It was easy enough. He slept most of the time and I dozed in the chair." She smiled. "Though it was not restful, and my back does not thank me for it. Are you here to see the ambassadors? Rodrigo told me they were coming again this morning, which is why he wanted to go home to bathe and change his clothes."

"I am not sure he is well enough to attend such an important meeting," Thomas said.

"I tell you, he is fully recovered. It surprised me too. He

is a fortunate man. I know about curare because of Baracoa and am aware of how deadly it is. When I went with Don Rodrigo last night to ensure he reached his house, I saw you and Jorge leave Luisa's building, then you returned. Did you stay the night with her?"

Thomas almost lied, then realised Rosa had always been honest with him. "I admit I stayed with her, yes, but this morning, not the night."

"That is good. You are a fine man, Thomas, and deserve some moments of pleasure. Luisa is the perfect woman for you. She expects no permanence."

"Which is what she told me. I want to speak with Baracoa again to find out if he managed to find Jayuya, and whether he thinks him capable of producing curare. Has he returned yet?"

"He stayed at my house last night," said Rosa. "I do not know if he is still there, but I return when I am finished here. If he is, shall I tell him you want to speak with him?"

"I would be grateful. I believe I may know where Jayuya has fled to, but if I am right it will be difficult to get to him."

"Mateo," said Rosa, smiling. "Do not look so surprised. Baracoa told me that is where he would go for shelter. Jayuya once served Mateo when he was first brought to Sevilla. Mateo would come to the docks as though he could scent incomers and bid for them. He bought Jayuya and two women."

"Jayuya came to the palace from Mateo's house?"

"Another transaction. I believe Rodrigo may have had a hand in it. He bought both the man and the women. You met them yesterday."

"Why would Mateo release them?"

Rosa shook her head. "I do not know and have never asked. Mateo puts up with me, but he reveals little. He sells me plants and seeds. I provide him with salves and cures." She smiled. "He has me prepare him a potion to make him a better lover. Not that he ever asked me outright, but dropped hints and suggestions."

Thomas laughed. "No doubt he knew someone who had difficulties and it was for them."

"Yes, that," said Rosa, starting for the door, bucket in hand. "I am finished here. Come to my house when you are done with your meeting and speak with Baracoa. I will ask him to wait for you."

Thomas went in search of the room the negotiations would take place in. He found them, but they were empty. He stood, listening to the sounds of the building. They were little different from those he would hear in London's Tower, in Ludlow Castle, or any of the other great places of state he had known. A low background hum of conversation. The occasional raised voice. Noises as items were moved. In England, there would be the clang of church bells at least every hour, but rarely in time with each other. Here they were the same, but with a different tone. More strident, but also more melancholy. He recalled the days when he lived in Moorish al-Andalus and the call to prayer would echo across the city of Granada. Sometimes it raised the hairs along his arms even though he believed in no religion.

He was still lost in thought when footsteps made him turn. He was surprised, almost shocked, to find Queen

Isabel enter the room unaccompanied. She stopped, stared at him, her expression unreadable.

"We should not be alone together," Thomas said.

"We should not." She looked around, as if someone might be hidden behind the drapes to spy on them. "I expect the others will be along soon."

"No guards with you today?" Thomas asked, which raised a faint smile.

"I am within the walls of my palace; guards are not needed. I am sure you will protect my honour, Thomas."

"I will do my best. Are the English ambassadors ready?"

"They are downstairs with the King, talking hunting. Fernando promises – or perhaps threatens – to take them hunting for boar and stags when we are finished here. More meat at the table tomorrow." She gave a small pout, clearly not enchanted at the thought. "How is Don Rodrigo today?"

The sudden change of subject set Thomas back a moment before he responded. "He is less sick than I took him for and has taken himself home. Rosa – I apologise, you will not know her, spent the night caring for him, She has cleaned up the infirmary and also gone home."

"If the Rosa you speak of is a fine herbalist, then I know her. Don Rodrigo is fortunate to be alive."

"He is."

The conversation drifted into silence, broken only when one of the remaining peacocks cried out, filling the air with its screech.

"Are you any closer to finding out who killed Don Alejandro?" asked Isabel. "Is it the same man who attacked Don Rodrigo and Diego Serrano?"

"It makes sense it is, Isabel." He called her by name without even planning to, but the sound of it tasted sweet on his tongue. Would have tasted sweeter still had he not lain beside Luisa mere hours before. Except, he did not consider it a betrayal, because what they had once briefly shared was a dream and nothing more. Blown to dust by the years and hardships he had endured since. He wondered what her memories of those moments were. It was not something he could, or ever would, ask.

"Do you need more help, Thomas? I do not know who will take Diego's place, but I am sure Fernando does. That is his responsibility, not mine. I will ask him to send whoever he appoints to talk with you."

"My thanks."

More footsteps sounded, heavier and harder than Isabel's. King Fernando entered first, Inigo Alvarez beside him. The English ambassadors and Spanish negotiators drifted in behind.

"What are you doing here?" Fernando glared at Thomas.

"He is here on behalf of the English King Henry, of course," said Isabel. "Also, I like to believe, on behalf of us as well. Are we almost ready?"

"We are."

"Thomas would like to know who you intend to replace Diego Serrano with so he can offer him help," said Isabel.

"Is he still meddling in affairs better left to others?" asked Fernando.

His wife made no reply.

Fernando turned to Thomas. "Have you made any progress?"

"A little, Your Grace."

"Good. Yes, that is good, I suppose. And Diego's replacement is the man at my side. Inigo Alvarez has long experience in the *hermanos*. Inigo this is–"

"I know Thomas Berrington, Your Grace. His reputation is spoken of among the *hermanos*. Though I am surprised to see him here."

Thomas noticed that Isabel's expression was set. Any opinion she might have on Diego Serrano's replacement would not be welcomed.

"I am merely offering what assistance I can," Thomas said.

Inigo Alvarez turned to talk with Fernando.

Isabel remained silent, as a good wife, even one who was a Queen, was meant to do.

Thomas crossed the room and offered his hand to Richard Foxe, Lord privy seal and close to King Henry. Thomas knew him as a man keen on the proposed marriage. His companion, Thomas Savage, who had not yet arrived, less so. But it was Foxe who steered the negotiations on the English side.

"You have not attended all our meetings, Thomas," said Foxe. "I feel more sure when you are here and can translate truly. I do not altogether trust the Spanish interpreters."

"And well not to," Thomas said. "They do not always speak the true meaning of their masters. I believe they do not wish to upset your graces."

Foxe laughed. "I would rather the unbridled truth, and today you will tell it me. I would like to return to England before the year turns and snow cloaks the north of this land. I suspect you wish the same. King Henry tells me you have performed several favours for him since you returned to your native land." Foxe cocked his head to one side. "Did you do the same for the Spanish King and Queen when you served them? You were made a Duke, I believe. A position many would welcome, but which I suspect you did not." Foxe smiled.

"I did my duty," Thomas said.

"And continue to do so, is what I hear. You are looking into the unfortunate death of Don Alejandro, yes?"

"I am, as are the *hermanos* now. I believe we have a suspect."

"A Spaniard or Portuguese? I understand no love is lost between the two countries."

"A native of the Indies," Thomas said. "Don Alejandro was killed by curare, which is a potent poison brought from across the sea. Only someone from those lands would know how to prepare it. Even then they would need to be a shaman."

"Heathens," said Foxe with a scowl. "The sooner Spain brings them to God the better. I believe priests accompany the voyages now and are having some success, praise be."

"Yes," Thomas said, uneasy. "Praise be."

He was spared the telling of more lies by the arrival of the remaining ambassadors and was soon too busy translating to think of anything else. The talks made a little progress. Perhaps they would make more if the ambassadors enjoyed the hunt Fernando promised, but Thomas doubted it.

The meeting dragged on, and Thomas was unable to

leave until dismissed. By the time he emerged from the palace the day was drawing to a close and the sun had already dipped below the eastern hills. He wondered if Luisa would welcome him into her bed as readily tonight as she had that morning. He lived in hope. In her arms he might be able to forget Jayuya and death for a short while. Tomorrow would be soon enough to take up the investigation.

THIRTY

"How are the negotiations going?" Jorge sat on the edge of a fountain, stroking his fingers through the water as Thomas emerged from the palace.

"Slowly. Neither side appears to realise the future of Spain and England are at stake. They bicker. They pick tiny points of dispute and make them large. But I did manage to speak with Richard Foxe when the meeting ended. He told me he was hopeful about progress. He knows how such things work and explained there will be bickering and unacceptable demands, but slowly agreement will be reached. It takes time, and no doubt even more visits to Spain for him. He blames the Spanish, of course. When I pointed out the English are not without blame he blustered but eventually agreed. He told me he was asked by Henry to stay in the background and allow others to press our case."

"I presume you told him to step forward, yes?"

"I did. Foxe wants what everyone wants. An agreement and a marriage. There are obstacles in the way, but none are insurmountable. He said he would speak with the others and asked if I can talk to the Spanish ambassadors in the same way I did with him."

"I thought they did not like you, Thomas, nor want you involved."

"That is the face they show to the world, but as individuals they are more amenable. I will speak with those I can, but not today. I need to see Baracoa while he is still at Rosa's house. You will come?"

"Do I have a choice?" asked Jorge.

"Do you want a choice?"

"No, but I thought I would ask to see if you might offer one. Of course I will come. I like Rosa, and Baracoa intrigues me. I do not know him as well as you but would like to."

"I believe if you want to know Baracoa well you must partake of his visions. I am not sure you are made for such madness. Your mind is too placid."

Jorge smiled. "Do you mean being myself is not enough?"

"Baracoa is different. He is hard, inside and out. But try, Jorge, you might succeed."

As they crossed the dockside, Thomas glanced towards Luisa's office and rooms but did not see her. Later, once he had spoken with Baracoa, he would try to find her. Rosa stood behind her stall, packing her goods into small wooden boxes which she stacked into larger ones. As she worked, she spoke with a man who glanced from side to side as if worried someone might see him. Thomas saw Baracoa in the shade of the doorway and offered a nod, which was not returned. He waited to one side until Rosa had finished her transaction, but before he could approach, a hand touched his shoulder. He turned to find Luisa. Her expression showed no welcome, but Thomas did not expect one. She was not a woman to show emotion. Except, last night, she had revealed herself fully to him, body and soul. Her outward hardness had melted beneath his touch and, perhaps, she showed her true self.

"There is someone who wants to speak with you about the deaths," she said.

"Who?"

"Come with me and you will see." She glanced at Jorge and said to him, "I would suggest you stay here."

"See if you can charm Baracoa," Thomas said, before following Luisa, who had already started across the dockside.

Instead of heading in the direction of her rooms, she approached a crayer pulled up to unload. Four men stood beside the workers. As Thomas caught up with Luisa, he recognised them.

"You did not say it was Mateo," he said, his voice low.

"Did I need to? He claims to have information useful to you. Are you coming to my bed again tonight?"

The sudden switch between the two topics made Thomas's head spin.

"If you wish me to, yes." He tried not to give her invitation too much thought, which he knew he was often guilty of. For once, he was trying to follow Jorge's advice and accept the gift of love when offered.

Luisa glanced at him and lowered her voice. "I enjoyed what we did this morning a great deal. You are a considerate lover and have remarkable stamina. So yes, I want you to come."

Her expression hardened as Mateo approached, his hand out. Thomas shook it, then Mateo embraced Luisa and kissed both cheeks. She stiffened, turned, and walked away without a word.

"I am told you may have something of interest to me," Thomas said.

"I have a man at my holding I believe you are looking for."

Thomas could think of only one. "Jayuya?"

Mateo nodded.

Thomas recalled the conversation about Jayuya and his wives working for Mateo when they arrived in Spain, but years had passed since then.

"Why did he come to you?"

"It was an accident rather than purposeful. He was wandering west, perhaps looking for his homeland, but good luck with that. My men saw him and brought him to me. His Spanish is good enough for an interrogation, but he revealed little."

"How hard did you question him?"

Mateo smiled. "It was a conversation between two friends, nothing more. No thumbscrews or knives."

"Did he tell you I was looking for him?" Thomas asked.

"He did not. I only discovered it when I came to trade with Luisa. She told me there had been another death and Don Rodrigo almost died. When I asked who was looking into them, she told me you were." Mateo offered a questioning look. "Did she speak the truth?"

"She did."

"Why you?"

"You already know I was searching for who killed Don

Alejandro. I am sure the attempt on Don Rodrigo is connected to that death. I am also sure Jayuya is responsible. I mentioned it to Luisa earlier today."

"As she said." This time Mateo showed amusement.

Thomas was sure Luisa would not have told him what they had done together, but Mateo gave the impression he knew. It was no great surprise. People would have seen him enter her rooms and not leave for several hours. Rumours spread fast, and they seemed to have reached Mateo. It was no matter, and unrelated to what Thomas wanted.

"What would you do if I rode out with you and arrested him?"

"Do not do it today," said Mateo. "I have not finished questioning him yet."

"I would prefer him alive when I get there," Thomas said.

Mateo smiled. "I will ask my men to be gentle. Tomorrow, you said?"

"I would prefer to come today, but it grows too late. I can question him in the morning."

"And I have business today," said Mateo, "I will stay the night in the city, so you can return with us tomorrow." Mateo looked across the docks to the offices, but there was no sign of Luisa. "You do not have to decide now, my business will take some time. If you wish to take up my offer, then come here at sunrise. Bring a horse, we do not have one spare. I did not think we would be returning with a guest."

"Do not do it," said Jorge when Thomas returned to Rosa's house. She had finished packing up her wares, and only Jorge stood in the lamplight. "I know you will, because you never see sense, but I have a bad feeling about the man."

"He wants something, so will not harm me."

"What can he want of you?"

Jorge's dismissive tone surprised Thomas. "Information. What else do I have to offer?"

"Your life?"

Thomas stared at Jorge. "You know this is what I do, put myself in harm's way to discover the truth. It is no different this time. In fact, I would say it will be less dangerous than many things I have done."

"That is not what Rosa told me, and I saw Luisa's expression when she met him. She does not like the man. Go talk to her, get her opinion. Unless you do not respect her opinions, only her body."

Thomas tried to mask his impatience and surprise. "What is the matter with you?"

"Nothing. Everything." Jorge ran a hand across his head and face. "I miss my family. I miss England." He gave a short laugh. "I never thought I would hear myself say that, but I do. I am also–" Jorge broke off abruptly.

"Also what?"

"Why did you submit to Luisa?" asked Jorge.

Thomas frowned. "Because you told me I should, and she made it more than clear she wanted me in her bed. And..." It was Thomas's turn to trail off.

Jorge smiled. "And?"

"You know why. This place, this land, is different. We are cut loose from the responsibilities of home. It also seems

I am cut loose from restraints. Is that what is wrong with you? If it is, find a woman. I am sure you can have almost anyone you want."

"I want Belia."

"Who you cannot have, not here. Loosen your restraint, or tighten it until you gain control of yourself, but I am going to do what I always do."

Jorge gave a short laugh. "Who would ever have thought we would come to this? You offering me advice on love."

"It is not love we are talking about," Thomas said. "It is sex."

Jorge turned and walked away without a word, an event unusual enough in itself to raise a small annoyance in Thomas. He wondered if he would take his advice or not. He suspected not, because it was his advice in such matters that Jorge was the master of.

"So you intend to visit Mateo Salto?"

Thomas turned to discover Baracoa and Rosa standing behind him. He had heard neither approach, which worried him. Except he suspected Baracoa, like Usaden, could approach as silently as nightfall when he wanted to.

"He tells me Jayuya is with him. I intend to bring the man back to face justice."

"Mateo will not allow that," said Rosa. "Had he wanted it, he would have brought him. It is you he wants. Perhaps he intends to have you fight his men again, but more this time."

"I did not sense that in him. The man confuses me. At times he is civilised, at others not."

"Which is why he is dangerous, but I know you will go

whatever I advise. Tell Luisa what you intend to do. And try not to get yourself killed. It would break all our hearts, but Jorge's most of all."

"Is that what is wrong with him? He should know by now I am a hard man to kill."

"But it does not stop him worrying. I suspect it never has."

Thomas made his way across the wide docks. He intended to tell Luisa of his decision, but also to ask if she could find him a horse. She might refuse, but he knew the palace could provide one if she did not. Thomas also knew he had the night to wait until Mateo returned to his estate. The thought of spending the time with Luisa quickened his footsteps.

THIRTY-ONE

As Thomas stood on the dockside at dawn, waiting for Mateo to appear, his mind was slow from lack of sleep. His second time in Luisa's bed had offered little rest but a great deal of pleasure. Perhaps it was because they knew each other's bodies better, or there was less tension the second time. Whatever the reason, their lovemaking had been slower, deeper, less frantic. It had taken a great effort of will for Thomas to slip from her bed and leave her sleeping. All, it seemed, for nothing. Where was Mateo? Thomas turned and surveyed the docks. Even at this early hour it was busy. He had never seen a time, day or night, when it was not. Wealth and power flowed through Sevilla, sparking greed and wealth. Commerce. Luisa had said as much in the brief moments they had caught their breath and spoken. She told Thomas she had information for him but would not reveal it yet until she had looked into it more. He would have been intrigued, but she made a move that distracted him so he forgot all about it. Now, it returned to him. Whatever it was, she might reveal more today and, if so, there would be no need to ride with Mateo. Who remained absent. Thomas decided he had waited long enough, and the thought of Luisa's warm body was enough to spark impatience. He strode towards the offices.

"Is she still in her rooms?" he asked on entry.

"I heard voices not long since," said one of the scribes.

"That would be me," Thomas said.

"This was after you left."

Thomas frowned. He had been with Luisa less than a half-hour before. "Did someone go up to her?"

"Not that I saw." The man looked around the offices. "Did any of you see someone go to Luisa?"

There was a flurry of shaken heads.

"Man or woman?" Thomas asked, wondering if Rosa might have called.

"Sounded like a man," said the scribe.

Thomas wondered if Jorge had come to find him, but if he had he would not have sneaked in. There was only one way to find out who it was. They might still be upstairs, and if not he was sure Luisa would tell him.

A few of the scribes watched him climb the stairs.

At the top he knocked on the door, but there was no answer. He hesitated, then tried the latch, which opened. He went inside to discover why Luisa had not called out to him, and swallowed hard.

Luisa lay on the wide bed they had sported in so recently, but would never do so again. The sheets were stained dark with blood, and she appeared to have two mouths, her throat opened to spill her life. Thomas went across, knowing there was no point checking her pulse, but he placed a hand on the back of her neck to judge if she was cooling or not. She felt as warm as she had when alive, which was no surprise. It had not been thirty minutes since he left her. Thomas looked around for any weapon but saw none. He went to the balcony and called down to the scribes to send for the *hermanos*, then returned to the room. He checked Luisa again, satisfied she had not been violated. Recovering himself, he walked the room, looking for any sign of blood other than that on the bed. He found some near the open window overlooking the river. Two drops on the floorboards, another smear on the sill of the window where a knife had rubbed against it. He leaned out but saw no one. The drop to the narrow walkway was close to twenty feet, and Thomas knew whoever had taken the fall was lucky not to break a leg, or worse. Unless they had leaped into the river itself. Yes, he thought, that made sense. He turned away, intending to look for signs on the walkway, but as he reached the top of the stairs he stopped because Inigo Alvarez stood at the bottom of it, accompanied by a dozen soldiers. He stared up at Thomas, then motioned him down. Thomas backed into the room, hearing Inigo's voice.

"Get him!"

Sounds of heavy feet on the stairs followed Thomas as he crossed the room. He stood at the window, making a decision, but when the time came there was only one. He climbed onto the sill, and as the men burst into the room launched himself as far out as he could, hoping he would clear the walkway below because he was falling head first.

Cold water closed over him. Thomas had no idea how deep the Guadalquivir was here but assumed deep enough to allow boats to dock. He swam below the surface until forced to breathe. When he emerged, he saw rowing boats start out in the wrong direction, but a shout from above soon turned them. Thomas swam as fast as he could, but the boats were faster. He was halfway across when they caught him, surrounding him so he had nowhere to go. He could have dived again, but knew there was only one end result, so he let men pull him none too gently into one of the boats. When they took him into the dungeons of Triana, they were even less gentle.

"Why did you kill Luisa Mercado?" Inigo Alvarez loomed over Thomas, who was strapped to a rack. So far, it had not been wound tight enough to pull his arms from their sockets, but the pain was sharp enough to persuade most in his position to admit to anything.

"I did not kill her. I spent time in her bed, I admit, but ask the scribes. They saw me leave her room just before dawn."

"Her scribes indeed saw you leave, but they also saw you return to her room shortly before we were sent for. Her body was still warm, her blood still liquid."

"Someone else was there before me. The scribes heard him."

"They said it was a mistake. That sound travels strangely in the *Casa de Contratación*. What did you do with the knife? Throw it into the river when you jumped through the window?"

"I had no knife."

"Why did you kill her? Was it a lovers' argument?"

Inigo nodded to one of the men at the head of the rack, who made a quarter turn of the screw. Thomas settled his arms, making no effort to resist the pull, knowing if he did, it would only hasten the damage.

"Have you questioned Mateo Salto?" he said, his voice taut. "He was on the dockside with Luisa last night. He is the man you need to talk to."

"We asked, of course, but Mateo and his men left last night. They were seen."

"He told me they had business in Sevilla and would not be leaving until morning."

"Do you have anyone to back up your claim?"

"Only Mateo and his men."

"That is most convenient." Another nod. Another turn of the screw. Now Thomas could feel his shoulders wanting to pop loose from their sockets. An easy enough process to return them, but only if he was doing it. It would require someone with both strength and knowledge to manipulate them back into place. And that would depend on how much more the rack pulled one them.

"Do you deny you and Luisa were lovers? You were seen entering her room and not leaving until this morning. Was she already dead then, or did you kill her when you returned?"

"She was alive when I left. Dead on my return." Thomas said through gritted teeth.

"Again, I have only your word for that." Inigo smiled. "Of course you would say that."

"Send someone to the palace and ask about me. Send a message to Don Rodrigo, or even the Queen herself. They will vouch for me."

"I believe you are wrong in that. Don Rodrigo knows you are here and has been sent for. I want the truth before he arrives. A confession would suit." Inigo nodded to the man at the head of the rack. "A full turn. Do it."

Thomas grunted as the pressure built. His left arm popped from its socket and he groaned. Inigo grinned before the expression drained from his face.

"What is going on here? Set this man free!" Don Rodrigo stood in the doorway. The two men working the rack looked sheepish; Inigo bullish.

"He was about to confess to the murder of Luisa Mercado," said Inigo. "Another moment and he would have."

"After you unseated his other shoulder? Let him free and be careful doing it."

Inigo touched Don Rodrigo's arm. "We should discuss this elsewhere."

"In front of the Queen, perhaps?" asked Don Rodrigo, shrugging off the man's hand. "Who I happen to know is close to Don Thomas. I would even go so far as to say they are friends." He leaned close. "Set. Him. Free."

For a moment Thomas, through his pain, was sure Inigo intended to argue. Then the man saw sense. Don Rodrigo could not be disobeyed, though Inigo might be too new in his post to have learned that yet. The two men glared at each other. The stalemate might have gone on longer, but the other men knew the truth and released Thomas. When he tried to stand, the agony of his dislocated shoulder made his head swim and he bit down hard to stifle a scream. One of the men offered assistance, but Thomas shook his head. He would rather manage on his own and avoid fumbling assistance. Eventually, he swung his legs over the side of the rack and, a moment later, stood.

"Inigo, return to your duties. Search for whoever killed Luisa Mercado, because while you have been torturing an innocent man a guilty one is escaping justice." Don Rodrigo turned to Thomas. "Lean on me if it helps," he said, allowing Thomas to choose, which he did, accepting no aid.

Outside, he said, "Take me to Rosa. She will know what to do."

"I have seen an arm set before. She is too slight to do it."

"Baracoa is there. He has the strength." Thomas spoke through gasps as each step seared more pain through him. His left arm hung slack, and he used his right hand to support it.

As they approached Rosa's house she came out, tears streaking her face telling him she had heard the news of Luisa's death. No doubt the entire city knew by now.

Baracoa stood in the shade of the doorway, with Jorge behind him.

"Thomas needs to have his arm set back in place," said Don Rodrigo. "I would offer to help but suspect he prefers a friend to do it." He glanced at Jorge. "You, perhaps, for he has no greater friend."

Jorge shook his head. "Thomas knows I cannot."

"I will do it," said Baracoa, stepping into the sun. "Jorge, hold him around the chest. Rosa, fetch him something for the pain for when it is done."

Without waiting, Baracoa stepped up to Thomas, raised one leg and placed it on the side of Thomas's chest. As soon as Jorge wrapped his arms around him, Baracoa grasped Thomas's arm and jerked.

Thomas went to his knees, gasping, trying not to throw up, but his arm was back in its socket and already the pain was lessening. He would have bruises, but they would heal. He took a cup from Rosa and drained it. Whatever it contained tasted foul, but that was to be expected. When he looked up, he discovered Don Rodrigo had gone, no doubt to remind Inigo he had a killer to find.

Rosa went into her house. When she returned, she had a length of linen and fashioned a sling for his arm.

"Try not to use the arm for at least a week if you can," she said. "The news of your arrest is all over the city." Her voice carried a soft sadness and her eyes remained red. "I would not be surprised if someone in the palace did not send Don Rodrigo to free you, though he too will have heard of it. When he first came to Sevilla I was unsure of him, but he is a good man." She touched Thomas on his uninjured shoulder. "You saw Luisa. Was it bad? Did she suffer?" Her voice broke for a moment, and Thomas would have reached out to comfort her if not for his injured arm. His words would have to do.

"It was bad, yes, but quick. She would have felt nothing."

"I am sorry for you," said Rosa. "Luisa warms to few men, but you were an exception. She was taken far too soon." She wiped at her face, making an effort to set her grief aside for now.

"Yes, she was." Thomas rose to his feet, considering his own grief, wondering why he had not done so before. Now it swept over him like a rolling wave that threatened to drown him. He fought it, setting the grief aside until he had time to give it the attention it deserved. Now, he was even more determined to find her killer. "Who might want her dead?" he asked.

"Nobody," said Rosa. "She was always thought of as stern, and let few get close, but she did not make enemies unless they tried to steal from her or the docks."

"Were there many of those?"

"There are always thieves and vagabonds, but Luisa did her work well and caught most. They reside inside the walls of Triana prison now, or are dead."

"Mateo was here. Did she ever fall out with him?"

"Not that I heard."

"Were you close to her?" Thomas asked. "Did you talk?"

"Yes, we were close. More so a few years ago, less so now she has..." Rosa hesitated, "...had become so busy. She would come to me every few weeks and pour out her frustrations while we ate. She showed a stern face to the world, but inside any harsh words or actions hurt her. She built a tough outer shell to protect herself and let few through. I had great hopes she might find solace with you, even if she knew it would be only temporary. Your life is no longer in Spain. She knew that."

Thomas was aware of Jorge watching, listening. No doubt he would have his own opinion to share later. A thought rose through his grief and he said, "Perhaps Luisa was killed as a punishment against me."

Rosa took a step back. Jorge said, "Not everything is about you, Thomas. But in this instance, you may be right. You have much grief but try to see past it."

“Of course I have grief!” Thomas snapped.

“Which distracts you from the hunt for her killer. Set it aside until you find out who it is and punish them.” Jorge’s words so matched Thomas’s earlier thoughts he knew he must try to follow the advice. He raised his injured arm, pleased when it did not pain him as much as he expected, but knew that would be the result of Rosa’s potion. The arm would remain weak for some time and he would need to be careful.

“Mateo Salto told me he has Jayuya held captive at his estate. He invited me to ride there with him and his men this morning.”

“You cannot go alone,” said Jorge and Rosa almost at the same time. Jorge smiled and shook his head. “I will come with you.”

“No,” said Rosa. “Mateo is a harsh man. One of the few not prone to your charm. I will accompany you, Thomas. He likes me, as you know.”

“You will not go where Jayuya is,” said Baracoa, who had listened to their conversation without comment until that moment. “He is a sneak, and clever. I will come too.”

“Mateo will kill you on sight,” said Rosa, reaching for Baracoa’s hand.

“Which is why I will not show myself. I will go with Thomas, but not to the house. I will watch from a distance and only help if needed.”

“Thomas will be unable to fight as he did the last time he was there,” said Rosa, “and you are no match for Mateo’s men. There are too many.”

“I do not believe he means me harm,” Thomas said. “I will go alone.” He expected more resistance, but none came. “I do not expect to be away more than a day. All I want to do is to speak with Jayuya and persuade Mateo to let me bring him back for punishment.”

“Mateo is not a man who allows others to inflict justice,” said Rosa. ”If you insist on going, take care. Take great care.”

THIRTY-TWO

Jorge and Rosa stood side by side in the dawn's pale light, watching Thomas as he walked across the dockside. He did not glance back.

"You should have stopped him going alone," said Rosa.

"I could have tried, but I have known him a long time and never been able to prevent him doing what he thinks is right."

"With that arm he will be unable to protect himself. He should not walk into Mateo's den in such a state. He is angry about Luisa's death. They might have become deeper lovers over time, but he needs to put it aside until later."

Jorge smiled. "Thomas has only ever truly loved one woman, and she too died. He might have thought he loved others, but Lubna was the love of his life, taken from him far too soon."

"How did she die?" asked Rosa, then held up a hand. "I apologise. It is none of my business."

"It is no secret, and Thomas will not mind if I tell you.

Lubna was murdered by the Spanish during the siege of Malaga. I thought I had lost him after that. He changed."

"Did he know who killed her?"

"He found out, and the man died at his hand. The doing of it almost killed Thomas, too, but..." Jorge shrugged. "I saved him. He was close to death when I found him, but it takes a lot to kill him. I will wait until he gets some distance ahead then follow and do whatever I can."

"You are a good man, Jorge, but you are no fighter," said Rosa.

"Which is what Thomas always tells me. But I have to do something!"

"Do not decide yet – I will speak with Baracoa. You cannot go alone. Wait here." Rosa turned and entered the house.

Jorge assumed Baracoa was inside but had not seen him since he set Thomas's arm. He thought of Thomas and grew afraid. He had seen him fight against terrible odds and triumph, but now he was older, he was weak, and Mateo was not a man to cross. Thomas's anger would weaken him further. Jorge wanted to follow but knew he was the wrong man to offer protection. Advice, yes. Love, even more so. But protection? No.

When Rosa emerged, she said, "Baracoa has gone to the palace. He says he will be less than an hour and then we can all leave together."

"Who are this we?" Jorge asked.

"You will see. You should get ready. Do you need to change your clothes? Fetch weapons?"

Jorge offered a short laugh. "I need no weapons, for

they do not suit me. I will do what I can and, if I have to, will die for that man."

Rosa touched his arm. "Do not do that. You would be sorely missed." She went on tiptoes and kissed him, which confused Jorge. He thought he knew all there was about women, but Rosa was a mystery to him.

When Baracoa returned to Rosa's house, half a dozen of the Kalinago were with him. Four men and three women. All three looked as if they could match any man if it came to a fight.

THIRTY-THREE

Thomas saw Jorge and Rosa talking together in front of her house but gave no indication. He did not want to involve anyone else in this dangerous enterprise. It was his task alone. He walked slowly because it was easier on his body. What he would do when he reached Mateo's estate might be another matter. He would be useless if challenged. Useless if someone even knocked against him. He suspected going was a mistake but had little choice. What Mateo's involvement was, and why, he did not yet know but intended to find out. Thomas knew the man capable of killing, but whether he had killed Luisa he did not know. Could he confront him, and if he did, would he die himself?

At the crest of the first low ridge, Thomas turned and looked back over Sevilla. Smoke rose from fires in houses and businesses. These last years the weather had been strange, colder than usual. Even here in southern Spain, which Thomas recalled as often too hot, there was a chill carried by the wind. Had he more mobility he would have pulled his coat about himself. As it was, he would ignore the chill. His eyes found the *Casa de Contratación* and reminded him of Luisa. They had lain together only twice and, he knew, there might never have been a third or fourth time but suspected there would. Despite the almost transactional nature of their coupling, he believed there was something more between them. Not enough to keep him in Spain when his job was done, but enough to keep him in her bed until then. He felt a sudden, fresh moment of grief. Her death had come so soon after their loving, which made it worse. Thomas wondered if she had died because of him, then recalled Jorge's comment. *It is not always about you, Thomas.* And he was right. Now, he thought of who might have killed her, and why. He could suspect Mateo but had already dismissed him. He needed Luisa for trade. She might have stopped his illegal business, but there was enough of the legal kind to make him richer. Thomas's thoughts were on Jayuya. He knew the man was violent. Knew he had attacked Diego Serrano and Don Alejandro. Perhaps they had crossed him in the past.

Yes, he would question Jayuya hard and make use of Mateo's men to help.

With a sigh, he turned and walked on.

The ground was rough beneath his feet and progress was slow. He knew he could have ridden, but also knew he would be unable to pull himself into the saddle.

He glanced at the sky; it was already gone noon. He tried to increase his pace but took one false step and a stone turned beneath his foot, almost pitching him onto his side. He slowed again. If darkness fell, he would wait and continue at dawn. But when late afternoon turned to dusk, he went on, progress even slower. He crested a ridge as the light began to thicken and saw the lights of Cantillano below, with Mateo's estate beyond it, lit even brighter.

The sensible decision would be to find accommodation in Cantillano, rest up and confront Mateo in the morning. But Thomas had rarely taken the sensible option. He passed through the town and ascended the steep slope that hid Mateo's estate from below.

Two men came out beyond the wall, intending to confront him, but one recognised Thomas and said he should come with them.

"Why is your arm bound?" asked the man, and when Thomas told him said, "You should take more care. Men have died in those dungeons."

Thomas was more than aware of the fact. The estate had a slight air of abandonment, and after a while Thomas realised most of Mateo's men were missing. They had always stood apart, but had been there as both protection and threat.

Mateo sat at a table beneath a canopy, two braziers heating the air, torches attracting insects. Sylph-like women brought food and drink. He rose when he saw Thomas.

"Sit, my friend. What have you done to yourself?"

"Not me," Thomas said. "Inigo Alvarez arrested me for the murder of Luisa Mercado." He sat, glad to be off his feet at last. He reached out with his good arm and took a glass of dark red wine. It was rich in his mouth and, he hoped, might numb the pain of his shoulder now Rosa's medicine had worn off. "You must have heard of her death because you were in Sevilla today." Thomas watched Mateo for any reaction but expected him to show nothing. The man was too skilled in deceit, honed over many years, to do so.

"Yes, and was sorely saddened to hear of it. She was a beautiful woman. Do you know I tried for her myself but was turned down? I hear you were more fortunate. She spent her last hours on earth with you, is that right?"

Thomas wondered who had passed the information on, and how they had known, though it did not surprise him. The *Casa de Contratación* had many workers, and neither he nor Luisa had made much effort to hide their intentions.

"It was why suspicion came my way," Thomas said. He wanted to move the conversation on. "I was released only when Don Rodrigo heard of my arrest. What business did you have in Sevilla?"

"Nothing out of the ordinary. Trade. I had some items to sell and others I wished to purchase."

"Wine?"

"I spoke about wine, but it has not yet arrived from Portugal."

"I did not think trade between Spain and Portugal was allowed."

Mateo raised a shoulder, making Thomas wish he could do the same.

"There is a difference between something being against the law and people looking the other way when it suits them. Portugal makes fine wines, cherished by some in Spain including, I believe, both the King and Queen. It comes at a price, so only the wealthy can afford it. I will send you a gift of a few bottles. It will help drown your sorrow and ease your pain. Are you and that eunuch still in the small house behind the docks?"

Mateo was making it clear he knew where to find Thomas. He could almost feel eggshells cracking beneath his feet.

"Where are the rest of your men?" Thomas asked.

Mateo shrugged. "Doing work for me, guarding a caravan of goods coming from Portugal."

"How do you manage to bring so much contraband in without being discovered?" Thomas asked, pushing on. He sensed no reluctance yet from Mateo, who possessed the ultimate confidence of a man who knew that in this place he held the power.

"You do not expect me to tell you that, do you?"

"You already have. How many men do you have here? A score? Two score? Enough to protect smugglers from any local *hermanos* or townsfolk?"

Two young girls approached with plates of food, thin slices of chicken cooked in a spiced sauce, salad leaves and sliced peppers which were still regarded as a delicacy, their seeds brought across the wide ocean on Columb's first voyage. Now they grew in Spain and elsewhere but were still expensive. Mateo was making a point: see how wealthy I am.

He leaned closer, his eyes dark jewels. "Tell me why you are really here, Thomas. Not to question me about smuggling, because I know you do not care. Do you suspect me of having something to do with Luisa's death? Or is it something else? It is not as if we are friends, yet here we are sharing fine wine and good food. I would offer you a woman or two for the night, but you do not look as if you could manage even one. Though you would need to do little."

"Did you kill Luisa? Or send someone to do it for you?" Thomas asked.

"Of course not. I told you, I wanted her, but I am no animal. I can control my urges. Besides, you have seen the women here. I am not short of companions."

"A companion is different to love." Thomas believed Jorge would be proud of him.

"So it is, but some men, like me, do not seek love. In my opinion it is overrated. I suspect what you and Luisa shared was not love, was it?"

Thomas had to agree. He tried to put thoughts of her aside, for she was not his only reason for being there.

"You told me you have Jayuya captive here."

"I do," said Mateo. "What business is it of yours?"

"I want to speak with him. I believe it is he who killed Diego Serrano and almost killed Don Rodrigo. I want to know why he acted as he did. I believe it would have been on someone's orders. I also wonder if he did not also kill Luisa."

"If he took orders, they were not mine," said Mateo. "As for Luisa, she was killed early today. Jayuya has been here since yesterday. He has already been questioned regarding Don Rodrigo and revealed nothing. These natives are stubborn people. They can be beaten almost to the point of death and not say a word."

"Have you beaten Jayuya to the point of death?"

"I have hardly beaten the man at all. He is held prisoner, I admit, but I have not yet made my mind up whether his actions are my business or not."

"Then release him to me."

Mateo smiled, but there was nothing of friendship in it.

"I cannot do that. He is my captive. Mine to do with as I wish. I have changed my mind. You must leave."

"When I have finished this fine meal and drunk my wine."

"Then you do so alone." Mateo rose. He clicked his fingers and two women came, one to take his food and glass, the other to embrace him.

Thomas watched him go, relieved he had not been made a prisoner himself. He sat back, aware Mateo might be watching from within the house. He gazed across the now dark hillside without relish at the thought of having to return to Sevilla without Jayuya or any new information. It made him wonder why he had bothered to make the journey at all. He had been a fool, not thinking straight.

He stood but did not move away. Yes, he was a fool, but even a fool could redeem himself. Thomas strode towards the house, its windows now lit from within by a soft glow. The door Mateo had entered through remained open. Inside, the air was warmer, and a fire burned at each side of the room. Three of Mateo's women lounged on a couch. They regarded Thomas without curiosity before returning to a conversation in their own language, one he did not recognise.

"Where did Mateo go?" Thomas asked. At first, he thought he would get no reply, then one of them raised a languid arm and pointed through one of the three doors leading deeper into the building.

Thomas found himself in a long passage. Doors were set in the far side, all closed. He was uncertain how to proceed, then heard someone cry out in pain. Jayuya? The sound came from the end of the passage and Thomas moved as fast as his injured shoulder allowed. The passage opened directly to the outside, and as he stood in the exit he saw Jayuya with two men. One of them was Mateo. The other held a sharp knife loosely in his hand.

Mateo sensed movement, turned and saw Thomas. He said, "Kill him." His voice was casual, as if it meant nothing.

The man raised the knife, but as he reached out to cut Jayuya's throat he suddenly slapped his free hand against his own neck.

"Do it!" said Mateo, more urgently. "Kill him before he reveals the truth!" He glanced back at Thomas. "You are too late to question him. You tire me, and I am deciding if you should be the next to die."

Before he could turn away, Mateo jerked to one side and did the same as his man, a hand to his neck. Thomas saw the other drop his knife and go to his knees. He swayed, then pitched over sideways. Mateo started in Jayuya's direction, but did not cover a quarter of the distance before he too fell to the ground. As Thomas started towards them, he saw figures emerge from the shadows. In the lead came Baracoa, a length of bamboo in his hand, a small leather bag on a string around his neck. Behind him came Jorge, then Rosa, and beyond them three Kalinago Thomas recognised from the palace. He went to a knee and touched Mateo's throat, searching for a pulse. He was half surprised when he found one but concerned at how slow it was. He moved and checked the other man and found the same. Two of the Kalinago passed him and grasped Jayuya before he could flee.

"Will Mateo and his man die?" Thomas asked Baracoa, who shook his head.

"They deserve to, but no. The mixture is weak, and mixed with other herbs. They will sleep for a few hours and wake with bad heads. We should go before any of his men come to seek out where he is."

Baracoa casually reached into the leather sack and withdrew a small dart. Thomas assumed it had already been tipped with poison. Baracoa pushed it into the end of the bamboo, then added a small twist of cloth. He held it ready in case he needed to use it. Meanwhile, Jorge and one of the Kalinago held Jayuya between them. Thomas started towards them before realising he would be of no use.

"Do we return to Sevilla with him?" he asked.

Baracoa shook his head. "My holding. We can watch for followers, but they do not know where I live. We will go to Sevilla at dawn, avoiding this place."

Thomas nodded agreement. He would benefit from another night's sleep, even if it was on hard ground. The Kalinago next to Jorge took rope from around his waist and tied Jayuya's hands behind his back, then hobbled his ankles. Rosa led the way. Thomas came at the rear alongside Jorge.

"Why did you come?" he asked. "I had everything under control."

"We saw you did. Baracoa knows Mateo of old and told us he would kill Jayuya."

"He was about to," Thomas said. "He said the man knew too much, but about what I do not know."

"Ah, no doubt that is still a mystery. Perhaps later we will find out. Baracoa has a plan, though he has not told me what it is. I trust him."

Yes, Thomas thought, *so do I.*

THIRTY-FOUR

Baracoa led their group along the flank of a steep gulley cut deep by frosts and winter rain. Darkness had fallen, but a near full moon hung above the surrounding hills to cast enough light to make their way by and, in the base of the gully, show a sparse glint of water. Here in the western hinterland beyond Sevilla, winds from the great ocean brought moisture that frequently cloaked the peaks, painting them white between November and March. There was no track that Thomas could discern, but Baracoa knew his way. Two of the male Kalinago held Jayuya tied between them. Three women, who had appeared from the darkness as they left Mateo's estate, followed. They sang softly, a song of their own land that fitted well in this scatter of rock shards and scrub. Rosa and Jorge walked with Thomas, offering help when he stumbled or slowed. His mind had stilled and emptied. It had held too much these last days and had finally turned off. He forced one foot in front of the other, climbing, always climbing. This was not the way he had come the first time in Rosa's company, and he had no idea if it was a better route or not. Then, Rosa had followed a ridge to come down to Baracoa's small hut from above. They would have stood out against the skyline then, and Thomas suspected Baracoa did not want to be seen now. Most of Mateo's men were protecting a caravan of illicit goods along the deep valleys from Portugal. When they arrived they might be sent out to track Jayuya, though what purpose Mateo had for the man must be ended if he meant to kill him. Unless there was unfinished business.

The journey passed for Thomas in a daze, until the slope lessened and they emerged on the narrow plateau cut into the hillside and he saw Baracoa's hut. Chickens huddled together in apparent sleep. Two goats stood, open-eyed but unmoving.

Baracoa directed the Kalinago to tie Jayuya to the gnarled oak, then brought cushions and blankets from his hut. Jorge helped Thomas sit, while Rosa wrapped a blanket around him. A flame was set to a pile of wood standing ready, and soon caught, offering a partial warmth that came and went with the wind. Baracoa set an iron pot over the flame and started to slice vegetables into it. He rose and went in search of more to add to it. Thomas adjusted his position until he lay back against a boulder and stared up at the moon, its light strong enough to wash all but the brightest stars into submission. The three women sat cross-legged together, singing a new song, which differed little from the others. If there were words they were unclear, but their voices wove across each other to form an emotion, though not one Thomas was familiar with.

Baracoa returned as darkness fell. Night enveloped them and the sky pivoted around a single point as Baracoa added more to the pot. The food would take some time, so Thomas rose and walked to where Jayuya stood with his arms pulled above him, a grimace on his face.

"Have you come to kill me or free me?" he asked.

"Neither. You remain Baracoa's prisoner unless you tell me what I want to know. Even then it is Baracoa who decides your fate."

"Then I will die. He hates me, as I hate him."

"Why such enmity?" Thomas asked.

"Because we are too alike, though from different islands. We were both *cacique*, which meant only one of us could command those of us in the palace. I thought it should be me. Baracoa disagreed."

"Is that why he left?"

Jayuya shook his head. "He wormed his way into the Queen's favour and eventually she gave him his freedom."

Thomas realised it explained some things, but not all. It was not what interested him at the moment, and he was aware Jayuya had distracted him.

"Baracoa told me only he could create curare, but he was wrong. How did you learn?"

"What makes you think I know how? It takes a strong shaman to make the poison."

"Because you used it to kill Diego and almost kill Don Rodrigo. Do not tell me Baracoa offered the poison to you because you have just told me of your hatred for each other. Why did you hate Don Rodrigo so much you wanted to kill him?"

"You do not understand," said Jayuya. "I do not blame you, but you cannot judge me."

"It is not me you should be concerned about. You failed

to kill Don Rodrigo, and he will not forget your attack on him, nor that you took Diego Serrano's life."

"It was not me," said Jayuya.

Thomas laughed. "Do you expect me to believe that? You were seen."

"Who told you I was?"

"Don Rodrigo, of course. If you wanted no witnesses you should have made sure he was also dead before making your escape."

"I had no hatred of Don Rodrigo. As for Diego I barely knew the man. My life in the palace is not perfect, but better than it would be outside it. I am Kalinago. Not of this land. Spaniards mistrust us because we are different but at least we are alive. I would not risk that. I miss my homeland and my people but know I will never see them again." Jayuya's gaze scanned Thomas from head to toe. "I see you have a knife. Use it to kill me, for I do not want to live anymore."

He wants me to feel sorry for him, Thomas thought. *But that moment is gone, if it ever existed.*

He turned and looked back at the others gathered around the fire. Baracoa was passing out bowls of the stew he had made, and Thomas wanted to join them, to become part of the group rather than stand here with a killer. For that is what Jayuya was, and he did not believe his words. This man had killed Diego and tried to kill Don Rodrigo. And how many others? There would be more, he was sure. He started to turn and at that moment Jayuya's strong legs wrapped around him, jarring his shoulder so a sharp pain ran down his side.

Thomas tried to break free but could not. Jayuya drew

him back, then lifted him from his feet. The two of them swung together, doubling the weight on the rope and branch. Thomas used his legs to swing more in an attempt to escape, but the rope broke. All at once, Jayuya was on top of Thomas and his hands ran across his side until they found his knife. Jayuya took it, rose to his feet and fled.

It took a moment for Thomas to return to himself. Everything had happened so fast, had been so unexpected, and yet he should have taken more care. He was aware of underestimating Jayuya.

Slowly, Thomas sat up, then knelt. He watched the others in the light of the fire. Heard their singing and laughter. Then he reached down and drew a second knife from inside his boot and got to his feet. When he turned there was no sign of Jayuya, but Thomas trusted himself. He had tracked men before through darkness and knew the skill remained. This land was unfamiliar, but so would it be to Jayuya.

Thomas took a moment to tug down the broken rope from the oak branch and wrap it at his waist. When he caught Jayuya he would bind him and take him back to Sevilla for punishment. He knew almost everything now. Jayuya had created curare and used it to kill Don Alejandro. He had done the same to Don Rodrigo and Diego Serrano. The only part Thomas did not know was the why. But he intended to find out.

Thomas did not call out or ask for help. The distant light from Baracoa's fire faded as he moved away, and slowly his eyes adjusted. What he had considered darkness was less dense that he thought. The sky was crystal clear and the stars and lowering moon still bright. Not bright enough to show much, but enough to move ahead with care. There was no sign of Jayuya, but he could not have gone far. Thomas slowed and surveyed what he could see, trying to put himself in the man's place. He would want to put distance between himself and Baracoa's holding, which meant he would have gone straight out, which was the way Thomas also went. His feet caught now and again on rocks, which gave him an idea.

He stopped, closed his eyes, and listened.

At first there was nothing, but then, in the distance, he heard the rattle of stones. He waited to be sure, and it came again, less loud this time, which meant Jayuya was moving away. Straight ahead.

Thomas started up again, trying to move silently but fast. He heard the distant sound of water, muffled because it came from far down in the gorge they had passed on the way up. Which meant Jayuya was making his way back to Sevilla. There he could disappear amongst the throng or take a ship to the coast. It was doubtful he would find passage to his homeland, but there would be other destinations where he would be a stranger without a past.

Another sound came, closer this time, surprising Thomas. Then Jayuya appeared from out from the dark, a hand raised.

Almost too late Thomas saw a large rock clutched in the hand. He raised his good arm and deflected the blow, but still it caught his damaged shoulder, and he cried out.

"You are weak, old man, so now you die," shouted Jayuya.

He swung again. Thomas ducked, but was too slow, or Jayuya too fast.

He remembered nothing else, felt no pain until later when someone pulled at him. Thomas struck out, fearing Jayuya would use his stolen knife to end his life. Someone caught his arm and rolled him over so he lay on his back. He heard voices, soft, lyrical. When he opened his eyes there was orange light and he saw everyone standing in a group at a distance. Only Baracoa and Rosa were close. She reached out and touched his brow and Thomas winced.

"This needs closing but I have nothing," she said. "I will bandage it for now."

"You are fortunate to be alive," said Baracoa.

"He stole my knife," Thomas said. "I am very fortunate to still be alive." He thought of sitting up and began to start, then slumped back.

"Are you dizzy?" asked Rosa.

"I do not think so but need to stand to be sure. Help me."

"Stay there as long as you want. Baracoa and some of the others intend to track Jayuya."

"Not until I can go with them."

"You are hurt," said Rosa.

"Not that much. Help me to my feet."

Jorge came forward and offered his hands. Thomas took them and heaved himself up. When he swayed Jorge held him close, the embrace comforting. He held on until Thomas said, "Let me try on my own."

Released, Thomas waited for the world to start spinning again, but it held firm. The wavering torches did not help, but he was grateful for the light.

"Give me a moment, then we go," he said.

Baracoa began to organise the group. Rosa would come,

as would Jorge. The three Kalinago women were to return to the camp in case Jayuya thought to circle back. "If you see him call out as loudly as you can. We will hear you."

Each nodded.

Baracoa led the way.

"Should we leave the torches?" Thomas asked. "He will see us coming."

"Good," said Baracoa. "He will also fear us. Jayuya is strong, but he is a coward and a bully. Bullies are always cowards once you confront them. We drive him until he can go no further, and then we bind him again, tighter this time."

"It was my fault he escaped," Thomas said. "I got too close and he took my knife."

"Did he stick you?" asked Rosa, one hand reaching out to touch his side.

"He did not." Thomas frowned. "Not even after he knocked me out. He could have cut my throat, pierced my heart. Why did he not?"

"We were coming by then," said Jorge. "I thought you had been gone too long and the others agreed. We discovered both you and Jayuya gone so followed. It was easy for Baracoa to follow your trail, as he follows Jayuya's now."

"He is not so far ahead now. Did you strike him?"

Thomas tried to remember, his head still not working well.

"I do not think so," he said.

"That is not like you," said Jorge.

"No, it is not. I must be getting old."

Jorge snorted a laugh but made no comment, for which Thomas was grateful.

From ahead the sound of racing water which had drifted in and out of Thomas's hearing grew louder, then louder still, and then they found Jayuya.

He stood facing them on the ragged edge of a vertical cliff. The sound of the water rose from the gorge, rushing, angry, hungry.

Jayuya said nothing, only stared at each of them. When his gaze met Baracoa he smiled and shook his head.

He leaned back until the darkness reached out and embraced him. He fell, swallowed by the night.

Baracoa ran forward and held his torch out. When Thomas reached him, they held to each other as first one then the other leaned out, but of Jayuya there was no sign. Baracoa let his torch fall. It guttered, illuminating vertical cliff faces, and then in a brief moment showed white, raging water before it was snuffed out.

"He is gone," said Baracoa. "Dead. Taken by the water."

"You are sure?"

"You saw it. No man could survive that torrent. Jayuya is gone, and I am pleased by it."

THIRTY-FIVE

It was a change in the light that brought Thomas awake from a sleep deeper than the grave. When he opened his eyes Jorge stood over him, shading him from the rays of a bright sun that stood higher in the sky than expected.

"Baracoa is cooking food if you have hunger," said Jorge.

Thomas rolled over, stood with some effort but grateful Jorge offered no help.

"I want to check the ravine first," he said.

"Baracoa has already been. He said there was no sign."

"All the same..."

Jorge smiled. "That is my Thomas. You never trust anyone's word until you have confirmed a fact for yourself."

Thomas returned the smile. "You know me so well."

"I should think so. I will come with you in case you have a dizzy spell. Rosa told me to keep close to you for today, at least."

"Are we not always close?" Thomas said, and Jorge nodded.

On the edge of the gorge, they both looked down. Light reached the water at the bottom, which was not as distant as the night had made it seem. Forty feet, perhaps less. Of Jayuya there was no sign, but the amount of water filling the cleft meant his body would have been carried further downstream. When he started to rise, Jorge offered a hand and Thomas took it.

He fell in beside Jorge as they walked back, the smell of cooking meat drifting to him. It made his mouth salivate and a sudden ravenous hunger filled him.

The others sat cross-legged around the fire as Baracoa sliced meat and placed it in a large bowl where each of them reached in and took what they needed. Thomas sat and surveyed them, aware of their eyes on him in return. They were silent, and he realised idle chatter was not something they indulged in. When Baracoa spoke, it felt like an intrusion, but he was right to do so.

"Jayuya is a trickster. Believe nothing he told you."

"He told me little. I wanted to find out why he attacked Don Rodrigo and Diego, but he claimed he did not."

"Curare was used," said Baracoa. "I did not attack them, which means only another Kalinago could have done it." He looked at the three women. "Did he ever show he might be able to create the poison?"

Each took a moment in thought, then each shook their heads.

"Never," said Yariel, "though that does not mean he could not. I know only shaman are allowed to make it, but I have sat beside one in my own land and seen what he used, how he mixed it. If I had the herbs and plants and roots I might be able to create some."

"There is more to it than that," said Baracoa. "Only shaman have the power to make it strong. The Gods flow through them to make it lethal."

"Could a woman not harness the Gods' power?" asked Yariel.

Baracoa appeared to consider her question before nodding. "I see no reason why not," he eventually said.

"Then Jayuya could also make curare."

Baracoa nodded again. "It seems he could. Now the knowledge of it is lost together with him. It is a good thing." His gaze turned back to Thomas. "He is dead, yes?"

"Most likely, but I would prefer to see his body."

"Washed away. Search if you wish, Thomas, but either way Jayuya is gone. He will trouble us no more."

Thomas agreed with the sentiment, but knew he had to look for Jayuya's body.

It was almost noon before the others began to gather themselves to return to Sevilla. Rosa led the way, saying she knew the quickest route that would avoid Cantillano and Mateo. Jorge went with them, walking beside the Kalinago women.

"You are not going with them, are you?" said Baracoa.

"I told you, I need to find out what happened to Jayuya."

"Search if you must. I can see it is part of you. A good part. Go to where you think you saw him fall and look down. I would caution you not to try to climb. The walls are vertical and slippery. If you cannot see him, travel downstream to a place where the water reaches a small lake. If it carried him away you should find him washed up there."

Baracoa held out his hand and they clasped arms. "Good fortune, my friend. Tell Jorge I like him."

Thomas laughed. "Everyone likes Jorge."

"That may be so, but I like few people. No matter, he strikes me as a man who would not care if I like him or not." Baracoa smiled and turned away, climbing the hillside to where his goats grazed rough ground.

Thomas returned to the gully and did as recommended. He found a stout stick and used it to balance with as he peered deep into the narrow defile. He saw water but no body. It was possible it had been caught beneath the rocks. If so, he would never know, so he followed the slope down until he saw the promised lake ahead. It was small, with an outflow at the far end. Baracoa was right. If Jayuya had been carried this far he should still be here. Did the fact he was not mean the fall had not killed him? If so, the man would flee and never be seen again. It was justice of a sort, and the only one offered.

Thomas glanced at the sky. Noon had come and gone and fresh clouds gathered to conceal the sun. Strong gusts of wind caught at him as he turned and began his return to the city. He walked east and followed the land, doing as the others had and making a wide detour around Cantillano. Rain began to fall, light at first, then the heavens opened and he was soaked within moments. He worked the sling from his arm and discarded it on the ground. His shoulder ached, but already hurt less than it had, and he could lift the arm now. He wanted to return to Sevilla as soon as possible and put thoughts of both Jayuya and Mateo behind him. The latter was a thief and a rogue, nothing more. He ruled in his small estate, traded in illicit goods, but was not the only one to do so, and would not be the last. Thomas could not see how it benefited Mateo to be involved in the killings, either of Luisa or Diego Serrano, or the attempt on Don Rodrigo. Tomorrow, the ambassadors would meet again and Thomas would be expected to be there. He was growing tired of Spain, starting to believe he should never have come. The country had changed, and so had he. He realised returning to England had brought a sense of belonging. He had walked away from his position in Granada without regret, but leaving had changed people's opinion of him. He needed to become more involved, to press both Spanish and English ambassadors to find an agreement. When he reached Sevilla he would bathe – though the torrential rain was already doing a good job of that – and, if possible, speak with each ambassador privately. Thomas knew his presence had been questioned when he attended the first meetings, but Isabel had made it clear he was a valued member of the party. On the English side, Richard Foxe and Thomas Savage were skilled and trusted negotiators, equally matched by the Spanish. Despite this, such matters were expected to take time. Haste would not be seemly. Thomas was also aware that despite the effort put into the negotiations, other approaches had been made from both Portugal and France. Spain was in the ascendancy in Europe, and a marriage with Catherine of Aragon was considered a catch worth almost any cost. There was a reason the Infante Duarte was hanging around the palace. Why he had tried to become closer to Don Rodrigo.

Thomas had neglected the task he was sent to carry out. Catherine's future was important. So were the deaths he had seen, but despite his claims of innocence he was convinced Jayuya had killed Don Alejandro, Diego Serrano, and attempted to take the life of Don Rodrigo. It was even possible he had killed Luisa, though the reason for that was less clear. The man had fled, or died in the attempt. There was nothing Thomas could do. The task of finding him was beyond his ability. In a few days, Jayuya could be anywhere. Even aboard a ship to his homeland, for it was not only the Spanish who sailed those dangerous waters.

It was time for him to do what he had been sent to Spain for and ensure the future of England through marriage.

THIRTY-SIX

Dusk shaded the air as Thomas crossed the Triana bridge to the dockside. Rising on his right, the palace and its high walls caught the last rays of the sun so it shone as if in some fairy tale. *There is where my responsibilities lie*, he thought. Except as he passed the *Casa de Contratación,* he wondered who worked there in Luisa's stead. And because it was the way his mind worked, despite often being more of a curse than a blessing, whether their appointment was the reason for her death. He glanced at the open doors to the warehouse, his footsteps slowing before he turned his gaze away and reluctantly walked on.

Shouting reached him from a group of men on the dockside. Half a dozen surrounded a taller figure, which with a jolt Thomas recognised as Jorge. Rosa was with him, trying to put her slight figure between the men and Jorge. Thomas moved faster, scanning the group for weapons but finding none. All his determination to turn away from trouble disappeared in an instant and he ran, even as he did so aware of the ache in his shoulder. He was still a hundred paces from the group when the men pounced. Two of them grabbed Rosa and dragged her away. The other four grappled with Jorge, who did his best to fight them off, but it was not in his nature, nor was he skilled enough. They punched and kicked, and Thomas saw Jorge's body go limp with the blows. Then they lifted him off his feet and threw him out into the river. By the time Thomas reached them all the men were running in different directions.

Rosa came to him.

Thomas stood on the edge of the dock looking into the water, grey with silt, spilled grain and flour. He could not see Jorge. The disturbance of his hitting the water had come and gone.

"Save him, Tom." Rosa pushed against him.

"I cannot see him."

"He went in there." She pointed at a spot no different to any other. "Can he swim?"

"He can, but not well. Apart from which he was unconscious."

Thomas wondered why he was even talking. He pulled off his boots, discarded his jacket, took four deep breaths and dived into the water. He kicked himself deeper, eyes wide, but barely saw his own hands as they dragged him through the murk. The keel of a ship passed him on the left, and then he was in deeper water, clearer here, and he saw something ahead. He stroked for it, his lungs burning now, and he would need to surface soon, but not yet, because as he got closer Jorge appeared, floating face down, lifeless. Thomas reached him, wrapped the fingers of his good arm around his wrist and kicked for the surface. The rise seemed to take an age, and by the time he emerged his lungs were empty. He gasped in great breaths, only then pulling Jorge after him.

Jorge did not move, hanging slack in the water, his face above the surface, his body a dead weight. Thomas kicked for a set of stone steps and made them with the last of his energy. When he tried to climb, pulling Jorge after him, he could not.

Rosa came to meet them. She added her lithe strength to what little remained to Thomas, and between them they got Jorge on to the dock.

Thomas rolled Jorge on his side and punched him hard in the back, but there was no response. The impossible occurred to him but he dismissed it. Jorge could not be dead.

He lifted him with his arms around his chest and pulled them both to their feet before heaving hard, ignoring the pain of his injured shoulder. *What pain?* he thought. There is only Jorge, and he is not dead. He cannot be dead.

And then Jorge coughed and ejected a great stream of water. He remained unconscious, but Thomas laid him down again and massaged his back as he started to breathe.

"Bring him to my house," said Rosa. "People are watching."

"Who were those men? Did Mateo send them?"

"I do not know, but they were not Mateo's. Bring him, Thomas, before they return."

"They will have me to deal with if they do."

Rosa shook her head. "I am sure they will be sore afraid. Bring him."

Between them they dragged Jorge across the cobbles and into the house. Rosa laid Jorge on a couch and prepared herbs. Thomas opened Jorge's eyelids and stared beneath them. Nothing. How long had he been without air? Too long? Or had those men beaten him too hard?

He leaned close and whispered into Jorge's ear, "You cannot die. I forbid it."

There was no response, but Jorge's chest heaved again. Thomas could still hear water in his lungs, so he turned him over, put his arms around his belly and lifted hard several times until the last of it came out. By which time Rosa came with warm, honeyed liquor, and a paste of herbs.

"Help me get these into him," she said.

"He does not respond," Thomas said.

"He will." Rosa showed none of Thomas's doubt, and that banished his own. Jorge meant too much to him, that was all. The thought of losing him was impossible. He helped Rosa as she pushed the paste far back into Jorge's mouth, then tipped his head back. The first draft of the liquor made him cough, the second did the same, but some was also swallowed. With the third Jorge made some effort himself, then fell back against the couch with a hard sigh and lay flat.

Thomas reached out to his neck and felt his pulse. It was strong, steady.

He sat on his heels and stared at Jorge, whose breath came in gasps that slowly steadied.

"Let him sleep," said Rosa. "He will live now."

THIRTY-SEVEN

"Who were those men?" Thomas asked Rosa. They sat outside on a bench, drinking wine. Dark had fallen but the dockside remained as busy as ever. Thomas's mind was clear, as if confronting Jayuya had wiped some of his concerns away. Lamplight glowed within the *Casa de Contratación,* and he thought of Luisa before pushing a fresh wave of grief aside. It would not bring her back, nor would it catch whoever had killed her, but doing that might offer a degree of closure.

"Might they have been sent by Mateo?" he asked Rosa again.

She shook her head. "I know most of his men and did not recognise them."

"Mateo could have hired others."

"It is not like him to do so," said Rosa. "He trusts only those close to him. Those he can control. I have no idea who they were, but paid men by the look of them. It started as we crossed the dock to come here. At first, we thought it was nothing more than hatred of Jorge being with Yariel.

They walked hand in hand. It was quite innocent, no more than Jorge being Jorge, but the men started jostling them, calling him a native lover–"

Thomas interrupted. "Could it have been no more than that? They did not like the idea of a Spanish man being with one of the Kalinago?"

"It did not feel that way, and then the punches started. It came from nowhere. There was nothing we could do. I would have run for help but they dragged me aside, and then Jorge was in the water. Which is when you came." Rosa reached out and touched Thomas's hand. "He owes you his life."

Thomas smiled. "In more ways than one. I am sure the attack has to be more than it seems. I wonder if they were making a point and I was the intended recipient. It is too much of a coincidence that it happened the moment I arrived at the dockside."

"They could have killed him," said Rosa. "They would have killed him if you had not come along." She drained her cup and poured more wine.

"What happened to Yariel?"

"She ran."

"Did none of the men pursue her?"

Rosa shook her head. "All their attention was on Jorge."

"Then it was not some random band of ruffians picking on a stranger. They chose Jorge, and I believe they did it knowing I would witness the attack."

Rosa looked at Thomas for some time before shaking her head. "Once more you make yourself sound too important. I know you are close to the palace, but that is no reason to attract such hatred. And it was Jorge who was attacked. I doubt the men even knew you were a witness."

"It was not some random act of hatred. It was planned. But you are right. They did not know I would arrive, but they did know killing Jorge would unman me.There is so much going on I cannot pull all the threads together to make sense of them. Jorge has done nothing to annoy people. He is Jorge; he never annoys people."

"Some wife who he teased, and she took it to heart? Her husband hired the men to get rid of him?"

"Perhaps," Thomas said, unconvinced.

"Did you find Jayuya's body?" asked Rosa, a reminder he had not told her what had happened on the mountainside.

"I did not, so most likely he escaped. If he did, I doubt he will return."

"So that is it? He walks free?"

"He walks free," Thomas said.

"After killing how many? Three? More?"

"Jayuya claims he had nothing to do with any of the deaths."

"You believed him?"

"I did. He knew his life here was done. There was no reason for him to lie."

"And he did not tell you who might have killed them?" asked Rosa.

"If he had, would I be sitting here drinking your wine? I would be tracking them down."

"Mateo?" said Rosa.

"He is dangerous, but I see no advantage for him in killing Don Alejandro, or anyone else who has been attacked. And I do not see Mateo acting unless there is an advantage to be gained."

"He was here with his men the morning Luisa was murdered," said Rosa. "Mateo would not do the deed himself, but any of his men would if asked."

"Why would Mateo want her dead?"

"Their relationship was always difficult."

"Did they have a relationship outside of trade?" Thomas asked.

"Mateo would have liked one but Luisa rejected every advance he made. I suspect he thought if he could seduce her she would turn a blind eye to what he was doing. As it was, she held him to account. Most of his trade was legitimate, but that which was not was more profitable. Luisa would have been a thorn in his side, but I do not believe he had her killed because he still held hopes he might be able to persuade her to his side. And she was useful to him in regard to the legal side of his business, which was large enough."

Thomas rubbed a hand across his head. "I am missing something, or there is something I have not yet uncovered. And now I hurt even more."

"Do you want me to make something up for you?"

"It is only pain and will go away eventually." Thomas rose to his feet. "I will check on Jorge. If he wakes, I would like to take him to our lodgings so I am with him in case anything else happens. I would not put you in danger if someone else comes."

"I have good neighbours," said Rosa. "One call and they will protect me. And if Jorge is not awake, he should stay here." Rosa rose and accompanied Thomas inside.

They found Jorge starting to wake. He tried to sit up but failed, and Rosa put a hand on his chest.

"Stay there. Do you recall what happened?"

"Every second, unfortunately. Who were they? And why pick on me?"

"I do not know. I take it such things do not happen to you often?"

Jorge tried to smile. "Not to me, no. To Thomas, all the time, but he deals with such things far better than I do. Who pulled me out?"

"Thomas, of course. He arrived after they threw you in the river. If not for him you would be dead."

"Then I owe him my life, yet again," said Jorge. He reached out and held Thomas's hand. "Thank you, my friend."

"Do you think you can walk if I help?"

"Only if you promise we go straight to our lodgings. I want no more excitement for at least a year."

"I cannot promise that, but will do my best."

When Thomas tried to support Jorge, who was rapidly improving, Rosa pushed him aside. "Do not be a fool. You are in a worse state than him. If Thomas is insistent you go with him then lean on me, Jorge. He can show me the way to where you are staying."

It felt wrong, but Thomas knew Rosa made sense, so he led the way to their house. She came inside and helped Jorge climb the stairs before leaving. Thomas embraced her at the door, and she kissed him on both cheeks.

"Let him sleep as long as he wants. You try to do the same."

"I will, but I have an early appointment at the palace."

After Rosa left, Thomas barred the door, something he had not done since taking the house a month before. He was starting to wonder if the attack on Jorge was a case of mistaken identity, but wanted to feel safer before he sought sleep. Except it did not come. He undressed and washed himself as much as his injured shoulder allowed, dressed in a loose linen robe, then checked on Jorge again. He continued to sleep. Thomas suspected it was an escape from what had happened. He wondered if Yariel had returned to the palace and knew he should make time to talk with her after the ambassadors' meeting. The argument, whatever it had been about, had not included her, but she might know something.

He wanted to act but knew he could not until morning. He went downstairs to curl into a chair so as not to disturb Jorge. The lack of comfort on the hard chair had its effect and he woke to daylight, stiff and aching, already late for his meeting.

THIRTY-EIGHT

Richard Foxe motioned to Thomas the moment he entered the plain meeting room where all negotiations regarding the future of Catherine of Aragon took place. Thomas nodded to King Fernando as he walked towards Foxe. When he came close, the man turned and led the way into a side-chamber.

"I take it you need to speak to me privately," Thomas said.

"Why are you standing so strangely?" Foxe asked.

"I assume that is not your reason for calling me across, but I dislocated my shoulder." Thomas saw no advantage in going into a long explanation or giving those responsible.

"You should be more careful. We are in a foreign land and I would not trust the physics here. But that is not what I wish to speak of. It is Princess Catherine, of course. Tell me, Thomas, why is an agreement not even visible in the distance? We meet thrice a week and have polite discussions, but nothing comes close to being decided. Do these people even want the princess settled?"

"I believe they do, Richard," Thomas said. "And settled in England, is what I understand, but you know there have been other approaches."

"France and Portugal, and perhaps the Netherland. None are as important as England."

"I have heard Portugal's approach is being considered," Thomas said. "The Infante Duarte is a better age than Prince Henry, but the boy is too unworldly to make a good husband. It is more likely there will be war than a marriage."

Foxe stared at Thomas. "Are we in danger?"

"Not here. If war comes, it will be a slow process. Skirmishes. Ambushes. Threats and counter-threats. I believe France is considered an unsuitable match for Catherine. If danger comes, it will be from Portugal."

"So why all the delay? Better to strike a deal and have done with it. I have business at home, and pleasant as this city is, it is not London. Far from it."

Thomas was not sure he agreed with the sentiment but knew better than to offer his own opinion.

"I was told you are closer to the Queen than to King Fernando." Foxe's expression showed what his opinion on such a relationship was. Unseemly, but in this instance useful. "Perhaps you can impress on her the importance of an agreement."

"It is unlikely I will be able to speak to her without several chaperones. If I manage to get a chance, I will state your concerns, but perhaps couch them as my own."

"Couch them how you wish, Berrington, but another month is all I am willing to give this and then we leave for home. Whether you accompany us is your own choice, but

I understand King Henry values your efforts on his behalf. Not that I have seen evidence of such here."

"My position is difficult," Thomas said.

"As far as I am concerned, your position is not required," said Foxe. "All the same, do as I ask and my mind might change." Foxe turned back into the room. Thomas stayed where he was, thinking through their conversation. It was not unexpected, nor anything new. He was well aware of the ambassadors' opinion of him. He was regarded as an outsider. Close to King Henry he might be, but not close to the wheels of power surrounding the King and which made England work. Those wheels also ground riches, which ended up in these men's coffers; though Thomas had heard Foxe was rigorous in refusing such.

He returned to the room where a long table stood with each delegation on either side. All the times Thomas had been asked to attend he never knew exactly where he should sit, so now, as always, he took a chair set against one wall and listened as demands and counter-demands, threats and counter-threats, flowed to and fro. He failed to understand how any matter could be settled in such circumstances but believed eventually it would. Not this time, most likely, but in the end it would. Next time the Spanish ambassadors might come to London. Whether home territory added to their entitlement, Thomas had no idea. He listened, aware of how the translators on both sides sanitised the demands of the other, but they did little harm. Threats were changed to flattery and flattery to something lesser. An hour passed, then another. Eventually, an equerry came and announced that a midday meal was ready next door, and everyone rose.

Thomas remained where he was. He wanted to use the

hour or more they would spend over the meal to follow up on his own investigations. He was in the palace and wanted to speak again with some of the Kalinago women. In particular, Yariel and Anacoana, who had been wives to Jayuya. Thomas believed the relationship had been one-sided. If so, they might be willing to provide information on the man. He had fled, and Thomas had already abandoned hope of finding him, but he had lived for many years in the palace and must have made contacts. Thomas doubted Jayuya had come up with the plot to kill Alejandro and Rodrigo alone, two men who held exalted positions in the palace. Both close to king and queen. If Jayuya had killed them, on whose orders? Yariel and Anacoana might be unaware they possessed information on who that person might be.

So involved in his own thoughts was Thomas that it took him some time to become aware someone stood in front of him. When he did, he was surprised to discover King Fernando waiting patiently – a state of affairs rarely witnessed.

"You were lost in thought, Thomas. I did not want to disturb you in case it proved fruitful. Did it?"

Thomas rose. "That I do not yet know."

"I take it you are not eating with us?"

"Not unless you command me, Your Grace."

"I do not. I want a word in private, if I may."

"Of course." Thomas was confused. Fernando generally ignored or insulted him. This was a side of the King he had rarely, if ever, witnessed. "I regret to say I am making little progress in the death of Don Alejandro or the attack on Don Rodrigo."

"That is not what I wish to discuss. These negotiations

draw my mind increasingly to threats against Spain. In particular that of Portugal. Their ambassadors make increasingly bold claims for Catherine to marry the Infante Duarte de Beja. He is a nephew to King Manuel so has royal lineage, but he is no king in waiting, unlike Prince Henry."

"I have heard only vague rumours," Thomas said. "What do your Spanish ambassadors say?"

"They say nothing, as no doubt you heard. Tell me, Thomas, do the translators speak true or not?"

"For the most part they speak true, but tend to flattery, as do your own."

"We take that into account, of course. All the same, this boy worries me. Rumours of soldiers gathering on our borders reach me. Of men finding hidden pathways into Spain that lead close to Sevilla. It worries me this boy, or more likely his uncle, the King, wants war, thinking they can win it." Fernando stared at Thomas long enough that he knew he must speak.

"Spain is too strong for them," he said, seeing how his words pleased Fernando. "But much else other than war is going on in the west. How much do you know of what I have been doing to investigate the deaths?"

"Nothing at all. I know you delve into matters not of concern to you, but recognise it is your way and allow it as long as it does not interfere with what you have been sent here for. Which is to arrange this marriage. As soon as possible."

"It will not be soon, Your Grace. Harry is too young."

"He will not be too young forever." Fernando shook his head. "You call him Harry, not Prince Henry?"

"The boy likes me," Thomas said.

"As my daughter also likes you and your family. Do you all call her Catherine?" Fernando tried not to smile.

"We do not, Your Grace."

"Good."

"We call her Cat."

Fernando burst into laughter, loud enough to bring an equerry running in from the corridor where he had been waiting to protect his master. The laughter surprised Thomas, too. He could not remember a time when Fernando had been in such a good mood. He wondered what the man wanted.

Fernando waved a hand to dismiss the equerry, then motioned Thomas to accompany him as he crossed the room. They walked onto the raised terrace that looked across the gardens. The noonday sun blazed down, early morning mist burned off hours ago.

Fernando pointed west to where low hills were just visible.

"Portugal lies that way, and they spoil for a fight. I mean to give them what they want. And soon. Better to stamp on a snake before it bites you." He glanced at Thomas. "We go soon, and I want you with me."

The request surprised Thomas. "Why me, Your Grace?"

"I hear you can still fight and can still save a man wounded in battle. I could do with someone like that."

"I have a weak arm, Your Grace, from when one of your *hermanos* decided to rack me."

"It does not show," said Fernando.

"I try not to let it," Thomas said. "But whether I can fight like you expect is uncertain."

"It will be at least a week before we ride, perhaps more

depending on what my spies bring me. Tell me, Thomas, do you know of a man by the name of Mateo Salto?"

Thomas hesitated, unsure if the question was a trap. He decided, or hoped, it was not.

"I do, Your Grace. I visited him not long since in an attempt to identify the dead man I believed at that time poisoned Don Alejandro. I now know it was a Kalinago poison, not anything known in this land."

"That I did not know," said Fernando. "What else have you discovered?" Before Thomas could respond, the King held up a hand. "No, do not tell me now. We will be able to talk when we ride to battle. For now, tell me if you trust this Mateo."

"No."

"Good. Neither do I. He claims to be an honest trader but I do not believe him."

"You believe right, Your Grace." Thomas decided to reveal a little more. "There is a Kalinago by the name of Baracoa I have become slight friends with. He–"

"I know him," said Fernando. "He came to Spain on Columb's first voyage and lived in the palace for several years. He asked to be released from our service and my wife allowed it." Fernando shrugged. "I would not have done so, but I could not take her offer back once made. I knew him as an honest and hard-working man."

"As do I. He showed me where the Portuguese bring contraband through the mountains to Mateo Salto. The same route would allow an army to approach within a few miles of Sevilla."

"You can lead me to this place?" asked Fernando.

"Baracoa can."

"Then ask him so I can send men to the west. They will inform me if an army approaches. It would be good to arrange an ambush. Ask this man, then wait for my call. I will try to give you a day or two's notice, but ride with me you will, as well as Baracoa."

"And if he refuses?"

"Then you will ride with me. Get him to show you these approaches again. Now we are done. I have stayed too long as it is and people will wonder what I have been plotting."

"The future of your daughter, Your Grace."

"You mean Cat."

"Yes, Your Grace, I mean Cat. Will King Henry see satisfaction before long?"

Fernando smiled. "Not yet, but as you said, soon. Both he, and we, want the matter settled. Both of us are aware Catherine cannot return to Spain so we must settle her. The Portuguese still press their claim, but the Infante Duarte is unsuitable. He is too low in the pecking order. Who better to settle our daughter with than the future King of England."

When Fernando was gone, Thomas left the palace to make arrangements. He would need to speak with Baracoa again. And then he would have to toughen himself up if he was expected to ride into battle. It had been some time since he acted as both soldier and medic, but the memory remained. Also, he hoped, the skill.

THIRTY-NINE

Thomas knew he had to check on Jorge but also wanted to speak to Rosa. With good fortune, Baracoa would still be with her and that was who else he needed to consult. As it was, fortune favoured him as he crossed the dockside to see Rosa and Jorge sitting outside her house. Making his way towards them he saw Rosa rise several times to serve customers, their needs met by already pre-packed sleeves of herbs.

Thomas pulled a chair out and sat, reached across and took a sliver of fowl from Jorge's plate.

"I see you are recovered," he said.

"Once again, my thanks for saving my life. I will never be able to repay you."

"I had no idea you intended to."

Jorge smiled. "I do not, but an apology costs nothing and earns respect."

"You know I already respect you, but..." Thomas stole another slice of meat.

"Here, eat your own food." Rosa set a plate in front of

him, before sitting. She set her elbows on the table-top and leaned closer to Jorge, her eyes scanning him.

"Not you as well," said Jorge. "I am fine."

"I will be the judge of that," said Rosa. "Both you and Thomas are injured. Is this a common state of affairs?"

"Hardly," Thomas said, and Jorge nodded agreement. "The last time I was badly injured was two years ago when I was stabbed. My daughter saved my life."

"I would like to meet this daughter of yours. Where did she learn her skills?"

"From me. She has fifteen years, but I would have died if not for Amal."

"It is a Moorish name," said Rosa.

"As was her mother, who died giving her own life for Amal's." Thomas's expression prevented Rosa from asking more about his past, for which he was grateful. "Is Baracoa still with you?"

"He was here last night but left a little time ago. Why?"

"I need to speak with him again. This time without partaking of his potions. It seems to me he sees and hears everything that happens near where he lives."

"He hears and sees everything wherever he is," said Rosa. "Again, why do you want him?"

Thomas wondered why Rosa was being so protective of Baracoa. He was sure the man was more than capable of looking after himself. Unless there were things she did not want Thomas to know. He did not want to tell her what Fernando had informed him of but could think of nothing else.

"The King also seeks Baracoa's advice. He told me he knows him of old and trusts his opinion."

"Opinion of what?"

Thomas sipped a little wine as he fashioned a version of the truth. When he set the cup down, he said, "I think Fernando knows about Mateo importing contraband and would like it stopped, but it is not his responsibility, it is that of the *hermanos*. He also believes Baracoa may know enough about the operation to be of assistance."

"I thought you knew him better than that," said Rosa. "Baracoa is not of this world. Its plots pass him by unless they impinge on his life. Mateo takes care not to cross him. In fact, I believe he does so deliberately because he fears him."

"Mateo fears Baracoa? Why?" asked Thomas.

"He is superstitious. He believes Baracoa to be a powerful shaman and would rather not antagonise him. This ignoring of each other works for both of them. I admit Baracoa seems to like you, but do not expect that to last if you press him too hard to do something he does not want to."

"I could at least ask the question," Thomas said. "How long since he left? Would I be able to catch him if I went now?"

"Only if I come with you," said Rosa. "And only if we go right now." She glanced at Jorge. "And you, my friend?"

"The last time I was not with Thomas it did not end well, so I will also come."

"The three of us then. Now. Both of you help me pack up my goods."

Between them they took everything inside the house. She lowered the shutters but did not lock them. She took a moment to change into hose and a leather jerkin, then led the way to Triana bridge.

"How strong do you feel now, Jorge?" she asked once they had crossed the river.

"I feel good," said Jorge.

"And you, Thomas?"

"Better every day."

"Then let us run. Baracoa only moves fast when he needs to, but covers a surprising amount of ground without appearing to make any effort."

Rosa started ahead and Thomas let her gain enough of a lead so she could not hear them.

"Did you sense any defensiveness from her when I asked about Baracoa?" Thomas asked Jorge.

"A little, yes, but only because she loves him. Before you arrived, she asked about you. She does not understand why you are not more upset over Luisa's death."

Thomas looked ahead to where Rosa continued to cover the ground like a faun. "Do you think I should be?"

Jorge laughed and slapped him on the back. "There's my Thomas. No, I do not, because I know you. You have not truly given your heart to anyone since Lubna, not even Bel, who was your first love. You have scars, Thomas, both inside and out. Rosa does not understand you like I do. I tried to explain it to her but she still does not. I said you would revenge her death, and that is your way of remembering her."

"What I had with Luisa was purely physical," Thomas said.

"I know. Rosa does not. She is a loving soul, like me.

You were that once, but no longer. Now, we had better follow before she disappears altogether."

Which Rosa did. She was more fleet than either of them, and Jorge was not designed to move fast, despite his elegance. When they next caught sight of her, she sat on a boulder next to Baracoa. In the distance, Mateo's estate was visible, crouched beneath the mountain slope. Both of them watched Thomas and Jorge approach.

"Your friend needs to run more, Thomas," said Baracoa, when they stood panting in front of him.

"He usually has no need. Did Rosa tell you I want to talk?"

"She did, but not about what. Pleasant as this day and the company is, I would rather be at my home than sitting here."

"King Fernando wants to speak with you."

"Why?"

Thomas smiled, because it was the exact same question Rosa had asked.

"About Mateo and the Portuguese."

"Does he not already know everything he needs to?" asked Baracoa. "The King must have many spies, and Mateo makes little effort to hide his activities. Some of the goods he trades in can only be found to the west. Portugal's influence across the ocean is in different areas to Spain, so their goods brought over the sea are also different, as are the people. And yes, like Spain, Portugal steals natives away from those distant lands. So what does he really want to talk to me about?"

"War," Thomas said.

Baracoa stared at him. He rose to his feet. "I want nothing to do with war." He started away.

Thomas caught up and fell into step beside him.

"I can run faster than you," said Baracoa with a smile.

"And I am determined. I know where you live."

"Do you forget I kill intruders?"

"I thought we were friends," Thomas said.

"What gave you that impression? Rosa is my friend. Beyond her, there is no one I cannot turn my back on, you included."

"You may want nothing to do with war," Thomas said, "but that will not stop it coming to you. Do you not have wars where you are from?"

"We are men, so of course we do. The world would be a better place if it was run by women. I try to think like them, but sometimes it comes hard."

"And how many times did you start those wars?"

"Skirmishes rather than wars." Baracoa leapt a narrow gulley where water ran fast from a hill. "And I will still not help you. Go back to the King and tell him my answer. He knows me of old and will know I mean what I say. Besides, I am but one man and the King has others better suited to fighting. Join him if you must, but this is not your fight either."

Thomas slowed, then stopped. Baracoa kept walking, covering the rock-strewn ground with ease. Thomas watched until he disappeared over the ridge before turning back. Rosa still sat on the boulder when he reached it, now with Jorge beside her. Their heads were together and as Thomas approached, they glanced up and laughed.

"Jorge told me you are stubborn to a fault," said Rosa with a grin.

"I prefer to regard it as being steadfast," Thomas said. "Do you intend to sit there all day, or shall we return to the city?"

Jorge slid down, then offered his hand to Rosa, who accepted it. She kissed him on the cheek but ignored Thomas.

As they approached the river, Jorge told Thomas to slow down and pointed to a substantial house set on the slope with a view across the city and palace.

"Yes, it is most impressive," Thomas said. "Do you want me to buy it?"

"Do you forget that we came here after speaking with Don Alejandro's household? It is the house of his eldest son."

"There were many calls on my mind at that time, but yes, I recognise it now. As I recall the man had gone away to the country."

"As Doña Carlita was away when last we called on her," said Jorge.

Rosa watched them both without expression.

"Don Gabriel returned a week since," she said. "He sent for some of my potions only two days ago and the girl told me they had visited his stepmother. Do you want to speak with him? He does not welcome approaches from strangers and has an overly high opinion of himself."

Jorge smiled, looking between Rosa and Thomas. "I visited Don Alejandro's house myself three days ago, hoping Doña Carlita might have returned. I thought you would find it useful to know her intentions regarding the inheritance of her husband's wealth, but she had not returned. It is possible Don Gabriel was with her. I heard the whisper of a rumour he might try for Doña Carlita himself."

"He is already married," said Rosa, and pulled a face. "Apart from which the Church does not allow a stepson to marry his stepmother. It is impossible."

Thomas thought of Catherine's position which, while different, still required a papal dispensation if she was to marry Prince Harry, the brother of her dead husband, Arthur. As far as he knew, the request was still being sought.

"I hear he is besotted with her," said Jorge. "I understand why. There are few women as beautiful, or dissolute, as Doña Carlita. It might not be marriage on his mind, but the wealth of his father which she no doubt also wants."

"What manner of man is Don Gabriel?" Thomas asked Rosa. "His father was hugely wealthy. Might the son want him dead so he could inherit that wealth?" Thomas was pleased to see she gave his question attention before responding.

"He is corrupt, but I cannot see him committing murder."

"He would not do it himself. I believe Jayuya killed Don Alejandro, as he killed Diego Serrano."

"It is possible he might have paid to remove his father," said Rosa. "But despite Don Gabriel's high opinion of himself it is difficult to believe him plotting such a scheme. But go talk to him when he returns and find out for yourselves."

Thomas watched her go, wondering if there was any point doing as she said. If Don Gabriel had been involved it would mean two men, at least, being executed. But it would not bring back the dead.

FORTY

Back at their lodgings, Thomas sat in the smallest room, staring at the blank wall of the house that backed onto the far side of the street. His mind felt as empty as the wall. He was still staring at it some unmeasured time later when Jorge poked his head around the door.

"Are you going to sulk there all afternoon or come out with me?"

Thomas turned only slowly. He wanted to remain wrapped in his own thoughts, few as they were, but wondered if distraction might cut him loose from this feeling of being lost. Slowly, he rose.

"Yes, let us go out and eat."

They found a house with a few tables outside. Like many such establishments, it bordered the docks, for dockers and stevedores grew uncommonly hungry. The establishment was run by a woman of indeterminate age and her daughter, who was pretty and flirted outrageously with Jorge.

Jorge spoke with the woman and her daughter. Thomas ate, drank, and gazed across the extensive docks. He glanced at the *Casa de Contratación* and thought of Luisa. What had she done to get herself killed? Or was it something she knew? Perhaps even something she was not aware she knew? In either case, how could it have been dangerous enough to merit murder? And hers was not the only one. There was Don Alejandro, which started everything. Diego Serrano and almost Don Rodrigo. Thomas considered the death of the gardener and his family. Was that connected or not? The others had been people of substance, the gardener a worker at the palace. Had the man witnessed something so had to die? Then there was the attack on Jorge, and Thomas's own arrest. He imagined he might have disappeared into the depths of Triana for good had Rodrigo not freed him. Had the same person carried out all the attacks? Or if not the person themself, then under the order of someone else? There had been too many deaths too close together for it to be coincidence. They hinted at a plan. But what manner of plan?

"You are thinking again," said Jorge. "How you can do so much of it without wearing your brain out is a mystery."

"It is like a muscle, my friend. Use it and it grows stronger. Do not use it, and it withers and weakens."

"Then my mind should be the size of a walnut," said Jorge with a laugh. "What were you thinking about?"

"Do not underestimate yourself. And I was thinking of all the links between the deaths. I cannot hold all the details in my head. Try as I might they keep slipping away."

"So write them down. That is what you always do."

"There are so many. Even put on a page of paper I am not sure they would make sense."

"Then try something else. I do not know what. Throw tacks at the wall. Glue pages to the wall. But try, Thomas, or whoever is guilty will go free to kill again. Next time it might be us. It was almost you, and it was almost me."

Thomas nodded. He drained his wine and stood.

"I need to speak with Rosa briefly. Do you want to come?"

"Of course I want to come."

Rosa's stall was closed up, but when Thomas rapped on the door she opened it.

"Did you forget something?"

"I need your advice. Where can I find good quality paper, a quill, and ink? And some tacks, and something to hammer them into a wall with."

Rosa laughed. "What are you intending to do?"

"Solve a murder."

"With those things?"

"It was Jorge's idea."

Rosa looked at Jorge and raised an eyebrow. "And I thought he was just a handsome face."

"Oh, I am much more than that. But the idea was really Thomas's. He had just not thought of it yet."

"Quill and ink I can give you," said Rosa. "I am sure good quality paper can be found in the palace if you ask, as can everything else you want. You can do that, yes?"

"Yes," Thomas said.

Jorge remained behind with Rosa because she wanted to talk to him. What about was not revealed, and Thomas's mind lay on the ideas that swirled through his head, and a means to control them into some kind of answer.

Thomas spoke with several people, none of whom could help, then in desperation he thought of the Kalinago. He recalled hearing how they had created their own huts from spare material in the palace and assumed they might know of what he sought. He found Rocio, together with Zoraida and Anani. It was Rocio who knew where tacks could be found, and Anani took Thomas to a storage room where piles of unmarked paper were stacked almost to the ceiling.

"They do much writing of no consequence within these walls," she said. "What is it you want paper for?"

"To write on, of course. Do you know of a room I can use where I will not be disturbed?"

Anani led him to an empty room and Thomas lit the lamps and found half a dozen candles. There were many such rooms in the palace, which seemed to have a great many of them for the few who resided there.

Thomas knew when the court was not present these buildings were home to only the few staff who kept it maintained, ready for its return. Thomas had witnessed the same at the Alhambra, as well as in Malaga and Cordoba. Even with the King and Queen present, together with their retinue and support staff, as well as the ambassadors and their staff, most of the rooms lay empty. Anani sat cross-legged on the floor.

"You can leave now," Thomas said.

"I want to stay. I am curious."

Thomas pulled a chair up to a large table which sat

beneath a window. He took several sheets of the paper and folded it, folded it again, then tore along the seams. He poured a little ink into a beaker, dipped his quill and started to write. Names. Locations. Methods of killing. When he had the main elements recorded he stood, poured some of the iron tacks into his hand and used them to pin the paper to the wall. It took longer than the writing had because he needed to re-arrange them several times. When he sensed someone beside him he looked down to see Anani had crossed the room. She stared at the pages without expression.

"Can you read them?" Thomas asked.

She shook her head. "What do they say?"

Thomas read them out, touching each in turn.

"I see," said Anani. "These are all ... what is the word, contacted?"

"Connected," Thomas said. "Yes, I believe they are. Exactly how I do not yet know." He stared at the papers, trying to see what linked them. Some were obvious. Don Rodrigo and Diego Serrano, both attacked in the palace garden. Jayuya and Baracoa. Also Rosa, linked to Baracoa.

Anani touched her fingertips to one of the sheets. "Are you and your friend also here?"

Thomas shook his head, realising they should be, for had they not also been attacked?

He went to the table, wrote their names down, then wrote down both Isabel and Fernando, drawing a crude crown beside the names to indicate their royalty. He added them to the wall, where Anani remained, her eyes scanning without comprehension.

Thomas pinned the new sheets, placing all four in the

middle of the others. He stepped back, trying not to think, trying to form a pattern and failing. They were names and places, nothing else. His eyes scanned backwards and forwards, attempting to hold some kind of relationship in his head.

"You are missing something," said Anani. She turned and left the room.

After she had gone Thomas laughed. "A harsh judgement, but true. What I am missing is enlightenment." A feeling grew in him that he might never be able to draw the threads together, never discover who killed Don Alejandro and the others. Who benefitted? Who feared?

He was still staring when Anani returned. She placed a tangle of coloured threads on the floor, knelt and began to tease them out. Red, blue, yellow, ochre, black, white, gold, silver. She stood and handed a thread to Thomas.

"What am I meant to do with this?"

Anani shook her head at his stupidity. "Which names belong to you and your friend?"

Thomas tapped the two pages in the centre.

Anani wrapped one end of the thread around the head of a tack, pulled it across and did the same on the other sheet. She broke the loose end from the thread and stepped back.

"Now you can see," she said, as she handed several of the threads to him. She remained at his side, a reminder of Thomas's stupidity.

His eyes scanned the sheets. He reached out and wrapped the end of one around the tack holding Don Alejandro, then did the same with Don Rodrigo. One had died. The other had taken his place.

A growing excitement filled him. He worked faster, unaware of the passage of time. Anani went to the wall and sat again so he could move more freely, a smile on her lips.

Finally, Thomas stepped back. Half the wall was filled with scraps of paper, each linked to several others with threads of different colours. Black for dead. White for friendship. Red for enmity. He stepped back again, trying to take it all in.

Anani came and embraced him. "Now you are clever," she said. "You do not need me anymore." She turned and left.

Thomas missed her calm presence. He knew without her he would not have done as he had. But did it tell him anything?

He went close, then stepped back until he was against the opposite wall. Distance brought the connections into clearer focus. He narrowed his eyes and nodded. He returned to the wall and tugged several of the sheets away and let them drop to the floor. They were not relevant. Don Alejandro's wife lay discarded but his son remained. Minor characters followed. As each was removed the remaining connections became clearer. Finally, Thomas knew what he needed to do next.

Before he could go in search of Jorge, a new figure entered the room. She stopped as if not expecting anyone.

"Oh," said Isabel. She glanced around, then her gaze took in the wall. "What have you been doing, Thomas?"

"Thinking."

She gave a small laugh, covering her mouth. Thomas knew they should not be in the same room together without the presence of servants or chaperones. If Isabel was aware of the breaking of protocol, she did not show it as she approached.

She crossed her arms and took in the entire wall, eyes flicking left and right, head turning.

"It is most pretty," she said. "Where did you get the thread?"

"Anani helped. She is one of the Kalinago."

"I do not know their names," said Isabel. She touched Thomas's name in the centre of the wall. "Why you and Jorge?"

"Because attempts were made on both our lives. I am also there because I want to uncover who is responsible for the deaths."

"How many other than Don Alejandro?"

"At least four, but there may be more. An entire family died, but I do not know if they are linked or not." Thomas tapped one of the sheets where no names showed, only 'dead family, palace gardener'.

"Children as well?" asked Isabel. "How many?"

"Three, all young."

She shook her head.

"Then find out who is responsible, Thomas. It is what you have done in the past and I trust you to do so again. Bring the culprit to Fernando and he will take their head."

"This wall tells me there may be more than a single guilty person." He ran his finger along a thick crimson thread until it reached the name Jayuya. "This man killed Diego Serrano and almost killed Don Rodrigo."

"Then bring him to us."

"I believe him already dead, but he may have killed others. May even have killed Don Alejandro through the use of poison. The Kalinago have much knowledge of plants brought from their world to ours, some of which can kill a man almost instantly."

"And you believe him guilty?"

"I am sure of it, but not yet sure if he is the only person. He is ... was ... an angry man. He is no loss to the world."

Isabel nodded. "Good. Leave this where it is. I will give instructions for it not to be touched in case you need to study it again. Now, Thomas, that Portuguese boy is here again demanding an audience. I thought we were meeting in this room, but I can see we are not."

"I thought he had been sent back to Lisbon with his tail between his legs."

Isabel laughed. "So we all thought. It seems Portugal wants him to try again."

"Do you want me to explain the facts of life, marriage, and such to him?"

Isabel cocked her head to one side, her gaze on Thomas. "Would Jorge not be better at that?"

Thomas smiled. "He would, but he cannot threaten like me."

"Then perhaps you should. It is worth trying, anyway. Come, let us find him. You can scowl and growl and tell him to leave us in peace. Catherine will marry Prince Henry eventually. It is all but agreed, but such things move exceedingly slow."

Thomas looked again at his work. "Do you know if this room can be locked? I do not want anyone interfering."

Isabel laughed. "I would not know that, Thomas, but will send someone with an answer and, perhaps, a key. You should wait here until they come, then ask for my whereabouts. You can take the Infante Duarte aside and have stern words with him. Tell him Catherine is not available. Not now, not ever, to one such as him." Isabel pulled a face. "What is Portugal thinking? They have stolen away one of my daughters already. They will not have a second."

FORTY-ONE

It was late before Thomas left the palace, his head full of connections and theories, few of which made sense. He walked without seeing the city around him. At their house, Jorge was already asleep and grumbled when Thomas woke him, but found sleep quickly again, which Thomas did not. He stared into the night, listening to sounds from outside, a few passers-by, the distant sound of work continuing at the docks. It never ended and no doubt never would. Trade was too important to the city. He knew he would not sleep and wanted to rise and return to the palace. The room was locked, but he had been allowed to keep a key for himself. He listened to the cathedral bell strike the hours until, eventually, a restless sleep found him.

He was woken by someone hammering on the door and rose, bleary-eyed, his body aching.

Rosa stood outside in the gathering light, her hands wrapped across her waist as if in protection. *Not from me*, Thomas thought.

"Do you want me or Jorge?"

"Baracoa wants to speak with you," said Rosa. "He did not tell me what about."

Thomas fetched a jacket, slipped a knife into his boot, and went with Rosa.

"Baracoa is an interesting man," he said. "It is perhaps that which draws me to him."

"You too are an interesting man, Thomas, otherwise Luisa would not have made a play for you. Do you grieve for her as I do? You do not show it."

"I am sorry she died. Sorry that some of it may have been my fault. But I have loved and lost before and learned that the pain lessens, even if not altogether. With Luisa there was less of love and more of lust. For both of us, I believe."

"Yes, so do I."

They entered the wide dockside and crossed to Rosa's house. Baracoa stood outside, staring into the distance, as still as one of the saints' statues that lined the square around the cathedral. He turned his head only as Thomas came close. Rosa stroked her fingers along his forearm before opening the shutters on her stall then going into the house.

"You want to speak with me," Thomas said.

"I need to show you something, but yes, also speak. We should leave so we get there before dark."

Thomas glanced at the sky. "It is not your holding, then?"

"A little farther than that."

"What is it I need to see?" Thomas wondered if he had the time or inclination to go with Baracoa but suspected the man would not have asked for him unless he considered it important. "Have you found Jayuya's body?"

Baracoa almost smiled. "Not exactly. Come and you will see."

"Do we need horses?"

"I do not. You may, but where we are going it will be as easy on foot." Baracoa looked Thomas up and down. "Are you recovered enough to walk..." he had to stop and work something out, and only when he spoke did Thomas realise he did not think of distance in the same way as he might, "...six leagues? That is what you call them, yes?"

"You know the distance, then."

"It benefits a man to know what he can about the land he has made home." Baracoa started off.

Thomas went into Rosa's house. "Tell Jorge where I have gone. Sometimes he worries about me."

Rosa smiled. "Only sometimes? Of course I will."

Outside, Thomas ran to catch up with Baracoa before falling into step at his side. The man covered the ground at a rate that made Thomas breathe harder.

On the far side of the river, they climbed the familiar slope. Thomas turned his gaze aside from their path to look at Gabriel Ortega Dominguez's house. The name of Don Alejandro's son had been on one of the sheets of paper tacked to the wall in the room of the palace, but few coloured threads linked it to anything other than his step-mother and, of course, Don Alejandro himself. To Thomas, that meant the man was not involved in any plot to kill his father, much as he would benefit from the death. It was the slips of paper with many threads linking them that interested him, and Thomas realised that as he physically distanced himself from them, the clearer some of those connections came in his mind. He knew, on his return, he wanted to rearrange them to create less confusion.

"Are you sure Jayuya is dead?" he asked Baracoa, who did not so much as glance at Thomas before replying.

"Are you?" he asked, which was no answer.

"You knew him better than me, which is why I ask. I saw him fall into the gulley where storm water raged. I did not find his body. What I witnessed tells me he died, but I have made the same mistake before and regretted it."

Frustratingly, Baracoa did not respond.

They walked on. Over the first ridge, onto a wide plain where the Guadalquivir turned back on itself so when they reached it they were forced to wade across at a shallows with a sandy bottom, where large fish swam lazily in a pool below the sandbank, their tails occasionally slapping the surface. Beyond, the ground rose more steeply and soon Baracoa slowed so he would not leave Thomas behind. The sun moved across the sky, dropping towards the west where the ridges of more mountains would meet it prematurely.

As they approached the crest of one more ridge, Baracoa held his hand up before going to his knees and crawling forward. Thomas, not being a fool, did the same.

He lay beside Baracoa, looking down into a wide valley that ran west to east. Glancing to his right, Thomas knew the valley would most likely lead to Mateo's estate. West it led to the border with Portugal. A small river ran along the valley bottom, other streams cascading down to add their contribution to its waters. Over one hundred men were camped on one bank, their horses left to wander the sparse patches of vegetation. There was no covering, no tents, so if rain came these men – no, these *soldiers* – would get wet. But soldiers were used to such.

"There are no women," Thomas said.

"Is that important?"

"Soldiers usually have followers to provide comfort."

"You mean sex. Say what you mean, Thomas. Does it matter?"

"It means they do not intend to stay long. They are a large enough force to cause problems if they come closer to Sevilla, but I see no other reason for them being here. Do you have any thoughts?"

"Does the King have many soldiers in the city?"

It was a good question, and one Thomas was unsure he had an answer for.

"Fernando gathers an army when he intends to fight. Depending on the nature of that fight, it might be a small army or a large one. I expect he could gather four score men from those in the city. If he needed more then he would have to recruit them locally or cast his net wider. Most likely in the direction of Córdoba, Granada or Malaga."

"Do the Portuguese fight well? I assume those men down there are from Portugal, yes?"

"I am not familiar with their uniforms, but they are soldiers and appear to have travelled from the west, so yes, they will be Portuguese." Thomas shuffled back from the crest. "I need to return to the city and tell Fernando about them."

"Not yet." Baracoa did the same, both of them rising once they could not be seen. "We go further west now, but not far."

Neither of them spoke as they followed a faint track

made by a small herd of Ibex, which could be seen in the distance. They would be aware of the men, but were shy creatures and would move on before they came close.

Eventually, Baracoa pointed at a softer ridge, and they climbed it and once more went to their knees. This time, Thomas looked down on a smaller group of men, no more than thirty. There were carts drawn by horses and oxen, each piled high with barrels and crates and boxes. Here there were tents. A fire burned, spiralling smoke into the air, and two men appeared to be cooking some game they had brought down.

One of the men looked like Jayuya. He stood apart from the others.

"Is this the reason you brought me?" Thomas asked. "Is it him?"

"It is. I went closer last night and saw him clearly in the firelight. He did not drown. What I do not understand is why he is down there. He appears to be heading towards Mateo's estate."

"The last time Jayuya was there he was about to be killed," Thomas said. "Whatever reason Mateo had for wanting him dead no longer appears to apply. Those men are traders. No doubt they are taking contraband to Mateo, and Jayuya being with them offers him protection. It also changes his worth to Mateo."

"Most likely," said Baracoa. "As far as I know he has removed all rivals. If those men are also of Portugal, then what they carry will be punished by death if they are discovered."

"So the soldiers are there as protection." Thomas said.

"I would say not."

Thomas glanced at Baracoa. "Why?"

"Contraband is brought through these valleys all the time. I watch and do nothing because it is not my business. Never before have I seen soldiers. And the presence of Jayuya worries me. He is wicked, and a killer. You know this. There are some Kalinago in Portugal, but most are natives of lands further south where ships of that country have trade routes. It would give Jayuya great pleasure to become the leader of a band of such people. He craves power and position. He also craves killing. It is in his nature, which is why he has to die – and this time be seen to die."

Thomas thought for a moment. Usually he would disagree, but in this instance he knew Baracoa spoke true. He recalled his thoughts as they had travelled here, of how he had dismissed Jayuya from consideration because he believed him dead, so could no longer be punished. That was no longer the case. How the man was still alive he did not know, but it concerned him that he was. How difficult he must be to kill.

"I believe Jayuya killed Don Alejandro," Thomas said.

"How?"

It frustrated Thomas that Baracoa always seemed to throw his questions back at him, but he knew it made sense. Thomas was closer to what had happened.

"He was at the banquet, I saw him there. And he also attacked Don Rodrigo and Diego Serrano. When I questioned him Jayuya admitted nothing, but I believe he must have the knowledge of how to create curare."

"If so, he kept it well hidden when I knew him at the palace. How would he find the plants needed? I grow them myself, but their cultivation is hard and requires much skill in this land. It is true he came from a different island to mine and I do not know what Jayuya learned there. But it needs not only the knowledge and skill but the ingredients as well."

"You grow the plants needed at your holding," Thomas said. "I know many others are also brought from your world and planted in the palace gardens. Might the same ones grow there that grow for you?"

Baracoa smiled. "That is a clever question, Thomas. Yes, they might, but I believed only I knew which of them could be used."

"If Jayuya knew how to make curare he must have almost known how to obtain the ingredients," Thomas said. "You would recognise them if I took you to the palace garden?"

"Of course, but I know the gardens are large and heavily planted. What we looked for we might never find."

"If we do not look we never will find them. Never know if Jayuya killed Don Alejandro. Though it is the why that puzzles me more than the how." Thomas started to slide back from the ridge, then stopped. A band of riders appeared around the turn of the valley to the east. Ten men, with one individual in the lead. He was dressed in fine velvets beneath a leather jerkin, his horse a white stallion, his saddle of the finest leather. Thomas recognised the Infante Duarte, whom Isabel told him was once more in Sevilla to plead his case. Clearly, he had been sent away without an audience if he was now here. It told Thomas that this valley was indeed a major route to and from Portugal. One more fact that would interest Fernando. Thomas expected the Infante to ride past the traders, but he did not. He held a hand up and halted his men, then dismounted. He walked across and spoke to Jayuya.

"Who is that?" asked Baracoa.

"The man who wants to marry Catherine."

"Catherine who?"

"The daughter of the King and Queen. She is about to be pledged to the English prince, but that prancing fool is not to be discouraged."

"He knows Jayuya."

"It seems he does, which worries me. I took the lad for a weak fop, but I may have underestimated him. It is even more important I return to Sevilla and tell Fernando what is happening here." As he watched, Thomas saw the conversation between the Infante and Jayuya end. The Infante offered a hand and pulled Jayuya up behind him on his horse, turned and rode away.

"He is riding to join the Portuguese soldiers," Thomas said. "The traders might be heading to Mateo's estate, but the soldiers are not."

"The valley they ride through will take them to Sevilla," said Baracoa. "I will return with you. I can start searching in the garden, but if there is going to be a fight I want to kill Jayuya myself."

Thomas grinned. "You may need to get in line behind those of us who wish to do the same."

"I need to go to my holding and prepare myself," said Baracoa. "I will have Rosa bring me to you when I reach the city."

With that Baracoa sped away, his bare feet flying across the harsh ground.

Thomas waited until he was out of sight then turned and headed back towards Sevilla, hoping he could remember the way. The setting sun cast his shadow long ahead of him.

War was coming, but not tonight.

FORTY-TWO

Full dark had almost fallen as Thomas made his way into the palace, which was lit as if the cycle of day and night did not affect it. He asked the first guard he saw if he knew where King Fernando was. The man looked Thomas up and down, seeing someone dressed in dust-stained clothes that looked more suited to a desert than the city.

"Who is asking?"

"My name is Thomas Berrington, Duque of Granada, and I must speak with the King."

The guard took some time before Thomas's words sank in and he replied, "I would not know where the King is, sir, but I will take you to my captain, who may."

Thomas wondered who that might be now Diego Serrano was dead. No doubt there would be a hierarchy from which a suitable candidate could be chosen. The man, when the guard introduced him, did not impress him much. He was short and overweight, his leather jerkin open because he was incapable of closing it. His cheeks were florid from drinking. He sat behind a small desk in an office at the rear of the palace. He looked Thomas up and down without expression, then waved the guard away.

"I am–"

"I know who you are, Thomas Berrington."

"You are unfamiliar to me, sir," Thomas said.

"As it should be. My name is unimportant. What is it you want?"

"I need to see the King."

"Why?"

"That information is confidential. If you cannot accept that, then take me to Don Rodrigo Vargas."

"I believe he is with the King at the moment, but I still need to know what reason you have to also be there."

"War," Thomas said.

"There is no war."

"Not yet, but come morning there will be, and the King and Rodrigo both need to know of it."

"War with who?"

Thomas's patience had grown thin, and he held back his first response.

He took a breath before saying, "That is also none of your business. If you refuse to help, then I will find them myself. I am familiar with the palace. And when I do find them, I will be sure to tell them how helpful you have been."

The man smiled. "But you do not know my name."

"I have no need to. The guard told me you are the new captain. I am sure Don Rodrigo knows your name."

"It is–" The guard started to say, but Thomas had already gone.

He went first to the royal rooms, but no one there had

seen the King all day. The Queen was present, but dining and not to be disturbed. Thomas tried other rooms without success, then as he walked along the upper terrace, he glanced across at the gardens and saw a fire burning, two indistinct figures standing beside it. He ran down the steps and out along the path.

Hearing fast-approaching footsteps, Don Rodrigo drew his sword and placed himself in front of Fernando. When he saw who it was he sheathed the weapon and stepped aside.

"Why the rush, Thomas?" he asked.

Thomas bowed to the King before saying, "How many men can you gather, Your Grace? I have seen a small Portuguese army camped not three leagues from the city. I believe they will attack at dawn. Both Jayuya and the Infante Duarte are with them."

"How small an army?" asked Don Rodrigo.

"A hundred and twenty men."

Don Rodrigo glanced at Fernando. "Not so small, then. We have the palace guards and a small number of soldiers, Your Grace, but will be hard pressed to gather more than four score. A few more if we call on the men of the city, but that would leave it undefended." He looked at Thomas. "When do they plan to attack?"

"I am not privy to that information, but Baracoa believes they will reach Sevilla by dawn tomorrow. A surprise attack, almost certainly at the docks. This is not a war between countries, but a war for trade. They will burn any ships moored there and destroy whatever goods they can."

Fernando turned to Rodrigo. "We can find enough men to protect the docks, yes?"

"We can, Your Grace."

"Then do it. Let them waste their energy. They will need to cross the Triana bridge and we can hold them there."

"It would be a mistake to be defensive," Thomas said.

"And how many battles have you fought and won?" sneered Fernando. "Moorish ones only, I suspect, and I beat those heathens over a decade ago."

Thomas could remind Fernando of all the battles where the Moors had triumphed against the odds but considered it a waste of time. The man would not believe him. There was nothing so blind as the victorious.

"It would still be a mistake, Your Grace. Letting them reach as far as the Guadalquivir will only show the citizens of Sevilla how weak we are." In the flickering firelight, Thomas saw Fernando's expression turn stern, but Rodrigo spoke before the King could.

"Thomas may be right, Your Grace. And suppose we cannot hold them at Triana?" He turned to Thomas. "What do you suggest?"

"We gather as many men as we can and ride out in the night. They are camped in a steep-sided valley, not so wide that two or three score men could not halt their progress. Stop them and they will have no alternative but to fight and risk defeat or retreat back towards Portugal. There will be a full moon tonight, so we will see them well enough. Push them back. Kill them if we can as a lesson to others not to try again."

"We attack them?" said Fernando. "Do you intend to ride with us?"

"If you will allow me, Your Grace."

"But you have been injured."

Thomas swung his arm. "And am almost healed."

"It is a good plan," said Rodrigo.

"And bring the Kalinago men," Thomas said. "Baracoa told me they can join him and help."

"We cannot trust natives," said Fernando.

"They will bring another dozen to the fight, Your Grace. But if you think you can manage without them, so be it."

"When?" asked Rodrigo.

"Two hours after midnight," Thomas said. "The sun will not rise until seven, so it gives us time to reach their camp by moonlight and attack as soon as we are gathered."

Fernando once more looked at Rodrigo for advice, and he nodded.

"It is a good plan, Your Grace," said Rodrigo. "I will go to make arrangements. We will meet beyond the Triana bridge and move out from there." Rodrigo ran off without waiting for confirmation, leaving Thomas alone with the King.

"This could be a trap," said Fernando. "Are you sure the men you saw were Portuguese soldiers?"

Thomas grew impatient with Fernando's questions, as if the man did not trust him. "Have I not served you and the Queen well over many years, Your Grace?" What benefit would it bring me to mislead you now? You know all I want is the best for Catherine. And what is best for her is a betrothal to Harry."

"Harry?"

"Sorry, Prince Henry, Your Grace."

"Yet you call him Harry, as I know you also call my daughter Cat on occasion, as do your children. Isabel is too soft on you. I would not allow it."

"Then I will stop doing so, Your Grace."

"If I believed that I would say yes to you, but I know you better after all this time. You are often a thorn in my side but have also shown you can be useful. But try, Thomas, like other men do. Now, I go to help Rodrigo gather our men. I suggest you prepare yourself. You talked of taking some of the natives with us, so that can be your responsibility. You know where they live in the palace. Go recruit them." Fernando smiled. "And tonight, we give Portugal a black eye for their temerity in threatening Spain." He clapped Thomas on the shoulder and strode off.

Thomas stared into the dying embers of their fire. He kicked at them and watched as sparks swirled into the sky before winking out one by one. As men fighting in battle could wink out one by one. He had fought in many battles, but only a few times had he come close to death. Once when he had little more than seventeen years and would have died if not for an old Moorish physician who lived high in the Pyrenees and saved him. Not only saved him but gave a letter of introduction to the Infirmaries in Malaga. A letter that changed Thomas's life forever and brought him to where he now stood.

He turned away to find the Kalinago and ask if they were willing to join the fight. If he told them it was Baracoa's idea, he believed they might. And then he knew he must tell Jorge what he was about to do. If he failed to return, Jorge could tell his children their father died bravely, if foolishly.

FORTY-THREE

Thomas returned to their lodgings to find Jorge once more sitting in the dark looking through the window at the cathedral square, which on this occasion was almost empty. He told him what he intended to do and saw it came as no surprise to Jorge. It was what Thomas did.

"I want to come," said Jorge.

"There will be hard fighting, and I will have no time to protect you."

"What if I want to come to protect you?"

Thomas considered the question required no answer.

"If you refuse me," said Jorge, "I will follow anyway."

Thomas sighed. "In that case, stay well back. I do not know if the Portuguese fight well or not, but safest to assume they can. You are not skilled enough."

Thomas saw he had hurt Jorge's feelings, but better that than hurt his body.

"I am going to sleep until midnight. Try not to disturb me."

Thomas left Jorge to his watching and lay on his bed.

Sleep came, but it was short and unsettled. When he rose, the bell on the cathedral was sounding twelve and he dressed for battle, strapped a sword at his waist, and slid knives into his belt and boots. He was about to leave when he stopped and took the tagelmust which hung from a nail and wrapped it expertly around his head and neck. He tiptoed to where Jorge had taken a cot in the other room. He peeked inside to see him fast asleep. Good.

Outside, he made his way to the palace training ground where he found at least three score men. Torches around the walls cast flickering yellow light across the gathering. The Kalinago, both males and females, stood to one side with Baracoa, who was passing out lengths of bamboo and small pouches. When Thomas went across, he discovered the pouches contained a small amount of curare mixed by Baracoa.

"Do they know how to use it?"

"They are Kalinago, so they do."

"Even the women?"

"Yes. Even the women."

"What if a band of men comes at you with swords and knives?"

"We will not be seen, Thomas, but close enough to help. Now go join the others. I see the King looking this way. No doubt he wonders why you are speaking with us rather than him. Go bend your knee. I will keep a watch on you when the fighting starts."

Thomas turned away. Fernando greeted him warmly and slapped his shoulder, making him wince.

"There are horses on the far side of the river," said

Fernando. "We cross the bridge then mount. You will need to lead the way for you know where this army is gathered."

"I may need the help of Baracoa to do that in the dark."

Fernando glanced across the square. "What is he doing over there?"

"Arming the Kalinago."

"We do not need women with us and cannot protect them."

"Baracoa tells me the women are equally skilled and that none of them will be seen. Where is Don Rodrigo? I expected him at your side."

"He is recruiting more men to bring after us. Some of those in the city have volunteered to join us and he is gathering them together, telling those who have their own horses to bring them. He will supply weapons from our armoury. We are well stocked, so it is not a problem. They will not fight as well as soldiers, but will make our number larger."

"Does the Queen know what we do?" Thomas asked.

"I have not told her. Time enough to do so when we return victorious. She worries too much that I am not as strong as I once was, but she is wrong. I am as hale as I have always been. Like you, it seems."

"I feel my years these days," Thomas said.

"I do not." Fernando turned away and began to issue orders.

Thomas returned to Baracoa and said he wanted him to guide them to where the Portuguese waited. He could share Thomas's horse, or have one of his own if he preferred.

"I will walk," said Baracoa. "We have time to reach them without rushing, and I trust my own two feet rather than the four hoofs of a horse." He glanced at the sky, but the guttering torchlight hid the stars and there was no sign of the moon yet.

Thomas knew what Baracoa was looking for and said, "The moon will rise soon, and is almost full. It will be at our back, so we need to be careful not to be seen, but it will guide our way."

Baracoa nodded. "I will meet you on the crest of the first hill to guide you, but will leave again once you know your way. Do not be concerned. You will not see us, but we will be there."

An hour later, Thomas crossed the Triana bridge in the company of an array of soldiers, citizens, and some who appeared to be there because they enjoyed a fight, whether it was theirs or not. In waste ground on the far side of the river many horses stood about, some fine, others sad and old. Thomas pushed through and picked the best he could, knowing he would not need to ride for hours. The moon rose, as promised. The sky above them was free of cloud, though in the west dark thunderheads towered. The wind blew from that direction, and it carried the smell of coming rain. Thomas rode on the edge of the others, trying to avoid the stink of their unwashed bodies and the horses, though the horses were the least of it. He only slowly became aware of a presence at his side. He turned his head, half expecting to see Jorge, but found the King.

"Have you seen Don Rodrigo?" asked Fernando.

"I have not, but he could be among the throng."

"I sent men to look, and they tell me he is not. He said he was going to follow and not to expect him until we came closer to our enemy. I would prefer he was with us now so we could discuss tactics."

Thomas rode on for a moment, thinking.

"How will he know which way to come?" he eventually asked. He realised he had neglected to add 'Your Grace' but supposed it would not matter overly much this night.

"I assume by following our trail. Even a blind man could track our passage, and Don Rodrigo is a skilled fighter."

"Have you witnessed him in battle?" Thomas asked.

"He has not been at court long enough and the last year has been uncommonly quiet. I suspect the Portuguese have been planning this for some time, and the French seem to have lost the balls for a fight. It does not surprise me."

"And Naples?" Thomas asked, knowing it was where Fernando had fought some of his most arduous battles.

"Has also been well behaved. It is as if the world is changing from a time of swords to a time of words." Fernando smiled at his turn of phrase, no doubt considering it clever.

"Perhaps it is because Spain is seen as master of the world now," Thomas said. "The wealth brought here from the new world is immense. Other countries are afraid of you."

"Is England afraid of Spain, Thomas?"

"England is too distant to be concerned, other than the pressing matter of your daughter's betrothal to Prince Harry."

"Isabel told me she asked about him and you told her he will make a good husband, like the brother who died. Is that so?"

"Harry is headstrong, handsome, and popular with the ladies of the court."

"How popular? Catherine cannot marry tainted goods."

"He flirts, nothing more." Thomas lied, knowing full well that, young as he was, Harry had tasted the forbidden fruit arrayed around him more than once.

"That will have to stop when they marry," said Fernando.

"So they will marry, Your Grace?"

"Yes, they will marry."

"Can I tell King Henry that?"

Fernando laughed. "Of course not. We must make him squirm a while longer yet to see what else we can squeeze from him." Fernando was clearly in a good mood, and Thomas wondered if it was the thought of the coming fight. Life had been uncommonly quiet, he had said. He probably meant uncommonly boring.

"You are unlikely to get any more out of Henry, Your Grace. It is well known how careful he is with the wealth of his country. It should not matter once our two great countries are united. Wealth will flow freely in both directions."

"Now you are speaking my language." Fernando turned in his saddle to study him. "Do you know what Isabel and I think of you?"

Thomas smiled. "I am not sure I want to."

"I will tell you anyway, so you may know it in case you should die tonight. We both think you are a clever, subtle man who is capable of rising to great heights in whatever you do, if only you want it. And your main failing is you do not want it."

"Why would I, Your Grace?"

"See? That is what you always say. You are a mystery to everyone. I take it you can still fight?"

"I hope so," Thomas said, realising he meant it.

As they crossed a low ridge, a shadowy figure ran towards them. Fernando reached for his sword, but Thomas raised a hand.

"It is only Baracoa, come to lead us to the Portuguese. I will ride ahead of your men to show them the way."

"If you see Don Rodrigo, send him to me," said Fernando.

Thomas nodded to Baracoa, who sprinted ahead, and he followed. The moon cast their shadows across the pale ground ahead, where death or victory awaited.

FORTY-FOUR

Thomas knelt on the edge of the drop into the valley, King Fernando beside him. They spoke in whispers, even though those below would not hear them. Baracoa had left Thomas an hour earlier and he had not seen the man, or the other Kalinago, since. A westerly wind had picked up, driving dark clouds overhead, their bellies dropping rain onto distant hills.

"They are close to two hundred," said Fernando. "You said little more than half that."

"Which they were when I was last here," Thomas said. "More must have arrived since."

"They mean business. We could do with Rodrigo and the men he promised."

"We have the Kalinago," Thomas said. "There are fourteen or fifteen of them."

Fernando made a sound through his nose. "Fifteen will make no difference."

"We do not know that Your Grace. I trust them."

"I am glad one of us does." Fernando looked back to

where his men waited on the far side of the slope, ready to descend to the mouth of the valley. "I wish we had that giant Northman friend of yours with us, but he remains in Granada with the main body of my soldiers."

"Olaf is still in Spain?" The news surprised Thomas. "I would like to visit him before I return to England."

"It is your time to waste. He is not here, so we will have to make do. Rodrigo could be bringing a hundred or more men, but it looks as if we will have to start without him. What do you think, Thomas – a direct assault?"

"Is one option."

"Do you have a better one?"

"The ridge we are on leads to a side valley. Half of us could descend there and come at them from the rear. Take them by surprise. When Don Rodrigo arrives, he can attack from the front to distract them. He will read the fight and know what to do."

"Then show me this place, so we can come on them with surprise."

Thomas led the way, which was not far, to a narrow valley that cut through the hillside, its waters raging white to join the river in the main valley.

"It is a hard descent," Fernando said.

"But possible, yes?"

"Yes, and I like it. We will take a score or more of them before they even know we are there. I like the idea of splitting our forces. When they turn to meet us, the others wait then come at them from the other direction."

"It does mean less in each group, of course," Thomas said, "but it is a good plan."

"Then let us carry it out. Already the eastern sky shows signs of the coming morn."

Thomas smiled. "And the western sky promises a storm. There will be heavy rain, which we can use to our advantage. The men will be inside whatever shelter they have so will not see our approach." He got to his feet and turned back. Fernando fell in beside him.

"I have still not seen any Kalinago," he said.

"You will not, but I guarantee they are here and will prove lethal."

"Poison darts," sneered Fernando. "It is not how a true soldier fights."

Thomas said nothing. He only hoped his faith in Baracoa and the others was rewarded.

They split their forces, and Fernando put the captain of the guard in command of those who would remain at the mouth of the valley, while he led forty men along the far side of the ridge. The ground was too steep and difficult for horses, so they left them behind, with two men to watch over them. The attack from the west would be on foot. And wet.

The first skeins of rain hit them as they descended the rocky slope. It came and went, and then arrived with full force, soaking every man. Descending, Thomas wondered if the rain would affect Baracoa's poison darts, then dismissed the thought. He would have enough troubles of his own to worry about.

As the slope lessened, he followed Fernando and a small group of his best men to where the torrent they had followed met the larger river. They turned east. Ahead of them, an array of tents, horses and carts. Of watchmen,

Thomas saw none. He suspected they were taking shelter as the rain grew ever more fierce, slashing across his face so he had to narrow his eyes. The fighting would be difficult, but when it might start was another matter. Fernando and his men approached the first of the tents, and the King pointed left and right. Soldiers slipped close to the tents then struck when commanded. The cries of those inside alerted others and the Portuguese poured from their tents and formed up, still strapping weapons to themselves, some lacking helmets or leather jerkins.

"Follow me!" Thomas yelled, knowing these first moments would be the most telling. He did not check to see how many came with him, trusting Fernando would not hold back. As Thomas met the first body of resistance his sword flashed left and right. Men fell back, and all at once he found himself behind the line of the Portuguese. Fifty paces ahead, he saw the other Spanish troops attacking. They were making harder work of it, and Thomas suspected the more seasoned Portuguese troops had been stationed there where, if an attack came, it would be expected from that direction.

Thomas turned and attacked men from behind, though by now there was no front or back, only a melee. Fortunately, all the Spanish wore red leather jerkins so could be picked out even in the dark. A faint light from the moon remained but would soon be covered by the approaching storm. Fires and torches cast guttering red light across the ground but it did not carry far. Thomas deflected a wicked blow from his left before running his attacker through. It had been some time since he fought, but was relieved to discover the cold had already filled him and his mind stilled. His damaged arm might hurt but he did not feel it. There was no thought, only reaction, and he trusted his body to do what he knew it could, and survive.

At one point, he found himself back-to-back with Fernando as they held off a group of a dozen men who had recognised the King and brought others to attack him. The rest of Fernando's men had moved on, finishing off stragglers, corralling prisoners, while the other battle continued. Soon there would be no opposition at the rear and they could attack from behind. If Fernando lived.

Thomas recognised the man's skill, which had been honed over a lifetime of battle, both in Spain and beyond its borders. He had not seen Fernando fight at close quarters before. He assumed, as King, he might have relied on his troops around him to do the bulk of the fighting, but the man was skilled. Almost as skilled as Thomas's friend Usaden. As skilled as Thomas had once been, and perhaps still was, for he remained alive. Which almost came as a surprise.

The dozen men were reduced to eight, and then five, who dropped their weapons and put their hands above their heads. Fernando grinned wildly, his face and arms blood-streaked, his sword dripping red. He called out to a group of his men to take the surrendered to join the others, then clapped Thomas on the shoulder and hugged him tight.

"By damn, but you can fight. I enjoyed that." He released Thomas and went to the prisoners. "Where is the Infante Duarte?"

No one replied, so Fernando drew his sword and threatened to run the first man through. It worked without needing to draw blood.

"He was here, sire, but left last night."

"Left for where?"

"He does not tell the likes of us. He went east, towards the city."

"Did he have men with him?"

"A score, sire. If he had stayed, and his men with him, this battle would have turned out differently."

Fernando laughed. "I should run you through for such impertinence, but I feel magnanimous in victory."

He turned away from the men and returned to Thomas.

"We had best join the others while there is still a fight to be had."

They stalked forward through the sheeting rain. As they did so, Thomas saw one of the Portuguese slap at his neck, stagger to one side and fall on his face. His legs moved, then fell still. Thomas searched for the Kalinago but could not see them. Another man fell, and he glimpsed one of the women duck behind a rock after using her bamboo weapon to spit a dart. *So*, he thought, *the rain does not affect the poison*.

When only thirty of the enemy remained, Fernando called a halt to the fighting. This remnant of men would live to become captives, pawns in a game of diplomacy, their return offered in exchange for silver and gold. Portugal had a great deal of both, as did Spain, from their explorations further south than the islands Columb had discovered. Thomas had heard rumours of strange lands there. Of tall pyramids and people who practiced blood sacrifice. Of a land dense with trees where half the animals could kill you. It was not a land those who went there were familiar with and many died, of disease, of snakes, at the hands of those whose land it was. Yet still they went, drawn by the promise of great wealth, and slaves.

Baracoa and the other Kalinago came into the open, to be congratulated by Fernando, but they stayed only a short while before disappearing once more.

The rain still fell, though not as hard. Even so, every man was soaked to the bone. Thomas's boots squelched as he walked, and his hair hung lank across his face.

Fernando set men to shackle and corral the captives, and they started back to the horses. The Portuguese could not be allowed to ride, so Fernando called Thomas and a few men to him, and they rode ahead. The King wanted to return to Sevilla in case there was a counterattack or unrest. It worried him that the Infante Duarte had already gone that way. They travelled as fast as conditions allowed, a few dozen men riding through the night. Until they met unexpected resistance. Led by a traitor.

FORTY-FIVE

By the time they had covered half the distance to Sevilla the sky was lightening ahead and the rain passing through. Progress had been slow, which angered the King. It seemed to Thomas it took little to anger Fernando these days. The Portuguese prisoners strained his patience with their mulish behaviour. Nothing came easily. At one point the King's temper flared and he had three of them brought in front of the others. Only one needed to be run through to change the minds of the rest.

There had been no sign of the Kalinago, but Thomas did not expect to see them.

The shoulders of the valley eased and widened. Soon they would see the Guadalquivir, and after that the city itself. A battle won. Prisoners taken. The prospect of more riches for the royal coffers.

When a band of men appeared on their left, Thomas was unconcerned. They were on horseback, but only twenty in number. None were in uniform, but the figure at their head was dressed resplendently. Thomas recognised the Infante Duarte. His horse wore a shining silver head-dress which matched that worn by its rider.

"Come on then, attack us," hissed Fernando at Thomas's side. "I want to run the little bastard through myself."

"He is not clever," Thomas said, "but I doubt him stupid enough to attack a larger force unless our prisoners turn and join him."

Fernando cursed. "I knew it was a mistake not to kill them all, but Isabel tells me I am too harsh a general. All the same, if they do turn it will be a bloodbath. They have less than a quarter of our men. We ride on." Fernando kicked his horse's flanks.

Thomas held back, scanning the slopes to either side. The Infante's men remained where they were. If they did not intend to attack, why had they even come? Did they expect the result of the battle to be different? Had they come to witness a great Portuguese victory with Fernando's head raised on a pike? One the Infante might claim as his own? Now all they did was sit and watch. Thomas itched to ride up to them and demand to know what they were doing, but twenty poorly trained men might prove too much for him alone, so he kept watch as he followed the King.

Fernando slowed, looked back at Thomas, and pointed to their right. A larger force appeared over the slope of the hill. Thirty men. Thomas recognised Mateo at their head, as well as some of those he had seen at the man's estate. He must have recruited mercenaries because he had not had thirty men before. The Infante had also seen them and started to lead his band down the slope.

"Thomas, take a third of our force and hold off the idiot boy," shouted Fernando. "I will take care of the other interlopers."

"It is Mateo," Thomas said.

"I know who it is, and the time has long passed to deal with that man with steel. Now go. I do not want to be worried about my back."

With that, Fernando called his men into a square, the prisoners encased within so any attacker that broke through would almost certainly kill some of their own.

Thomas pulled his mount around and called a smaller number of men to him. Ten only, but it would be enough.

The Infante descended carefully, picking his way over rocks and gulleys. As he drew close the expression of disdain for those he saw creased his face. The man did not even have twenty years but acted as if he was a general of great renown. How the boy thought he could win Catherine of Aragon's hand was a mystery to Thomas. He kicked his horse into a canter and drew his sword. As he approached, he saw a group of Kalinago run from hiding and cross the valley. They climbed the far side, more than half their number with Baracoa in the lead, going to Fernando's aid. It was the right move.

At their head, three female Kalinago used their darts on the descending Portuguese and men fell. Four in total, then as others rode at them they disappeared as if they had never been.

The two forces met, steel on steel. Blood sprayed. Once

more, Thomas's mind stilled and his body grew calm. He had no need to think because he could fight without thought. His body knew what to do and he trusted it.

The fighting went well, and as the number of Portuguese lessened Thomas called a halt. The Infante Duarte sat astride his horse, but his arrogance had melted away. Eight of his men remained alive, and Thomas had their hands tied before he rode up to the Infante and stared into his eyes.

The boy looked away, as well he might. Thomas's expression was stern, his face blood-streaked.

"You do not deserve Catherine," Thomas said. "You deserve nothing but death, but I will not offer you that gift." He looked across to the hills. "Tuck your gilded tail between your legs and scurry back to Portugal. Tell them that all your men were defeated, and if more are sent they will also be defeated. If you ever return to Spain you will die, slowly and in great pain." Thomas slapped the rump of the Infante's horse with the flat of his sword and, whether the boy wanted to leave or not the beast reared and galloped away along the valley floor.

When Thomas turned to see how Fernando was faring his heart sank. Not because Mateo's men were victorious, but because a new force rode into the mouth of the valley. Sixty men this time. A larger force than Fernando had, even when the exhausted remnant with Thomas were added to their number. Thomas saw this had all been planned. Pick away at the Spanish little by little, all the while bringing in more forces as their men tired.

The two groups faced each other along the valley floor. Thomas knew Fernando's men would be as exhausted as his own. Their prisoners recognised this and a few dashed for freedom. Not all made it, but the diversion allowed others to escape.

"Let them run," shouted Fernando. "We will kill them again soon enough." He turned to Thomas. "Take the left flank, I will work the right. Try a pincer movement and pick off enough for a frontal assault."

For a moment, Thomas believed the forces arrayed against them would not attack, but they had only been judging their enemy. Their ranks parted and Don Rodrigo Vargas rode through. His face was without expression as his eyes scanned their number. Thomas's mind went dull with shock. He could barely believe Rodrigo's treachery. The man had fooled them all. Thomas most of all. He had liked Rodrigo. Respected him. Damn, but he had been clever. Too clever for Thomas.

"Traitor," hissed Fernando, then louder in a shout, *"Traitor!"*

Don Rodrigo smiled but made no response other than to wave his men forwards.

It would have been a rout if not for the Kalinago. Don Rodrigo's soldiers dismissed their threat, which was foolhardy. Baracoa sprinted close, used a dart and withdrew to be replaced by another. Fernando attacked hard, driving men back, making them part as he rode among them, a sword in each hand flashing to bring death. Thomas matched him on the left flank, a wild madman with eyes of ice, filled with anger at the betrayal. His sword slashed, stabbed, opened necks, chests and bellies. He lost track of time and place. All he saw were enemies, which grew slowly less. He came face to face with Mateo and swung at him, opening his neck. Anger flared through his calm for a moment. The man had wanted more than riches. He sought power. And now he lay on the ground with his lifeblood draining into the tainted water of the river.

Thomas looked around, searching for Don Rodrigo. How long had the man been planning this betrayal? And why? Had he ordered Don Alejandro killed so he could take his place? It made no sense, because the man had been old and sick. Don Rodrigo would inherit the position before the year was out. Thomas wanted to face him and ask why, but he could not see him. He pushed through the attackers, who moved back to allow him to pass. They had seen how he fought and feared the demon dressed like a Moor.

Don Rodrigo was nowhere to be found.

Thomas rode to join Fernando, who was organising his remaining men to gather the prisoners. The fight was over. All courage had drained from their attackers.

"I cannot see Don Rodrigo," Thomas said.

"He was over there a moment ago. I thought you had taken his head."

"He is gone now."

"Fled to save his own cowardly life." Fernando spat on the ground. "There was always something wrong with the man, but Isabel liked him well enough. Just as she likes you." Fernando shook his head at the notion of such a thing.

"How many men did you leave to protect the palace?" Thomas asked.

"A dozen, it was all I could spare. Why?"

But Thomas made no reply. Instead, he urged his horse

into a gallop and flew along the ground. He knew where Don Rodrigo was going, and why.

King Fernando was meant to have been defeated. No doubt his life would have been taken. Leaving only the Queen. A frail woman. Unprotected.

Thomas urged his horse into more speed, leaving the King and his men behind.

FORTY-SIX

As Thomas rode from the valley a lone figure stood on the riverbank, and he pulled back so his horse came skidding to a halt.

"Where are you going in such a hurry?" asked Baracoa.

"Don Rodrigo has ridden back to Sevilla. I fear Isabel is in danger. I ride to offer her protection."

Baracoa nodded and offered his hand. Thomas took it and pulled him up onto the rump of the horse. Baracoa wrapped his arms around Thomas's waist.

"Now ride." His voice was soft. "The Queen has been good to my people. I would see her live."

Thomas urged his horse into a canter, and then a gallop. Without seeming to hold tight, Baracoa sat comfortably behind him. They skirted Mateo's estate because it was the quickest way to Sevilla and there would be no one there now to bother them. Even so, as they passed, Thomas saw the tall brute of the man he had fought, but no others. Mateo must have taken all other men. The women remained. Ten or eleven stood on the terrace, watching as they passed. The big man raised a hand, but Thomas was too busy to respond, though he did wonder what would happen to them now Mateo was dead.

"Did you see what happened back there?" Thomas asked as he eased his horse into the river. It swam, the water rising to their thighs.

"If you mean Don Rodrigo then yes, I did," said Baracoa. "It is a shame. He was always respectful of our people. I liked the man."

"So did I, but no longer. I wonder how long he has harboured this evil?"

"It explains why he did not die when Jayuya darted him," said Baracoa. "They must have worked together and less curare was used on him. Or perhaps none at all. It is possible to fake the symptoms."

"He would know you would cut him."

"Some men do not mind the pain in search of something bigger."

"He cannot believe he could ascend to the throne," Thomas said. "He must be working for someone else. Someone with a claim. Such as..." He hesitated. The answer was obvious, but ridiculous.

"The Portuguese boy," said Baracoa, and Thomas thought of how he had let him ride away to freedom.

They emerged from the river sheeting water and started to climb the final slope. Soon they would reach Sevilla and, he hoped, be in time.

"He is young, but it makes no sense for it to be anyone else."

"The people would not accept him," said Baracoa.

Thomas knew it was a statement only someone unfamiliar with the ways of royal marriages would make. Catherine was in no position to choose. Thomas doubted King Henry had even consulted her regarding her future. She was a woman, little more than a girl, and would do as she was told. Her life ceased to be her own the day she came into the world. The day Thomas saw her for the first time, and on many days since. There were times it felt as if she belonged more to his family than her own, but those days were long past. He had seen Catherine perform her duty, and perform it well. She would do whatever was demanded of her. *That* was the way of royal marriage.

Thomas did not think the Infante Duarte would recognise such rules, if he even knew what they were. That the boy could hold any hope of the marriage seemed impossible. Yet if Don Rodrigo pled his case, was it? Royal marriages were not like others. There was nothing of love in them. Would joining the two new powers trading with the new world be such a bad idea? Perhaps not. Except whatever plans had been laid now lay trodden into the mud of the valleys behind. Unless Don Rodrigo meant for neither the King nor Queen to survive this day.

Thomas urged his horse into a faster canter as they descended to the river and the Triana bridge. Beyond it, the palace lay pristine, washed by the rain that had fallen then moved on. Early morning sunlight shimmered along the stonework and roofs.

Thomas abandoned his horse beyond the palace gate. They were admitted at once after Thomas enquired whether Don Rodrigo Vargas had been seen.

"He entered not half an hour since," said the guard. "He appeared to be in a hurry. I expect he had news of the King's victory, yes?"

"I expect he did," Thomas said, wondering if he spoke the truth.

They stayed together as they walked the corridors, for to split up might have them find Don Rodrigo sooner, but better they were both there to deal with him. They started on the second floor because that was where Thomas had seen the Queen more than anywhere else, and Baracoa confirmed the same.

"How long since you lived within these walls?" Thomas asked. The palace was unusually quiet, and they saw only a few servants as they moved through the chambers.

"Many years. I stayed two when I first arrived, then left."

"That was when the Queen gave you your freedom? Was it offered to any of the other Kalinago?"

"I was the only one she offered her gift to. I might have asked about them, but I have no need of company. In truth, I prefer to be alone."

"Yet Rosa is close to you."

"She is. But she has no hold over me, as I have no hold over her. You must have known the same, yes?"

Thomas thought back over his relationships. There had been one, once. He had lain with women before and since, and hoped he might again, but none that touched his heart as Lubna had. He felt responsibility for Luisa's death, and wondered yet again if he had been the cause of it.

"You lost someone close to you," said Baracoa.

"Yes." Thomas felt no need to add more, and Baracoa did not pursue the question.

They finished on the second floor without sign of either Isabel or Don Rodrigo. They asked those servants they passed, but they had not seen either of them.

"Where else would Isabel go?" Thomas asked, not sure if he was asking the right person or not.

"She used to like the gardens at this time of day, before it gets too hot. There is a place I have seen her in before. It catches the morning light, and the plants there are beautiful. They will be even more so for the rain that passed. We can try there."

Descending the steps the way they had come, Baracoa led them through a maze of corridors Thomas knew he would be unable to follow without the man. They reached the small enclave where the Kalinago lived. Five women had returned, and Thomas recognised Yariel and Anacoana. Baracoa went to them for a moment, speaking in their own language. When he returned, he said, "I have asked them to follow us but keep out of sight. If we are attacked and about to be defeated, they are to fetch the guards."

"Why not fetch them now?" Thomas asked.

"We have not found Don Rodrigo yet." Baracoa seemed to think it answer enough, and Thomas supposed it was. When he looked back there was no sign of the women, but he knew they would be there, just as they had on the hillside.

A man appeared from a path, but it was a gardener, not who they sought.

"We are looking for Don Rodrigo," Thomas said.

"Then you are in luck, sir. I saw him with the Queen not long since. Don Rodrigo wanted to show her some of the recent plants from the new world. A few are coming into full flower, and mighty strange they are too."

"I know where his garden is," Thomas said, starting forward.

"The one by the gate tower?" said the gardener.

Thomas frowned. "He has two?" Then, "Where?"

The gardener seemed surprised at his brusqueness but pointed to their left. "Take this path, turn right at the wall and you should find them easily enough. Unless they have moved on. There are–"

But Thomas did not hear what else the man intended to say because he and Baracoa had moved off, not running yet, but almost.

They reached the high wall and turned right.

Soon they saw a clearing ahead and slowed, but when they entered the space it was empty. The flowers were indeed both impressive and strange, but not what Thomas sought. And then he heard Isabel's voice.

"I have no idea what you are trying to do, Rodrigo, but you will lose your head for this."

The man laughed, the sound clear. "It is not me who will lose their head."

"You cannot speak to me this way!" said Isabel, her voice filled with the power she held in her slight body.

"I will speak to you however I wish. You do not impress me. You and Fernando have failed Spain. Failed Iberia. My master will correct that when you are both dead."

"Who?" asked Isabel.

Thomas moved closer. He glimpsed Rodrigo with his back to them. Beyond him, Isabel stood on a narrow ledge twenty feet above the garden, her back pressed to the stone of a tower that rose ten feet above her. The ledge was barely wide enough for her small feet to hold her there. To her right lay a narrow opening, which is how she must have been forced to her current position. A noose was tight around her neck. The other end of the rope was tied to a metal spike set into the tower. Any slight movement and she would lose balance and fall. There was enough slack in the rope for it not to tighten until she almost reached the ground. Almost, but not quite. The fall would snap her neck. A second, thinner rope was tied around her waist where it also wrapped around her wrists. Don Rodrigo held the other end. He jerked it and Isabel teetered, then leaned back, but her toes were over the lip of the ledge now.

Thomas drew his sword.

Baracoa had no weapon, not even his pipe to send a dart into Don Rodrigo's neck.

"Catch her," Thomas whispered.

Baracoa shook his head and held out his hand. He nodded at the sword.

"Do you know how?" Thomas asked, barely a sound at all.

"I have seen one used." Baracoa's reply was even softer.

Thomas knew it made sense but was reluctant to hand over his weapon. Except he knew, strong as Baracoa was, he was slighter than himself and would struggle to catch Isabel if she fell. He accepted the change in their roles and turned his sword to offer the hilt to Baracoa.

"Make it fast," he said, not waiting for a reply.

He stepped to one side, looking up, judging the distance, judging where Don Rodrigo stood. He knew if Baracoa failed, Rodrigo would send Isabel to her death and still have time to attack Thomas. There was one chance only, and its moment was now.

Thomas ran, glimpsing Baracoa doing the same. And then, beyond him, Yariel appeared with a length of bamboo to her lips.

Don Rodrigo sensed, then saw them. He pulled hard at the rope he held, and Isabel swayed forwards, backwards, then lost her footing and fell. Thomas was six feet away and knew it was too far. Except he had no choice. He flung his body forward, twisting as he did so. He grasped Isabel around the waist as the noose tightened at her neck. She would have cried out if she could have found breath to do so.

Thomas lifted the Queen, barely any weight at all. He managed to raise her by an inch, and then another. He had no idea what Don Rodrigo was doing, whether Baracoa had run him through or Yariel had let fly her poisoned dart. If they had failed, Thomas expected to feel the agony of a knife in his side, but there was nothing he could do but act as he did. He lifted Isabel again. Against all protocol he forced an arm beneath her while he reached for a knife. He found it and cut the rope.

He lowered the Queen to the ground, where she stood rubbing her neck.

"Again, Thomas? You have saved me yet again? It is becoming a habit I am starting to admire in you even as I wish it were not so."

Thomas laughed and turned to find Don Rodrigo still

on his feet, with Baracoa on the ground, blood spreading from a wound in his chest. A great deal of blood.

Rodrigo grinned, then laughed. He went to one knee, took the sword from Baracoa's limp hand and came at Thomas.

He pushed Isabel behind him, judging where Rodrigo would strike, working out his response. Rodrigo was almost on him when Thomas saw Anacoana rush at him, but too late and she fell on her side from a fearsome blow with the hilt of the sword. Rodrigo ignored her, all his attention on Thomas, who raised an arm, knowing as he did so it was foolish for a strong enough strike would take it off. Except the strike did not come. Baracoa, despite his injury, had found a rusted hand scythe left by Rodrigo, for Thomas knew now this was his hidden garden where he grew the plants needed to make curare.

Thomas sprinted across the ground and threw himself at Rodrigo, but managed only to trip him so he fell on his face, the sword twisting away. Baracoa lunged and the blade of the hand scythe went through Rodrigo's boot, through his foot. Pinned for a moment, it offered Thomas the chance to grab the sword, but Rodrigo hit him hard on the side of his head and his senses spun. He rolled over, expecting another blow, but instead Rodrigo pulled the scythe free and ran off, limping as he went.

Thomas rose and went to Baracoa. He pulled at his loose clothing to reveal a deep wound which, while bleeding, had missed his heart or any vital organ. Thomas ripped Baracoa's clothing and wadded it, then pushed hard against the wound to stem the blood.

He glanced up. "Get someone here now. I can save

him." He spoke to either of the women, but it was Isabel that ran off while Anacoana, a livid bruise covering one side of her face, knelt beside Baracoa. She kissed his face.

"He will not die," Thomas said.

"If he should," said Anacoana, "in the afterlife he will remember the touch of my lips."

FORTY-SEVEN

Thomas ripped Baracoa's single item of clothing into strips. He padded some, then wrapped the rest around the man's chest. When he looked up Anacoana and Yariel were staring at him.

"Go fetch me water, and needle and thread."

He expected them to object, but they turned and ran off, slim and lithe, light on their feet, and he wondered for a moment what their lives had been like before they were brought across the sea. In their own lands they might have been people of importance. Or more likely ordinary but living their own lives in their own place. Here, they were chattels.

He sat on his heels and watched as blood seeped through the makeshift bandage and feared Baracoa would die. He had forgotten about Isabel, so was surprised when she knelt beside him and took Baracoa's hand in hers.

"Will he live?"

Before Thomas could reply, Baracoa said, "I am hard to kill, Queen. Thomas and Rosa will repair me."

Thomas wished he felt as confident as Baracoa, but knew the suggestion of seeking Rosa's help was sound. He considered lifting Baracoa and carrying him to her shop but knew he must wait and do what he could first.

None of them spoke.

Baracoa's chest rose and fell, and after a while he closed his eyes.

Thomas reached out, but there was still a pulse in his neck.

"How long has Rodrigo been a member of the palace?" he asked Isabel.

She took a moment to answer before saying, "He came to the palace eight or nine years ago. He was a young man then and had a letter of introduction from my uncle. He proved himself useful, and clever. It was Fernando who liked him at first, but he was also popular with the ladies of the court. He is most handsome and possesses a silver tongue." She offered a small smile. "Unlike you, my Thomas. But you have other attributes I approve of even more."

"I am glad to hear it. You had no doubts about him?"

"None at all. His position as Don Alejandro's replacement was about to be made permanent." She looked into Thomas's eyes. "Why did he act as he did? He would have attained one of the highest positions in the land and grown rich beyond the dreams of most men."

"He wanted more, Isabel. He wanted to stand beside a new king and his new bride. Did he not say anything to you when he held you captive?"

"He spoke only words I cannot repeat. His hatred was a

writhing snake within him. Why did he hate us so much, Thomas?"

"I suspect it was Spain he hated, though I expect that included both of you because you and Fernando represent Spain. He wanted the Infante Duarte to marry Catherine and unite Spain and Portugal. Together they would become the most powerful country in the world and control both this and the new one."

"The Infante is a boy. He has enough years, but is still a boy and acts like one. Catherine would not have him. And we would not allow the marriage."

"You would have had no say because Rodrigo would have killed you both. It is likely the crown would pass to your daughter, who is married to the Portuguese king."

"Then he has failed. And when we capture them, both will lose their heads. Fernando will see to it. I have given a daughter to the Portuguese crown, but this is too much. If King Manuel had any hand in this then it will be war."

Isabel opened her mouth to speak, but before she could Yariel and Anacoana came running. They went to their knees, four of them now around the dying man, except Thomas had saved dying men before and had no intention of giving up on this one.

He wetted a cloth in the bowl of water Yariel had brought. Then he peeled away the temporary binding and washed the wound. It continued to bleed, and he knew whatever he did now would be a battlefield repair. Still, it had to be done. He took the needle and thread and did he could. Baracoa's eyes opened, but he made no sound even though the work must be agony.

When he was finished Thomas asked for more bandages, but the two women removed their own clothing and handed it to him before walking away hand in hand.

"They are most enchanting, are they not?" said Isabel, and Thomas laughed but said nothing as he rebound Baracoa's wound. When he was done, he lifted the man and carried him through the gardens. Isabel followed for a while, but when he approached the gates, she turned aside without a word and disappeared into the palace.

At Rosa's house she cleared a table and put water on to heat. When Thomas unwound the bandages, Rosa paled.

"This is bad," she said.

"It is, but between us we will save him."

"I am not sure that is possible."

"Then he will die with friends, but let us not allow that to happen. We both know what to do. I need my tools, so clean him as best you can."

At their lodgings Thomas found Jorge, who insisted on returning with him. When they entered Rosa's shop he stood to one side but did not avert his gaze as they worked on Baracoa. Rosa had made him drink hashish and poppy to soften the pain, but still he writhed as Thomas cut into his wound to seek what damage had been done. He found two blood vessels cut through but managed to tie them off. Others would do their work from now on. Rosa packed the wound with a preparation of herbs.

"Leave the wound open until we are sure there is no infection," said Rosa.

"I agree. Two days, perhaps three. You can care for him that long?"

"I can care for him forever if needs be. You will help?"

"As much as possible, yes."

Rosa was silent for a moment, then a tear gathered and fell from her eye.

"If not for you he would have died. Thank you, Thomas." She embraced him, holding him a long time, and Thomas made no move away. He knew she needed this moment. When he glanced at Jorge he nodded in approval.

"Will you be able to manage if I leave for a while. There is something I need to do."

"He is in the hands of his Gods now," said Rosa. "But do not stay away long. Where are you going?"

"To discover if King Fernando is in need of my skills."

Thomas rose before Rosa could reply. Jorge followed him outside and asked, "Who attacked Baracoa? You did not say."

"I hardly had time to say anything, but it was Rodrigo."

Jorge was silent a moment, then said, "I saw him. I was watching the cathedral square, and he crossed it at a run. He was limping. I was curious so went out and followed until he left the city, but I went no further. His foot was bleeding and he left a trail."

"Which direction did he go?" Thomas asked.

"North. At least I think it was north."

Thomas set the information aside for the moment. When Baracoa recovered, even if Baracoa did not recover, it could be examined again.

They fetched horses from the palace and rode west but did not have to ride far. Beyond the ridge that separated the two giant meanders of the river they saw a rag-tag band of men riding slowly. Thomas tried to count their number and came up short of what he hoped, but at least a blood-streaked Fernando rode at their head. He looked beyond exhaustion.

FORTY-EIGHT

Five weeks had passed since the battle that ended the life of Mateo Salto and discouraged, for the moment, the ambitions of the Portuguese. Thomas had withdrawn from the negotiations regarding the marriage of Catherine of Aragon to Prince Henry and suspected he would not be missed.

For ten days after his injury Baracoa hovered between life and death, but Rosa's care, and Thomas's oversight, slowly paid dividends and the man began to recover. Now he could be found sitting beside Rosa's stall while she worked, his face turned up to the weak winter sun. He showed no sign of wanting to return to his holding in the hills yet.

Thomas had ridden to Mateo's estate to find it abandoned. Someone had tried to set fire to the main building, but it had been built too well and failed to burn. Of the giant man Thomas had fought there was no sign, nor of the African women who had stood on the terrace the last time he rode past. In a few years, unless someone took ownership, it would fall into disrepair and eventually crumble into the dry earth. No doubt the contraband Mateo brought across the border would be handled by someone else. Trade was trade, whether legal or not.

Don Alejandro's son, Gabriel Ortega, was appointed to replace his father. He was unlikeable, but had trained in the law and might prove the best candidate, though after the deaths of the two previous occupants of the post applicants were few and far between. Gabriel would line his own pockets, but that was only to be expected.

Thomas knew that soon he and Jorge must leave for home, but not yet. He already knew, from what Jorge told him, that Don Rodrigo had left Sevilla heading north. After making enquiries from those who had worked with Don Rodrigo they travelled in that direction, into the heart of a little-populated area bordering Spain and Portugal. Baracoa came with them, his one allowance for his healing injury to ride a horse. They went in search of the traitor Don Rodrigo Vargas, wanting to discover what had brought him to Sevilla and turned him to hatred. It took several days to track down any sign of him. If they found him Thomas knew he would kill the man rather than return him to Sevilla.

At most hamlets and farmhouses, mention of his name brought blank stares and shakes of heads. An offered description mostly did the same. The Spanish spoken in this hinterland was hard to understand, which did not help. But occasionally they heard of a tall man riding a fine horse. At first Thomas dismissed the reports as being someone else, but they came often enough to make him think they were on Rodrigo's trail.

When they camped for the night on the slope of a sunblasted hill with a view across an undulating plain to tree-shrouded mountains in the distance, Baracoa wandered off as he always did, saying he was searching for signs. He had not yet found any, but on this evening he did.

The wind was cold. The year had turned, and January brought snow even to low-lying Sevilla and across most of the land. It capped hills and gathered in hollows. Jorge sat with a fur cloak around him, and Thomas had a blanket over his own shoulders. Baracoa ignored the weather, as he always did.

"You must come with me, Thomas," said Baracoa when he returned.

Thomas did not need to ask why. He left Jorge by the fire and followed the Kalinago shaman. They walked a mile then Baracoa paused and knelt at a cleft in a rock face. He pointed into it.

"I left it as I found it. Tell me if you think as I do."

Thomas knelt beside him and peered in. It was dark in the cleft, but enough light remained to show something pale, and he caught a faint smell. He reached in and drew out a cloth that had once been white. Now it was stained, both with dirt and dried blood. Thomas held it to his nose and sniffed, then turned and spat.

"He is dying, yes?" said Baracoa.

"Yes, he is dying. That is your doing when you struck him with the rusted tool." Thomas saw Baracoa smile, then continued, "It might be possible to save him if his leg is removed, but I will not do it. Let him die." Thomas tossed the cloth away, its message given. "This was discarded not long ago, which means we are closing in. He must have travelled slowly for us to have caught him up."

"He would be in pain, yes?"

Thomas nodded. "Great pain. Not just from his wound, but the corruption it has brought. His leg will be an agony, turning black and putrid." He smiled. "You did well in your choice of weapon, my friend. Not just rusted, but coated in the dirt of the man's garden."

Baracoa nodded. "It was good fortune, nothing more. I hope he does not die before we find him."

"So do I. I have many questions."

"Which he will not answer," said Baracoa.

"If he is dying, he might."

Baracoa only shrugged and started back to their camp. Thomas remained for a moment, watching as the last of the light leached away to the east to continue on across the wide sea to where Baracoa's land would still bask in its warmth.

FORTY-NINE

In a small town crouching on the banks of the Tagus river which marked the border between two countries, they stopped at an inn to ask the usual questions, expecting the usual answers, but this time luck favoured them.

"If anyone knows of who you speak it will be old Paco," said the owner of the inn. "You will find him at Ramon's bar next to the river. Paco likes to talk, so I hope you are a patient man."

Thomas knew he was not, but in this new life, without ties or responsibilities, he was starting to learn to be. Besides, Jorge was with him, and he would be content to talk to someone until midnight. Hopefully, that would not be necessary.

Outside Ramon's bar sat a short, grizzled man whose age it was impossible to determine. He might have been thirty, or one-hundred-and-thirty. His hair was long and matted, shot through with grey, but his face was almost unlined even after a lifetime in the Spanish sun. He sat in shade on the north side of the bar. An empty beaker sat on a table beside him. Baracoa had wandered off again so when Jorge approached the man and asked if he was Paco, he touched the beaker and said, "That depends which Paco you are looking for. We have a choice of seven."

"Old Paco," said Jorge.

"Then that would be me." He touched the mug again and Thomas went inside for a fresh jug of ale. When he came out Jorge had made the mistake of asking how they could tell the seven Pacos apart if they were not the old one.

Old Paco smiled and held his mug out for Thomas to fill before replying.

"There is young Paco," he said, "then short Paco and tall Paco, fat Paco and thin Paco, and of course, blind Paco."

"If blind Paco has clouded eyes," said Thomas, "that might be helped if there is a Moorish physician nearby."

Old Paco drained his mug and Thomas refilled it.

"He went to one but it did no good," he said. "It is his own fault. He got drunk one day and passed out in a field. His eyes were half open, and they stared into the sun too long. He has grown used to not seeing and makes do." Old Paco looked at them both. "You are not from these parts, and this village is on the road to nowhere. You must want something."

"We do," Thomas said, before Jorge could speak. "We are seeking information on a man by the name of Don Rodrigo Vargas. He will stink, for he has a rotten leg."

Old Paco stared across the river for a long time.

Thomas refilled his mug once it was empty.

Eventually, after a long silence, Thomas said, "Is the man familiar?"

Old Paco shook his head. "What makes you think he came to Cedillo?"

"We have tracked him for ten days. He came this way. I also believe his father once farmed near here. The family was attacked and only Rodrigo survived. He left to seek his fortune."

"Did he find it?" asked Old Paco.

"In a way." Thomas hesitated, then saw no harm in providing more. "Until he turned to the dark side. He had attained a powerful position serving the King and Queen." As an afterthought he said, "Of Spain."

Old Paco nodded. "What age had he? Can you describe him again?"

"He was–" Thomas started, but Jorge interrupted.

"He is tall for a Spaniard. We never knew an age, but I would say he has forty years but looks younger. Someone does not reach his position young. He can fight well." Jorge glanced at Thomas. "Is that right?"

"Yes, he fights well," Thomas said. "Better than most men."

"A man like that rode through here four days since. He did not come to the village but I saw him pass down there. And yes, he favoured one leg and I could smell something rotten. Did he tell you anything about this land his father worked?"

"That it was hard land, dry, the soil not much softer than rock. The river was nearby, but they had to carry water from it to irrigate their crops."

"That also does not help. Most land here is hard. He must have had a mother," said Old Paco.

"He must have, but never mentioned one, other than I think he may have said she died giving birth to him."

Old Paco smiled. "It is not unusual, but what is will be a father who does not abandon the child or give him up to a barren couple."

"Rodrigo told me he had two older brothers who were killed when bandits attacked. He tracked them down and killed them."

Old Paco smiled but said nothing.

Jorge went inside for more ale. Thomas drank some of his own. "I believe Rodrigo knows he is dying and has returned to his roots to do so. Some men are called there." He waited for Old Paco to speak.

"There was one," he eventually said, "but his name was not Rodrigo, and his family name was not Vargas, it was Martinez. Miguel Martinez. Everyone called him Mio, but he did not like it. He had no brothers and I have never heard of bandits attacking their farmstead. Miguel was young when he left here and was popular with the girls in the town. More than one of them pushed out babies after he left. And yes, his father died, and that is the reason he left. Because he killed him and left his body to rot among the crops. He would have had..." old Paco stared into space, "...yes, fifteen years. He fought well enough, as you say, and often needed to, for he was not popular. He considered himself better than everyone else."

"Where was this land?" Thomas asked.

"There is nothing there now," said Old Paco. "A few stones, a lot of weeds. It will tell you nothing."

"I believe he will be there," Thomas said.

Old Paco shrugged. "Follow the road south from here.

When you reach the river, turn east. Half a league and you might see what is left of the house. If not, there is a small dock for crossing the river. It might be there still, but no one has visited the place since he left. Why would they?"

Thomas thanked the man, bought more ale and offered him some coin, which was accepted.

A westerly wind had brought a warmer breeze which melted the frost in the hollows. Baracoa descended a slope and joined them as they rode south, then turned to follow the river.

The remnant of the house was sounder than promised and, with some work, might be possible to live in again. Why someone might want to was another matter. Thomas walked the land, but old Paco had been right. It told him nothing. He had half expected to find disturbed ground where Don Rodrigo's father was buried, but if it had ever existed it was no longer visible. He descended to the riverbank and found the old dock at once, in better shape than the house. Beside it was the upturned hull of a rowing boat mouldering away. Thomas stood and stared across to where another dock sat on the far bank, in Portugal, a boat in better condition tied to it. He stood for some time trying to work out if there was any significance to it but failed. He did not know enough about who Rodrigo had been, or his father. Was the son a product of the father? Thomas knew he was far from that but had experience enough to recognise it often happened. In particular, a father might be too hard, or too violent, on his children and turn them away from the light. Was that why Don Rodrigo killed him?

Thomas sighed and started to turn away when Baracoa,

who stood twenty paces along the riverbank from him, said, "He is over there."

Thomas stopped. Baracoa was pointing at the boat tied to the far dock. Thomas waited, watching, and eventually saw it. Not Rodrigo, but his presence. The boat rocked, an unnatural movement not caused by the languid current. Thomas bent and started to turn over the boat on his dock, but it broke apart as he did so.

"Jorge, ride to the village and ask for a boat. Tell them we need to cross the river."

"I am not good with boats," said Jorge, "particularly small ones. You must go, Thomas."

"I will do it," said Baracoa. "It will not be a canoe, but I will manage."

After he had gone Thomas went to the remains of the farmhouse and went inside. The roof was mostly intact enough to keep out the worst of the weather. Inside, furniture remained. A table, chairs, two cots pushed back against opposite walls, one larger than the other. A soot-stained fireplace where a metal pot still hung from a hook above it. At one time this had been a home.

He brought out two of the chairs, testing them before sitting and offering one to Jorge.

"Baracoa may be a while."

FIFTY

It was almost an hour before they heard the splashing of oars and Baracoa appeared. He brought the small rowboat close to the shore, unwilling to risk the rotting dock, and Thomas and Jorge walked down to the bank.

Jorge stared at the boat and shook his head. "I am not getting into that."

"Then wait here." Thomas reached out for Baracoa's hand and stepped in, the boat rocking wildly before he managed to sit. Baracoa pulled on the oars and set out.

Rodrigo lay in the bottom of the boat on the far bank. His face was deathly pale, his eyes were open, and his chest rose and fell. The stink of rotting flesh filled the air, but Thomas had always been able to ignore it, and Baracoa showed no revulsion. Thomas stepped onto the dock and knelt to look in. Rodrigo had cut his trousers away on his left leg, which was black and swollen, the skin split to release a dark wetness. Rodrigo had tried to bathe it, but it was beyond any help. A metal cup sat in the bilge, an empty bucket beside it.

“I can no longer move,” said Rodrigo. “Help me and fetch more water.”

“It will do no good,” Thomas said.

“It has before.”

“But no longer. You are dying.” Thomas’s gaze studied the leg. A week before he may have been able to remove it, but no longer. The putrefaction had already risen into Rodrigo’s belly. The pain would be terrible.

“Then kill me. Offer me that mercy.”

“Like you offered Don Alejandro? Like you offered Luisa? How many others?”

“I cannot think for the pain. Help me and I will tell you what you want to know.”

Thomas considered the request. How long did the man have? Would easing the pain speed his passing or not? Would he talk without it? There was only one way to find out.

Thomas reached for the cup and filled it from the river. Not clean water, but that hardly mattered. He drew a leather bag from inside his jacket and crumbled hashish and opium into it, judging the right amount, then adding more. When he sat Rodrigo up the man screamed, but gulped down the liquor. Thomas laid him back and waited.

After a while, Rodrigo’s laboured breathing eased and his eyes closed.

Thomas prodded him. “Do not go to sleep on me.”

Rodrigo opened one eye. “Ask me your questions and I will tell you true. I had such hopes, but all are dashed. All is lost and soon, so will I be. When I die let the river take me to the sea.”

“Why should I, after what you have done?”

"Because you are something I am not. A good man."

Thomas was unsure that was true but knew he would do as asked. The man would be dead soon. What did it matter? He asked the question that concerned him the most, the one he could not understand at all.

"Why Luisa?"

"You," said Rodrigo.

"Was it jealousy because she chose me?"

"Do not overestimate yourself. She came to me and said she was going to reveal the relationship between Mateo and me. She told me to leave Sevilla and never return. She was tired of our schemes and wanted them ended. What she did not know was how closely Mateo and I worked together. If she told you enough you might have been able to tie the pieces together, so she had to die. It was not difficult to enter her room and cut her throat." The poppy was working hard now, and Rodrigo smiled. "She squealed your name as she died, as if in accusation. I considered killing you as well, but it would have been a step too far. The Queen would not have rested until she found your killer, and I could not risk that. I almost managed to have you killed in any case by making it look as if you had murdered her."

"Except you saved me."

"So you would have no suspicion of me."

Thomas almost hit him then. He had to breathe deep and let the words wash over him and away. They were a lie, and if not it was too late to be moved by them.

"What was she going to tell me?"

"Everything. Who I was: a mask to hide my true self, which is a nobody. I also told her I worked with Mateo to enrich myself. I told her if she let Mateo trade openly some of the wealth would reach her."

"You told her all of that?" Thomas said.

"When we lay together, like you lay with her. I expect you were a disappointment to her after she had tasted my skills as a lover. But she was sly. She teased everything from me, and more. I would have killed her then, but everyone knew we were lovers. I had to wait."

"How long?" Thomas asked.

"A year. I did not know it would be you, but it would be someone. Luisa chose rarely, but carefully."

"Except for you," Thomas said. "Did she also rebuff Mateo?"

"She did, which angered him greatly. He was too greedy for his own good. Does he live?"

Thomas shook his head. "He does not."

"Good. I never liked the man. Spain is finished now. Princess Catherine will never marry the English boy. She will marry no one and die a crone." Rodrigo's eyes closed and he breathed softly for so long Thomas was sure he had fallen asleep. Then he said, "My only regret is I did not kill the Queen or the King. I was not strong enough."

"You were not clever enough."

"I wish to die now," said Rodrigo. "Before the pain returns. It remains but is distant. How long until it comes for me again?"

"An hour. Time enough for more questions. Why did you kill Don Alejandro? Was it to take his place?"

Rodrigo was quiet for so long Thomas again suspected he might have fallen asleep, but finally his eyes opened but remained lidded.

"I did not seek his position, and if truth be told I would still live if I had not been offered it."

"So why?"

"Because he discovered what I wanted – which was the destruction of Spain and the Infante Duerte on the throne of a united Spain and Portugal, with me as their advisor."

"How did Don Alejandro find out? Did he know who you were?"

Rodrigo looked as if he wanted to shake his head but lacked the energy.

"It was an accident. A stupid accident. Don Alejandro went to Mateo to ask him to get Portuguese wine of the highest quality. It was two weeks before the banquet, and he wanted to impress the King and Queen, as well as the gathered officials of England. You included, Berrington, though you are not important."

"Mateo knew of your plans?" The idea surprised Thomas.

"Of course not, but that fool of a lad the Infante Duarte was at Mateo's estate. He is never able to keep his mouth shut. He was boasting and revealed who I was and what I wanted. He was not even aware of what he had done, but for all his age and failings, Don Alejandro was no fool. He confronted me."

"He would reveal you to Fernando, yes?"

"No. He wanted money. No money and he would unmask me to the King. I played along, then had Jayuya dart him." Rodrigo almost smiled. "It fooled you, did it not? You were sure the wine had poisoned him. Which of course meant the cupman also had to die. He was nobody.

A foil, nothing more, but your reputation preceded you and I could not have you questioning him."

"So you killed him as well."

"It was too easy. He waited in the yard for payment and I caved his skull in and cut his throat for good measure. I wanted everyone to believe Don Alejandro had died of poisoned wine once you suggested it."

"Who did the cupman work for?" Thomas asked.

"On that night, for me. On other nights for Mateo. He would do anything for payment. Jayuya concealed himself behind a curtain and used a dart to kill Don Alejandro. It was a merciful death. I wish for the same."

Thomas rose and walked from the jetty and sat on the slope above the river. Baracoa joined him. Neither spoke for a long time.

"Do you think he told you everything?" Baracoa eventually asked.

"Not everything, but enough. There is more, but I know the worst of it now. And that worst is Luisa, who did not deserve to die, and that I played a part in her death."

"Do not think that way. You did not wield the knife."

"You heard everything?" Thomas asked.

"Everything." Baracoa reached down to the wrap at his waist and drew out a small clay pot. "Do we finish him now?" He twisted the top and showed Thomas the black, viscid liquid inside. Then he showed him a wooden dart. "One touch and he will die."

"Not yet," Thomas said. "He does not deserve such mercy. We wait."

Dark fell. Thomas had watched Jorge leave the far shore and ride towards the village. He would no doubt find food and lodging for the night. Thomas did not ask Baracoa if he wanted the same because he knew what his answer would be.

Stars sparked into life. The moon rose and climbed high. Time passed, and eventually Rodrigo cried out.

"More, Thomas! Give me more!"

Thomas nodded at Baracoa, then went to kneel beside the boat.

"I have no more but will offer you something better."

Rodrigo writhed, the pain engulfing him.

Baracoa reached down and scratched along his arm.

Rodrigo jerked, looked down.

"What did you–" But his voice faded away.

They watched his chest rise and fall, then grow still. Thomas reached out to Rodrigo's throat, felt there and nodded.

"It was too much mercy," said Baracoa. "I would not have offered it. I did it for you."

"Then I will accept the burden of it," Thomas said.

He untied the rope tethering the boat to the dock and pushed it out into the current. They watched it drift, turning, until a bend in the river carried it from sight. Then they climbed into their own boat and rowed across to the other side where their horses waited patiently. They mounted and went in search of Jorge, and in the morning, they would start their return to Sevilla.

Except as they rode, Baracoa said, "I will not come back with you, Thomas."

"Why not?"

"I have had enough of this land. You told me you could help me return to my own, or was that a lie?" Baracoa's expression showed no disappointment. Such emotion had been scoured from him long ago.

"Come with me to Sevilla and I will write a note to Columb asking him to find you passage across the great ocean. I will even take you with me when I deliver it. He will do this for me."

Baracoa inclined his head. "My thanks."

"What about Rosa?"

"I will ask if she wishes to come. There is much for her to learn in my land, and great beauty. But if she does not wish to then I will go alone. That might be for the best." Baracoa stared into the dark. "And you, Thomas? What will you do?"

"I will also return home, now I know where my home lies."

HISTORICAL NOTE

Little is known about the Kalinago (also referred to as Taíno), who are generally regarded as having died out completely, although some sources dispute this. They were inhabitants of the first Caribbean islands discovered by Christopher Columbus on his initial voyage. It is recorded that he brought several of them back with him, but almost half died.

I use the word *sayapa* for the poncho like cape worn by Baracoa and other Kalinago in Spain. I base this on the more contemporary word sarape which developed from an older native word. I made up *sayapa* to be consistent as the names of such garments are lost in the mists of time.

For fictional purposes, I have shortened the period of negotiation over the marriage of Prince Henry and Catherine of Aragon. In reality this lasted several years and would have undoubtedly made for boring reading. However, both Richard Foxe, Lord Privy Seal, and Thomas Savage, Archbishop of York, were present at several of the negotiations regarding the royal betrothal.

The Infante Duarte de Beja is a creation of my own, but a Portuguese prince of the right age and contacts would have made a suitable alternative suitor for Catherine and might indeed have united the two greatest powers in the world at that time.

By late 1502, trade between the new world and the old was regular and frequent, and many new plants, animals and people were being brought across the Atlantic. Spanish ships tended to explore the Caribbean islands and, later, southern Mexico, where at that time Aztecs ruled. The Portuguese traders and soldiers explored the northern areas of South America. The riches of these lands were bountiful and much fought over.

The next book in the Thomas Berrington series, *Life and Sacrifice* will be released in 2026.

Glossary of terms (s: Spanish, k: Kalinago)

alguacil s: sheriff

cacique k: chief/leader

ABOUT THE AUTHOR

David Penny published 4 novels in the 1970's before being seduced by a steady salary. He has now returned to his true love of writing with a series of historical mysteries set in Moorish Spain at the end of the 15th Century, and 16th Century Tudor England. He is currently working on the next book in the series.

David also writes The Izzy Wilde Crime Thrillers series under the name DG Penny, and the Unit-13 paranormal Spy Thriller under David G. Penny.

Find out more about David Penny

www.davidpenny.com

ALSO BY DAVID PENNY

The Thomas Berrington Tudor Mysteries

Men of Bone

A Death of Promise

The Hidden Dead

The Beasts of the City

The Thomas Berrington Historical Mysteries

The Red Hill

Breaker of Bones

The Sin Eater

The Incubus

The Inquisitor

The Fortunate Dead

The Promise of Pain

The Message of Blood

A Tear for the Dead

The Thomas Berrington Prequels

A Death of Innocence

The Thomas Berrington Bundles

Purchase 3 full-length novels for less than the price of two.

Thomas Berrington Books 1-3

The Red Hill

Breaker of Bones

The Incubus

Thomas Berrington Books 4-6

The Incubus

The Inquisitor

The Fortunate Dead

Thomas Berrington Books 7-9

The Promise of Pain

The Message of Blood

A Tear for the Dead

Writing as DG Penny, the Wilde and Ward Crime Thrillers

The Murder Trail

Writing as David G. Penny, the Unit-13: WWII Paranormal Spy Thrillers

An Imperfect Future